Overtime

ST. CLOUD HOCKEY SERIES

MARI LOYAL

Book Cover by Enni Amanda at Yummy Book Covers

Edited by Beth Lawton at VB Edits

 Formatted with Vellum

HEAT LEVEL AND CONTENT WARNINGS

Before reading this book, I encourage you to first read this section to determine whether it's the right fit for your personal circumstances.

This book is closed door, which means there is innuendo, kisses are descriptive, and characters don't shy away from their attraction. While there are no on-the-page explicit scenes, I caution more sensitive readers to avoid Chapter 24 as the characters (spoiler ahead) swim in a lake in their underwear and kiss passionately (end spoiler).

There is mild to moderate use of cuss words, particularly in emotional moments. However, there is no use of f-bombs, religious blasphemies, or known ableist terms.

The heroine of this book is comfortable defining herself as both fat and chubby, and also suffers from fatphobia from peers and relatives. She also suffers from extremely painful periods that are relevant to the plot. The hero is Venezuelan and has brown skin, and he's on the receiving end of a couple of instances of racism.

If any of these topics are troublesome for you, please

protect yourself and read a book that better suits your situation.

Visit my website mariloyal.com for general content warnings that apply to all my books.

CHAPTER 1
ARAN

f only I could get to the ice ASAP, it would transform this crappy day into a halfway decent one.

I run my badge by the scanner at the front doors of St. Cloud's training facility, home to the Thunder Bolts and the Thunder Strikes. The sign above the entrance saying all that jazz still looks brand spanking new, courtesy of boosters who have really been enjoying the hockey program since my older sister's generation put it on the map. I couldn't give two flying turds about the prestige of the program or the school, though.

All I want to do is play hockey. And maybe have a few casual dates.

A-freaking-las, I have to go to school, where I get a failing grade on my essay for the useless business class I never wanted to take in the first place, if not thanks to my sisters.

When they said that I'm such an unfeeling robot that I couldn't pass a Captcha to save my life—even though I showed them on my phone that I damn well could—they challenged me to take a class that had more words than numbers. Apparently, the fact that I can stand still while disks made of vulcanized rubber are being shot at me makes me less human. And so is the fact that I'm studying Accounting. Also, that I can't commit to a single relationship.

Now here I am, with my first big F. Coach Green will no doubt have words about it.

On top of that, my phone hasn't stopped buzzing all day, and unfortunately, the messages aren't offers from the pros. Because guess what? The casual date is now upset she's still casual. Even though I told her from the beginning that I don't do serious.

"Watch out, you guys," a familiar voice says as I walk into the locker room. "Our captain looks like a solid five on his bad mood scale."

I throw my duffel bag on the bench by my locker. I set my stick down with more care. It's my favorite.

"When is he not in a bad mood?" asks another clown.

"Hence the scale." The original jokester chuckles. Unfortunately, his locker is next to mine. And he's my assistant captain. And also my roommate. "What's got your panties in a twist this time, Rodriguez?"

I unzip my coat with a grunt. That's all he's getting from me. I'm minutes away from the ice rink, and until then, my mood could easily tip closer to a ten on my bad mood scale. Especially if they catch wind of why I'm so annoyed.

But Archie Bracken doesn't give up. It's why he makes a stellar left winger and assistant captain, and why he tolerates me off the rink. He and Ryan are the only ones.

"Let me guess," he says with a hum. "Did someone corner you in the bathroom and ask for your autograph again?"

I hang my coat and unwind my scarf from around my neck, balling it up and stuffing it in the pocket of my coat. As I peel off my hoodie, some of the other guys join in on the ribbing.

"My turn," Jamal Amadi, my other assistant captain, chimes in with laughter in his voice. "A pretentious professor implied you're yet another stereotypical jock? Because that literally happened to me this morning."

Several murmurs of "me too" erupt. Half of the student body, most of them female, may have become big fans of the team over the years. But the majority of the school staff still think we're a waste of space. And I may have just helped their case with my flunked paper.

"No, no," says the drawling voice of Harrison Edwards, the backup goalie. "This has something to do with a girl. What are you at, girl number fifteen this year alone?"

"Why are you keeping track?" I ask while taking off my jeans and socks. "Waiting for your turn in line or something?"

"Oh, burn!" Archie hollers.

"You wish." Edwards scoffs and turns his back again. He's a classic can-dish-it-but-can't-take-it kind of guy.

I toss my street clothes into the bottom of my locker and kick my boots under the bench. I manage to change into my compression underwear and hockey shorts just as a commotion starts. A yelp from a manly voice is weird enough that I glance over my shoulder and… promptly wish I hadn't.

Because in the middle of the men's locker room is none other than my casual date.

Kelsey, in her pink coat and high-heeled boots, stands out in the locker room decorated in St. Cloud's blues and grays. More pairs of eyes than I need for whatever this is are trained on her. And she doesn't care about the various stages of undress all around her, or my own.

I draw in a deep breath and turn to face her. "What are you doing here?"

Kelsey's eyes get their fill of my bare torso, and the guys start whistling. I'm not sure if it's at her or at me. With these stooges, you never know.

"I had to make all this effort since you're not picking up your phone."

"See? It was a girl all along. Pay up." Edwards offers his upraised palm to Archie.

"No one made a bet. Get that paw away from my face so I can watch the show."

I run a hand over my buzz cut and down the back of my head, trying to massage the tension in my neck. There's some pleading in her eyes, as if she expects that by doing this, she'll convince me to change my mind.

"I responded to you last night," I say, leaving out the part where last night was the *third* time I said we should part ways.

She takes a deep breath and blurts out, "Breaking up with me by text is such a dick move!"

"Really, Rodriguez?"

"I'm disappointed, Cap."

"That's too harsh, even for me."

"Dude, shut up. You can't even get one date." A round of snickers.

I breathe even deeper. I could tell them that the first time I tried to break up with her was definitely in person, but what does it matter? The people want a show, and I'm not happy to oblige.

Back to rummaging through my duffel bag I go. I find my socks and drop them onto the bench. Next is the performance shirt. I pull it on first. Then I make the mistake of checking to see if she's still there. She is. Guess I should be thankful she didn't show up a few minutes earlier, or she'd have found me buck naked.

Still, I ask, "Why are you still here?"

My tone must've come out harsher than I meant, because even Archie hisses and looks away. I'll get a scolding at home tonight, no doubt.

"Because I'm trying to make an effort here." She stomps her foot. "We have great chemistry, and I can't be the only one who thinks it's a waste to end things here."

"Yeah, you are. Chemistry isn't enough for a relationship, and I don't want one of those anyway." I sigh and jerk my chin at the door. "Do you mind? This is a men's changing room."

"Bro…" someone whispers. I'm not sure if it's a warning or a reprimand. I'm not in the mood for either.

"Then change, because I'm not leaving! We're having this conversation right here, right now."

"Fine."

So I say, but this conversation is over for me. I don't acknowledge Kelsey anymore, even as she starts tossing out lies about how bad I supposedly am in bed. Which contradicts her argument that we have chemistry, anyway. Besides, we didn't even sleep together. I'd look pathetic if I start trying to defend myself, though, or if I attack her instead. I don't care if Edwards and his buddies want to use this to give me crap. I'd rather wait until she runs out of fumes than engage and make it all worse.

I finally sit down to put on compression socks, and she screeches. "Are you really not going to say anything?"

I wince a little but move on to lacing up my skates.

"Word of advice," Archie whispers in a *very* loud voice. "They don't call him Aran 'the Iceberg' Rodriguez for no reason. And you don't want to end up like the Titanic, do you?"

"Why don't you date me instead, babe? I promise you I'm much hotter," one of the younger guys says while flexing his arms like a peacock.

"Shove that *babe* up your ass." Kelsey turns to me. "And you—"

I know exactly what she's going to do before a single one of her muscles moves. It's in the fury in her eyes, how her nostrils flare. But I let her, because I know this is the closure she needs to move on and leave me the hell alone.

I let her slap me.

The room hisses. Every Bolt felt the blow as if they'd gotten it instead.

Turning my head back around, I test my jaw with my hand. It doesn't hurt too much, like this was just a show for her too.

"You done?" I ask in a gruff tone.

"Now I am. Don't come crawling back to me when you regret this." She turns around, and I notice her heeled boots don't click-clack against the thick carpet. No wonder I didn't hear her come in.

But just as I start feeling some relief, Kelsey walks by Coach Green. He's leaning against the door, chewing gum and glaring daggers at me. It probably means he witnessed most of this little episode.

"Captain, a word." He motions with his finger at me to follow.

Mierda, this will hurt much more than the slap.

"Yes, Coach."

"Oh, *now* you're in trouble." Edwards laughs.

The urge to tell him to piss off is strong, but I ignore him.

I'm missing my top pads and jersey, but when the Coach says to walk, I walk. We don't make it far from the locker room, just enough that eavesdroppers won't find satisfaction.

"What the hell was that?" is the opener of the conversation.

"I'm still wondering so myself," I mumble.

"Rodriguez, you're the captain of the Thunder Bolts. I've never seen a guy who can command a room without a word the way you do. And I've never met a more talented goalie in my life." His eyebrows are as pinched as they get during bad games. "But what kind of example are you setting by bringing your girlfriends into the locker room?"

"First of all," I say, shifting my weight to one leg. "I didn't bring her in. She sneaked in all on her own." And now I wonder if it was when I badged in, but that's irrelevant. "And second, she's not my girlfriend."

"Well, obviously not after that slap."

"Or before."

He gives me a pointed stare. "The point is that this isn't the first time one of your girl-*space*-friends has pulled some kind of stunt that disrespects this institution."

He's referring to the time during my sophomore year when some freshman girl I didn't even know wrote my name across her chest and flashed everyone during a game.

I scowl. "That wasn't my fault either."

"It's never your fault, but somehow it keeps happening to you, huh?" Coach sighs so hard he blows a raspberry. "I'm going to give you a warning, and this time, if you don't follow it, I will suspend you for three games and put Edwards in."

I grow as stiff as a plank.

"His save percentage is one point four below mine. You'd hurt the team to teach me a lesson?"

"Yes, I would if it means you'll finally keep it in your pants and focus only on school and hockey. I'm doing this for your own sake. Women, alcohol, drugs, or whatever can completely derail your career now and in the future." He points at me and lowers his voice. "One more scene that messes up this team or your studies, and you're suspended for three games. Even if it's in the playoffs. And even if there are scouts watching. You understand?"

"Crystal clear," I say through gritted teeth.

"Hockey. School." He punctuates each word with a slash of his hand. "Nothing else."

"What about family?"

"Don't be cheeky with me, boy."

I press my lips into a tight line. It was a legit question. "Hockey and school, got it."

"Good." Coach Green nods. "Now go get ready for practice."

"Yes, sir."

Now my bad mood is set at a firm seven on the scale. About to turn seven point five the second I step into the locker room and face the hyenas. But I'm not that worried about that part.

If Coach finds out I got an F on a paper—in a class that is graded entirely on essays—he's going to bench my ass and put in our subpar goalie who hates my guts and got drafted thanks to his daddy's connections. I can't let that happen. I have scouts to wow because *I* didn't get drafted.

In the quiet of my mind, I make up a plan. Step one, swear off girls for the rest of the season. Step two, do some overtime schoolwork with the help of a tutor to salvage the useless elective. Step three, tell no one about steps one or two so people keep their noses in their own business.

Should be easy.

CHAPTER 2
MADDIE

'm going to write a hockey romance. As soon as I figure out both the hockey part *and* the romance part.

In theory, I already know how to write a love story. After all, my debut novel, a traditionally published young adult romance that is like *The Princess Diaries* but with a fat princess, is set to release in a few months. The heroine bullied by mean classmates until—surprise!—she turns out to be the long-lost daughter of a remote country's king. When she travels there, she falls in love with her bodyguard, a super-hot boy her age who was assigned to act as her friend while protecting her from the bad guys. They work together to unravel the secret group that has been trying to dethrone her father, and they fall in love at the same time. Easy peasy lemon squeezy.

Except romance between two seventeen-year-olds is a bit different from adults. Or at least that's how it looks in books. I wouldn't know IRL. But I've consumed every hockey romance I could get my grubby hands on, and I have a solid grasp of the tropes and such. Consuming books doesn't replace the lived experience but, eh, it's not like I can hire a guy to show me the ropes. Heaven knows I can't find one for free.

What I'm still relatively clueless about is the hockey part. But I have a plan.

I sit near the end of a long table in the loud part of the library. This section is too far from the librarians who regularly shush students, but it's my favorite because people are more interested in their conversations than what others are doing. No one minds me as I pull open the athletic department's website and begin researching the hockey teams.

"Write what you know, they said," I mumble to myself with a mocking giggle.

What I know is young adult books. I live and breathe YA. I read about a hundred fifty per year. In fact, the reason I'm majoring in English at St. Cloud, despite the monumental debt I'm accumulating, is because it's the only college program I could find that is geared toward modern genres, including YA. Here, professors and other classmates don't look down on me for wanting a traditional career in that age category. Without the encouragement of several professors, I wouldn't have queried my book, landed an excellent agent, and sold it to a Big Four publishing house.

The problem is that the first cut of the advance only covered my rent for a few months. I won't see the next payment for a while yet, which poses the need for a side gig. Or *several*. I already have one as an English tutor, but I need a hybrid career self-publishing as well if I want to keep a roof over my head. Preferably a different roof from the one I'm living under now.

That's how I decided I should write a hockey romance. While I know squat about it, it's what everyone online is obsessed with. I've seen what authors in this genre are making on different platforms. If I could get just a fraction of that, I'd be able to move away from *my* bullies.

As I jot down the numbers of players on each team and their respective positions, the conversation around me shifts into a different cadence. A single murmur rises in a wave approaching my end of the table. I lift my head and don't have to wonder what the deal is for long.

The textbook definition of tall, dark, and handsome walks toward me. Although he's obviously not looking at me. His attention is set on one of the free chairs by the end of the table. Behind him, he leaves a trail of hushed whispers.

"What is *he* doing here?"

I catch that one easily. It comes from a girl with stars in her eyes. The *he* in question either doesn't hear or acts as though it isn't shocking to see the captain of the Thunder Bolts in the library. Which it is, because these are my haunting grounds, and I've never seen him here, unless you count his face on my computer screen, that is.

My pulse spikes as he pulls up the chair two spaces away from me. I lower my head back to the screen and change the roster to the Thunder Strikes, because, whew, I am not immune to Aran Rodriguez. And the up-close, in-person version is overwhelmingly better than his picture.

And also way bigger. As he stretches out his arms to remove his thick coat, I figure his huge wingspan helps him catch a lot of pucks.

Hmm, that's a good note to make for a future hockey player character. I jot it down in my journal.

"Take a picture," someone whispers, and sure enough, the sound of a shutter echoes around the silence his arrival has brought over the table.

I cringe. I don't know who's worse, the obvious stalker snapping pics of a campus celeb or the covert one like me. Except I'm doing book research. I'm not being a creep. And he doesn't have to know what I'm up to. In fact, I'm probably invisible to him.

Which is why I figure this is kismet. I said I'd write a

hockey romance, and *voilà*. The universe has dropped the perfect inspiration in my lap.

Lowering my head, I use my laptop screen to do some discreet people-watching. I've only seen the Bolts' captain on campus from afar and once at a game I was dragged to last year. I could not appreciate the sheer scale of him in those circumstances. After hanging his coat from the back of his chair, he sits down and has to push the chair beside him away so he can squeeze in.

I jot down *are all hockey players huge?* and underline the question. I'll fork up tickets to a game to get this answered.

I glance around my screen again. He's now pulling a laptop from his backpack. There's already a clear bottle with some green concoction on the table before him. A protein shake? Obviously, athletes need a ton of protein and calories, which isn't something I think about on a daily basis. That's good to know, since I'm doing the reverse of writing what I know here.

My phone buzzes against the table with a racket. I pick it up, fearing it may be yet another text from mother dearest, but it must be my lucky day, because the text is from my boss.

BOSS WHO IS NOT A LADY

Hey, are you busy right now?

Technically, I am. But I don't know how to explain to her that I'm trying to design a tall, dark, and handsome character out of a real-life TDH.

ME

I'm studying at the library. What's up?

BOSS WHO IS NOT A LADY

I may need your help urgently. Stand by.

I emote with a thumbs-up and set my phone down.

Back to my so-called studies. College or adult romance is a

lot more physical than a typical YA romance, and not just because there may or may not be intimate scenes. It's just that when you're a certain age, you're a bit bolder. You know what's what. Longing stares and blushing while holding hands isn't enough. You want to *know* the other person inside and out, and it's always easier to start with the outside first.

Which is why checking out Aran Rodriguez is book research.

I use the old trick of stretching my back to scope out the situation. He's not paying attention to me whatsoever, as expected. A thick textbook now lays spread out by his laptop, and he runs his finger softly across the page while he reads. Huh, I wonder what that feels like against skin.

Wow, okay. Now I'm being a creep for sure.

Be objective, Maddie.

Okay, so he's big. He needs extra space to sit, which at least I can relate to, even if, in my case, it's more girth than height. And he drinks protein shakes while he studies. What else is useful?

His mechanical pencil looks tiny in his hand as he makes notes directly on the textbook. What a monster. I would never dare to deface a book. But that's not a fact I can use. He's a leftie, and that's not a big deal either. He pauses to twirl the writing instrument between his fingers at a speed I could never achieve. Okay, so even his fingers are athletic. That may be a useful fact.

Heat explodes in my face at the image my brain conjures. I am definitely a creep now, but I still make a saucy note in my journal about how an elite athlete may use his deft hands away from the court. Or the pitch. Whatever it's called.

My phone buzzes again, and I grab it at the speed of light, now desperate for a distraction from my own thoughts.

BOSS WHO IS NOT A LADY

Okay, I do need you.

Wyatt won't make it in time for the new student
appointment.

I'm switching you around.

It's a command, not a question. After working for Melinda
for a couple of years, I know that when she says something like
this, it means she already checked my timetable and it works. I
trust her. Plus, she also knows I'm desperate for more students.

ME

I'm game.

BOSS WHO IS NOT A LADY

Great, let me confirm that the student
agrees too.

So, I already stretched. How do I make sure the subject's
attention is still elsewhere?

A cough!

I twist toward his side, away from the more populated right
side of the table, and fake a cough into my inner elbow.
Thankfully, he's chugging down his green shake and doesn't
catch sight of my smooth move.

Oh. My. Word. I didn't know a human could have so many
neck muscles. Is his whole body chiseled like that? Why must
we be smack dab in the middle of winter? If he weren't
wearing the thickest hoodie known to humanity, I'd see the
answer easily. His Adam's apple bobs as he drinks, and for
some reason, that makes my face heat up even more.

But then I freeze.

Dark eyes find mine above the rim of his shaker bottle.

Crap. *Crap.*

I've been caught.

I cough—this time it's for real, because I'm choking on my own saliva.

Where's my own bottle? In the middle of a bad coughing fit, I knock my pen down the table as I paw around my things. Now the whole table looks at me, including the subject of my research.

I squeeze my eyes shut as I down half of my water bottle in one go. At least it means that a) I definitely stopped staring at him, and b) I don't have to apologize for staring if I can't freaking talk.

When I dare open my eyes, I find that he's already moved on and is reading something on his laptop. I'm tempted by the sharp, square-cut of his jaw to keep staring, but I can't possibly endure those deep-set eyes on me again.

I should retreat. I can do the rest of my research from a safer distance. A few coughs escape from my chest while I start packing up, and my phone buzzes again right as I reach for it.

> **BOSS WHO IS NOT A LADY**
>
> The student agreed to the swap. I'm sending you his profile right now.
>
> He's already waiting at the library, and we're about 15min late.

Yikes. That means I'll have to finesse this guy into extending the first lesson for an extra fifteen minutes so I get paid for the full session, but I'm not above begging. It should be fine as long as I locate him quickly. I switch over to the email app and find the student's profile from Melinda sitting pretty at the top of my inbox. I click on it and my phone nearly slips from my grasp.

Aran Rodriguez's picture looks up at me from the screen.

I squeeze my eyes shut and shake my head. But no matter how hard I blink, that's his face and name on the student profile, all right. Wyatt was supposed to tutor him on essay writing starting fifteen minutes ago. And now…

Oh, no. No. *No.* He lifts his head up from his laptop screen, and those deep-set eyes, dark as an abyss, meet mine once more.

I'm rooted to my chair as the Bolts' captain pushes his chair back. The scrape against the floor catches the attention of the other students again. We all watch as he slowly stands to his full height—the whole six-foot-four-inches of it, according to his player profile. He doesn't break eye contact even as he sweeps all his stuff on the table in my direction with one hand and takes the seat right across the table from me.

I open my mouth to say something. Nothing but air comes out.

That's what happens to awkward turtles like me when the number one hottest guy on campus—as voted by students on the student portal over the summer—pays a modicum of attention to them.

He tilts his head to the side. A deep, husky voice that feels like velvet comes out of his mouth.

"Were you staring because you're my new tutor, or was it something else?"

And I proceed to die.

CHAPTER 3
ARAN

This time Strawberry doesn't choke. She does open and close her mouth as if she's forgotten how to use it.

After clearing her throat, she finally says, "Something else. And I'm sorry. That was rude of me."

I lean back in my chair. That was unexpected. The usual responses to something like this would be excuses or vanishing acts. But she doesn't bullshit her way through, nor does she leave. Rather, she takes out a few of the things she'd been packing in her backpack. A strawberry keychain hangs from the pull of its zipper, matching her earrings.

"Um." She tucks her brown hair behind her ears, making the earrings jut out next to her cheeks. Which are just as red. "Could we please start on the right foot?" She sticks her hand out for me to shake.

"That's a hand, though," I say, just to be annoying. When she starts pulling away, I reach out with mine and shake it. "I'm Aran Rodriguez, your new student."

Her eyes are wide. The brown in them looks almost translucent under the sunlight streaming in from the window. Her hand is so cold I'm tempted to lend her my gloves. But she gives a firm, strong pump to my hand and lets go. A good, professional handshake that doesn't make her whither into a fit of giggles like it would the other stalker at the table.

That makes me curious about what the something else was. If it were related to the tutor swap, she'd have easily explained herself with that. But I'm not curious enough to ask, especially if it could make things so awkward that I end up having to find yet another tutor. And I really need to get this new essay started before the next away game.

The only problem is that she's a she. Which goes against Step One of my plan.

"Madeline Berkley. You can call me Maddie." She lowers her eyes to her phone screen. "So, Aran—"

She mispronounces it, so I interrupt. "It's not pronounced Aaron. It's Ah-ran, with emphasis on the *ran* part."

"Oh." She tests it on her tongue without spewing a sound for a moment, then attempts it. "*Aran*? Is that correct?"

Not quite. She's as American as apple pie and the Spanish *r* sound will never come naturally to her, but at least she has the *a*'s straight.

"Good enough," I concede.

Her lips stretch into a smile that reaches all the way to her eyes. It transforms her face from that of a meek little mouse into something I can't describe. Something blinding and alluring like the sun is. Something I have to fold my arms to resist.

Okay, so what? Strawberry's cute. But I don't do cute. My type is girls who are looking for a good time and *only* a good time, which this girl is the antithesis of. So even though I specifically requested a dude for a tutor, this swap shouldn't put Step One of my plan at risk.

"So, Aran," she continues with more confidence. "I'm afraid that with the last-minute change, I haven't been able to look at your profile in detail to find out what your needs are.

And on top of that, I know we're starting this lesson twenty minutes after the agreed time—"

Eighteen, but I don't interrupt this time.

"Which is why I'm wondering what you'd prefer to do. I could take a few minutes to review your file and come up with a lesson plan, and then we could start today's session but do the full forty-five minutes. Or—" Here she pauses to draw in a breath. "We could just meet for our first session tomorrow. I can try to work around your schedule if that's what you'd prefer."

I run a hand over my head. Is she always this chatty, or is this just the standard introduction?

"How many minutes is *a few minutes*?"

"Ten to fifteen?" She cringes a bit and, without pressure from me, says, "I can try to keep it to ten maximum."

"Fine."

There's the smile again. "Great, I'll get right on it."

I grab my kale shake and take another big gulp as she fires her laptop back up. The smile naturally fades as she focuses on my file.

I had to explain why I needed someone to tutor me in essay writing when I approached the student center, which meant showing my essay in all its embarrassing glory. My profile probably contains interesting tidbits like: total bonehead, lives up to the reputation of a stereotypical jock, can barely string together a coherent sentence in English—and often chooses not to, anyway—code red: needs to be sent back to elementary school.

Strawberry scribbles in the yellow journal she was poring over before. When she does, she leans forward so much her long hair falls over the table like a curtain. I stretch a bit to see if I can catch what she's jotting down. Or whatever she wrote before when she was observing me. But her hair ruins my plan.

Another whisper comes from the eavesdroppers at the

table, and it mispronounces my name. No matter how many times I explain the correct way, people still botch it. At least tutor-girl made an effort and got it mostly right.

Her pen flashes against the light as she taps it against her chin, and lo and behold, the end cap is shaped like a big strawberry. I snort, and the sound makes her look up in a panic.

"Oh, is the time up already?"

I glance at my laptop's clock. "Nah. You have two minutes left."

"Okay, thanks."

Her face scrunches up as she tries to speed write the rest of her ideas. She looks fiercer than some of my teammates.

The right corner of my lips twitches. How interesting. Attitude comes out when she faces words. But when she's up against people, she retracts.

I polish off the last of my shake and stuff the bottle back into my backpack. Next, I close my auditing textbook and set it aside. She's gone over a minute already, but fortunately for her, I'm free for the next two hours. Unfortunately for her, I'm not generous enough to share that info.

Just as I'm about to cut her off, the crease on her forehead grows until she comes up for air like the Little Mermaid. She even pushes her hair back and away from her face as if she's been underwater. "So here's the plan. Take a look." With a flourish, she turns her journal upside down and slides it over to me.

Two forty-five-minute sessions the first week. The first would be centered around the general methodology for writing essays, and the second one would help me flesh out the content of my current class assignments. Then from week two and on, we'd alternate. One week, she'd correct last week's essay, and the next, she'd help me revise it or flesh out the new one, per my class assignments. At the bottom, she lists the time slots she has available per week. There are so many that this girl either has no social life or isn't taking many courses this semester.

"What do you think?" she asks.

"I honestly have no clue what I'm doing here," I admit with a shrug. "You tell me. Is this what I need to pass this elective?"

"I think so." She nods at her computer screen. "The ideas in your essay look pretty solid. It's just that you basically put zero effort into fleshing them out the way professors want. That's probably why Melinda—that's my boss, by the way—assigned you to Wyatt and now to me. We're English majors, not business ones, you know? You don't need help with the concepts, but with the execution."

A few giggles echo off to the side. My so-called admirers seem to be finding this amusing. No doubt I'll wake up to a fresh round of hockey-players-are-knuckleheads comments in the morning.

But Strawberry's expression holds no trace of mockery. In fact, if anything, she thinks I'm lazy. Which I've definitely been with this class.

I pick my mechanical pencil back up and circle the two time slots that work for me. One is this one, Tuesday morning, and the other one is Wednesday afternoon before practice. As I slide the journal back to her, the page blows over, and I catch the letters TDH underneath, where she was scribbling while she was snooping on me.

Tutor-girl smacks the page back down and jerks the journal back up to her.

Sus.

I force my lips to stay in a straight line as I ask, "What's TDH?"

She sucks in air through her teeth, and at the same time, her eyes go wide as saucers.

Well, that confirms that it has something to do with me. I

place my forearms on the table and lean closer. I won't ask again. This is usually enough to get people to spill.

"Nothing," she says in a high-pitched voice.

I narrow my eyes slightly, and all she does against the pressure is press her lips tighter. Strawberry has some spine. I'll give her that.

Faint but frantic steps distract me for a moment, as if someone is running in the library, which *I* know not to do, even though this is like my second time here. A guy rounds the corner around a bookshelf and immediately locks eyes with me. I recognize the blond mop of hair from the tutor profile I got when I was signed up for the service.

"Aaron, I'm so sorry I'm late!"

I grit my teeth.

Strawberry turns around. "Wyatt! You made it." I'm not sure if that's relief or disappointment laced in her words. But they're charged with something.

"This morning's been a mess." He plops onto the chair next to Strawberry with a huff. His coat is askew as the strap of his bag slides off his shoulder and he drops the whole thing to the carpeted floor. "Some jerk rear-ended me at a red light. Can you believe that?"

"That sucks. Are you okay?" Her forehead creases as she scans him down and back up.

"Yeah, I'm good. Getting the insurance stuff sorted out just took a while." Finally, the dude faces me. "Sorry about that. I can talk with Melinda and switch you back to me if you want."

"Oh." Strawberry whispers this word, and this word alone. This time, the disappointment is clear.

I tilt my head. She scratches one finger over the surface of the journal containing a neat little timetable written in rounded loops in blue ink. She put that together in hurry after a whole hockey player was added to her plate out of the blue. She's crafty and surprisingly direct. Not to mention, her rating from previous students is a whopping 4.9, compared to this dude's 4.7. I'm a numbers guy, and the choice is pretty obvious. So even though I requested a dude, I think this girl is better suited to the task of getting me out of the flunk zone.

"Nah," I say loud and clear. "I already agreed on a plan with Strawberry, here."

She splutters, "Strawb—"

"But," tutor-dude says. "It's really no big deal. Right, Maddie?"

"Um, actually—"

"I mean, don't you already have three other students on your plate?" He gives her a cringey smile that is as clear as if he were begging with words. "I only have two right now if I include Aaron."

"Actually," she says firmly before I'm able to correct the other guy. "Melinda just swapped our new students, so you will still have a second one, even though it's not going to be Aran. Pronounced as Ah-*ran*, not Aaron."

I raise my eyebrows.

"Oh, cool. Should've said so from the beginning." The fight leaves the guy, and he deflates on the chair before glancing at me again. "So, I guess we're cool, Aaron."

"Not if you keep calling me by the wrong name."

Something in my voice makes him pale.

"Yeah, dude. That's rude." She whispers the admonishment to him and then turns to me. "But so is calling someone else by something that is not their name."

This time I don't fight the smile. The amusement hits me harder than a slapshot.

"Look at that!" someone whispers aggressively, pointing a cell phone at me.

My lips flatten right back. I turn to the cohort of giggly girls and snap, "Take your damn pictures once and for all and go."

One of them squeaks. Another one pulls at her two friends until they scramble and go.

"Yikes." The tutor-dude mumbles as low as his voice can go. He stands back up slowly, as if I'm a feral animal that could jump at him any minute. And I will if he dares call me Aaron again.

Sighing, I face my new tutor again and find her blinking rapidly, like her brain can't process me.

Bienvenida al club, fresita, I think to myself.

"So, Maddie." My voice comes out gruff with residual annoyance. "Are we getting to work?"

"Uh, right." She clears her throat, fills her lungs with air, and launches into the first lesson.

CHAPTER 4
MADDIE

My heart beats as fast as a rabbit's as I rush toward the exit. Our table mostly cleared after he snapped at those annoying girls, and with Wyatt also gone, it was just Aran Rodriguez and me for forty-five minutes more.

And he's intimidating as heck.

He has this really intense air about him. Something about the way he observes every detail in complete silence. It made me rant like I never have in my life just so I could busy myself with anything other than panic. Because that's what I felt the second he asked what TDH is.

In my hurry, I didn't even bundle myself properly, and once I leave the building, I regret it. The January air feels like tiny needles stabbing my exposed neck and hands. I leave a trail of puffs in the air across the parking lot until I locate my Beetle and hide in it. I turn on the engine and set the heating to the max, watching the library's front door.

Of course he doesn't follow. Why would he?

I expel a sigh of relief. Is it just me, or is it even hard to breathe in front of him? I wonder if this is how his opponents feel when they face him. This overwhelming certainty that his eyes can see through to their deepest flaws.

Strawberry, huh? I fiddle with my favorite earrings, the ones I wear when I need a little spark of joy. Now I feel childish.

My phone buzzes in the pocket of my dress and keeps shaking while I pull it out. I accept the incoming call from Wyatt. "Hello?"

"Did you survive?"

I snort. "Barely. Did you time the session so you could make this call?"

"I totally did." He laughs a bit. "I was too curious. How did it go?"

"It went well, I guess…" I trail off a bit because objectively, it did. Once I started the session, there was no more teasing or snapping. Aran gave me his undivided attention, which is the problem.

"You guess? Don't tell me he was like…" Wyatt draws in air, though I don't know if it's for drama or because he's taking a brisk walk. "A bully?"

"Goodness, no."

"Okay, cool. I was a bit concerned based on how he reacted to those girls."

"So was I, to be honest," I mumble, fiddling with the hem of my coat. "But I think he's just kinda grumpy."

He chuckles. "Grumpy isn't how I would describe him."

"You're right. He deserves at least a full paragraph of description." I laugh, because I have a whole page of notes about him in my journal.

"I confess I'm a little glad I won't have to tutor him now, but I'm worried about you." He hushes his voice, like maybe he's in a building and not alone anymore. "Did you see in his profile how he specifically requested a male tutor?"

"I saw. What's the deal with that?" I mumble in return while I fasten my seat belt.

"I don't know. Moreover, I don't know why Melinda reassigned you to him."

"Maybe I was the only one available."

"Maybe." Wyatt pauses. "Just be careful with that guy, Maddie. He has a reputation." The way he says the last two words is as if he capitalized them, and I know exactly what he means. Aran Rodriguez is a player on and off the ice.

"Don't worry. That has nothing to do with me."

"Hmkay, hopefully those won't be famous last words."

I huff a quick farewell after that. While I appreciate his concern, I can also take care of myself. Ish. Extremely good-looking guys with bad-boy reputations and a stadium-full of broken hearts have never been my kryptonite. It's not that I'm invisible to them. I'm just someone they glance around on their search for a hot girl who fits next to them.

That's probably why it didn't matter to him that he was reassigned to a girl, despite requesting a male tutor. I'm basically the same as Wyatt in his eyes. And to me, he's like looking into the sun. It's nice to know he's there, and certainly heated me up, but so far out of my reach I won't even contemplate the possibility. I put my car in drive and leave the parking lot, determined to leave him behind for the day.

But dang, does he make great character inspiration.

TDH, foul-mouthed, self-confident, bottomless eyes. I can't wait to get home and flesh out some backstory. What would fit a character like this best? Surely something tragic. So what if it's nerve-racking to sit with Aran Rodriguez for almost an hour, two times per week? If it means I design the ultimate hockey hero for my new book, it's worth it. In fact, I should probably pay him for the service.

Optimism returns to me on the drive back to the apartment. I have no classes for the rest of the day, so I can spend a bit of time on developing my first-ever hockey romance before switching over to my coursework.

Even better, my roommates do have class this afternoon. I'll have the whole place to myself for a few hours.

I pick up my fave veggie lo mein on the way and wolf it down at the kitchen counter in our tiny apartment. After I'm done, I bag up the trash and toss it into the building's trash container by the parking lot. Last time I threw the cartons in the kitchen trash and my roommates saw it, they said this was why I was so fat, and that if only I'd stop eating takeout, I could get healthier and lose weight, when, in reality, I can't afford takeout more than once a week.

Back inside, I change out of the marigold cashmere dress I found at a thrift store and chuck my leggings across the room. I put on my comfiest pair of sweatpants and a sweatshirt that fits me like a tent because it's a men's 4XL. And with this freedom, I decide to enjoy the only good feature of this apartment. The glorious couch.

Rebs was my roommate at the freshman dorms, and we hit it off. The dorm room was too small for all our junk, and she knew I was having a hard time with the shared bathroom situation. So, at the first chance we got, we looked for options and found this place. The problem was that it has three bedrooms, so we needed one more person to help us carry the expense.

Insert Tiff. She found us through the roommate-wanted post we made on the student portal, and there were no red flags from her. But that's because the red flag was Tiff's bestie.

Lori.

Good ol' Lori is what fat phobia would look like if it could transform into a living, breathing person. She's one of those girls who's hot and knows it. And if you're not at her level, she will let you know. Repeatedly. Until you either start hating yourself, run away from her as fast as possible, or turn into her so she can accept you. I'm currently trying to do the second one of those options because, even though she's not my room-mate per se, she spends most of her time at our place hanging out with Tiff and Rebs.

Lori's the author of the takeout comment, which was obnoxious and expected of her. But the next day, I came home with a few leftover cookies from the office and made the mistake of offering them to Rebs and Tiff.

I still remember how Rebs's expression turned all concerned and she said, "Are you sure you should be eating this, Maddie? Maybe you should watch your calories a bit more."

And that was the first time I exploded. Rebs was my best friend. She knew that my mom made comments like that all the time. She knew how much they drove me nuts and how they hurt. And how they made me shrink in on myself. Two years of atta girl-ing me when I vented to her about my mom went down the drain the second queen bee Lori walked into our lives, deeming Rebs a *hot* and me a *not*.

So yeah, I have to get out of this place. But first I'll enjoy the feather-soft couch Rebs and I bought when we moved in for a little longer.

I brew myself a mug of lavender and chamomile tea, because I worked myself up to a froth just thinking about the mean girls. The aromatic steam settles my nerves. I put the fluffy blanket over my legs and settle in.

My laptop fires back up, and it still shows the site with the Thunder Strikes info that I'd minimized once I felt a little guilty over stalking Aran and his team. But now, in the privacy of this apartment, I look up his player profile once more.

This time I don't stop at his pretty face. Except I don't understand his stats at all. Are they good or bad? I've heard people say he's a great player, but this is all gibberish to me. I open a new tab on my browser to start looking up the terms and soon discover that he's not just great. Aran is the cream of the crop of Division I players. My tea goes cold as I fall into a rabbit hole of YouTube clips of games. I have no idea what I'm watching, but it's fast, and I'm enthralled.

I pause to heat up the tea in the microwave and make a note in my journal that says *hockey players must have good eyes, because the puck is small and fast.*

Huh, that must be how Aran spotted the letters TDH on another page of my journal. And maybe how he knew I was staring, even though he only made eye contact the one moment that made me choke.

The microwave pings, and I retrieve the mug. I remake my nest and brace myself. *Aran Rodriguez* pulls out a shocking number of results. The first one is a video feature in *SPORTY* magazine—a magazine even I've heard of—from last year.

I watch the whole ten minutes of it with my mouth hanging open. It starts with a montage of various trainings. Aran lifting weights that look as big as me. Lacing up his skates in the locker room. Getting *white* pucks fired at him in rapid succession—and him catching every single one like a machine. That has to be edited, right? But then they show him at a gym in normal clothes, catching a barrage of tennis balls someone flings at him from behind the camera, like it's a party trick. The words *prodigy* and *hottest goalie prospect* are bandied about every so often. They get some action shots of him that I rewind to watch again. Not my fault they got his best angles.

"Whoa!"

I jump in my seat. One of the action shots shows him shirtless and lifting what looks like thick, heavy ropes in rapid succession. And my question from earlier is answered eloquently.

Yes, a human apparently can be *that* chiseled.

His brown skin gleams with a sheen of sweat under the gym's harsh lights. It marks deep shadows in the ridges of his muscles, which shift and flex under the effort. Thick drops of sweat trickle from his chin, but his expression is exactly the same as when he's sitting at a library, watching me rant my head off. Calm but intense. And even though he's more or less crouching as he lifts the ropes up and down, his stomach doesn't bunch into a little tire like mine. No, sir. His is a map of tight muscles that belongs to a museum. I can even see the V shape that disappears into his sweatpants.

Wait, his sweatpants are quite tight. Are those muscles around his knees? I didn't know knees could look like that.

Would it be creepy if I paused the video to stare?

Bah, no one's watching. I hit pause and even make the video full screen.

"Oh no, Maddie. You shouldn't have done this," I mumble to myself. It's going to be hard to face him tomorrow and not imagine what I've now seen is under his clothes. Maybe Wyatt's concerns weren't as unfounded as I thought.

Keys jiggle outside the door, and it opens with a bang. I slam my laptop shut, looking like a deer caught in the headlights.

"Gee, are you looking at something for adults?" Tiff asks with a laugh she tosses over her shoulder. Sure enough, the other two also cross the threshold into the apartment.

"Of course not." But almost. I curl my hands around my warm mug of tea and take a casual sip. "Why are you all back early?" Unfortunately, my question goes ignored.

"Wow, Maddie. I didn't know you were into that." Rebs wiggles her eyebrows at me, playing along with her friends. Their twinkling little laughs chafe me raw.

Sighing, I start collecting my stuff. Meanwhile, Lori throws her bag at the foot of the couch and plops onto the cushions as if she were the owner.

"Aw, you don't have to go!" Lori pouts in an exaggerated manner. "But then again, if you prefer privacy to watch your naughty videos, I understand. Just don't let us hear you. Am I right, girls?"

Tiff snorts. "Ew, yeah."

I wish I didn't have paper-thin skin that so easily gives away when I'm feeling a strong emotion. But as I clutch my laptop and journal against my chest with one arm and pick up my mug with the free hand, they can all see how red my face is, and they laugh even harder. But actually, this is a flush of anger.

I slam my bedroom door shut with my heel. I'm angrier at myself than at them. I wish I could tell them off once and get them off my back for good. But every time I try to stand up for myself, Lori's comments get more and more insulting, and Rebs and Tiff get meaner too. It's worthless to even try anymore.

I don't want to max out my credit card to move out, but I may have to. Even taking in an extra student won't get me there quick enough. I sit on my bed and open my laptop back up, about to check my bank balance when there's a soft knock on my door.

The only one who'd ever bother is Rebs, the lesser of all the evils. Taking a deep breath, I say, "Come in."

She pushes the door open and pokes her head into my room. "Hey, we're heading out to O'Malley's soon and will probably be out of your hair all night, okay?"

Not an invitation. Not an apology. Or even an acknowledgment that her friend was awful—again.

"Yeah, whatever" is all I say. My door clicks shut, and Lori's laughter echoes from the living room, disrupting the quiet in my room.

I'm officially done with this.

CHAPTER 5
ARAN

Shit, Coach drove us too hard today. Even I'm eyeing the infamous puke barrel. Assistant Coach Thomas brings it out every time practice is going to be more medieval torture than hockey training. At least half of the team has left their own offering to the barrel today, but I can't let myself join their ranks. As the captain of this team and as a senior, I have a reputation to uphold. I swallow down the rising bile and focus on breathing through my mask.

"If you think this is hard, wait until you make it to the championship," Coach Green says from the center ice, frowning as another of the freshman guys dashes for the barrel and empties his guts there. "You'll be facing gradually stronger teams that will be trying to crush you. One mistake, and you'll wish you hadn't skated like an absolute ninny today."

"Anyone else need the barrel?" Assistant Coach Thomas asks, knocking his knuckles against the metal frame of the nightmare vessel.

A chorus of groans answers him.

Coach Green shakes his head. "Fine, get some rest now, you tender little babies. I'll see you tomorrow bright and early for dryland." Coach Green blows the final whistle, and the staff are first to file out of the rink.

I rip my mask away and draw in a big gulp of air. I blink hard under the steady stream of sweat trickling down my forehead. Unbidden, the image of a massive, juicy burger pops into my mind. It's what propels me to slide my ass away from the ice, even when my gear feels ten pounds heavier while sopping wet.

"Is this what death feels like?" Archie asks while we trod slowly down the hallway to the locker room.

"Bro," Jamal says while panting. "Pretty sure death feels like nothing. But this? This feels like too much."

I grunt in agreement.

Slowly, I lower myself to my bench and just breathe for a while. Anyone would think goalies have it easier because we don't have to skate around the ice all game long. But the coaches still make us join skating practice—while wearing bigger, heavier pads. I can't be faulted for needing a moment.

Glad to report Edwards visited the barrel today. Twice. But I don't even have the energy to heckle him. I wish a crane could remove my jersey for me.

I grit my teeth and push through as I always do. Not a peep comes out of my mouth even though everything hurts like hell. My jersey makes a wet slapping sound as it hits the floor. I remove my pads at a snail's pace, one by one. The hardest part is peeling off the undershirt that has fused to my skin. It takes me several tries and a growl before I'm able to tear it off.

"Mierda." I grunt when I look down at myself and no further layers have magically removed themselves.

"C'mon, the faster we get naked, the faster we can get a cold shower," Archie says to the room, immediately bringing people's motivation through the roof. They should've made him the captain instead. I couldn't motivate a mosquito to bite me right now.

Eventually, I manage to haul my bare ass to the showers. I don't even have enough energy to jump when the freezing spray of water hits my feverish skin. I wipe my face with my hands. This time a basket of steaming salt-sprinkled rustic French fries pops into my mind. And you know what? After this puke-inducing practice, a burger and fries sound perfect. Maybe with a shake.

Wait, no. A beer. Stout. With frost on the glass. And there's only one place nearby that sells this exact combo.

"Who's up for O'Malley's?" I ask.

A roaring chorus of yeses bounces off the bathroom walls.

My muscles ease under the freezing shower. By the time I'm dressed up and out the door, I start feeling almost normal. Except for the fierce growling in my gut.

"You read my mind, Rodriguez. O'Malley's is exactly what the doctor ordered," my roommate says as he falls in step beside me. "In fact, this girl from class texted that she and some friends will be there."

I cut a glance at him and almost blurt out that I'm only going for the food, but that would be too big a bone to throw at this gossip hound. In a second, he would zero in on the *only* and turn it on its head.

We toss our bags full of rank pads into the trunk of my car and join a few guys from the team for the walk over to the only bar on campus. There are many others downtown, but that's too much effort. And that's why O'Malley's is packed every day and night of the week.

Tonight is no exception. There isn't a single free table in this damn place, but I will eat my burger standing in a corner if I must. I break off from the group and head to the bar to place my order, starting with the stout.

"ID?" the bartender asks, even though I'm here practically every other day.

Sighing, I fish for my wallet and open it before him. He

appears as bored as me as he checks my birth date and nods. I turn, leaning my elbows on the bar to scope out the situation. If anyone looks remotely like they'll be done with their meal or drinks, I will hover over them like a storm cloud until they scamper off.

Waving catches my attention. Archie motions me over to a table with three girls and a handful of Bolts. Moreover, the surface space is pretty clear.

"Here," the dude behind the bar says, slamming a tall glass of stout onto the bar.

I grab it, enjoying how my fingers stick to the icy surface, and make my way through the crowd to the table.

"Here he is, the infamous Bolts captain in the flesh." Archie makes a grand sweep of his arm toward me that actually helps clear up space. I slide up to the tall table and finally take a swig of my drink.

"Oh my goodness. It's such an honor to meet you, Aran," a girl says, extending a slim hand with very long nails. "I'm Lori Schmitt, and these are my friends, Tiffany Peterson and Rebecca Newman. They go by Tiff and Rebs."

She called me Aaron. Normally, I'd consider giving her a pass because she's hot and potentially interested. Today, I don't give her a pass for precisely those reasons.

When it's clear I'm not going to shake her hand, Archie chimes in. "Tiff and I have class together, and I figured her friends are our friends, you know?" He gives me a look, the kind that means *be nice or else*.

"Double cheeseburger and fries?" a waiter asks, and I raise my hand.

The vultures lean in while I set the basket of food on the table, and I give them a warning look. Except the Lori chick must be worse at reading cues than me, or she maybe does it on purpose. She grabs a fry and pops it into her mouth with a smile.

It's official. She's on my blacklist.

Her smile falters under the force of my glare. "It's just a fry!" She titters a high-pitched laugh.

But it's never just a fry. It starts with one. Then it's half of the ration. And then it's *why don't you tell me you love me?*

I know her type. It's the same kind that got me slapped in front of the entire team a few days ago. The exact type that got me in trouble with Coach. And that I always gravitate to because they seem easy-going at first. We do a little fooling around, and then they want to screw me over.

"First rule of Bolts club is," Archie starts in a serious tone, "never mess with anyone's food. Unless that's their preference."

People laugh. I eye the bar for any empty spaces.

Fortunately, I don't have to make the effort. The conversation picks back up to what it was before I arrived, and no other fries are nicked by manicured hands. Even though I keep my attention on the meal, I note from my periphery that Lori keeps eyeing me. Not my plate, but me.

"Dude," Archie says, digging his elbow in my side once the girls have gone to the bathroom as a unit. "What the hell is your deal? Lori's totally into you, and you're acting crankier than usual."

"Yeah, I'd say you're like an eight right now," Mark Webber, one of the defensemen, says from across the table, referring to my infamous bad mood scale.

"I just wanted to grab a meal in peace, that's all," I say while wiping my fingertips off with a napkin.

"Well, great. You grabbed one meal, and you can have a different one if you stop being so prissy." Archie runs a hand through his red hair. "Or at least dial it down and let us have the meal this time."

"What the hell are you talking about, Archibald?"

"What he's trying to say," adds Jamal from my other side, jerking his head toward the other assistant captain. "Is that the rest of us don't have that *je ne sais quoi* that attracts women like flies—"

Archie nods. "Exactly. That *ye nay* whatever."

"So if you could just bring it down to like a four or something, you might not scare these girls away for us."

I frown. "Why do *I* need to work for *you* to get girls?"

Jamal gasps and puts his hand on his chest. "There is no *I* in team, captain."

"Whatever. I'm going home."

"No!" the three of them scream at me. Half the bar turns in our direction.

"Don't you dare move from this table, Aran Jose Rodriguez." Archie narrows his eyes as if he's getting ready to tackle me. Mark goes as far as spreading his arms wide and blocking my exit.

As a creature of math, I do the numbers. Three girls. Four guys. One openly uninterested guy. This is an ideal scenario for the guys. The second these chicks get their undivided attention, they'll forget about me. After all, every girl who has dumped me in the past has said I'm more boring than watching paint dry.

"Fine," I grumble.

"Okay, great." Archie turns to the others. "Just so you all know, I'm into Tiff."

"Rebs seems nice, so dibs, I guess," says Jamal.

"I mean, Lori's super hot, but she hasn't looked at me once." Mark winces.

"You'll have to work—And here they come." Archie clears his throat and plasters on a blinding smile. "Hi, there. Are you ready to order?"

"Oh, yeah. Totally!" The girl called Tiff sidles up to Archie, her own expression mirroring his.

My roommate's a dork. He thinks he has no game, but this girl is already putty in his hand.

I pull out my phone and check the time. It's pretty early, and my stomach is still open for business. Maybe I'll order a salad this time.

"Wow, you're so tall."

A waft of perfume hits me from behind right after that line. I don't even need to look up to confirm that it's coming from the newest addition to my blacklist. Jamal, the polite fool that he is, makes way for her to squeeze between. I sweep my eyes around her and catch the attention of the same waiter from before.

"Great, I'm starving," she says, grinning up at me as if I flagged the waiter for her.

"Guys, do you have plans after this?" the Tiff chick asks.

"Not really," Archie responds too eagerly.

"Cool, because we have a Play Station at home, if you wanna join us."

"Wait," the third girl cuts in. "I thought we were staying out all night."

"I mean, we could." Mark winks.

I give him a look. We have practice early in the a.m.

"It's honestly too loud in here," the girls' head honcho says, wrinkling her nose. "It would be better if we could get to know each other in a quieter place, right?"

"Yeah, that would be great!" Archie says a second before the waiter arrives to take everyone's orders.

I consider peacing out early, but going home and making my own salad would take much longer at this rate. So I stay for the food and end up getting dragged to some strange apartment just so my friends can try to score. Along the way, I grumble that there is an *I* in captain, but they ignore me.

CHAPTER 6
MADDIE

I wish I could say I'm strong enough to not let anyone's crap sour my mood, but that would be a lie. I am as tender as a half-melted marshmallow.

After they leave, I table the hockey romance plans for another day and wallow in my misery by doing something that is also miserable: I start my homework.

This is one of my hacks for not breaking down. Between a heavy senior-year workload, my job as a subject tutor, the behind-the-scenes work for my debut book, and now all the strategizing for a parallel career as an indie author, I have no time to stop and think about how much of a loser I am.

And I have a massive *L* hovering over my head. No friends aside from Wyatt and Melinda—and I'm not even sure they count. No boyfriends outside of the ones on book pages. A relationship with my body that's more melodramatic than having a bad boy for a boyfriend.

I can only escape from myself through my journal, my laptop, or my work. And I exercise them a lot.

I catch up on my readings for an elective on Women's Fiction vs. Women's Studies: What's Real and What's Fiction.

After that, I need to lie on my bed and stare at the ceiling in silence. The fresh reminder that it's hard to be a woman in real life, in books, and in the book industry—for more reasons than bleeding out of our vajayjays every month—knocks the wind out of me for a moment.

With some effort, I pick the pieces of myself back up and sit straight once more. The room is pitch dark, so I make my way around using the dim light from my laptop screen. I flip on the lamp and the fairy lights hanging around the edges of the ceiling. Now bathed in a cozy light, I hop back on my bed, which doubles as my work desk. Unfortunately, my desk is covered in too many piles of books to be used as intended. I didn't have enough money to buy a proper bookcase, and I don't dare install shelving on the walls because I'm hoping I can get part of my deposit back.

"Speaking of," I mumble to myself, opening my bank's app.

Ugh, it's time to do math.

So, subtract a mother who is still angry that I'm majoring in creative writing instead of something serviceable like law, like my older sister did. Then subtract the first cut of my book deal advance, which is already spent. But add the next cut, which I expect in March, when my book hits the shelves. Add the extra wage I'm earning now that I'm tutoring one super-hot hockey player. Weigh all that against how much the average rent is, plus the security deposit and the movers' cost, and…

"April," I say with a groan. I can't gather enough cash any earlier. Unless I max out my credit card, kick my credit score to the deepest abyss, and accumulate interest.

Could I handle another student? What if I start donating blood? Should I shave off my hair and sell it? It's my only objectively beautiful feature but, eh, it'll grow again.

Just as I'm laughing at myself, my phone starts buzzing

against my comforter. I feel around until my hand bumps it to check who the caller is.

I would turn into a raisin if I could cringe any harder. After taking a few bracing breaths, I pick up the call. "Hi, Mom."

"Madeline Berkley, I know you read my text. Why haven't you responded?"

"I'm doing great. Thanks for asking. Living my best life as a soon-to-be published author, acing my classes, helping out my fellow students." My voice comes out in a deadpan.

But Mom knows this is as far as I'll rebel, so she just snorts in response. "Madeline, this is important. It's for your sister's wedding."

I stifle a sigh. All our conversations are about Megan's wedding. If not, they're about my many shortcomings.

"Sorry, I really needed to sort out my semester calendar first."

"It's been two weeks since I asked you when you'll be available for a dress fitting."

"And it's been two weeks since the semester started. See the correlation?" I mumble.

"Fortunately for you, you have a mother who cares," she says in her snippy voice that grates on my nerves and gives me headaches. "So I went ahead and ordered dress samples in your size. Unfortunately, they take more time to be ready than straight sizes."

I hate that term. It sort of implies that anything else is an abnormal size.

"Which means," she continues, "they'll only be available the weekend after next. That's the first weekend of February, so mark it in your calendar."

"Fine." Wow, okay. I guess I'm happy it takes so long to get XL or XXL sample dresses. It gives me time to prepare for this torture.

"Your sister will join us too. She wants to make sure you'll look perfect. Or, well, as perfect as you can."

Oh, great. Beautiful, favorite child Megan will be there too.

Okay, I'm not being fair. I would give a kidney for my sister and she'd do the same for me. It's not her fault that Mom often uses her as an example of how lacking I am. For example, Meg will point out that the sleeves of my blouse are weird, and Mom will say it's the shape of my arms that's weird.

This will be awful. I wish I had a solid excuse to get out of it. But if not next weekend, then the following, and so on until my mother gets what she wants.

"Do I have to be sober for this thing?"

"Maddie…"

"Okay, okay." The whine I'm trying to hold back filters through my voice anyway. "Text me the address."

"No need. I'll pick you up, and we can make a day out of it."

That's the very last thing I want. A whole day of my mother nagging me about why I can't lose weight for the wedding? Hard freaking pass.

"Sorry, Mom, but I'm seriously busy with school and work. We'll have to hang out later, okay?" It's not a lie, but I still feel crappy.

That's what happens when I talk to Mom. I either feel crappy because of what she says or what she implies, or I feel crappy because I can't fully tell her how much those things upset me without her blowing up. It's like walking through a field full of land mines.

She lets out a sigh that could break records. "See? You wouldn't have to work so hard if you'd picked a more sensible degree."

"Did you forget how Meg had to study for like ninety hours a week when she was in school?"

"Yeah, but that was for a good purpose."

And there it is. The cold knife of parental disapproval thrusting into my heart with clinical precision, right where it hurts the most.

I wish Mom understood that books are a good purpose. The best. Books are an escape. A friend. The fantasy you know you'll never get to live in real life. The parent or the teacher you need during hard times. A window into a different world. And the honest living of so many people.

She acts like I'm the only fool who wants to pay the bills off dead trees. But she sure enjoys the occasional Nora Roberts off the supermarket shelf, huh?

"I have to go."

"Maddie, you know I just worry about you. I wish you would—"

"No, I really have to go. My boss is calling me." A complete lie for lack of a legit exit.

"Oh, okay," she practically chirps, oblivious to the fact I'm about to cry. "I'll see you in eleven days, then. So exciting!"

"Yes. Super exciting." I clench my jaw and squeeze my eyes shut.

"Bye, baby!"

"Bye, Mom."

I end the call and fling my phone onto the pillows.

No, I'm not going to cry. I've gotten over every passive-aggressive or plain-aggressive comment about my looks or choices for twenty-one years. This isn't a new hurt. I can get past this easily.

"Shut up," I hiss as my phone starts buzzing again.

I can't find the annoying thing, though. I run my hands over my pillows and under, and nothing. It buzzes incessantly until it stops. I squeeze my hand into the space between the mattress and the wall and voilà.

This time the caller was Rebs. That's weird. We barely talk in person, forget on the phone. Still, I call her back. Twice. And she doesn't pick up. A butt-dial, maybe? But that would only work if she made her butt the feature her phone recognizes to unlock. The mental image is so ridiculous it lifts my mood for all of a minute.

Next thing I know, the banging of the front door opening and slamming against the wall cuts through the quiet in the apartment. Followed by voices. Many. Including male ones.

I rush to my bedroom door and glue my ear to it.

"Make yourselves at home, guys!" a voice that is distinctly Lori's says. So obviously, these aren't burglars.

"Where's the PS?" a guy calls out. That's the last I discern before the chatter grows louder.

A knock on my door startles me, but then Rebs's voice sounds from the other side. "Hey, it's me."

I open the door a crack and whisper, "What the heck is happening?"

"Change of plans." She wrinkles her nose. "Tiff's Play Station was apparently more interesting than a night out partying and drinking."

It's only Tuesday, I want to say, but I don't. Nobody wants a homebody's condescension.

"Okay."

She pushes her blond hair behind her ear. "You can hang out with us if you want."

I recognize the olive branch for what it is, and yet I push it right back.

"I don't think that's a good idea."

"The guys are super nice," Rebs adds in a hushed voice. "They're also hockey players so, like, super, super hot."

I choke on my own saliva.

I've gone almost four years without crossing paths with a single hockey player, and now they're everywhere.

"Exactly." She sighs.

"Uh, I'll still pass." I offer a smile I know is watery at best. "I'm kinda busy, so…"

"Okay." She shrugs. "Just join us if you change your mind."

Still smiling, I close my door and sag against it.

If I weren't a frumpy mess. If I hadn't let my mom or Lori or the bullies of the world get in my head. If I were a confident awkward turtle. Maybe then I'd have what it takes to casually chat with hot guys without making a fool of myself.

I'm dragging my feet back to my bed when my eyes zero in on my empty mug on the night table, then on the empty water bottle beside it. On cue, my stomach grumbles, demanding something. Anything.

"No," I whisper down at the traitor. I can't believe my plan of staying holed up in my room for the rest of the night has been foiled so quickly. I rummage through my bag and come up blank on snacks or surprise water bottles, so a trip to the kitchen must be made.

Not to be dramatic, but when I open my bedroom door, it feels as if I'm about to embark on the quest to get rid of The One Ring. Suddenly, my bedroom door is pushed open by a force that doesn't come from me, and I stumble back.

There, in front of me, is the hottest hockey boy—again.

"Whoa, there." Aran Rodriguez does a double take. "Strawberry?"

"What are you doing in my room?" I squeak out.

He makes a casual sweep of my surroundings with his eyes. "Obviously this isn't the bathroom."

"Obviously not!" I squeeze myself between the doorframe and the door, pulling it closed behind me. Which leaves me far too close to him, seeing as he hasn't moved away. I crane my neck back to meet his piercing eyes.

"You're not stalking me, are you?" he has the nerve to ask.

"How could I possibly be stalking you when you're the one who barged into my bedroom?"

A corner of his lips twitches.

Dang, he has pretty lips. Wide. Thick. Moisturized. I wonder if he wears lip balm. I should make a note about that in my journal. I bet hockey players' lips get chapped easily.

"I did not barge in. I've stayed out here the whole time." His voice is the perfect companion to the work of art that is his mouth. Rumbly. Deep. A bit raspy. "Where's the bathroom?"

I fix my attention on his eyes and say, "Door behind you."

Finally, he takes a step back and points at me. "First door, they said." He shifts his finger backward. "Should've said first on the right."

"Ha ha, yeah."

Those glorious lips stretch just a smidge, but then they disappear as he turns around and heads into the bathroom I share with two other girls.

Oh no. The bathroom's a disaster zone. What if he sees the hundred pots of acne creams I have on the counter? I should've picked up when Rebs called. Maybe I'd have had time to…

Who am I kidding? No matter what I do, I'll always be a mess. And I don't have to bust my butt trying to impress this guy or anyone else; I should just be myself, no matter what. I push my shoulders back, lift my chin, and march to the kitchen.

CHAPTER 7
ARAN

Well, well, well. I never imagined I'd get to know my tutor this intimately. But there, as a welcome sign the moment I step into the bathroom, is a bra that can only belong to Strawberry. The other girls are smaller.

I snort, and a laugh threatens to burst out.

Also never would've imagined her as a lace girl. Not that I've tried to picture what her underwear is like, but if I had to, I'd have said it would be some pink stuff. Possibly with strawberries for decoration. But this is some proper silk, lace, and wire, in a creamy color that would blend with her skin and make her look naked.

I clear my throat.

After that, I make a point of not looking at the garment again. But it's imprinted in my mind, and I happen to have top-notch spatial vision. I now know exactly how big her chest is. And I'm not sure I can wipe the knowledge from my mind.

After washing my hands with fruity soap, I close the bathroom door and am assaulted by chatter coming from the living room. I stand there for a second, staring at Strawberry's door. There was a shocking lack of the infamous fruit in the decor, and the whole space was filled with books. But it smelled similar to this hand soap. I don't know why I realize that now.

I lift my hand to my nose again and take a good whiff this time. And, of course, it's strawberry. The woman is obsessed.

"Dude, stop. You're doing the character dirty," Mark is saying to Archie as I walk back to the living room.

"Dirty how? I've played this game a million times before."

"Yeah, in your sleep." Mark snatches the control from the other guy. It doesn't seem to bother Archie, because when he leans back against the couch, he's right up against the girl he's into.

Jamal and Rebs handle the other control. The girl whispers something in his ear that makes his face shift from amused to ultra-competitive, as if he's on the ice, facing a Bulldog or something and not about to play some video game against Mark.

"You're back."

I pull my hands out of the pockets of my jeans, ready to push this Lori chick away bodily if I have to. But she's sitting on a barstool, legs crossed and facing me.

"Yeah, not for long," I say, glancing around her until I find my tutor.

"What do you me—"

I tune out the rest of her question while striding around the kitchen island. I lean against the fridge and fold my arms. My tutor freezes in the middle of assembling a sandwich. Slowly, she glances up at me with wide eyes, like I caught her doing something wrong. And I have.

"Where's the meat?" I ask, momentarily distracted by the spread of food on the counter.

She blinks fast. "I'm vegetarian."

Clicking my tongue, I shake my head. "We can't be friends, Strawberry."

Her mouth flattens into a tight line for a second, but when she opens it to talk, someone else cuts in.

"Do you two know each other?"

I forgot whatsherface was also in the kitchen.

"No, we actually don't," Strawberry says quickly. Then she gives me a look I can't decipher.

"Hmm." I lean closer to her and lower my voice until only she can hear it. "Since we don't know each other, maybe I shouldn't warn you that your bra's hanging in the bathroom."

The gasp she draws is enough to capture the attention of everyone in the apartment. The knife she was using to spread mustard on the bread slices clatters to the floor as she makes a dash out of the kitchen. Her bunny slippers skid against the floor as she rounds the kitchen island.

She's faster than some of the newbies on the team.

I smack my hand against my mouth, but there's no hiding the shake in my shoulders. Archie cocks an eyebrow but has the decency to keep his yap shut. Or maybe his teasing game is off while he has a girl leaning against his arm.

"What's so funny?" Lori leans on the counter, presenting her cleavage as a trophy. She must've slid down the zipper of her sweatshirt in preparation for the move.

"If it had been for your ears, then you'd have heard it."

"Fine." She lifts a delicate shoulder. "I'll get it out of Maddie."

A door slams shut, and then a second one does in quick succession. Stomps echo out of the hallway, and Strawberry appears again, huffing like a beast about to charge.

Ah, shit. I want to laugh.

Her eyes narrow, as if she can read my mind.

"Maddie, are you okay?" Lori swivels the stool around. "I've told you; you need to exercise more so you don't run out of breath so easily."

Tutor-girl cuts a fierce glare at the head honcho that tells me these two aren't friends.

I check my phone. I'll stick around for exactly ten minutes more of this awkward mess, but then I'll I peace out. The guys are sufficiently installed here. They don't need me anymore. I might have considered investing five more minutes in giving my tutor crap if this chick didn't make me grind my molars.

Speaking of, Strawberry picks up the fallen knife and tosses it into the sink. She stops to regard me with vaguely murderous eyes and speaks through gritted teeth. "If I make you a sandwich, will that shut you up about this little incident for the rest of our lives?"

I mull it over. The salad at O'Malley's was more lettuce than anything else, which was disappointing, because the burger and fries were already not filling enough. I could do with a snack.

"Not a vegetarian one, though."

"There's"—Strawberry grimaces—"ham in the fridge."

"Deal."

"So, you two *do* know each other." The obnoxious voice sounds right behind me now. "From where?"

Strawberry expels a deep sigh. "We only just met today at—"

"School," I finish with a cutting tone and a warning glance. Strawberry clamps her mouth shut, and her forehead creases, but fortunately, she leaves it at that.

"Really?" Lori checks me with her hips to squeeze into the tight space between the kitchen island and where I stand beside Strawberry. "That's so funny, because Maddie studies English, but you're in accounting."

"How do you know that?" I frown.

"Dude, everyone knows that," Jamal calls out from the living room. Apparently, the game isn't as interesting as this conversation. "In fact, everyone at school knows your height, blood type, and girl type."

"Especially the latter," Archie chimes in.

"Exactly." Lori sweeps her eyes down my body. "Especially the latter." She curves her lips in a way that makes it clear she thinks she's my type.

I turn back to Strawberry and say, "Hold the mayo."

She narrows her eyes at me. "Please."

"Please," I add.

For the first time since I opened her bedroom door, she smiles. Too quickly, she shifts the full power of it down at the second sandwich she's making. It's like she enjoys putting me in my place. But I don't mind, because I'm getting a free sandwich out of the deal.

"It's so good you're finally making friends, Maddie," the other girl continues, as if we were paying attention to her in the first place. "You can't keep being a little cave troll forever, you know? Even if you often do look like one. Those sweats just don't do you any favors."

Strawberry stills. Her grip on the knife tightens so much her fist shakes.

"Aran." Her voice comes out tight. "Your sandwich is done. Just put the ham in it, okay?"

Strawberry tears a piece of paper towel from the roll and slaps it on her sandwich. Glaring both at me and at the other girl, she picks up her plate and a steaming mug, then squeezes past us out of the kitchen. I watch her go until she disappears into the hallway.

There's a whole lot of silence in the apartment, aside from the *pew-pew* of the video game.

Since I'm not a total monster, I close the lid on the mayo and bag up the rest of the tomatoes and lettuce. I have no idea where they go in the fridge, but better in the wrong place than rotten. I find the sliced deli ham on top of a carton of eggs and set out to follow Strawberry's instructions.

"Sorry about that." Lori sighs. "She's just so sensitive, you know? Can't ever take a joke."

"That didn't sound like a joke to me," I say as I pull two slices out of the pack and throw them on top of a big tomato slice. It didn't go unnoticed to me how Strawberry stacked up my sandwich with more food than her own. I like generous people far more than conniving ones.

"No, it totally was a joke." She lets out a tinkling laugh like the one earlier, when she stole my fry. "That's how we girls play around."

I take a bite out of the sandwich and turn around. While chewing, I say, "Screw that. I have two sisters, and they never talk to each other like this."

Someone chokes, and it's not me. It also isn't whatsherface. Her mouth hangs open, and she reels back as if my words punched her.

"Guys," I call out over her head. "I'm leaving after I eat."

"Yeah, okay." Archie looks at me with eyes as wide as saucers.

Lori splutters. "But—You just got here."

I use every ounce of tact I possess, which isn't much, and say, "Yeah, I know," rather than what I truly want to say. Which is *yeah, but you're really stinking obnoxious.*

With the sandwich hanging between my clamped jaws, I make the trek around the kitchen and back to the hallway with four doors. I knock on the first one—on the left. There's some shuffling on the other side, and as I wait, I take another proper bite. Strawberry must be a good cook, because the ingredients wouldn't taste this good if I put them together myself. I'm another bite deep and about to knock on the door again when it finally opens.

The annoyance on Strawberry's face falters. "Oh. It's you."

"It's me." I raise what little's left of the sandwich. "This is really good."

"Don't tell me you want another one."

"Not right now. By the way, you have mustard on your face."

"Oh, crap."

Strawberry scrambles back into her room and snatches the balled-up paper towel from her empty plate. She keeps her back turned to me as she wipes her face. Her brown hair is a curtain behind her. A thick one. And it stops right atop her ass. Also a thick one. But then she twirls around, and I stuff the remainder of my sandwich into my mouth.

Nothing to see here. Nothing happened. I was *not* checking out my tutor.

"How about now?"

I grunt.

She tilts her head, and a strand of her hair caught on her shoulder drops to her chest. The chest I now have the perfect measure of in my head.

"You do that a lot, you know? Grunt like a caveman."

I nod. I *know*. I do it so I don't blurt out what's going through my head. Which right now goes against Step One of my plan. And I need to remind myself that Strawberry here is a major player in the success of Step Two, so I shouldn't be standing here wondering if her underwear matches the bra I can now see tossed over a chair in the corner.

I clear my throat. "Anyway, you good?"

Her eyebrows rise and her face scrunches up. She scratches her elbow. But then she lifts her chin. "Yes, I'm good."

And I'm Ken Dryden.

But this is none of my business. Just like how her under-wear isn't any of my damn business. I lick a drop of mustard from my thumb and tear my eyes away from the bra.

"See you tomorrow, Strawberry."

Annoyance takes over her features. "Don't make me call you Aaron."

A girl who can take it *and* dish it back, huh?

I grin. "See you tomorrow, *Maddie*."

I don't know whether I should be amused or worried that tutoring sessions won't be a drag after all.

CHAPTER 8
MADDIE

rush through the buildings in the central campus area at a brisk walk. My white Dr. Martens squeak with every step as they shed the residual slush from outside, but I'm happy to trade potential slips for noisy boots that make people stare. Pushing the door to the student center with my shoulder, I pause for a second to relish the warmth. Melinda always keeps it a notch too high, but it's snowing outside, and this is the next best thing to a roaring fireplace.

It's close to noon, so the place is mostly deserted. One of the tutors frantically types something on one of the office computers. Beyond the counter, I see my boss in her office. She's on the phone, though, so I'll have to wait to have this conversation with her.

But I spot Wyatt coming out of the break room. Jackpot.

"Wyatt," I whisper and motion with my mitten-covered hand.

He lifts his head away from a steaming cup of gross hot chocolate, more commonly used to warm our hands than as a drink. "Hey, Maddie. What's up?"

"We need to talk." I glance around. The other tutor is watching, that snoop. "In private."

"Oh, sounds intriguing."

Never one to back away from a good piece of gossip, he follows me into the one meeting room in the student center. I take a seat across the table, finally catching my breath. I've been high-strung since this morning, but I have a plan now.

I wait until he takes a seat and sets the paper cup on the table before I speak. "Is there any chance we could swap students so we have the ones we were assigned to from the beginning?"

The way his eyebrows rise pulls his eyes as wide as saucers. "Wait, did something happen after I left?"

"No." But he starts leaning away, and I figure it'll be harder to convince him if I'm not honest. "Not after you left. Later. Many hours later."

"Oh?" Wyatt leans forward.

I huff, blowing a strand of my hair away from my face. I try tucking it behind my ears, but my mittens are too thick. They also feel too good to remove just yet. My hair will have to stay messy.

"You're stalling, so this must be good."

I whine. "I have embarrassed myself beyond comprehension," I say, dropping my face into my mittens.

"Did you already develop a crush on him, then blurt it out or something?" he asks with a chuckle.

"That's not what happened. It's much worse." I lower my hands to the table and do the same with my eyes. "Promise you won't laugh?"

"Do I have to?"

"Wyatt…"

"Okay, okay. I promise."

I pin him with a hard stare. "Also promise that what you're about to hear won't leave this room."

"Cross my heart and hope to die. Scout's honor."

"I know you weren't in the scouts, but I'll take it." Drawing a deep breath, I spit it out. "He saw my bedroom. And my bathroom. And my bra!" At this, I collapse into my hands again.

"*What?*" Wyatt snorts, but a glare from me is enough to hold his laughter back. "I'm going to need a few more details. How did Aran Rodriguez end up seeing your bra the day you met him?"

"I don't know. I don't know how any of this happened. But I can't possibly face him again." I melt on the table, using my arms as pillows.

"Maddie, I didn't know you could move that fast, but I approve."

"It's not like that. My roommates brought him and a few other Bolts to our apartment last night without giving me any warning. And my bra was hanging in the bathroom as it dried. And he saw it. And I want to die. The end."

"Please, please, *please* let me laugh. The one who is dying here is me."

"Fine. Laugh," I mumble.

He lets out a great guffaw, followed by kindergartener-type giggles.

I scrunch up my face. "You wouldn't be laughing if it had happened to you."

"First of, that would've never happened because I don't have boobs." His whole frame shakes with laughter. "Second, I can't trade you now. Sorry."

"What? Why?"

"Turns out the girl you were supposed to tutor is my soulmate."

I sit up straight and blink like an owl. "Okay, now you spill."

His lips stretch into a smile that reaches his eyes, and it's like he's stopped seeing me. Instead, his mind must be set on an image of this mystery girl.

"She's a jock too, actually. Tennis, though." Sighing, he rests his chin on his hand. "Like, I've always been into the more artsy girls, but she and I hit it off from the get-go in a way that's never happened before…"

"Oh my."

"Anyway, I want to see where this goes, so Aran Rodriguez is all yours."

"He's not—Ugh. Fine. I'll see if Melinda can trade me with someone else."

"Yeah, good luck with that. The two other tutors quit, so I doubt she'll have anyone to sub in for English."

"Well, this has been extremely helpful." I roll my eyes and push my chair back to get up. "But I have to go bury my head in the sand now. Bye."

"Good luck."

I leave him to his laughter and go mope in the cafeteria while I have lunch. My mind keeps churning the scenes from last night, even during class, as if it's more important than paying attention to the lecture. I take the long route out to the library after class, knowing I might even be late for the next session with Aran. But it feels like my shoes are filled with lead, and every step I take makes my breath turn more jagged.

Not to be dramatic, but I think I may die of embarrassment if I see him. But I have to. Because I'm his tutor.

Unless… What if I convince him to ask for a replacement? Melinda may be more willing to swap me if the request comes from him. And yeah, maybe it will make my rating tank, but I'm desperate.

"Crap," I mutter to myself as I hide behind one of the bookshelves. For Aran Rodriguez is already waiting in the same spot as yesterday.

This time the table is fully empty, though. Which is even worse.

He already has his laptop on. It's one of those big models that must weigh a ton but looks small against his hands as he types on it. Several textbooks are open all around him and there are some wrappers balled up next to them, like maybe he's been parked here studying for a while. Maybe he won't notice that I'm late. Maybe he won't notice if I don't show up at all.

No, I'm responsible. And brave. And strong. I can face him.

I almost make a U-turn when he lifts his eyes for a second and locks them with mine. But he focuses back on whatever he's doing, and the relief alone is enough to propel me forward until I sit across the table from him.

"Hi." Regretfully, my voice comes out like a squeak.

The only acknowledgment I get is another brief glance.

I busy myself removing my coat and hanging it from the back of my chair. I take off my mittens and scarf, a matching marigold set I knitted last year. Then I sit back down, but I don't take any of my stuff out of my bag. Hopefully I won't need them because he'll agree to requesting a different tutor.

Manifesting, I tell myself as I breathe in deep. We can do this.

"Give me a moment while I finish," he mumbles, more to himself than to me.

"Give me a moment, *please*," I blurt out, correcting him again.

A corner of his lips curves up slightly. "Sure, take your time."

"Ugh."

My hopes start deflating. He seems to fully enjoy antagonizing me for sport.

The half smile stays locked in place, even as he continues working. He pauses to circle something in his textbook with his mechanical pencil, then he's back to fiddling with his computer. I stretch myself up to glance at the textbook. It's a love festival of numbers. Just looking at it makes me dizzy.

What was it Lori said yesterday? That he's studying accounting? That didn't feature in his player profile, but it must be true.

So, Aran Rodriguez is a smarty pants, and not just because of the crap he says all the time.

He snaps the textbook shut and slides it away before tearing his eyes away from his screen. Showtime, I guess.

"Hi," I say with more strength.

"You said that already."

"Ha ha. Yeah, so…" I trail off. "Can we talk for a moment before the session?"

"I'm all yours."

How can he say something like that so nonchalantly?

I clear my throat. Unlike Meg, who is a master of spoken language and can talk circles around the heads of a jury, I tend to wither when I have to express myself aloud. It's why I always gravitated to the written form as a kid. I can only express myself properly if I have the time to think about each word. Which is why I had to prepare all my talking points in advance, and why I couldn't concentrate during class at all.

Here goes the first one. "So, I noticed in your profile that you specifically requested a male tutor, which I'm not—"

"I noticed."

"And I was wondering if you'd still prefer to be tutored by a guy?" I cross my fingers under the table. *Please say yes.*

"I don't care anymore." Aran shrugs those big shoulders of his, making the fabric of his sweatshirt stretch from his neck.

"What? Why?" This may or may not have come out as a whine.

"What I really didn't want was someone who may start hitting on me or something," he responds, using that cool inflection that betrays no feeling. It's like he's talking about the weather and not saying something that sounds super pretentious.

Except, in his case, it's not showboating. Dude has a serious fandom in this school. And from what I found online yesterday when I was doing book research, they can be a bit too much.

"Uh, but I'm not what you requested…" I'm grasping at straws.

"A new tutor may be weirder than you, though."

Aran folds his arms on top of the table, and they distract me. Mom wouldn't have anything bad to say about them. In fact, she'd be wondering what I'm wondering. What's the name of that muscle that curves on the outside of his upper arm?

"Are you planning to hit on me?"

"No!" The shout echoes around the library.

Oh my word. Did he catch me checking him out again? Maybe I should've said yes. That would've convinced him to ask for a new tutor right away. Although I would never! Heat rushes up from my chest. A cocktail of embarrassment and panic churns in my gut.

"B—But I definitely don't want to make you uncomfortable, you know?" Next argument I prepared: "You deserve the best care, and I'm just not sure I'm the right person for the job."

"Your rating says otherwise."

Why is he so good at picking apart my arguments with so few words?

Maybe because they're flimsy. That's why. I may have to use the tactic I least wanted to use.

"Listen, I'm going to be fully honest with you." I draw in a deep breath, and in a solemn way, I say, "I'm absolutely dying of mortification."

Aran leans forward a little, those intense eyes unwavering. "You should get that checked out."

The urge to kick him is strong. "C'mon," I whine.

"Why? Because I saw your room?"

"Not because of *that*," I mumble with a frown.

"So what? I saw your bra. Everyone has boobs. Half of the boobed people wear bras. It's no big deal."

"It's a big deal for me." I drop my face into my hands again. "How can I possibly act professional now?"

"Want me to show you my boxers to level the playing field?"

"Aran!"

"Or I can show you my boobs instead."

"Are you trying to kill me?"

The grin on his face is criminal. It's a gesture that steals hearts and sanity. He should register that and only use it when he has a valid permit.

"Look, if you hadn't brought this up, I wouldn't be thinking about your boobs right now, and we would've started the lesson like normal."

I groan and collapse on the table. He's right. I'm the one who made it awkward. He had probably forgotten all about it. He's probably seen countless pieces of lingerie on or off countless girls. There was probably nothing memorable about mine. Why did I have to overreact?

"Can we please forget this conversation happened?"

"Now we can't, no."

"Great," I grumble, my face smooshed against the table. "Is there really no way I can convince you to find someone else whose humiliations you haven't witnessed?"

"Nope. And I have class soon, so we better get cracking."

"Fine. But promise me something." I pause not for drama, but so I can steel myself. "You won't tease me."

"I can't promise that," Aran responds factually. There's no malice in his eyes, only amusement.

I purse my lips. "Then promise you won't bring it up in public."

"I *can* promise that. I didn't do it last night."

"And thank you for that. Lori would've eaten me alive." I sigh and grab my bag, because I'll need my things after all. "I guess we can start the lesson."

CHAPTER 9
ARAN

For the first ten minutes after the session finally starts, I can't concentrate on what Strawberry's saying at all.

My normal scale of emotions is a spectrum that ranges from mild annoyance to virulent, volcanic rage. I've only felt the latter once in my life, the night Luz got hurt. But I normally oscillate between levels near the lower end because even though good things happen every day, I can't help feeling the bad ones more strongly. I'm like a caveman primed for danger and misfortune all the time. So a bird shitting on my car will leave me sour for the entire day, but acing a quiz will only tip me out of my bad mood scale until the next annoying thing happens.

But three times now, Strawberry has yanked me out of my bad mood and forced me to hold back laughter.

That's… rare.

"Aran Rodriguez, I need you to focus on the lesson." She pokes the table with the tip of her index finger in what I assume is meant to be an irritated gesture. She's been trying really hard to be cool, calm, and collected. Except her face is as red as that fruit she's obsessed with.

I point at her yellow earrings. "What happened to your strawberries?"

"I assure you I like other things," she mumbles, trying to push the pencil case decorated with a very predictable motif from my view.

I snort. "I don't believe you. Even your hand soap smells like strawberries. I bet your shampoo's the same."

A little gasp. "Did you look into the shower?"

"I didn't have to."

"Do you seriously want to spend the rest of your session talking about my toiletries?"

"Does it get me out of writing this stinking essay?"

"No. Stop stalling." She points at my computer. "I hope you wrote down everything I said."

"You know I didn't." I've been sitting here, staring at her and trying not to laugh. One of my hands was busy pressed against my mouth. The other one was resting on the table.

"Okay, write it down now."

I comply. She repeats her entire thought process about structuring writing. She must've read the case study I sent her in advance, which surprises me. I thought reading it would be part of the work she was supposed to do in-session.

"Wait, you're speaking too fast for me," I say with a frown at my laptop screen. My notes are full of typos because I can't type as fast as she speaks.

"Oh, sorry. Where did you lose track?"

"The part about presenting the thesis."

She blinks. "You're a slow typist."

"Yeah, I am. My hands are fast at other things," I say in a droll.

"I bet."

She stiffens, as if shocked that those two words came out of her mouth.

I tilt my head. "Is that a veiled insult?"

"What? No!" She shakes her hands in the air. "It's a compliment! You're a goalkeeper. You catch super-fast pucks, that's all."

"Goalie."

"What?"

"The position I play is called goalie."

"Oh. Right. I knew that." She clears her throat. "Anyway, keep typing."

"Yes, ma'am."

That gets a spark of amusement from her, just the tiniest arch of her lips that possibly means she's finally relaxing.

I try to focus on writing down the sequence of ideas, but I stumble again. My fingers know the lay of my keyboard to a T, but in the numerical section. I can keep my eyes locked on an Excel workbook without once glancing down to ensure my fingers are typing the correct numbers, but it's not the same case with the letters. At this, I'm fully incompetent.

My previous good mood has gone up in smoke, and when I have to ask her to backtrack for the fourth time, I start fantasizing about flinging my laptop out the window.

"Let me see your notes," Strawberry says at the end.

I grumble something incoherent and turn my computer around so she can read it. Bracing herself with her arms, she leans over the wide table and squints to read.

"You could just grab the laptop, you know? Or you could sit next to me."

She grimaces, and for a second, I think she's going to shut that suggestion down, but she straightens and starts packing away. "Actually, good idea. It looks like a beast I'd rather not have to lift. What if I drop it?"

"It would break the table," I mumble as I watch her stuff her laptop, the same journal from yesterday, the pencil case, and a water bottle into a knit bag. As she walks around the table with her coat hanging from her arm, I wonder if she'll sit close enough that I'll catch the strawberry scent in her hair so I can tease her about it.

I hold my breath as she sits to my right and have to tell myself, *don't forget Step One, you bonehead.*

"Okay, let me see."

I push my laptop to her, glad she's sitting at a good distance. The light from my laptop screen illuminates freckles on her cheeks and across her nose. She's just a strawberry herself, huh?

"You're missing a few things. May I?" She lets her fingers hover over my keyboard, as if it was a living, breathing thing she needed consent to touch.

I rub the top of my head. "Go ahead."

At the speed of light, she types up a sentence here, another there. Her fingers move faster than any fingers have a right to.

"Are you sure you're not a goalie?" I ask.

Strawberry tears her eyes away from the screen. "Huh?"

"Because your hands are really damn fast."

That gets me a full-blown smile. "Wow, that's the best compliment I've ever gotten."

I could give her more, but they'd make her blush to the roots of her hair again. I need to take a page from her book and be professional here.

Instead, I say, "Any chance I could pay you to type up my essays for me?"

"Absolutely freaking not." If anything, she beams even more. "Good try, though."

"Bummer."

"It's all yours now." Her nose wrinkles as she picks up my laptop to hand it over. "Geez, is this made of lead?"

"I don't like small things."

"Makes sense. You're so big."

I watch as color rises up her throat in real time. My bad mood level plummets until I'm firmly in the rarely used good mood category.

"I didn't mean to make it sound weird. It's just my awkward turtle talent, that's all." She focuses on unpacking her stuff again.

I bite my lip. There are nineteen minutes left in the session. All I need to do is focus on the coursework, no matter how viscerally I hate it, and not on making my tutor blush again, even though it's so easy. And amusing.

Wait a damn moment. Have I been flirting with my tutor?

I put my elbow on the table and rest my forehead on my hand for a moment. If I could roundhouse kick myself, I would.

"It's not that bad," she says all of a sudden. "Just type the first sentence and call it a day if you want. That one's usually the hardest."

I grunt. If only that were the struggle.

Okay. Let's focus. I can pretend this essay is a Bulldog forward, and it's not going to defeat me. Strawberry has basically given me a map to write this miserable thing. And it will be over sooner if I start it.

How do I start it?

Shit, why can't I just say the CEO of this case study's company was a tool who made every bad decision possible? Should I ask for help already? Am I going to look even more incompetent than the CEO if I do?

But my tutor's busy. Her cell phone sits on the table between us, the calculator app open. In her journal, she has a table with categories and numbers she's adding up and subtracting. She pauses to count something in her mind with her fingers, frowns, and then strikes through the total at the bottom of the table.

"Need help with math?"

She jerks her head up. "Oh, no. It's okay. The math isn't the problem."

"You sure? You look like you're in pain."

"It's not as painful as when you're thinking about what to write."

"Touché."

Strawberry leans back against her chair with a sigh. "No offense, but math sucks. Especially when it's about money."

"Full offense taken."

"In accounting classes, do they teach you how to pull money out of thin air? Asking for a me."

I snort.

"So that's a no, then? Shame."

I type a couple of words. Delete them. I have bone-deep regret over having let Luz and Olivia get in my head with the whole robot thing. I should've never taken this class. So I grab the distraction being presented on a silver platter.

"What do you need to multiply money for?"

"So I can move," she mutters, jotting another line at the bottom of her list. *Sell old clothes*, it says. Then she writes *100?*

"Is this because of Lori Schmitt?"

"How did you—Oh, right. You met her last night."

"Very charming girl," I add, my voice flat.

Her eyebrows go up. "You didn't like her?"

"Hell no."

"Oh, maybe we can be friends, Aran Rodriguez, even if you're a meat-eater." She leans closer to inspect my laptop screen. "But first, don't forget I'm your tutor. Why haven't you written anything?"

"Because it's a nightmare I want to wake up from."

"Do your work, Aran." Her face twitches like she wants to smile but is fighting it.

I try. I *really* try. But all I manage is to type a paragraph that basically summarizes the abstract of the case study, and then her alarm goes off, signaling the end of the session. I'm only too glad to slam my laptop shut.

We both stand up from our chairs at the same time. I put my laptop in my backpack while she stretches, and her gray dress snags on the page of her open journal. It stays open to that list she's been working on, which includes what she makes per student, her itemized expenses, and a bunch of things she's apparently willing to sell. At the bottom, she has underlined the words *it's not enough, ugh*.

Before I think too hard about it, I say, "I can help you with that."

"Oops." She snaps the journal shut. "No, it's okay. I don't need an accountant. I also couldn't pay you for your time, as you clearly just saw." An awkward laugh follows after that.

"Not with that. With moving."

She releases the handle of her bag, and it flops back onto the table. "What do you mean?"

"My friend Ryan's looking for a roommate," I say as I wind my black scarf around my neck.

"Oh. I, um. I'd prefer to room with a girl."

"She'd be amused to hear this." I shrug into my coat.

"Oh, wow. Please don't tell her I put my foot in my mouth before I even met her."

"You do that a lot," I say, mimicking her from when she pointed out my grunting.

She winces with that tiny smile of hers. "Yep, that's me. Never a dull moment. Anyway, I don't know if I could afford it, but I'd love to talk to Ryan."

"Then meet me after practice outside the arena."

"What, today?"

With my chin, I gesture to the journal still on the table. "I read the letters ASAP, and I know my eyes didn't deceive me."

"What time does your practice end?"

"Six thirty."

"Got it. See you there."

I shrug on my backpack, and with a nod, I turn away. And bury my face in my scarf so no one can see how hard I'm freaking smiling.

CHAPTER 10
MADDIE

Sometime in the past twenty-four hours, the world has tilted on its axis. That's the only reasonable explanation as to why I'm going to meet the captain of the Thunder Bolts for a fourth time. This is the St. Cloud equivalent of, I don't know, suddenly meeting Chris Evans at a bar and then agreeing to hang out again the next day.

It's wild.

Also wild: the fact that I don't know what to do with myself. I already tried walking into the building, but the doors are locked. And it's cold enough out here to freeze my nose hairs. But I can't afford the gas it would take to run my car for so long. So I've been alternating between hanging out in my car for a bit and hopping outside and moving my body so it stays warm. I only stop when I skid on black ice in the parking lot and figure spending money on gas is better than spending money on a trip to the ER.

Because it's nearing seven p.m. and no one's out.

All the lights are on, though, so I don't think Aran lied to me. He doesn't seem like that kind of person. Gruff and grumpy, sure. A bit cutting sometimes too. And he revels in my embarrassment. But his intimidating air doesn't translate into being a jerk, like I feared at the beginning.

No, Aran is... The school may revoke all my credits because I'm a creative writing major, yet I'm coming up blank with how to describe him. *Nice* doesn't fit him. He still makes me much more nervous than any other guy I've ever met, and it's not because of his gorgeous face. He just gives me the impression that I won't be able to hide anything from those sharp eyes. He's an intense person who is intensely hot. Who wouldn't freak out?

He's also late, though.

I check my phone, and it reads 6:52. I wish I'd thought to ask for his number so I could contact him to reschedule. But then the front door opens, and two guys come out dressed in thick coats, with ginormous duffel bags hanging from their shoulders.

Should I get out of the car now? Would it look weird if I wait for him outside the door? But what choice do I have? It's not like he knows what I drive.

Gathering my nerve, I turn off my car again and climb out. More people stream out of the building, guys and girls alike, all carrying big bags and equipment. And apparently, all of them much taller than me.

I attract a few stares as I park myself by some benches at the entrance. I don't sit because they have ice on them. My breath comes out in puffs that cloud my vision, but even if I don't see him, Aran will spot me easily. And it won't be because of his super vision. It will be because I'm the only short, chubby person not carrying any equipment here.

But I spot him right away. His is the only tall head with a buzz cut. He keeps the door open for a girl to walk through. They're chatting, so I clamp my mouth shut and don't call out his name like I intended. He turns around, as if he'd already seen me, and heads my way without hesitation.

"So this is her?" the girl asks, motioning toward me.

Aran nods. "Maddie, this is Ryan Avery. Ryan, this is Madeline Berkley—goes by Maddie and doesn't like it when I call her Strawberry."

"Gotcha." Ryan's eyes sparkle under the light of the lamppost. She offers her hand, and I shake it and, wow, she's strong. "It's great to meet you, Maddie. I've heard a lot about you already."

"Uh-oh." My eyes are wide.

"Nothing terrible. Only how you're keeping my boy here out of trouble."

My boy?

I didn't know he had a girlfriend.

"Uh…"

Aran expels a little cloud from his mouth with a sigh. "I had to explain how we met. So she knows you're my tutor."

Of course. I mean, girlfriends like to know these things. I think.

"Apparently," Ryan continues, her tone conspiratorial, "he doesn't want anyone else to know he's about to flunk an elective."

"A bullshit elective, to be more accurate," Aran mumbles.

"Don't worry. All your secrets are safe with me." She jams her elbow into his side so hard it makes him grunt. "Unlike the bunch of gossips you call teammates, am I right?"

"Unfortunately." He shakes his head with a deadpan expression and hoists his duffel bag higher on his shoulder. "So, Strawberry, are you ready?"

"Will you ever stop calling me that?"

"Probably not."

"And he won't be apologetic about it," Ryan adds. At the same time, she hooks her arm with mine. "But if you can put up with his crap, you'll have a solid friend for life."

"I, uh…"

Aran rolls his eyes wide. "She's looking for an apartment, not for some buddy-buddy bullshit. Are we going or not?"

"Lead the way, Forrest Grump."

I choke on a laugh.

Without a word, Aran turns on his heel, and I follow, pulled by Ryan.

"Don't let him fool you," she says in a whisper. "He's all bark, no bite."

"I do bite," he chimes from the front, and Ryan shakes her head at me.

They're cute. Behind the teasing, it's obvious they each understand how the other ticks. I should make a note in my journal that this is how couples act when they've truly meshed. A little pang in my chest makes me wonder when it'll be my turn for this.

"Bro, where you going?" a familiar voice calls. The redhead who was all over Tiff last night cuts through the people walking out of the building and heads over to us.

Aran jerks his head back, which makes the guy glance over.

"Oh. Maddie, was it?" He falls in stride on my left.

"Yeah, hi." I cringe. "I didn't catch your name last night, sorry."

"Archie Bracken. Left winger. Assistant captain. And the saint who puts up with Aran's crap on a daily basis. A.k.a. his roommate and best friend."

"No, I'm his best friend," Ryan says in return from my other side. "You're just the one who does his laundry."

"That was only once after I lost a bet." Archie sticks out his tongue.

I cough to hide a laugh. These two seem like the perfect balance to Aran.

Speaking of, he stops by the back door of a black SUV. I can't tell what make, since it has a hefty coat of snow from the day. It must be a kind of old one, since he inserts the key into the lock to dump his equipment in the back. Ryan releases me to do the same.

"Anyway, doofus. You weren't invited to this party, but are you coming?" Aran asks his roommate.

"Where to?"

"Ryan's."

Archie blows a raspberry. "And here I thought it was something more exciting."

"Hey, don't make Maddie think my place is a dungeon or something."

"Anyway, no. I just wanted to know if you wanted to come hang out with us again," Archie says to Aran.

"Again?" he asks.

"Yesterday's crew." Archie turns to me. "And Maddie, you're more than welcome to come too, of course."

I offer a stiff smile. "Thanks, but we already have plans, so…"

"It's cool. I might catch you later if Ryan's dungeon doesn't trap you." He grins.

Ryan folds her arms. "Rodriguez, send your underling away before I cut him."

"Shoo" is all Aran says to his friend.

Archie waves us off and whistles as he beelines around parked cars.

Meanwhile, Aran shuts the back door and heads over to the driver's side. I follow after Ryan, but she gets to the back passenger door first, and I stand there like a plank.

"Hop in the front so you can watch the way," she says. Then she slides into the back seat without leaving me a choice.

I don't know why my pulse flutters in my veins as I hoist myself up by the handle and climb into the passenger seat, but it does. There are butterflies flitting all over my body. Maybe it's because I'm too cold. I shut the door, and the smell of his car slams into me.

It smells like boy. Not that I know how guys smell, in general. That's just the impression I get. It's like soap and something a little rich, and when Aran leans my way slightly to pull at his seat belt, I catch the exact same soap scent coming off his skin.

I quickly turn around to pull my seat belt too. But now the smell is imprinted in my brain. And my brain is melting like caramel under too much heat.

"Anyway, Maddie. Tell me about you."

Ryan's sudden comment snaps me back to reality. A reality where I can't start going mushy over a guy who smells mouth-watering, because he has a freaking girlfriend.

Goodness, what is wrong with me?

"Um, so. I'm not very interesting? Creative writing major. Twenty-one. I knit?"

"And you love strawberries, from what I've heard."

I laugh a bit. "Yeah, they make me happy."

Aran cuts a quick glance at me but says nothing as he turns the vehicle on, and the heating starts with a roar.

"Creative writing sounds cool, though. What do you write?"

"Fiction books. Mostly YA." I clear my throat. "That's young adult, in case you don't know."

"So like, *Twilight* type of thing?"

I shift a bit so I can glance over my shoulder. Ryan looks curious rather than mocking, so I relax.

"Not quite, but same age category."

"So when will we see your work in bookstores?"

I'm at a loss for words, because there's genuine excitement in her voice. None of the mockery I get from my mom or anyone else who is also not in this writing life. I peek over at Aran, and he looks chill too. Like we're talking about something totally normal.

"Oh." I sag into the seat, more overwhelmed than I want

to show. "Um, actually, my first book comes out in less than three months."

At that, Aran shifts his attention to me for a second.

From the back, Ryan says, "Get out! For real?"

"Yeah."

"That's remarkable!"

"It's no big deal," I mumble, turning away so I can blink back tears. I wish Mom had reacted like this when I broke the news to her last year.

"No, that's pretty amazing, Strawberry."

Hearing that from Aran robs me of breath.

"You'll have to give me your autograph," Ryan continues, not noticing that I'm about to break down into tears. "I'll add it to my collection. Although, so far it's only been jocks."

"Her collection is full of autographs from friends," Aran explains. I wipe my face quickly so I can turn to him. My eyes catch on his hand where it's turning the wheel as if it's someone he's caressing. "She thinks one of us will hit it big and she'll be able to sell the autograph for a hefty sum."

"It's what my dad did." She laughs. "One of his childhood friends became a pretty well-known singer, and with the money from the autograph, he bought me my first car."

I like Ryan. She's a chatterbox like me when I'm not being an emotional butt. And she seems genuinely friendly.

A small smile plays on Aran's lips. He must like her a lot too, huh?

Ryan picks up where she left off. "Anyway, that's probably the most interesting thing about me. Other than that, I'm also twenty-one. I'm a bio major. And I'm varsity Strikes."

"The captain," Aran finishes off.

"What?" I whirl around as far as my seat belt lets me. "You're the Strikes captain?"

"Yup. It's how I met this weirdo." She jerks a thumb at

Aran. "Captains often have to share duties. Mainly, keeping our kids in check."

"Whoa." I glance between them. "I'm among St. Cloud royalty. I am not worthy."

"Hush, you dork." Ryan waves a hand. "The only royalty here is Aran, who is a royal pain in the—"

"And we're here," he interrupts, cutting the engine.

I missed the last stretch because I've been watching Ryan, but I recognize the place immediately. It's one of the apartment complexes closest to campus. Even though it's older than where I currently live, it's always in higher demand because it's cheaper. Not a single unit was available back when Rebs and I were looking.

They haul their bags and equipment up the stairs without issue. But I lag behind with my tongue hanging out like a cartoon character. I don't know if I can live without an elevator.

After a moment, Aran climbs back down until he reaches me. "You good?"

Wow, this is embarrassing.

I close my mouth, although he could probably hear me panting all the way.

Ryan jogs back down too. "Don't worry, it's just one more flight. You'll get used to it."

"Will I?" I push myself to keep going. "Because I'm not an elite athlete like you two."

"First month or so, I got winded too," she says. I don't know if it's a white lie, but it does make me feel a bit better.

Finally, we reach her front door. Aran and I wait as Ryan takes off a glove and fishes in the pocket of her knee-length coat for the keys. I'm curious about why Aran doesn't help, since he probably has a key too. Maybe he's not a super affectionate boyfriend.

Ryan opens the door with a "ta-da!"

She walks in, and Aran motions at me to go first. I step into the apartment as Ryan flicks the lights on.

"It's Spartan because I don't actually spend a lot of time here. You can put your stamp on it as much as you want," Ryan comments from the kitchen.

The whole place is painted white. The floor is imitation wood throughout, and the only furniture in the living room is a cream-colored sofa and a TV stand with a flat screen on top. Floor-to-ceiling curtains cover an entire wall. Probably a balcony.

"It's pretty big," I say.

Something bumps against my back, and I jump. But it's only Aran's duffel as he's turned around, shutting the door.

"Let me show you what hopefully will be your room."

I follow after Ryan, casting a glance back. Aran has set down his bag and stick and now has his head poked into her fridge. The boy is always hungry.

"This here is the bathroom." Ryan points at the door immediately after the kitchen. "And the next door is the laundry room."

"Oh, what a luxury. We have a shared laundry room at my current place."

"Right?" She grins. "It used to be a storage room, but my previous roomie and I converted it. And the door across from it," she says, pointing at the farthest one on the left. "Is my room. Yours would be this one."

She opens the door across from the bathroom, with the shared wall to the living room. Even though it's completely empty, I hazard a guess that it's smaller than my current room, but it's free of the Loris of the world, so it looks beautiful to me.

"Um, so what's in the fine print?" I ask.

"Fifty-fifty split on everything except food because I eat like a horse."

From the kitchen, Aran says, "She does."

"You're one to talk," she retorts and shakes her head at me. "So, anyway, your rent would be about…"

My eyes bulge out. I make her repeat the sum. And once more for good measure.

"Are you pulling my leg?"

"Why? Is it over your budget?"

"No!" I gasp. "It's a hundred fifty bucks cheaper than I'm currently paying, and that's with one extra roommate."

"So you're interested then?" Ryan clasps her hands as if she's praying. "Say yes, please. I like you and I really need someone to split the bills with, like, *yesterday*."

"I'm about to say yes, but…"

"If your concern is Aran, he won't bother us. Much." She blinks cutely, which is in contrast to the whole badass look she has going on with her pixie haircut and ear piercings.

"No, I mean. You can have your boyfriend over as much as you want, that's not—"

Someone chokes. Aran, from the kitchen.

Ryan starts cackling.

"What?" I ask, confused as heck.

"Boyfriend? Aran? Mine?" She screeches. "That combination of words is just—nope. Don't make me drink bleach."

I hear coughing from the kitchen. In the middle of the fit, Aran asks, "You thought Ryan was my girlfriend?"

"Well, I—Yes?"

The two of them laugh. Which isn't shocking from Ryan, considering what she just said. But I haven't heard Aran laugh a single time before, and it's jarring. Because it's a good laugh —hearty and entirely unhinged.

My face probably looks like a stop sign. "I take it I was wrong."

"Severely." Ryan smacks my shoulder a few times as she calms down. Wiping a tear off her face, she adds, "I mean, we did try to date during sophomore year, but it was like trying to date a cousin."

"Do you want me to barf all over your kitchen?" Aran asks, his voice still weird.

"Anyway, if it's not about this jerk, what's the holdup?"

"Still money." I bite my lip. "I don't have enough for a deposit or for movers."

"We got you." She puts her arm around my shoulder, steering me back to the kitchen where Aran's chopping up vegetables as if this is his house. "First, there's no deposit."

"For real?"

"Yeah, I'll just add you to my existing contract. And second, you see that guy over there?"

I face Aran, who pauses what he's been doing and raises his eyebrows.

"Um, yes?"

"See all those big muscles on him?"

"Well, no. He's wearing clothes."

His eyebrows rise another notch, and I wish I could've worded it a different way.

Ryan grins at me. "True, but you know they're there just by how he's built, yeah?"

And also because I saw them on a video, but this I have the decency to keep to myself.

"Well, guess what? He'll help you move. And I'll sweeten the pot. He'll get all his goons to help you move as well. For free. How's that?"

I blink hard. All Ryan is missing are twinkling lights around her. That's how pleased she is with her own idea. Meanwhile, Aran resumes cutting vegetables.

"Uh, I couldn't possibly—"

"It's no big deal. Right, Aran?"

He shrugs a shoulder. "Sure, it's not like she has a lot of stuff."

My jaw hangs.

"Great! So when are you moving in?"

"I'm free this weekend," Aran says with his usual gruff voice.

I flap my mouth closed. Open it again. Closed.

They're both so strange. Just absolutely unlike anyone I've ever met. I've only known the guy for a day, and this girl for all of an hour. And yet here they are, casually offering to help me with something I've been agonizing over for months.

Oh, no. Here come the water works.

CHAPTER 11
ARAN

This is what I get for helping. Having to help more.

"You didn't have to do all this," Strawberry says behind me, watching as I unravel a wire tie from around a nail she used to hang lights around her room. "But," she adds, "thank you for being tall."

"I didn't grow tall for you," I deadpan, and she snorts softly.

"Okay, what's next?" Archie walks into the room. I hear him shuffle something and then grunt. "Whew, this box is heavy."

"Please don't get hurt!" Her voice fades as she follows him.

I finish untangling the wire and stuff it into my pocket. Another section of the string lights falls to the floor. I'm done with one wall and have one more to go. The position is annoying because it makes my shoulders sting and I have to basically glue myself to the wall to reach. Strawberry probably had to get on a stepladder to do this, and I hope she had supervision. If she did this on her own, she could've really hurt herself.

"Captain, my car's loaded up, so I'm headed to the base," Mark says from the door.

I flash him a quick thumbs-up before getting back to work.

After Ryan volunteered me and the guys, and after seeing Strawberry's eyes well up like fountains with a glitchy valve, I had no choice but to agree to help her move. This is why tears are my kryptonite. I get this visceral need to make them stop any way I can. Which is very annoying when, say, I'm trying to break up with a girl I haven't clicked with. Can't fix the tears if I'm the one causing them.

But this case was easy. All I had to do was get a few of the guys to haul her stuff in their cars and deliver it at Ryan's. No biggie.

"Maddie, is this really necessary?" a voice calls out from the hallway. It's one of the roommates, but I don't know which one.

From the corner of my eye, I catch as Strawberry fully steps outside the room. But the walls are paper thin, and no matter how much she lowers her voice, I hear everything.

"Yes, it is."

There's an exasperated sigh. "We should've talked about this. What are we going to do now that we're down a roommate? You should have at least given us warning so we could find someone."

"Rebs, I told you last month that I was considering leaving," Strawberry hisses.

"Your literal words were 'I don't think I belong here anymore' and that's not the same!"

"It is, because I don't!" Strawberry grunts in a way that sounds remarkably like me.

I pause for a second, contemplating whether to close the door and give them privacy. But it'll be quicker if I just finish this and go. If only this damn tie would just unwind, I'd be quicker. I yank it instead, and out comes the whole nail.

"Oops," I mumble, picking it up from the carpeted floor.

"I'm sorry this is an inconvenience to you, but the way you and Lori have treated me for years has inconvenienced me more. So just move her in and be happy together. Bye."

My tutor marches back into the room just as I'm winding the string lights around my fist. A flush has taken over her face, and there's a dangerous sheen in her eyes. A door closes somewhere in the hallway, maybe from the other girl going back into her room.

"Are you going to cry?"

Strawberry presses her lips. "Probably. But not right now."

I feel genuine relief as I busy myself looking around. The only thing left is the bed frame. Books, clothes, shoes, and even the mattress are already gone. "Do you have everything?"

"I think so." She extends her hand, and it takes me a moment to understand she wants her silly lights. I place the bundle in her palm. "Can't take half the couch with me, unfortunately."

"What about bathroom and kitchen? I know the hand soap is yours."

She winces. "I'm not that petty."

Oh, I would be. I'd be the pettiest little ass if I'd been treated the way she has. I got a sample of that the night I was here, with that Lori chick making passive-aggressive comments that made even me uncomfortable. And then, when I took Strawberry to Ryan's and she started crying, she shared some stories that made Ryan and me want to smash something.

Jamal strides in. "Truck's ready downstairs. Let's finish the job."

"I'll bring up the rear," I say.

As Jamal and I pick up the metal bed frame, Strawberry scampers away to give us space. Maybe we should've disassembled the thing, but it's the sturdiest bed I've seen, and Jamal's truck is big enough that we can just tie it up. Even better, it has no headboard, so it makes the job of climbing down the stairs relatively painless. We're still as slow as snails, because nobody wants to get hurt here.

My arms shake a little by the time we're hauling the frame into the bed of the truck. We tie it up real tight and put the little flag at the end of the bed frame as required for long loads. Nobody wants to get a fine either.

Jamal brushes his hands off and stuffs them into leather gloves. "All right, I'll see you both at Ryan's."

Strawberry holds her hands to her chest as she says, "Thank you so much, Jamal."

"Thank me with food. I'm starving," he says as a farewell. I stuff my hands in the pockets of my jeans and watch as he starts the truck. The ropes are secure, and the frame doesn't move an inch. Good.

I turn to Strawberry. "Where's my thanks?"

"How does pizza sound?" She smiles and sniffles against the cold. The tip of her nose is as red as…

I wonder if strawberries are in season. She's making me crave them.

Then again, maybe I'm just hungry too.

"If they're from Romano's, I accept."

She nods, all solemn. "I'm willing to fork over the cash today, so Romano's it is."

"Great. I want a meat lover's," I say, because I know it will gross her out. And sure enough, she sticks her tongue out in disgust.

"Fine, but first, let's go. I'm freezing my butt off." She whirls around and heads over to her yellow Beetle. Her butt is well covered by a long coat, though, which is a shame. I don't know why she's complaining.

Shaking my head, I head over to my 4Runner. Inside, I crank up the heat and take a few of my tutor's boxes full of books for a joy ride back to her new place.

I drive right behind her. At a red light, I catch her wiping at her face a few times. I wince a little, because there's nothing I can do about her crying when she's in her car and I'm in mine and we're in traffic. Not that I *should* do anything about it, either.

It takes us until well past noon to bring her bed frame into her new room and empty all the junk from five cars into her new apartment. But considering we started the move midmorning, right after practice, I'd say this was a record.

True to her word, Strawberry orders pizzas from Romano's for all five Bolts, two Strikes, and for herself. She's the only one with a small veggie pizza, while the rest of us ravenous beasts fight over pepperoni and meat lover's.

"This is very generous of you," Archie says with his mouth so full it's hard to guess what he's saying.

"This is nothing compared to all your help." She offers a cute little smile that melts him like an ice cube in the desert.

I attack my pizza as if it owes me money.

"Maddie." Jamal gulps down his food to speak again. "You should come watch us play tonight."

"I'm sure she has better plans," Ryan says with a shrug. "Like watching *our* game tonight."

"You should definitely come watch us," says Christine Freeman, one of the forwards on Ryan's team. "Athletic girls are so much hotter than these knuckleheads, am I right?"

"Too right." Ryan offers her forearm, and the other girl bumps it with hers.

I reach out for another slice of meat lover's. The rivalry between the Bolts and the Strikes will probably go on until the end of time, but at least no one's maiming each other anymore.

"Um, actually." Strawberry clears her throat, sets her slice down on the almost empty cardboard box, and lifts wide eyes to us. "I don't really know anything about hockey other than the names of your teams."

One by one, jaws drop, eyes pop, and gasps come out.

I blink real hard. I get it. Not everyone in the world is obsessed with hockey. It's not even the most popular sport in this country. And yet…

This town is in the middle of hockey nation. We're halfway between two Original Six teams. Shit, my parents are Venezuelan and grew up in a baseball culture, yet two of their kids live and breathe hockey like it's our family's legacy. I couldn't possibly conceive of a life without it. In fact, when I get too old to play it professionally and I have no other choice but to earn my living through accounting, I'll still play for some minor league or coach kids or *something*.

I take a deep, bracing breath so I don't spill any of this like lava from an erupting volcano. I guess it'd be the same if I admitted to her that I don't really read books.

Ryan takes a big swig of her water and sighs as if she's just guzzled a beer. "Girl, you shouldn't have said that aloud in a room full of hockey nerds."

"That's it." Archie smacks his own leg. "Let's watch a game together. We'll teach you all about it."

"Will you?" Why does she look so hopeful asking this?

"Yes, let's go." He grabs a slice and relocates to the couch, pawing at the remote with his greasy hand. "Hey, Ryan! Do you have film from one of our games?"

"Why the heck would I have a Bolts game?"

"Try ESPN first," Jamal suggests. "There may be some reruns from the pro season."

Mark shakes his head. "Man, are you implying we're not as cool as the pros? Because unfortunately, you'd be right. Did you see Max Cassiano's game yesterday?"

"Off the charts, I admit," Christine says.

I grunt. My future brother-in-law is teaching the league

exactly what this town is made of. And I'll be next. I don't give a shit that no one drafted me. I'll be the hottest free agent the league has ever seen. Teams will be fighting for me.

"Um, give me a moment. I need my journal."

Strawberry rushes over to my side of the counter and ignores me completely while she washes her hands. But I'm standing in the way of the towel draped over the oven's handle. She blinks up at me, and I stuff the last chunk of crust into my mouth, still firmly in the way.

Her hands drip, and she narrows her eyes, as if she knows what I'm up to. "Excuse me."

I shrug. "You're excused."

"Don't make me bodily push you away."

"You couldn't if you tried."

"You're probably right." Strawberry sighs in an exaggerated way.

But then she reaches over and wipes her hands with the front of my hoodie. And gives me a brilliant smile. Then she turns away and leaves the kitchen.

I stop chewing and glance down at the wet splotches that turn the blue fabric darker. I clamp my mouth tight so I don't laugh or shout. I'm not sure which one.

When I glance up, everyone is still wrestling over what video to watch. Except for Ryan. She's watching me, her brows raised and eyes turned into slits.

Fortunately, she gets distracted by her new roommate, who reappears with journal and strawberry pen in hand. "Okay, let's start with the basics, please."

"Why do you need to write all this down?" As Archie asks, he scoots to the end of the couch and motions at the free space. When Strawberry joins him, Ryan turns back to me, as if checking for my reaction. All I give her is a good view of me chugging down a sports drink.

"I'm going to write a hockey romance."

I choke.

"A what?" someone asks, but I can't tell who, because I'm coughing.

"A hockey romance," my tutor explains in an airy tone. "It's a romance book with a hockey theme. The hero will be a hockey player, but I don't know enough about the sport yet to get started."

I pluck a memory from the back of my mind. The first time I met her at the library, she was staring at me and writing things down. The something-else was what, studying me for her book?

And fine, that's not a big deal. Certainly not the wildest thing I've experienced. It shouldn't annoy me and yet…

I'm a solid four on the bad mood scale.

"Don't worry. If you base your hero on me, you'll have a bestseller in your hands," Archie says with a laugh. It tips me to a five.

"Look, I've been voted the sweetest guy on the team," Jamal counters. "You should base him on me."

"How about me?" Mark points at himself. "I have a baby face but abs of steel."

I'm at a six now. I need a freaking nap, or the scale is going to keep going up.

"Anyway, I'm going home," I announce, then head over to the pile of coats by the door to find mine.

"Already?" Strawberry murmurs something, and the next thing I know, she's wading through the sea of legs to join me.

I don't put on my coat. There's no point. But this catches her attention and a crease appears between her eyebrows.

"Yeah, have fun learning hockey. I'm going to take a nap." Over her head, I say, "Keep it down, you goons."

Ryan volleys back, "Wear earplugs."

Now Strawberry is full on frowning. I open the front door and motion her over. She only makes it to the threshold because she's wearing socks. At the contact with the freezing air, she shudders.

She pops her head out. "What—"

Her question fizzles as I insert the key into my apartment door. Which is right next to hers.

"My bedroom butts up to your living room, so make sure they keep it down," I say, pushing the door open.

"Wait, what?" She opens and closes her mouth. Then her voice comes out in a squeak. "We're neighbors?"

"Yup. See you around, Strawberry." And with that, I walk into my apartment.

CHAPTER 12
MADDIE

Not to be dramatic, but having a period is like being subjected to medieval-style torture every month.

Of course it had to arrive literally when I'm having the best time of my life. This week's study sessions with Aran were precisely what they should've been all along. I explained something; he put it to practice. We worked together side by side in an easy-going silence. No teasing from him. No putting my foot in my mouth on my own.

Ryan is the coolest person on earth. She doesn't mind that my strawberry obsession—as Aran calls it—is starting to take over the apartment. And she cooks mouthwatering food in industrial quantities that she doesn't mind sharing with me. In fact, a couple of days ago, she made this incredible veggie couscous and offered some to me. I heaped a big spoonful of it, and she literally screamed at me to take more, which is a concept I'm not used to. People telling me to eat more.

I knew the happiness had an expiration date of one week, corresponding to the appointment with my mother and Meg. I just didn't know it would be that *plus* my murderous period.

The car behind me honks. The streetlight has turned

green, and just pressing the accelerator hurts like a birch. The second my Beetle starts moving, the impatient driver passes me aggressively fast.

I try to press against my clothes a bit harder so the heating pad glued to my skin gets hotter, but that hurts more, so I stop.

The whole drive from my new apartment to the bridal shop would typically take about thirty minutes. I take an extra twenty, pausing in random parking lots first to take some more ibuprofen or to just breathe. Breathing is really freaking hard when there's an alien trying to claw out of your uterus.

Finally, I park right next to Mom's platinum sedan outside the shop. I leave my car running for a bit more and close my eyes. I tried canceling this morning—she knows just how severe my period pain is—but, of course, she didn't let me. Dresses were hard to get, blah, blah. The store won't hold them forever, blah, blah. You can't keep putting this off, yada yada.

"Fudge me." I grunt just like Aran does as I unbuckle my seat belt. I'm starting to see the appeal of his one-sound form of communication. "Oh, son of a birch." A horrible groan tears out of my throat as I shift to my side to exit the car. My back hurts too. I blink tears away from my face and wade through the parking lot. I cannot wait to get back home, slide into bed, and not move for the next twenty-four hours.

I open the shop's door with difficulty because it's very heavy and I am a weak, weak girl. An attendant appears before me like magic.

"Welcome to Tule and Silk! Are you with a party?"

"Yes, Berkley." My voice comes out in a croak.

The woman eyes my hand on my back and my stomach. "Oh, you must be expecting! We have really comfortable chairs in the dressing area. Can I get you some water? Herbal tea?"

"Tea, please. Although I'm not expecting anything other than a bad time," I say through gritted teeth.

"Excuse me?"

"Um, nothing. Do you mind taking me to my party?"

She plasters on an artificial smile. "Right this way."

Oh, how I wish I had a cane. I hold on to every sturdy surface as I follow her to the back of the store while a wave of dizziness hits me. I need to sit for a bit and not do anything. Only breathe. Maybe blink. Eyes closed would be best. I hope Mom and Meg are busy trying on all the things already so I can rest.

But no. They're both seated on a powder pink sofa, sipping something bubbly from champagne flutes even though it's barely eleven in the morning.

"Maddie, you made it!"

As if I had a choice.

Mom spreads her arms open for a hug I'm not in a position to give her, but I sit down next to her and let her pull me to her side. I clench my jaw so I don't spew out a curse.

"It's so great to have the three Berkley women together for a change," she says.

"You two can come visit me in the city any time, you know?" Meg laughs.

"Ugh, you're always so busy, baby." Mom pats Meg's knee before turning to me. "Ready? We were waiting for you."

I wince. "I need a few minutes."

"What for?"

"I'm in a lot of pain, Mom."

"Oh, nonsense." She waves a hand and releases an exasperated sigh. "That's nothing compared to the thirteen—"

"—Hours of labor when you gave birth to—"

I say "me" just as Meg says "Maddie." This is what Mom says every single time I complain about my cramps.

"Not Meg. She was such an easy baby, even during the pregnancy."

My sister leans back around our mother and gives me a

grimace. I just shake my head a bit. Nothing we can do about Mom.

"Excuse me, miss? Are we ready to start?" Mom asks the attendant, who comes with a steaming cup of tea for me.

"Oh, thank you." I accept the mug and bring it close to my face. Peppermint. Not my favorite, but it'll do.

"Yes, we're ready and so happy you have chosen us for your big day." The woman smiles so wide her face must hurt. "Between one daughter getting married and the other one expecting, you must be so happy, Mrs. Berkley."

"Wha—" Mom turns to Meg, as if doing the math. Here's the one daughter getting married. But who's the one expecting? Then she turns to me and screeches. "Madeline! Are you freaking pregnant?"

I rasp out a laugh. "Goodness, no." I haven't even found a willing man to kiss me more than once. Forget about sex.

"Then what is this all about?"

The attendant's smile drops into an abyss, and with it goes all the color from her face. "Oh my gosh. I am *so* sorry. I just thought…" As she trails off, she looks pointedly at my stomach.

Mom presses her lips tight and casts her patented disapproving state. Famous in at least two states. "Maddie, this is why I begged you to lose weight before the wedding."

"Mom!"

Meg clears her throat. "How about we change into the first option, huh?"

"You two go ahead. I'll drink my tea first."

"Maddie!"

"Let's go, Mom. Maddie looks really pale and probably needs a moment to feel better." Meg stands up, pulling at Mom's arm. "I'll try on the first dress and then you two try yours. How about that?"

Bless her. My sister is the only person who has seen me

faint from my cramps, and ever since, she's been a true believer in just how severe my pain is.

Mom grumbles something and stands up. But a second later, she turns to the attendant. "Please inform me if my youngest here attempts to make a run for it, you got it?"

"Yes, ma'am." The woman gives me a wince, which I guess is all the apology I'll get.

They leave me to my tea for a bit. It apparently takes Mom and the shop's employee to help Meg wrestle into one dress, which I can already tell won't be the right one. If it will take Justin that much effort to take it off, it won't work.

The tea is really potent, but it warms up my insides and eases the tightness in my muscles, giving me enough strength to remove my coat, scarf, and hat. I leave them scattered on the sofa, along with my bag, and heft myself up. Slowly, I walk over to the party but stop when Mom rushes out, all emotional.

"Oh, Maddie. You sister looks so beautiful."

But beautiful is not enough to describe it. Meg comes out in this concoction of fluttery, feather-soft white fabric that drapes around her torso like a second skin. It cascades down her hips in a twist that doesn't seem accidental. As she moves, the twist remains intact and shimmers under the light. Megan's natural fiery red hair streams over her delicate shoulders. I don't know whether it's the exertion or that she's in her feels too, but her cheeks and her pointy nose are as red as apples.

She looks majestic. Ethereal. Soft, but at the same time strong.

Dang, maybe this is *the* dress. Justin will have to be patient.

"Oh, wow."

"You look stunning, Miss Berkley," the attendant says, and this time it's a genuine compliment.

Meg sighs when she looks at herself in the mirror, a soft smile playing on her lips. "I love this dress. But I'm curious about how the next one will fit."

Slowly, I pull out my phone. "Wait, let me take pictures. We can compare more easily that way."

"Oh, smart." Meg winks at me through the mirror.

I snap a few pictures from different angles, although it takes me a long while to do so with how slowly I move.

"Okay, okay. You're stalling now." Mom pushes me into the next dressing room. "Please bring the extra *extra*-large bridesmaid dresses."

"Mom, she knows which ones to bring. You don't have to be extra *extra* clear," I say with a whine.

"Shush, Madeline. Your mother knows what she's doing. You don't want to get down to your skivvies and try to put on a dress that doesn't make it past your thighs, do you?"

I grunt. I certainly don't.

In the dressing room, I take my sweet time removing each layer of clothes. I immediately miss the warmth of my wool dress with little cats on the bottom fringe. But I leave my thick leggings on. There is no force on this round earth that will make me remove them today.

"Ready, miss?" the attendant asks from outside the curtain.

"As I can be."

She slides in a truly hideous fuchsia number, and I say, "Please tell me there are other options."

"Oh, you don't like this one?"

It looks like Barbie's curtains, but I don't say this aloud.

"Um, maybe I should see the whole range and pick?"

The whole range turns out to be only three other dresses. All of them are varying shades of pink, though they're at least less offensive than the first one. I lift one in nearly the same powder pink hue as the sofa. Actually, the fabric feels similar too.

I snort a laugh. It figures that they'd dress me to match the furniture. Very on the nose. But praise! I can pull it over my head. I don't have to bend down!

It's a bit too large, which I guess they'll have to fix, but it makes trying it on easier. The bust area hugs my boobs perfectly, even without zipping it, though. Almost as if it was tailor made. In fact, the way it holds them makes them look ah-mazing and defines my waist more clearly.

"Hmm, not bad, sofa-dress," I mumble.

"Do you need help?"

"Yes, please," I respond to the attendant. "Can you zip me up?"

"Of course." She squeezes in as if there are people other than my family outside. "Oh, it looks very nice, miss."

Not an effusive compliment, but I'll take it.

"I actually like it."

Then she zips it up, and like I thought, it needs to be taken in about half an inch on each side. But the color works well with my pasty skin and almost makes it look healthy. My hair is more brown than red, so it doesn't clash either.

Still walking like a duck, I make it outside and wait for the verdict.

Meg gasps. "Maddie! You look unbelievable. Guys won't take their eyes off you."

I wrinkle my nose. What guys? Our old uncles?

"Or guy? Have you found a plus-one already?" My sister wiggles her eyebrows.

"Puh-lease. You and I both know my dancing partner will be Kevin." I'm referring to the ten-year-old son of Meg's best friend from work.

"I don't know." Mom's frowning. "The fat under your arms is too visible."

"We have some delicate boleros that would pair with this dress very well."

"Actually, that sounds like a great idea," I tell the employee. "I'm getting cold."

"Shall I fetch a few samples?"

"Yes—"

"Isn't there another dress that covers your arms?"

I close my eyes.

"Well, I love this dress on Maddie," my sister says, which I know is her way of supporting me without antagonizing Mom.

And yet, I have to open my big mouth and say, "Mom, it's not a crime if people see my arms."

"Of course not," she snaps. "It's just a bit *too* much skin."

"Why isn't it too much skin on Meg? She's also wearing a strapless dress."

"It's different."

"How?"

Mom and I glare at each other in a Berkley standoff. The next few seconds will dictate whether this outing will end in at least a week-long impasse.

"Um." The attendant coughs delicately into her hand. "I'll go fetch some boleros."

"Can you please bring more champagne?" Meg asks with a serene smile. "I think I'd like to get plastered for the rest of the fitting."

If I hadn't driven, I'd ask for a whole bottle for myself. Instead, I opt for the healthier version. Which is marching into the dressing room and not coming out until I've tried on the rest of the dresses without an audience.

CHAPTER 13
ARAN

This douche thinks that trying to shove his ass in my face will rattle me. A whole Zamboni could be speeding up to me and it wouldn't get me away from the posts. My eyes zero in on the puck with laser precision. The play is moving closer, and so is this Bulldog guy.

Now he's joined by another. They're trying to turn the crease into their party, and it's not gonna happen. But where the hell are my D-men? They better be doing their jobs, or else.

Or else turns into a shot. I don't know why they call me Iceberg when I'm so clearly a frog catching flies. I catch the biscuit with my right glove as if it were coated in glue.

Hot tidbit: it isn't. I'm just an impenetrable fortress.

But we're tied at a grand total of not-a-single-goal, and if we don't score in the next two minutes and seventeen seconds, we'll go into overtime. I don't mind. I never feel more alive than during OT or shutouts. The problem is that not all the guys can handle the pressure.

For example, Webber keeps turning that baby face of his to the boards as if looking for an exit. That's his habit when he starts to get tired and feels like time's running slower. Amadi's accuracy goes down. And sure enough, his pass gets intercepted, and here come the Bulldogs again. I stop a weak shot with my left knee.

Bracken positions himself to take the next faceoff, and I glare daggers at his back. What is he doing, not scoring against Brighton College jerks? They've been weak all night. Bolts should be skating circles around them.

The ref drops the puck, and Bracken wins it with the kind of aggression I wish he'd have used all game long. My pulse spikes as if I'm the one breaking away from the Bulldogs' dirtbag D-man.

"Payback time," I mutter to myself.

The Bolts have formed a whole scramble in front of the Bulldogs' goalie—same strategy they tried on me a minute ago. Bracken makes a pass, and lo and behold, the buzzer goes off.

The arena roars with noise as Bolts finally get one for the house. Sure, it was a garbage goal, but we'll take it.

I brace, though, because I know our opponent. I've watched countless hours of film on them as far back as the Cassiano era. There's something very douchebaggy about how they're coached that makes them play even dirtier when they're down.

But I'm an asshole, so I push just enough away from the net to bait them.

Coach Green hates when I do this, especially because it can backfire. But the Bulldogs have been trying the most today and have failed each time. They're frustrated and tired. Probably embarrassed too. They never get booed as hard as they do when they're playing in St. Cloud.

The annoying guy from earlier bites.

In fact, he bites so hard he tries to trip me without even having the puck.

The ref blows a whistle. "Interference!"

"Ref, are you blind?" the guy yells, and if looks could kill, my whole bloodline would be dead.

Alas. Now we're in a power play for the last minute of the game.

We score a second goal, and the celebration all around the arena threatens to blow my eardrums. I'm sure Coach Green will be screaming at me too, and it won't be from happiness, even if I got the job done.

The final buzzer goes off. As I skate away from the net, I'm intercepted by half the team. They slam into me, raising their sticks and their voices as if we've just won the national championship.

"Dude, that was sick!" one of them says.

"Shit, you should've gotten an assist for that."

"It was stone cold, bro."

I snort. Maybe that's why they call me Aran "the Iceberg" Rodriguez. And here I thought it was because I'm hardheaded.

"Yeah, yeah. Get off me." I shove my stick at the nearest guy, and one by one, they peel off.

"Duuude!"

I would recognize that voice in my sleep, even if I hadn't already seen him. Whirling around, I head for the back of my net, where my little sister Olivia and her best friend Brooklyn parked themselves. They had ample view of my ass during most of the game.

"I have no words," Brooklyn says, shaking his head as I brake before him and my sister. "How could you even think of leaving your net like that? Like, bro, you have some cajones."

"It's cojones, you fool." She smacks his arm. "With an o."

"Cowjones?"

Aceituna rolls her eyes at her friend. Sometimes, they come watch my games with other kids from Brooklyn's high school hockey team, and a couple of girlfriends that my sister tolerates. This time, it's just the two of them.

I trap a glove against my side with my elbow, and with the free hand, remove my mask. "Is this a date?"

Neither of them reacts right away. Until, as if rehearsed, Liv bursts into cackles and Brooklyn's mouth gapes.

"What? No!"

"As if." My sister snorts between laughs.

I hum. Luz and I have long suspected that these two have a thing, but we haven't caught them *infraganti*.

"Right, don't be out too late. And Brooklyn?"

"Yeah?" He frowns a bit.

"If you get my little sister in any trouble, I will skewer you with this stick." I lift the weapon. "Got it?"

"Got it. Not gonna happen."

"Get her home early."

I push away from the boards and file off the ice. Some people remain in the stands, and there are claps as I head into the tunnel.

By the time I make it to the locker room, Coach is in full swing.

"—for the last three minutes, this game would've been a bust!"

I consider standing by the door and letting the worst of his screaming blow over, but just like I have a built-in radar for the puck, he has one for me. He turns around and points directly at my face.

"And you. What the hell was that, Rodriguez?"

It was the manifestation of my cojones, but I don't say squat.

He delivers a few choice words. None of them are profane or insult my mother, but they're annoying, nonetheless. Something about responsibility and being the leader of a team that doesn't have an *I* in it. I sit at my bench and watch him in silence. Tomorrow, he'll tell me in more muted terms how it was a good game but one that shouldn't be replicated. We know the drill.

After he leaves, Archie starts chuckling next to me. "Coach Green is gonna Coach Green, huh?"

"I'm convinced the man just doesn't know how to be happy," says Jamal from Archie's other side.

That's a good point. He screams at us just the same whether we lose or win. But we can't all have a Coach Young like the Strikes do. She's level-headed even when she's tough.

"Anyway, it's Saturday night and we just won a big game. Guess what that means?" Archie pauses in the middle of removing his pads to wag his eyebrows at me, then at our other assistant captain.

"O'Malley's?"

"I'll pass," I say.

"What?"

Half the room turns my way.

They can stare all they want, but I focus on removing my leg pads between grunts.

After spluttering, Archie says, "You pass? What do you mean you pass? This is the perfect opportunity for you to find Kelsey's replacement."

"After that last play you pulled off, I'm sure at least half of the arena is salivating over you, man," adds Jamal.

I doubt most of the audience even understood the nuance of that play. Forget about salivating.

Pulling off my jersey, I dump it on my growing pile by my feet. I decide to give them a morsel in the hopes that they'll leave me alone. "I'm busy."

"With what?"

"Oh, do you already have someone? You lucky dog."

Yeah, I have someone. A useless essay to finish. A quiz to prep for. A guide to read through.

None of those responses would be acceptable to these

horndogs. Granted, I'm one of them. If the roles were reversed, I'd mock the tar out of them. If Coach weren't keeping his laser beams on me, I'd be hitting up O'Malley's and maybe a bar downtown too until I found someone to let off some steam with. That's how I've been living my college life. And that's how I've been getting in trouble so consistently that Coach intervened.

I already pissed the man off during the game. It wouldn't be a good idea for him to find out I've picked up a new distraction. Not when Edwards is also watching my every move.

Speaking of, he glares at me from across the room. Acknowledging his existence was a mistake, because he takes it as an invitation to speak.

"Don't be so cocky. Next time you pull that shit, someone's going to bust your teeth, and I'll be right there, ready to replace you."

"Must suck to suit up for every game and only get to trash talk in the locker room, huh?"

"Guys, guys." Archie raises his hands as if Edwards and I had been about to come to blows. "Why can't we all just get along?"

"Piss off, Bracken."

I roll my eyes at Edwards's overt attempt at showing his testosterone.

"Let the record show that I tried." Archie turns back to me. "Anyway, are you sure you don't wanna score tonight?"

I wanna score, all right. I think about scoring every waking moment. My dreams are turning even more explicit than usual. But no girl is worth letting Edwards take my spot.

"Already busy." My tone is cutting enough that Archie finally drops it.

Instead, he turns to Jamal. "Whatever. Let's invite Maddie instead. She's way more fun than this grouch."

My whole body tenses as if there's a Bulldog all up in my grill.

I clench my jaw hard enough to hurt. If I let even a molecule of air pass between my lips, I will fully open them and tell them they better not be thinking about scoring on Strawberry tonight. Or tomorrow. Or the next day. Shit would get too complicated if any of them start tangling with my tutor. I mean, they may even find out she's *my tutor*. And that I'm flunking a class. And…

Scratch that. She's not like our usual groupies and wouldn't give them the time of the day. She's the keeper kind, not the one-and-done kind.

But I know how these stooges think. If I give an inkling of concern about her, they'll pounce on me and try to unveil the status of my interest. Which exists, yes. Because I'm interested in Strawberry's well-being as a friend, like Ryan predicted. And none of these dipshits is right for her. I don't know what kind of guy is right for her, but it's not some foul-mouthed, foul-smelling, foul-playing hockey horndog.

Incluyéndome a mí.

The thought slams me in my mother tongue and makes my head spin. I rush through the rest of the undressing process so I can stand under the cold spray of water in a shower stall. I open my mouth to it, trying to wash off the bitter taste in my mouth.

Of course I'm not right for Strawberry either. I'm not even playing for her. I'm just her reluctant student. A friend at best. She's not my type. I don't even like eating fruits.

I'm losing my head.

I fiddle with the shower knob. Can this get any colder?

The answer is no. But the air outside is punishing. I walk slowly to my SUV, taking the sharp air into my lungs. It doesn't cleanse me, though. I still have a pit in my stomach.

A group of Bolts exits the building. Some clap my back.

Others bid me a good night. They discuss which bars to hit. Someone suggests crashing a party at someone's house. Another gives a play-by-play of how he's going to chat a particular girl up.

I stand in the parking lot by my car, rubbing my gloved hand up and down my head.

Nah. There's no way I have a thing for my tutor.

I open the back door and toss my duffel bag and my stick in. Hop into the driver's seat. Start the engine. Leave the heater as low as possible.

My heart beats like a freaking rabbit's.

"No," I say firmly to myself as I drive away from the facilities. I've only known her for, what, two weeks? Less, even.

It has to be the whole abstinence thing. I'm used to doing whatever with any girl I meet who also wants to do whatever with me. That stopped two weeks ago, and the only new girl I happened to meet during that time was Strawberry.

Wait, there were her three former roommates. But they were kind of douchey, I reason with myself as I drive into the parking lot of my building. If they'd all been decent, I might've hit it off with whoever wasn't interested in Archie or the others. That's it.

I park the car and turn it off. I'm calm now that I understand this is just the hormones talking. I only have to be strong for a couple of months more until we win the national championship and the semester ends. Then, once I graduate, Coach won't be able to say shit about my dating life. And I obviously will have passed the elective, which means I won't need to see Strawberry again.

My hand flies up to massage my scalp again.

A yellow Beetle drives into the parking lot and slides into one of the spots closest to the entrance. I watch as the plume of smoke from the exhaust wanes into nothing. The driver's door opens, and out comes my tutor. Slowly. Too slow. I frown. Is something wrong?

It doesn't matter. I don't need to hover over her.

I drop my arm and turn off my car. I open my door and check to see whether she's still there. With how slowly she's moving, I'll probably catch up to her easily. But should I?

No. I hang back and tell myself, "Aran, you're not a helicopter."

My eyes are glued to her as she traverses the parking lot at a snail's pace. Something is definitely wrong. I need to not engage, though. But just as I'm about to turn on the car to drive anywhere else, Strawberry throws her arms into the air. And then she disappears from view.

A breathless moment passes until my brain clicks.

She slipped on ice.

She's on the ground.

In a dark parking lot.

I rush out of my car at full speed.

CHAPTER 14
MADDIE

Wow.

There are stars in the sky. Even though a second ago, it was dark gray from clouds loaded with snow.

Wait, no. My eyes are closed. It just hurts like a bi—

I groan. The sound awakens me to a reality I can't believe. I must've slid on black ice, and sure enough, as I paw around, that's the cold asphalt beneath me. Now I'm not sure what hurts more: my womb, my butt, my head, or my ego. Hopefully no one witnessed this.

Something odd registers. It takes me another second to make out approaching footsteps. I finally open my eyes right as someone drops to their knees beside me. Did I hit my head so hard that I'm hallucinating?

"Where are you hurt?"

Nope. I would recognize the voice that is smooth like velvet and rich like a wine and makes me feel heady. Or that last part could just be the headache sinking in.

"Aran?"

He pauses his inspection. "Glad you recognize me."

Just my luck that the hottest guy I've ever met has been selected by fate to witness every one of my humiliations. I don't know whether to laugh or cry. Sliding my elbow up, I attempt to sit, but his hand on my shoulder pushes me back.

"Stop." At the strength of his command, I have no choice but to obey. "Don't move. It could be dangerous."

"Huh?" I blink hard.

"Where did you hit yourself?"

"Um, my butt and my head, I think. Maybe my elbow too?" It's throbbing like a toothache.

The lampposts cast a weak light around the area, which is probably why I didn't notice the frozen patch. Even so, I can make out how Aran's expression darkens almost to the point of anger.

"Let me check a few things before you move." He leans down the opposite way, and I feel his hand cinch around one ankle, then the other. "Felt that?"

"Yeah." Like brands on my skin, but I don't say this part.

"Move your feet for me."

I will move a mountain for him if he keeps talking all soft and concerned like this. Clearing my throat, I stretch out my feet a little.

"Okay, lift your arms."

I do.

Sighing, he holds on to my hands and slowly pulls me up. I didn't bother putting on my gloves before getting out of the car, because it's hard to fiddle with my keys while wearing them. But he isn't wearing any, either. The heat of his skin is shocking against mine. It feels feverish, but he looks healthy. Maybe he just runs hot in more than one way.

Too quickly, I'm on my feet and swaying. His hands abandon mine to steady me by my upper arms.

"Whoa, are you dizzy?"

"A little," I admit.

Air hisses between his teeth. "Depending on how hard you hit your head and where, you may have a concussion."

"I don't think it's that bad—"

"And I don't underestimate blows to the head or the spine," he snaps.

He lets go of me and takes a step back, as if I'm the one burning. His breathing grows harsh in the span of a few seconds, and he sucks air deep into his lungs to slow it down. Now that he's not looking at me, he finds my bag on the ground and picks it up before turning away.

"C'mon, you're going to my place."

As I brush away gross slush from my coat, I ask, "Why?"

"Because I'm going to make sure you don't fall asleep tonight."

His response is so shocking that I stumble. With a yelp, I land against his back.

I feel him shift slightly, and his voice comes over his shoulder. "My, my. The little Strawberry has a dirty mind on her."

"Ugh." I push him away, glad he can't see how my face is probably turning scarlet. "You're the one who said it all weird. And I'm fine. You don't need to bother."

"Yes, I do. No one's getting hurt on my watch." He grunts at me or at his keys. Or at both.

Aran opens the building entrance and holds the door open for me. The automatic lights fire up and cast deep shadows on his face. He's still concerned. It's kind of cute to find out he's capable of that feeling.

At the stairs, the tiniest moan escapes me. Climbing up four floors isn't my idea of passing the time while on my period. But then I sense a massive wall of heat beside me. Aran waits to see if I need help. Something deep inside in my chest squeezes.

I focus on the steps one at a time. The slow, silent trek to our floor helps me clear my head. One of my many problems with guys is that the moment they're kind to me, I develop an instant crush. It's taken forever to understand that just because a guy is decent once, that doesn't mean *he* has feelings for me. And even though I'm still mechanically climbing stairs, I recognize this moment as the crossroad it is.

On one side, I could fall so fast for Aran that I break myself in the process. That's my usual pattern. On the other side—the harder, seemingly less interesting one—I could recognize that this is just him being a good Samaritan. As a hockey guy, he's probably seen terrible injuries, and if he witnessed anyone else slip and fall, he would no doubt react with the same concern.

So what if he looks like a spicy fantasy come to life? With his broad shoulders and his chiseled everything. With a face that deserves whole photoshoots. With a mouth that begs for sonnets whispered right against it. With hands that could do who knows what.

So what if he's actually *nice*? With an odd sense of humor, a die-hard loyalty to his friends, and a steadiness that gets him called 'the Iceberg.'

Aran doesn't have any interest in me, other than to make sure I don't die in my sleep tonight. He's just a good guy. The only reason he's giving me his attention is because I keep making a mess out of everything around me.

By the time we make it to his door, I'm so winded I wish I could run away and hide. But first, I know he won't let me. And second, I need to prove to myself that I can be around a decent guy—particularly this one—without nosediving straight into a crush. I take a bracing breath and follow him into his apartment.

"Why are you walking funny?"

I startle at his question. "Uh, I'd rather not say."

He stops in the middle of removing his coat, and his eyebrows rise all the way.

"Oh, my gosh. It's not like that, you perv!" I hide my face behind my hands.

"Why am I the perv? I didn't say anything."

"Your eyebrows implied it!"

His snort comes from behind me. I try to turn, but he steadies me by the shoulders. "Stop squirming. I want to inspect your head."

Even though his touch is as delicate as a beefy guy can handle, it still makes me wince. He shifts my hair around and digs his fingers softly into my scalp.

"Well, you're not bleeding."

The murmur would make me shiver if I were a weaker woman. But I tighten every muscle in my body and hold still. "I told you it wasn't that bad," I say through gritted teeth.

"Lucky you."

His heat moves away, and I can breathe again.

Tentatively, I glance over my shoulder in time to catch him unzipping his hoodie. He flings it across the living room, and it lands neatly on the enormous blue couch that swallows up most of the space. Underneath, he's wearing only a black long-sleeved T-shirt, which is now too little in the way of clothing, in my opinion.

"Sit." Aran motions to a barstool. "I'm going to cook and you're going to keep your eyes peeled open the whole time."

Sure will. I won't miss a single detail.

I bend down to leave my bag on the entrance floor with less difficulty than before. Maybe the blow to my head sucked in all the pain my body is able to produce, which is why my uterus is starting to cooperate. I shimmy out of my coat and turn it around to inspect the back. The vibrant emerald I so love has turned into gunky, brown splotches. Even worse, I can perfectly see the shape of my butt in them.

Ugh. I'm going to have to dry clean it. And if that doesn't work, I may cry. It's my favorite one.

But then something else occurs to me. "Aran, tell me the truth."

His response is to grunt, but he keeps washing his hands as if I haven't spoken.

"Is my hair a cakey, slushy mess?"

"Why do you think I'm washing my hands?"

I expel all the air in my lungs. Great, now I'll have to wash my hair tonight, even though I wasn't planning to wash it for another couple of days.

"This day really is the worst," I mumble as I climb onto the barstool.

Aran chooses to latch on to my words and asks, "Why?"

"You mean aside from how I showed an elite hockey athlete my abysmal skating skills?"

"I would not call that skating."

It's as if a dam breaks, and I explode into laughter. It's either this or bursting into a fountain of tears. Aran watches me in impassive silence as he dries his hands with a cloth towel.

"Okay, I will reveal all my secrets to you, Aran Rodriguez. I'm walking funny because I'm on my period and it hurts. Like someone's trying to shovel their way out through my womb."

I keep snort-laughing. If that's not enough to formally friend zone myself, I don't know what else would.

"Then I had to go to the first dress fitting for my sister's wedding. Which is great. Don't get me wrong! I'm super happy for Meg and Justin, but super miserable for myself because it means putting up with my mom as she criticizes every inch of my fat body. Like critiques alone have the power to smooth it all down to a perfect size four or something, you know? Oh! And that's excluding the veiled mockery about how I can't even find a plus-one for the freaking wedding. It's only two months away, Mom! Where am I going to find a boyfriend that quick? I'm busy getting ready for my book release!"

He hangs the towel back on the oven handle and slides over to the fridge, where he starts grabbing stuff to put on the counter by the stove.

"And that whole torture should've lasted, I don't know, a couple of hours, max?" I expel an exaggerated *hah* and continue. "Of course not. Five hours. Five freaking hours of trying on one hideous dress after another, because apparently, if you're of a certain size, you deserve to be punished with ugliness. And then—"

Aran sets a large bowl on the kitchen island across from me. He blinks up, as if surprised that there's more.

"I was supposed to meet with one of my students. But he canceled, because guess what? Apparently, he doesn't need tutoring anymore, which, good for him, I guess, but now I'll have less income. Which is just exactly what any student not on a scholarship needs, am I right?" I throw my hands in the air. "All I want is to write my silly little hockey romance without much drama—I mean drama in my life. The book will have plenty of it. Is that too much to ask?"

Aran presses his hands against the counter, which moves him a smidge closer to me. Even though there's a whole slab of granite between us, it feels like he's too close. I clamp my mouth closed. Heat spreads across my cheeks. It's half embarrassment at my outburst and half because of his sheer physicality.

This must be what I feel when I glance at him. It's not a crush. It's good old-fashioned attraction. The biological kind you can't help but feel when a superior specimen of your desired sex flaunts in front of you.

"I know you're vegetarian, but do you have any food allergies? Intolerance?"

"Um, no?"

"Is that a question or a statement?"

"A firm no." I scratch my head and wince.

"I can help you with some of your problems," he says as he grabs a yellow bag and opens it carefully, without spilling any flour. "Ibuprofen for the pain."

"Oh, yes. Actually."

"And also with the hockey romance." We both remain suspended in silence for a moment. Then he blinks real slow. "With the hockey part, I mean."

I sag a bit.

"Of course. And that would be great, actually!" Oh no. Am I giggling? That's way overdoing it for how awkward I feel. "Your friends are lovely but not super helpful." At least this is true. After the move, while Aran was napping, all his friends did was share glory stories about themselves. I jotted some of them down but don't really understand most of it.

Pouring a little flour into the bowl, he mutters, "Good thing we have all night, huh?"

CHAPTER 15
ARAN

What am I thinking?

Am I even thinking?

No, the answer is absolutely hell no. My brain shut down the second I saw her go down, and only my amygdala has kept me going since.

I let her rant as I gather all the ingredients to make arepas because, unlike my brain, my body is still fully functioning and is starving. My hands are on autopilot as they dump Harina P.A.N. into a bowl without measuring. Based on the size of her sandwich the first time I met her and how much pizza she ate last weekend, I have a good gauge of how much she'll eat.

Good thing we have all night *my ass*. It's a bad thing. A very bad thing. The whole point of me coming home tonight instead of hitting the town with the guys was to behave well. Keep myself out of trouble.

Strawberry is trouble. Especially when she looks up at me with shiny eyes and a tentative little smile that makes me want to do whatever it takes to see it grow.

"Are you sure"—here she drags out the letter *u* until her

voice breaks—"that you want to help me with my book research? I'm talking about super basic stuff like, for example, what the heck is icing?"

I stop. "You're kidding."

"No." But she's smiling, so I'm confused. "I watched bits and pieces of a game with the guys, and a whole game on my own later, but everyone kept saying *icing this* and *icing that*, and I only know about the kind that goes on cakes."

Biting down a smile, I set aside the flour pack and roll up my sleeves to my elbows. "Fine, I'll answer all your questions."

That perks her up. "All of them?"

"About hockey."

"Hmm."

Sneaky little Strawberry. What was she thinking about?

Curiosity gnaws at me as much as hunger, but asking would be too close to flirting. I try to concentrate on the dough I'm making with a pinch of salt and water. I had never cooked a thing until I left home for college, and even though my parents live across town, I couldn't spend my off time making trips home so Mom would feed me. I had no other choice but to learn.

"I'll ask you non-hockey questions too, though. Feel free to grunt when you don't want to answer."

I don't grunt.

The dough is consistent enough that I can shape it. I grab a good handful for her arepa and mold it into a neat ball. Then I slap it between my hands until it flattens into a disk.

"First question. What are you making?"

This one's harmless, so I say, "Arepas. It's the national dish of Venezuela, the country my parents came from."

"*Oh*. Okay, color me intrigued. Next question—"

"Too many already," I cut in with a deadpanned voice.

"Well, we have to do something if I've got to stay up all night long, right?"

Shit.

Every fiber of my being stops except for two things. My heart, which is busy pumping blood down south. And my eyes, which narrow.

She gapes. "Is your mind in the gutter all the time?"

Yes. Except for when I'm on the ice. And lately it's getting worse.

As for her answer, I grunt.

"Lettuce backtrack." She clears her throat.

"Did you just say *lettuce*?"

"I, too, am hungry," Strawberry says solemnly. "Next question. Can I help you with anything? I feel bad just watching."

"No, your job is to stay alert."

Strawberry gives me a little salute. "Yes, sir."

Once I'm done forming the three arepas, I rinse my hands and change gears to find her the pain reliever. I slide the bottle over to her and grab a clean cup from the cabinet to fill with water from the fridge dispenser. And then another one for me.

I quench my thirst—at least this one—watching over her as she takes a couple of pills and chugs water like it's beer. She even sighs hard at the end.

"Last non-hockey question for tonight." She squirms, and that worries me. Doesn't look like it'll be an easy one. "Or maybe I shouldn't ask. I mean, if you didn't comment on it when I talked about it, it shouldn't be a big deal."

What, among the verbal diarrhea she subjected me to in the past ten minutes, could she possibly want to revisit? The thing with her mom? The romance part of the hockey romance? And who the hell decided writing a romance book about hockey was a good idea? Hockey is the least romantic sport I could possibly imagine. It's a bunch of sweaty, stinky dudes slamming against each other or across boards, and a thousand ways to bleed. The cutesy shit that belongs in romance books should be figure skating or something.

Strawberry sucks in her lips and starts pulling away.

"Just spit it out, woman."

"Well." She tucks a strand of her messy—and, yeah, slightly gross—hair behind her ear. "How come you didn't blow a fuse about the period stuff? Like, most guys immediately want to fling themselves out the window at the mention of it."

"I'm not most guys," I say with the shake of my head. "Also, I have two sisters."

"Oh."

"Now you answer this. Cilantro, yes or no?"

"Oh, yes."

I try, I really do, to not find an innuendo behind that. But it's not my fault her voice came out all throaty and sigh-y, or that my blood was already pumping. I turn around and pull open the fridge with more force than necessary, just so I can stick my face in it ASAP. I know exactly where every single thing is, but I pretend like I can't find it just so I can cool down.

Finally, I grab the bag with the handful of greens and rinse the tomatoes I left soaking in a bowl in the sink.

"I love everything green," she continues saying, as though we hadn't just suffered a dangerous lull in the conversation.

It's just because you're out of the game, I remind myself. Nothing more, nothing less. Strawberry's not doing anything special. She's literally just sitting there, bundled up in a thick dress that fits her like a sack of potatoes. There's no cleavage, no hint of her curves, no flirty glances. She's not even wearing makeup. Her hair has mud in it. There's a whole kitchen island between us.

And yet...

For the first time in my life, I find the need to keep talking. If I'm the one filling in the silence, then my head won't have any choice but to stop this hormonal loop I'm trapped in.

"I'm not a fan of green stuff or fruits," I say in a rasp, as if it's the first time I've used my vocal cords all day.

"No way. When we met, you were drinking some green gunk I probably wouldn't even want to smell."

I dry the tomatoes with a paper towel and keep my eyes on them at all costs. Which is a good idea, since I'm about to use a knife anyway.

"If you like green shit, you'd like it more than I do."

"What's in it?"

I wrinkle my nose. "Kale, celery, apple, orange juice, and some green protein powder just so I'm not hitting up dairy all the time."

"Huh, that doesn't sound so bad."

"This will be better." I slice the tomatoes in half and take out as many seeds as I can with one swipe of the knife. I hope she's not testy like my little sister, who can't stand a single seed.

She shifts, and I dare glance up in time for her to rest her chin on both hands, elbows on the counter. The picture of innocence. The drastic opposite of the thoughts in my head.

"How's your head?" I ask a tad too loud.

It makes her startle. "Hurts a little, but not too bad."

The moment she slipped in the icy parking lot comes back to my mind like a bucket of cold water. She looks, sounds, and moves normally, but you never know with head or spinal injuries. My chest constricts as if it's being squeezed by a cold hand.

"My older sister, Luz, was the captain of the Thunder Strikes the year the team was created." Even though I pause, she keeps quiet, probably sensing there's more since there was no lead-in to this. "Which is nothing short of a miracle, since for a while before that, she couldn't walk."

I only hear her sharp intake of breath.

For a moment, all I can do is focus on dicing tomatoes without maiming myself.

"She got checked against the boards at a weird angle when she was twelve."

"Oh, no." Another gasp. "But she recovered, right? I mean, if she was the captain of the Strikes…"

"Yeah, it was pretty much a miracle." I dump the chopped tomato into a fresh bowl and grab an onion. "So, that's why I'm being intense."

"I get it. Um, I'll stay awake all night and send you picture proof if you want."

"No need. You're staying under my supervision."

She laughs. "You don't need to stay up all night too. Don't you have practice tomorrow or something?"

"Nope. Not tomorrow." Besides, it wouldn't be the first time I went all night long without sleep.

"Has anyone told you that you're really stubborn, Aran Rodriguez?"

"I'm unmovable like an iceberg, remember?"

Her scoff sends her reeling back. "Unfortunately for you, icebergs are melting faster than ever."

Yeah, that's kind of the effect she's having on me.

The onion fumes hit me, and I have to look up and blink really hard for a moment, which she decides to take advantage of.

"Oh, are you crying? Did I make the big, bad boy cry?"

"You don't stink bad enough to make me suffer like this," I say with a sniffle.

"So, I do stink?"

I glare, and it makes her burst into a giggling fit. With her eyes closed, she misses the lightning quick smile I manage to tamp down.

Back to work I go. I bag the rest of the onion and dump a small handful onto the tomatoes. I wash the cilantro and wring it out with my hands, which I find brings out the flavor better.

Then I chop just enough and mix it with the other veggies, adding salt, pepper, vinegar, and a dash of olive oil.

"Whoa, that looks amazing already."

"It's pico de gallo."

"Pico de gallo?" Of course she butchers the pronunciation of it, and I have to repeat myself two more times. As she practices the pronunciation, I turn the kitchen burner on and set a buttered pan on it. And off the arepas go.

"I didn't know guys who cooked this well existed outside of books," she says in a joking way.

I don't tell her about the Venezuelan saying my mom mocked me with the first time she saw me cooking. Ya te puedes casar. Which maybe one day, when I find the one woman who can put up with my bull crap long term, I will. Though it will definitely not be anywhere between now and graduation.

"You don't cook?"

"Eh, so-so," she admits. "I bake a mean casserole, but I'm extremely adept at burning pancakes."

I snort and flip the smaller arepa first. "How come you're vegetarian?"

"Ugh. Meat is the most disgusting thing that's ever been on my tongue." Gagging sounds.

"Strawberry." My voice carries a warning. "You keep saying things that are very easy to tease you about."

"Oh. Um. Maybe you're the one with the problem."

Definitely me. But I need help. What do we do?

"Anyway." She clears her throat once. Twice. "Maybe let's start the reverse tutoring."

I turn over my shoulder, cocking an eyebrow. Her face was already flushed to the roots of her hair, and it only grows warmer.

"On hockey! Oh my gosh. Do we need to wash your brain with bleach?"

"Maybe." I shrug and go back to flipping arepas. As they hiss against the heat and the oil, I slide back to the fridge and pull out a container. "I hope it's just the taste you don't like, because it's about to smell real meaty once I pop this into the microwave."

"Your house, your rules."

I file that one away for future reference and instead say, "So, why hockey?"

"Everyone's going nuts about it right now." I must've pressed the right button because she goes on. "My debut book is a young adult—that's fiction for teens—and it sold pretty well, but the way things work in trad—that's traditional publishing—is that they chop up the payments into checks smaller than those vegetables you diced. So I need to keep paying my bills until my next check, you know? And soon I'll have to start paying my student loans, which means I have to write what's popular even though I don't know squat about it."

She sucks in air and finishes off with, "And on the day I decided to write a hockey romance, I met you. It was fate!"

My eyes are as wide as saucers. I imagine if the sun could smile, it would look like this, with gunky brown hair framing it, a pink glow to its cheeks, and sparkly eyes.

"Fate, huh?"

Strawberry nods rapidly. "Yes! Everyone says write what you know, but I didn't know, and now I will, thanks to you."

She… could compete with my sisters when it comes to who speaks faster.

My head spins with her words and I try to train it on not burning the food. I pop the container with pulled beef from last night into the microwave and set the timer.

This confirms my suspicion. She was taking notes about me not because she was an analog stalker, but for book research.

"What's TDH, then?" I ask.

Only silence greets me. I let her be until the microwave

pings. Even as I take out plates and set them on the counter. I glance at her and almost laugh at how tightly she's biting her lips.

"If you want me to answer hockey questions, you'll give me that one."

Her brow crashes. She looks freaking adorable. "This is bribery."

"I call it building trust."

With a clean knife, I slice the three arepas, and before much of the heat escapes, I stuff each one with a mountain of cheese. To hers, I only add pico de gallo and put it on her plate. Then I load mine with the rest of the veggies and the meat.

"Thank you. It looks amazing." She's a clever one, watching how I wrap a napkin around my first arepa, then doing the same. She picks it up and takes a big bite.

The moan that comes from deep in her throat almost fells me like a tree.

I swallow hard one, two times. A third. Eyes on my food. Food in my mouth. Make it busy with that. Not with saying what I want to say. Keep it in my brain. That way it's only awkward there.

"Oh my word. This is so delicious. You'll have to teach me how to make them!"

"But first," I say with difficulty. "What's TDH?"

Strawberry groans. "You'll never let me forget it, will you?"

"Nope."

"Fine." She sets the food down and lets out a great sigh. "I will confess. But you must promise me—"

"I'm not going to promise shit. Just say it and deal with the consequences."

"Talldarkandhandsome." She says this so fast the words jumble into one and all I hear is gibberish.

"The what?"

Gasping for air, she says it again, this time more slowly. "Tall. Dark. And handsome."

My arepa is suspended in the air. I need to set it down for this.

I burst out laughing.

"This is what I didn't want!" Strawberry screeches and throws her balled-up napkin at me. "Stop looking at me like that."

"Like what?" The question comes out squeaky between guffaws that refuse to stop.

"Like I'm one of your groupies and you caught me red-handed!"

"I know you're not a puck bunny—that's the term. Write it down." I'm still chuckling as I add, "You don't even know what icing is."

"And you haven't explained it."

I put a dirty knife on the counter, then put the salt dispenser on one side and her cup of water on the opposite side. "This is the middle line and the two goals. If you're a player here, on your goalie's side," I say, pointing at her empty cup, "and you shoot the puck all the way here." I poke the spot behind the saltshaker. "That's icing, in a nutshell."

Her eyes widen. "Oh. Hold on. I need to write all this down."

I keep eating as she rushes over to her bag at the door. She returns with the same yellow journal and the strawberry pen from day one, where she jotted down that I was TDH.

The tall part, check. I'm at least a foot taller than her. Dark? Double check. My brown skin is several shades darker. I also wouldn't describe myself as a ray of sunshine. The handsome part? Well, I'm not in the business of lying. I guess I'm a TDH, huh?

"So, were you going to base your character on me?"

She does not meet my eyes. "Obviously not on the real you. That would be supremely creepy."

A corner of my lips goes up. The guys will be disappointed when they find out.

"And what exactly do characters do in a hockey romance?"

"They play hockey all the time." She looks up, blinking innocently in an exaggerated way.

"With their tongues?"

She gasps.

So I add, "Surely not with their sticks."

"Aran!"

"Any other hockey questions?" I take another bite of my food to shut myself up.

"Um, I mean. Lots. What made you choose hockey? Or did it, like, choose you?" An awkward laugh. "What's it like when you're playing? Have you been hit by pucks before? Why did you decide to be a goalie? Is your training different? I mean, I guess it must be—you're not shooting pucks, but catching them. And—"

"First of all, breathe. Second, it's probably better if you experience it."

"I plan to watch your next game."

That makes me oddly excited, but not as much as when I say, "I mean some firsthand experience."

Strawberry blinks fast as her brain processes. "There is no way in heck I could possibly play hockey. I don't even know how to skate."

"Excuse—" I do a double take. Triple. "Were you born and raised on the beach or what?"

"No, here. But not everyone is good at sports, you know."

I shake my head. "Fine, I'll give you a reverse-tutoring plan too. First step, I'm going to teach you how to skate."

"But—"

"No further hockey questions will be answered until then."

"What about non-hockey questions?" A slow grin spreads across her lips when she paraphrases our earlier conversation.

And like then, all she gets from me is a grunt before I take the last bite of my first arepa. My stomach is rumbly, but this time it's not because of the food.

CHAPTER 16
MADDIE

"Are you sure this isn't a date?"

Ryan sits on my bed, watching me braid my hair so it doesn't get in the way later for what I've told her a million times is *not* a date. I press my lips tight and give her A Look through the mirror. The same one I've sent her way the past two times she asked.

She puts her hands up. "I'm just saying it looks an awful lot like one. A guy and a girl going ice skating together on Valentine's Day? I mean, c'mon. I can't be faulted for thinking it might be a date. Your denial makes it all the more sus."

"Aran and I clarified that this is just for book research." I wrap a pink hair tie at the end of my braid. It matches the knit cable sweater that took me all last year to make.

"If so, why is it just the two of you?" She smirks.

"Because——" I interrupt myself with a long-suffering sigh. "I've told you I don't want anyone else to witness my awkwardness."

She dips her chin and gives me an incredulous look. "But it's okay if Aran does?"

"Yes, because that's all he's done——watch me make a fool

of myself over and over," I say, turning around with a great huff. "I mean, I even talked about my period with him. If that's not enough reason to put him off me, then there's *everything* else."

Tilting her head, she asks, "What's everything else?"

I gesture all around me, as if it's self-explanatory. But confusion takes over Ryan's expression, so I add, "I'm just not his type."

"Based on what? Did he say so?"

"No, but I know. I've seen one or two of his girlfriends on campus. And like, he dated you, and you're absolutely freaking stunning, fit, fun, and kind, and… I'm just not like that. I'm short, fat, flabby, and a walking embarrassment." I cringe.

Ryan coughs and splutters to the point where she has to thump her chest before she's able to talk. "Okay, first of all, that's bullshit."

"No way. You really are all that!"

She smiles from ear to ear. "Okay, maybe not that part. I am pretty cool. But the whole thing about you not being his type is the bullshit."

I shake my head. I saw Aran with one girl near the cafeteria once, like a year ago. They were tangled in a very public display of affection where I saw a whole game of tonsil hockey. I remember being stunned at first that they didn't care who may be watching. But then I figured two super-hot people probably wanted to pounce on each other all the time. Because the girl was leggy, with a tiny waist and a huge behind—which one of his hands had been dangerously close to. The other one was lost in the confines of her black hair. And she had the whole air of a girl who had her pick of guys.

I couldn't even get a kiss like that from the one guy who showed some interest in me in the past. And he was a normal-looking guy in the creative writing program too, not some Roman statue come to life.

Oblivious to my thoughts, Ryan continues, "In fact, my concern is quite the opposite."

"Huh?"

She observes me in silence for a moment, so I finish up fastening my fanny pack around my waist and grab my scarf. This one's white, like my Doc Martens. I'm wearing faded blue jeans from Torrid that don't stab into my gut, and I'll wrap myself and the look up with a thick down coat in a cream color and a white knit beanie with bunny ears. Nothing about this outfit screams date.

"I've never seen that stubborn ass open up to a girl the way he's done with you."

I wind the scarf around my neck as I say, "That's because I give him no choice but to talk. Because he's obviously not going to use his mouth for anything else with a girl who is not his type."

"Puh-lease." She unfolds her legs from under her and gets up, passing me my coat before I can reach it from the chair. "You have the smile of an angel. I've already seen it getting him to do things he's never done for anyone else."

"Ryan, we are *friends*. That's all."

"No, you're friends with Archie and the others, but it's different with Aran. He's not like this with anyone else."

I'm fully dressed to brave the February cold, and it's warm in the apartment, but I stand in my room observing my roommate. Aside from the few jokes in the conversation, she's been pretty serious throughout. And even though Aran is waiting in his car, I need to ask.

"Um, don't get me wrong, but… why are you so worried about this?" I bite my lip and play with the zipper of my coat. "Do you still have feelings for him or something?"

"Ha!" Ryan shakes her head. "Okay, I'll answer the second question first. Do you wanna know why Aran and I didn't work out?"

"If you want to share, sure."

I am low-key *dying* to know. But I'm trying to act chill and not freak her out.

"Because we weren't interested in each other that way. Him, because he's been incapable of forming a deep connection with a single one of the many girls he's dated. And me because I realized while being with him that I'm ace and aro."

My eyes go wide. "Oh."

"So I'm asking because I'm worried he will break your heart like he's done with almost every girl, and then I'll have to murder him."

My chest fills up with something warm that rushes up my face and to my eyes. I rush forward and give her a big hug. "Thank you for being my friend, Ryan."

She pats my back. "We can still make this a party of three, you know."

"I know." I pull away, wrinkling my nose as I mull over that scenario. "But if I change the plan at the last minute, he'll suspect something's up. The last thing I want is for him to think I may have feelings for him."

"Do you?"

"No, it was hypothetical. Besides," I add with a shrug. "This is so not a date that we're not going to the big outdoor ice rink, but to his former elementary school. We'll be surrounded by little kids and families, and not by smoochy couples. It's the least romantic skating date ever."

"So you admit it's a date, huh?" She elbows me.

I huff. "It's not!"

"I'm just teasing." With shocking strength, she turns me around by my shoulders and pushes me to the front door of the apartment. "Go enjoy your private humiliation with your friend who you definitely have no feelings for."

"Ryan…"

"And also, protect your head if you fall. Unless you want

him to stay awake the whole night with you like last weekend. Which I'm sure he did out of the goodness of his heart."

I open the front door and turn over my shoulder with a grumpy expression. "Stop teasing me."

"That's what friends are for."

With a final wave, she closes the door. I stand there for a moment, biting my lip. It's like Ryan could read my mind and make me voice every thought. Yes, this does feel an awful lot like it's going to be a date. I couldn't even sleep well last night because of how much I was anticipating it.

But also yes, Aran is not into me in that way. He acted normal even during the study session and movie marathon we had Saturday while we were making sure I didn't have a concussion. Sure, his mind was in the gutter a few times, but not about me. It was because I kept putting my foot in my mouth. We sat a foot apart on the couch, and he didn't look at me in a salacious way, because there's just nothing salacious about me.

I'm the kind of girl he can comfortably be around with no pressure. Like Ryan. Or maybe even like his sisters. I don't know.

Standing by the exterior balcony, I immediately locate his black SUV. The headlights are on, the beams dancing in the falling snow. As I head down the stairs, I'm glad I spilled the beans to Ryan. It was a good last-minute reminder that I'm not the kind of girl Aran Rodriguez goes for and that there will be nothing attractive about me learning how to skate.

The cabin is dark inside his car, but I make out his silhouette easily. I don't know if he watches me as I round his car, but when I open the door, his eyes are fixed on his phone as he texts with someone.

"Hey."

One of his caveman sounds is the response I get.

Yep, definitely no romance in the air.

I heft myself up into the seat by the door handle and buckle up. "Okay, ready when you're ready."

He nods, though I don't know if the gesture is to me or the phone. After a quick moment, he drops it in the cupholder and turns up the music a bit. His eyes stop on me for a second, but then he sets the car in motion, and off we go.

In full silence.

Aran is the picture of relaxation as he drives. Left elbow on the door, hand loosely on the steering wheel. His right hand is the one doing the steering, which I find interesting.

"How come you drive with your right? I thought you were left-handed."

"I'm ambidextrous, actually." The rumble of his voice fills the cabin.

"So you can write with your right?"

"Yeah."

"Wow, I wish I had that superpower."

Dark eyes flash to me for a second and then focus back on the road.

I regret having zipped up my coat all the way. My phone's in my fanny pack, and I really wish I had something to do with my hands so they'd stop fiddling with my hair or the seat belt.

"Nervous?"

I jump a little at his question, which gives him the answer. Laughing an unhinged little laugh, I say, "Yes, actually. Mildly terrified."

"Skating's not that hard."

The knives on my feet aren't what I'm nervous about.

Still, determined to not let Ryan become a murderer, I say, "Easy for the hockey player to say."

"Just trust me. I wasn't born wearing skates."

And I do trust him. Maybe that's the problem.

Once upon a time, about two and a half years ago, I had a crush on a guy in my department. He was smart, funny, and a year older, which, back then made him seem so mature. And he was such a nice guy to everyone, including me. Of course, I took that to mean more than it did. And because back then, I had a lot more illusions—or delusions—about guys than I do now, I developed a huge crush on him.

One time at a party, I got a lil bit tipsy and confessed my feelings to him. He admitted that, even though he saw me as a friend, we could go on a date and see how things went. I was over-the-moon excited. I even got Rebs to do some fancy makeup for me that later made my face break out. Anyway, the date went well because we talked about writing and books and our plans for the future.

But that wasn't enough. And I felt it when we kissed on our second date. Our lips touched, and it was as if we'd both forgotten how to move. Like maybe his lips were a square and mine were a round peg.

Things were awkward after that, and we obviously didn't keep going out. But we also stopped being comfortable with each other. And that broke my heart even more.

I just don't want a repeat of that with Aran.

When we get to the school, I've worked myself down to normal. The parking lot is packed with cars, and I have to be careful not to bump the one beside us with the door as I get out.

Aran heads to the back of the car and returns with his massive duffel bag. He says, "There are no rentals here, so I brought my older sister's skates for you."

"Crap, I didn't even think of that. What if they don't fit?"

"They should be okay. You're a couple inches shorter than her."

But fatter. What if my feet can't even squeeze in?

With that new worry unlocked, I walk with him into the school. The corridors are lit up, and we make our way through them at his pace, which means we find the ice rink pretty fast and I'm a little winded.

The noise that hits us when we enter is unexpected. Here, the suburban half of town congregates on the seats or on the ice. Groups of kids play around, chasing each other. A parent teaches their kid here and there. Someone takes pictures of a big group in the middle.

I walk behind Aran as we descend the steps to an empty corner in the front row. He motions for me to go first. It makes sense. With his long legs, he'll need the aisle.

I take a seat, and he does the same. First, he unzips his thick black coat. Underneath, he's in a gray St. Cloud hoodie and black jeans. His thigh bumps into my knee as he bends down to open the bag and take out his black skates. He sets them aside and digs for a smaller pair.

"When you're done putting them on, stuff your shoes in the bag."

"Yes, sir. Captain, sir." I salute.

He snorts a little as he sets out to follow his own command.

I take a page from his book and open my coat so I can bend forward easily. After making quick work of removing my boots, I discover the good and the bad news. The good news is that his sister's skates fit. The bad news is that I'll now have to learn how to skate.

Aran surprises me by grabbing my ankle and squeezing his finger into the skate. "You're tying them too loose. You could break your ankle like this."

"Oh, okay. I guess I'll—"

Before I can finish the sentence, he gets up on his feet. Or rather, on his skates. I crane my neck back, because he's impossibly taller. But then he lowers to his knees, and my heart stops.

His knees surround my foot and hold it tight so it doesn't jerk up with the motions. The tendons of his hands flex and release with the movements, fingers working with deftness as he undoes the strings of one skate and laces them back up *tight*.

"I could've done it myself, you know," I say in a choked-up voice.

"Sure. And maybe you'd have broken something that way too."

I smile. "No one's getting hurt on your watch, huh?"

"Damn right."

He pats my foot when he's done. I don't know if he even realizes it. Then he moves onto the next foot and starts all over again.

This is such a boyfriend move. Not that he's... I mean, for my book. I'll make a note of it.

"Thanks," I say as he stands up when he's finished.

"Get up."

"Okay, okay." I take a deep breath, brace myself against the seats beside mine, and stand up.

For all of one second. It's like my brain can't feel the whole bottom of my feet touching a flat surface and decides I'm free-falling. Which I sort of do—straight into Aran's chest. Face first.

I yelp at the pain in my cheekbone. It takes me a second to realize I'm still upright, and it's because he's holding my upper arms.

Slowly, I ease my weight back on my heels. Trying to break the awkwardness, I look up and mumble, "Dude, is your chest made of stone?"

"Not just any stone. Marble." His lips twitch, but he doesn't let himself smile. "Ready for the ice?"

"Hey, so. Since this is all for book research, I have a question."

"Are you stalling, Strawberry?"

Totally. I'm terrified of breaking my teeth on the ice.

"I'm just wondering all of a sudden how good a skater a goalie is. Maybe I didn't pick the best teacher."

The expression on his face says *really?*

"I have to practice skating just like the rest. In fact, my edge work is amazing."

Sighing, I say, "Oh, I bet. You're probably good at everything, huh?"

I blink hard as a little smirk curves his luscious lips. And that's when I realize his words carried an innuendo I played into far too well. His smirk widens the hotter my face gets.

He leans a little closer to my ear and whispers. "I'm not just good. I'm *really* good."

Wow, okay. Never imagined heart attacks felt this delicious.

I clear my throat. "Great, I think I've got enough inspiration for my book already. Let's go home."

Aran clicks his tongue and pulls away. "No can do. We didn't come all this way just to lace up." He drops his hands, which somehow doesn't make me fall. "See? You're ready."

"Is it too late for me to just look up some YouTube videos about how to skate or something?"

With a few long strides, he slides onto the ice, and with the momentum, he makes a neat turn back to face me. "C'mon, little Strawberry. Be brave."

With shaky legs, I shuffle over to the barrier by the entrance to the ice and clutch at the frame. "First of all, I'm not little. Second of all, I'm not brave."

He folds his powerful arms across his chest. "So you are a strawberry?"

Top heavy, easy to turn red, and likely to get pimples when stressed? Sure. I blow out air and glare—until he extends a hand and flexes his fingers, ordering me to come.

Heat explodes in my belly, and the shrapnel feels like butterflies all over. That little gesture, Aran telling me to join him in his element, is doing something to me. It's a shame that it would look very weird if I took my gloves off so I could touch his skin directly.

Slowly, I reach out with one hand until he grabs it, saying, "You can't be this stiff when skating."

What he doesn't know is that it's either this or turning to putty in his hand.

"This is still probably a good time to mention that I barely passed gym class."

Aran offers his other hand, and I hold it automatically.

Oh, no. He's leaning back.

"Wait, wait, wait—"

"You're more likely to fall if you don't relax."

"How can I relax?" I screech.

"Look up at my face."

Absolutely the wrong way to relax. Yet, with no excuse in my mind, I obey. Fortunately, Aran's attention is fixed on my feet. I allow one skate to touch the ice. The lack of friction freaks me out, and my weight tilts forward. Fast.

Pulling up my arms, Aran slides me out onto to the ice until I crash into him again. Upon impact, his hands move away, but before I can make a grab for them, they're on my waist. Under my coat.

"Look, you're standing on the ice."

I cannot see anything other than the gray of his hoodie and the upper portion of the *S*.

"If you let me go, I will kill you."

"I'm not letting you go."

Feeling his voice rumble against my body, the clean smell of his skin and of the laundry soap on his clothes, the heat of his body where it touches mine, his hands firmly clasped around my waist... is too date-like.

Swallowing thickly, I lean back until my feet start sliding. Every time that happens, my heart rate goes up. I make the mistake of tipping my head back.

Aran is smiling. "Maybe you actually suck at this."

"I'm afraid of falling. How do I get back up if I do?" I ask, breathless without even having skated an inch.

"I'll lift you up."

Maddie, this is not a date. Pull yourself together.

We're just talking mechanics here. Nothing about feelings or anything like that.

I swallow with difficulty. "Um, I'm really heavy, though. I wouldn't want you to get hurt."

"Please." He snorts. "I could bench-press you."

I glance at his thick biceps, his hard chest, his broad shoulders. "You do look strong, but—"

"Stop panicking, Strawberry. I got you." Aran grabs my waist a little tighter, which is both horrifying and thrilling. He can probably feel all my fat rolls, but it's the first time a guy has ever touched me there, and I don't dislike it. Not at all.

"Um, all right."

"Good. Now I'm going to skate back. Eyes on mine. Don't think about your feet."

I nod, and I do not think about my feet during the rest of the night.

CHAPTER 17
ARAN

'm so damn pissed, I'm about to lose my cool.

I don't even need to look up at the board to know we're losing miserably. An early goal put the Falcons of Northern State on the board. We tied it in second period, but I let in two more like a stinking sieve. And one of them was a weak wraparound I should've been able to stop with my eyes closed.

Worse, as if my wall crumbling caused an earthquake, the rest of the team has been a mess. Webber missed an easy pass. Amadi got sent to the sin bin for high sticking. And we're ending the second period in a PK that is testing me.

As I follow the play, I breathe in deep and try to calm my tits. Bodies scrimmage before me, and I bite harder onto the mouth guard. This game should've been a cakewalk. The Falcons are good but not as good as we are. We're the Frozen Four contenders, not them.

Even if I have to stop the puck with my face, I will.

I block a shot at my five-hole with my right knee. From the corner of my eye, Falcon number 4, a forward, approaches with the intent of picking up the garbage. I stack my pads. The guy crashes into me from the side, and I eat the net. Something digs into my side hard enough I feel it even through the pads. It tears a grunt out of me.

The weight comes off. As I sit up, Webber turns out to be the reason. "Get the hell off our goalie, asshole!"

"What goalie?" Falcon number 4 laughs and shoves Webber with enough force to down a tree. "All you have is a monkey that couldn't even catch a banana."

And then I lose it.

One second, I'm down and the next, my mitts are off and my fist connects with the dipshit's face. Then he's on his ass.

Bodies slam into mine, and I don't see. I don't reason. The shouting around me is a buzz. I struggle against hands, sticks, my own pads.

"Calm down!" someone yells in my ear. "Stay calm, man."

"Ref, number four said racist shit against our goalie!"

"Shouldn't that get him suspended?"

I shake my head. Hard. My mouth guard rattles against the cage of my mask. My knuckles are already bruising.

Someone jostles me, and I scope out the situation more clearly now. Bracken slashes one hand across the air as he talks with the ref and a linesman. The benches cleared, but thankfully this didn't turn into a fender bender.

Amadi gets in my grill. "You okay, man?"

"Yeah," I rasp out.

I pull up my mask without removing it all the way and spray water in my mouth and on my face. As if I have a built-in radar for her like I have for pucks, I spot Strawberry in one shot. Her hands are on her mouth as she watches me. Or the melee near my goal. I hate that this is the first game she's come to watch. And I hate that she came with that little sucker who was almost my tutor. Forgot his name the second he couldn't get mine right.

I tighten my jaw so hard I jam the mouth guard back in so I don't break the chiclets.

Because I'm the Bolts' captain, the ref delivers the verdict to me. A minor for me—that the Falcon captain has chosen Webber to serve in the bin, because of freaking course; take our best defenseman, why don't you—and a major and misconduct for Falcon number 4.

Doesn't matter. We're still on a PK.

The game devolves into dirtier play during the last seconds of the period. I manage to catch all the shots out of spite alone. But when the whistle blows and I join everyone filing off the ice, I can't even keep my head up.

"What the heck is wrong you bunch of toddlers?" Coach Green screams once we're in the locker room. "Especially you, captain!"

I toss my helmet on the floor and run my hands down my face. "I'm sorry. I know I'm screwing up the game."

Coach chokes a little. Silence takes over the locker room.

Saying that felt like a hand reached into my mouth and ripped out a lung or something. But it's true. My head hasn't been in the game from the beginning.

All it took was a turn around the ice before the game and seeing Strawberry sitting all cozy next to some guy. We haven't talked much since I taught her how to skate, outside of tutoring sessions. I didn't even know she was coming tonight. I'd have appreciated a heads-up. That way I wouldn't have kept glancing at her to see if her attention was on the game or on her date.

I'm a clown today, and I know it.

Before Coach or anyone else can say anything, I get up and wade across the room, past Assistant Coach Thomas and over to the bathroom. Stopping before the first shower stall, I turn the knob to the coldest setting and stick my head under the spray. My whole body locks under the assault. I stay put because this punishment is exactly what I need to clear my head.

"Dude," Archie says from behind me. "What's going on with you?"

I wish I knew.

No, I know why I've been dialed all the way up to an eight. And I have no right to feel that way. I pull away from the shower and turn it off. My heavy breathing echoes around the room.

"Talk to me, Rodriguez."

I shake my head, spraying water around like a dog.

"Is it serious, at least?" he asks, frustration evident in his voice. "Because if you're injured or something, I'll get Coach to pull you."

"No, you won't."

"Then say something, you knucklehead! This isn't like you at all. We're worried."

"I won't let it affect the third period."

He frowns. "So there *is* something."

Yeah, there is. And it's big. The size of this whole place. And it crept up on me when I didn't realize it. And I don't know what to do because this really isn't like me at all. I don't let anything interfere with games. Least of all girls. *Especially* not girls I'm not even dating. And yet…

Was Coach right when he banned me from dating for the rest of the season? Except, shit, I don't remember getting twisted into a pretzel over the Kelseys in my life. Was he wrong, and now his mandate has turned into a self-fulfilling prophecy?

Archie's expression shifts into worry. "You look ill. Maybe we should let Edwards in—"

"Don't you dare." I take a step forward, looming over him. "I will finish the game. Make sure the guys score."

He hits my chest. "In case you haven't noticed, douchebag, we've been having your back all night."

I'm letting the team down. Some captain, huh?

I have enough shame to ease off. Just a smidge.

"Is this about what number 4 said?"

"No," I answer. "But I don't want to talk about it."

"Okay, great. So it isn't about the game. That means it could be about a million other things no one can possibly guess at." Archie pulls at his red hair. "One day you'll have a breakdown if you keep bottling shit up like this, Aran, and it won't just affect your game. I'm your best friend. You can talk to me."

"Maybe later." Maybe never. But I add, "Definitely not when we have a game to salvage."

He throws his hands in the air and walks away. Wish I could walk away from myself too.

I wipe my face with the sleeve of my jersey and join the rest of the team. Coach keeps laying down a play for the opening minutes, but when his eyes catch me, they promise murder.

I lower mine to the *C* on my chest I no longer deserve.

"Keep playing like this, and I'll be starting next game," Edwards says while we head back out after intermission.

"Shut up, man. Everyone has off days," Archie spits out at him.

Yeah, everyone does. But not me. That's why they call me "the Iceberg." I'm supposed to be an impenetrable, unmovable block of ice. Today, I'm lava. Just oozing all over the place and destroying everything in my path.

"Rodriguez." I immediately hold back for Coach to catch up to me. "Is everything okay at home?"

I do a double take. That wasn't what I expected at all.

"Yes, Coach."

"Then what the hell is your problem today?"

That's more like it.

"I'm focused now."

"Better late than never, I guess," he says, his words dripping with sarcasm. "I'm sure the scouts will completely forget how you allowed three goals and got into a fight in the first two periods."

I wince. "Scouts?"

He gives me a textbook sarcastic expression. "We're regionals contenders. What did you expect? Of course there are scouts watching. You more than anyone should be busting your ass out there to show them not drafting you will cost them."

"I—" But I clamp my mouth shut. I have nothing to say. No excuses. I've sucked, and I know it.

Turning my head back to him by my mask's grill, Coach says, "Tell me you're going to play like a brand-new man in the third period so I don't have to pull you in front of those scouts."

"I will, sir." I clench my jaw and my fists. "I won't let the team down."

"Good. Go out there and break their wings."

Brutal mental image, but it does the trick.

I skate back out to the same side I had during first period. I know I'm closer to her now, but I force myself to keep my eyes on the ice.

Even though number 4 gets checked so hard toward the end of the game that he gets taken away by the medics, even though I make a save during PK that gets the whole arena roaring, we still lose three to two.

I'm so angry at myself that I march into the locker room, change out of my skates and into boots, grab my shit, and head right out to my car, all smelly and wet like a rat. But I can't be around anyone right now. If Edwards so much as runs his stinking yap in front of me, I'll probably break his face and get suspended from school altogether.

Plugging in my phone, I find the angriest hard rock band I listen to and drive away. It's dark out, but the night is clear, not a snowflake in sight. On a Friday night like this, while every St. Cloud student hits the bars or whatever house party they can find, I drive as far away as I can. Away from Coach's disappointment, from Archie's eagerness to talk, from my teammates' exhaustion. Away from Strawberry.

The second I make it to my secret spot, I'll put in a request to cancel the rest of my tutoring sessions. I already know enough to not flunk my essays. I'll say hockey has me too busy and that they should assign someone else to her so she doesn't lose income. And yeah, she's my neighbor now, but not seeing her on purpose will help. It has to.

It better. I can't keep playing like tonight. Coach was right all along. My professional hockey career is on the line.

My heart slams against my rib cage as if I'm still in the middle of the game, even though I'm pulling down the back road that leads to my favorite spot by the lake. Here, it's pitch black, the only illumination coming from the stars in the sky. Normally, I relish in the dark and the quiet, but tonight I'm just determined to be abnormal, huh?

The music cuts off, and I flinch. I ignore the ringtone for a moment because 99 percent of the people who could be calling me right now have to know I'm in my worst mood.

But I glance at the screen on my dashboard. Turns out I'm getting called by the 1 percent.

Pulling over, I turn on my hazard lights and pick up.

"Hey, Aran."

"Why are you calling me?"

"Geez." I can practically hear her roll her eyes. "Is this how you should be greeting your favorite little sister?"

"Yes, because you never call me." It could be because tonight has been a fiasco already, but hearing Olivia's voice puts me on high alert. "Something's up."

It's not even a question. But she evades it.

"How was tonight's game?"

"Don't even try me, Olivia. I know you don't give a shit about hockey. What is happening?"

"Well…"

"You better start talking right this second."

"Fine." She clears her throat. "So, Brooke is taking me to the hospital."

"*What?*"

"Deep breaths, big guy. It's just preventive care. I, uh, may have accidentally sipped from a peanut butter smoothie."

"You did freaking what *accidentally*? I will murder that kid—"

There's a little gasp, and then my sister's voice sounds annoyed. "Brooklyn didn't shove the straw in my mouth, you know."

"He should've been watching!"

"It's not his job!" Olivia takes a deep breath. "Anyway, come to the hospital, because I'll need an adult. But don't tell Mom and Dad."

"The hell I won't." I grit my teeth, turn off the hazard lights, and make a U-turn in the dark. "I'll take care of the paperwork. But then I'm taking you straight home to our parents, who will ground you until you graduate."

"But—"

"Brooklyn?" I bark.

The boy responds with "yes, sir?"

"You better make sure my sister gets to the hospital alive, because I don't give a shit if your father's rich. I will get you."

"Um, yes, sir."

I tap the screen to end the call. As I drive away from my spot, my insides turn icier and icier.

CHAPTER 18
MADDIE

"Wow, that was intense." Wyatt basically has to shout to be heard over the din from the throng of people vacating the arena.

I'm shaky as I follow. I've already seen enough clips of hockey games to know sometimes they get violent and the audience revels in it. Like tonight, for example. When Aran socked the Falcon player, the whole place almost went down. Meanwhile, I sat ramrod straight.

I wonder if he gets into fights a lot. One blow, and that's all it took for the other guy to go down. But, I mean, Aran's strong enough that he could literally haul me up if I was about to fall, and I weigh two hundred pounds. That other guy stood no chance. And the fact that it took half of the Bolts to hold Aran back gave me chills. I'm not sure whether they were good or bad. It was just the realization that I've been treating him as a pal when he's an untamed, testosterone-filled entity I don't really understand.

And what little I know of him makes me worry. Because what does it take for impassive, nonchalant Aran Rodriguez to snap like that?

I wonder if he's okay. I hope his hand's not hurt. Maybe I'll text him when I get home.

Wyatt keeps talking, oblivious to the fact that I'm fully in my head.

"Not gonna lie. At first, I was confused. Then I was kinda scared? But *then*—" He puts emphasis on the last word. "Then, I was kinda excited."

"Wyatt!" I smack his shoulder, and he chuckles.

"You can't tell me you didn't feel anything."

I can't. Because it's wrong of me to admit that, yes, Aran's intensity does things to me. Those chills might've been what Wyatt is talking about. Maybe my lizard brain wondered what Aran is like when he uses all that sheer power for something else. When those deep eyes of his are looking at you like he wants to eat you up. Just not in an angry way. I dig my face into my fluffy scarf when I feel heat traveling up my neck.

Wyatt checks his phone. "Anyway, thanks for keeping me company while I waited for my date to be done with practice."

"Well, thanks for the emotional support, I guess."

"See you later, Maddie!"

I wave at him, and we part ways in the parking lot. My head still churns as I get in my car and drive home.

Yeah, so I'm as attracted to Aran, like he and I are magnets of opposite polarity. Who isn't? At least half of the stadium probably swooned too. But this changes nothing. He's still completely out of my reach. And more importantly, he's my friend. How awkward would things get for him, for Ryan, and for everyone else, if I start drooling over him?

I'll just have to drool in private. Forcing myself to ignore this hasn't helped at all.

I get home and climb the four floors with relative ease now that I've been living here for a month. The apartment is dark, cold, and silent as a tomb. Ryan and the Strikes had an away game, so she'll come back home pretty late.

"Should've watched that one. But no, you had to choose the home game because it'd be easier that way," I mumble to myself as I ease off my winter clothes.

Easier my behind. I chose the home game because Aran was playing in it. And now look—I'm home alone, my blood is still roaring in my ears, and I want to cry.

Pulling my phone from my bag, I decide to at least attempt to be a good friend. I find Aran's contact near the top of my list on the text messaging app.

ME

Hey, are you okay?

I hesitate a little but hit send. Friends are allowed to be concerned about each other. And their primary function is giving encouragement when needed, right?

But maybe Aran doesn't want any. In fact, I spend about five minutes checking to see if he's at least read it, and nothing.

After pouring a tall mug of tea, I trudge to the couch and fire up my laptop. I'm in the perfect mood to write the first truly dramatic scene that happens in chapter ten of my hockey romance book. I finally started it a couple of weeks ago, and between talking about the sport so much with everyone, the skating non-date, and now this, I've had plenty inspiration to churn out one chapter after the next.

I let my mind transport me away from this weird feeling in my chest, and I immerse myself in what my characters are experiencing. In this chapter, the hero sees the heroine with another guy—who later turns out to be her brother—and gets disproportionately jealous. It makes him realize he has feelings for her, even though he swore to himself he would never love another woman after his ex.

Some readers live for the happy moments, the domestic bliss, the spicy scenes. I live for the angst that makes my chest twist. That makes me wonder how they could possibly get together against the odds.

In romance books, the happy ending is guaranteed. Not so much in life.

As I write some stream of consciousness about what the hero is feeling, keys jangle in the door and I hear it open.

"Hey! How come you're here by your lonesome?" Ryan locks the door back up and adds, "I thought you'd be at O'Malley's with everyone."

I lift my head for the first time in—and here I check the clock—two hours. Wow. My spine cracks as I stretch.

"Um, no. I don't know if they were in much of a mood to celebrate."

Her eyebrows go up while she unzips her coat. "Don't tell me the losers lost?"

I smile a little. Even though they get along well, and there sure are enough couples between the teams, the Strikes and the Bolts still give each other crap like this on a daily basis.

"Well, I wouldn't call the Bolts losers, but yeah, they didn't win tonight."

"Huh. You should've come to watch us instead. We beat the Sirens five-nothing. It was almost embarrassing."

"Next time I'll definitely go watch you."

Ryan grabs a sports drink from the fridge and heads over to the couch, plopping beside me. "I bet they're drowning their sorrows at O'Malley's. Wanna go? Some of my girls are hitting it up too."

"And you?"

She leans her head back on the cushion. "I don't know. I really busted my ass in the game."

"I'd rather stay home," I say in a mumble, running my hands across my laptop's keyboard as if I were cleaning it.

"How come?" She cracks one eye open. "I thought you'd

be eager to do book research about what happens after a team loses."

My lips curve, but with little humor. "I don't think it's the best moment for that. The Bolts seemed pretty down about the loss, and after Aran got into a fight, I just don't know how—"

"Whoa, whoa. What?" She screeches, sitting upright with a lot of energy for someone who is supposedly exhausted. "Aran what?"

"Got into a fight." I add, "At the game, I mean."

"I want all the details."

I relay them as well as I can, which isn't much, because she asked me if Aran got a penalty, and I don't even know how to respond to that. I didn't understand a lot about what happened after that.

"Dude, this is big." Ryan lifts her hips to fish for her phone in her back pocket. As she sends furious text messages, she says, "Aran never gets into fights. I wonder what happened."

"Never?"

"No. He's so stoic he might as well be a robot." A crease appears between her eyebrows. "Huh, he's not responding to me either. Archie says he hasn't seen him since the game ended. Apparently, he walked out of the locker room without even showering."

I scratch my head. So maybe Aran was leaving the place at the same time as I was. But I didn't see him in the parking lot. Doesn't mean we were parked nearby, though.

But if he doesn't respond to his best friends, he obviously won't respond to me either.

"Um, do you think he's okay?"

"Yeah, I'm sure he's fine." Ryan tosses her phone onto the couch and tries to smile, even though her brow is still creased. "Sometimes he disappears like this and then returns as if nothing happened. Archie and I think it's when he gets too overwhelmed by something."

"You… think?"

Sighing, she says, "Yeah. Because the dude just doesn't talk."

"Meaning," I muse aloud, "that something did happen during the game."

"Probably." Her phone pings, and she picks it up. "It's Mark. Oh! He knows what triggered the fight."

We glue our eyes to her phone screen, watching as Mark's three dots appear and disappear as he types.

MARKY BOY

A Falcon douche spewed some racist bullshit at Aran

After that first text, he adds another one with quotation marks around what the opposing player said. I blink really hard and read it again. Ryan draws in a sharp breath. Something inside me snaps.

"What?" I jump off the couch, pointing at the phone in her hand. "I will murder that asshole Falcon!"

"Um, Maddie—"

"How dare he—" I interrupt myself with a gasp. "No wonder Aran punched him in the face. That's the least that little asshole deserves!"

"Wow, I've never heard you cuss before."

I clamp my hands over my mouth, eyes wide.

Ryan's face twitches like she wants to laugh. Instead, she clears her throat. "Unfortunately, players fling about all sorts of distasteful slurs during games. Aran's been called worse before."

"So." I wince a little. "If crap like that is so commonplace, then why did he snap?"

"I don't know. And now I'm a bit worried. Archie sounded like he was too."

Slowly, I lower myself back to my seat and check my phone

again. Aran still hasn't read my text, but I send him another one.

ME

We're worried about you

I hope you're okay

Say *grunt* if you are

But even after more attempts from the three of us during the course of the night, he doesn't respond.

CHAPTER 19
ARAN

Mom sets a staggering plate with the chunkiest cachapa on the planet in front of me. It's like a thick corn pancake stuffed with a slab of queso de mano and several layers of ham and is drizzled with nata—which I know is also called cream, though it doesn't taste the same when I think about it in English.

I've been camping out at home ever since picking Liv up at the hospital after they flushed out her gut. That was probably enough punishment, to be honest. But then I yelled at her some more in the car just in case. And then our parents freaked out when I arrived home, basically carrying my little sister in, and presented them with a brand-new hospital bill.

Needless to say, she got grounded. And because our parents hover very high on the neuroticism scale, they kept her home from school yesterday. And because Luz is also the textbook definition of intense, she threatened to drive over when she found out about the whole thing. To save her the hassle, I volunteered to stay home for a few days so I could keep an obsessive eye on our sister.

That, and so I could avoid my life for a bit.

But the back and forth between school and home is getting old. And maybe because I'm also done with acting like a freaking child.

Liv glares at my plate, as if upset that her portion is so much smaller. Not that she could eat all this. I mean, shit, I'm not even sure *I* can. But Dad blesses our meal, and I dig in.

"Are you sure you're feeling okay?" Mom asks Liv.

My sister hasn't said a word to me in days, but she does respond to Mom. "I've told you a million times already. I'm fine. I don't need all of you to guard me like dogs."

"Of course you do," Dad says with a gruff voice I inherited. "You and Luz are delicate."

I wouldn't exactly use that word for either of them. Stubborn, reckless, and a danger to themselves? Sure.

Olivia rolls her eyes and sags against the chair. I keep stuffing my mouth with food, because anything I say would bring everyone's bad mood up to my own six.

Mom reaches over and pats my hand with her much smaller one. "I'm so glad we don't have to worry about you, Aran." Dad nods in silence to second that.

Right. I'm the solid, dependable one. The one who doesn't break. The one who doesn't need anything, ever. I've always been proud of being my parents' most low-maintenance kid. That's also why I came home for a few days. I knew they'd be too fussy about Olivita to even ask me why I was here. Unlike Archie, who's tried to corner me before or after every practice, or unlike some of the others, who have been blowing up my phone.

Except being home didn't dial my shitty mood back to a manageable level. If anything, I feel worse. I don't want people to fuss over me, but I also don't want them to pretend I'm okay. I just don't freaking know what I want.

After breakfast, I toss my duffel bags into the back of my

car and slam the door shut. I turn around and almost jump, because Mom stands on the curb beside me, quiet as a ghost.

"Can you take your sister to school this morning?"

I wrinkle my nose. But I note the lack of please and thank you, just as Strawberry would've pointed out.

"Why?"

"So you can make up."

I sigh and run my hand over my head. My hair's getting longer and my patience is getting shorter.

"Fine."

She reaches out and instinctively, I lower myself so she can pat my cheek. "Gracias, mijo."

Nodding, I grab her hand and straighten back up. "I'm not coming back tonight after practice."

"Good. Go resume your life." Chuckling, she bundles up into her cardigan. "Then I'll go back to cooking normal amounts of food, no?"

The sensitive little prick in me is still very much awake, and it takes issue. As if Mom had no right to get used to me being out of the house.

"Chao," I say, rounding the car and getting into the driver's seat.

Mom doesn't take my curt farewell as a big deal. She waves at me and heads back into the house. I hear her muffled voice calling out to Olivia.

I rub my eyes and run my hands up and down my face, wishing it was enough to wash away this embarrassing sentimental loop I'm trapped in. I'll drop Liv off at school, and that'll be the end of this episode. And then I have one more to close before I go back to my usual self. Before I can fully focus on hockey and nothing else.

The passenger door opens, and I drop my hands to turn on the vehicle while my little sister buckles up. I do the same and set us in motion.

The radio is off, and neither of us changes its status. We don't fill the silence with our voices either. Mom's hopes will be crushed when she realizes two people can't make up if neither of them thinks they were wrong. Because I sure as hell wasn't wrong in freaking out. And Liv has said a million times that it was an accident. Which I believe, because she's the one who stands to suffer the most from deadly food allergies. But it still doesn't satisfy me.

From the corner of my eye, I see her fold her arms and fix her attention out her window.

"You can't control everything and everyone around you, Aran. Sometimes things you don't want will happen, and there's nothing you can do about it."

The first words to come out of my sister's mouth that are directed at me stab into my core and make it bleed.

I tighten my hands on the steering wheel. "But sometimes I can."

"Yeah, this isn't one of those times. You can't stop me from getting hurt. And you also can't go feral if I do."

I frown. "Is this because I scared Brooklyn off a bit?"

"A bit?" She snorts. "He's nearly as big as you and plays defense, but I've never seen him as scared as he was when you squared up to him."

"I would've killed him if it'd been his fault," I mumble as I pull into the high school parking lot.

"And that's precisely the problem I'm trying to illustrate, you Neanderthal." She unbuckles her seat belt and gives me my own patented deadpan stare. "Would it kill you to be more sensitive sometimes?"

Yes.

Yes, it freaking would. That's what got me into this mess in the first place. If I hadn't acted like a sensitive little shit during the game, I might've kept my head screwed on right after.

"I'm your older brother. My job is to keep you safe, not to paint your toenails."

Huffing, she rolls her eyes. "Te odio."

"Me too. Don't forget your scarf."

She slams the door shut with shocking strength and flips me the bird, but then she winds her scarf around her neck. What a brat. My lips curve.

I switch on the radio and get back on the road. I have a half hour to drive around town and get to the St. Cloud library, where Strawberry will be waiting for me to start the tutoring session. The one that will be our last.

The smile drops away from my face. Instead of taking a right turn where I should, I drive straight down the longest path back to college.

At a red light, I focus away from the road for a second and find my old elementary school on the right. My pulse spikes at the onslaught of memories of that night. My hands on her waist. Her face buried in my chest. Her small hand grabbing mine for dear life. The smile on her face when she finally managed to skate a stretch on her own. Her arms around me after she almost fell.

"Ah, shit."

At the first chance, I do a U-turn and take the short way back to school. I need to nip this in the bud. The faster I get to the library, the faster I can tell her I don't need her to tutor me anymore. Not like a coward, like I almost did over the weekend by simply canceling the service online. But head-on. Just like I've done with every imminent breakup.

Except this is not a breakup. And we'll still see each other. Just less.

Ryan can teach Maddie all about hockey. It'll be easier that way, since they live together. I'll see her occasionally coming in and out of our apartments. Maybe at O'Malley's. Even less at school. English and accounting are a world apart on campus. It'll be fine.

The last three words repeat in my head as I cross town. I park near the library entrance and grab my backpack from the back seat. I tie my black scarf close to the base of my neck and take a step forward.

"It'll be fine, jerk. Why are you hesitating?"

Of course, no one answers my question. Not even my own brain.

I force myself to move ahead. I take a bracing breath as I push the heavy entrance door open. I flash my student ID at the scanner and walk past the information desk. Massive rows of bookcases occupy about a third of the ground floor. I cut through the middle of the long tables by the center and pivot to the stairs, taking two or three steps at a time. My heart gallops, but the little effort isn't enough to justify it.

I'm low-key freaking out. Once I get to the farthest tables on the top floor, I'll have to—

I spot her right away. She sits in the corner by the massive window. Sunlight from the clear morning streams over her, making her hair glow red. Her face is set in a grumpy expression as she furiously taps on her keyboard, and like magic, it makes the corner of my lips tip upward.

Tension leaves my body, even though my heart is still racing against itself.

Then, as if she senses me, Strawberry's eyes tear away from her computer and skewer me. That's how it feels when a smile blooms across her face.

My resolve wanes with every step that brings me closer to her. I was wound up like a coil when I was farther from her. Am I going to transform into an angry beast after I put a firm, permanent distance between us?

And then what's going to happen to my game? Am I really going to concentrate better if I'm always this worked up?

"Aran! I'm so glad you came." Her cheeks are still rosy from her smile, even when she narrows her eyes a bit. "I wasn't sure you would, since you've been ignoring all of us for days."

I pull up the chair across from her and take my sweet time divesting myself of my coat, scarf, and gloves. Finally, I take a seat. For the first time, I meet her eyes.

And I'm toast.

"Are you okay?" Strawberry asks, worry evident on her face. "You don't have to say anything other than yes or no. And if you say no, I won't nag you. I promise."

"Yes."

I am now. I'm okay. I know exactly what I'm going to do.

I open my mouth and speak.

CHAPTER 20
MADDIE

"Can we start the session?" Aran asks.

"Yes, of course. Although, um, you didn't send me your assigned reading in advance this time."

I swallow hard. The truth is I'm about to explode from nerves. I knew he was alive because Archie caught glimpses of him at practice and fed us what little info he had. But I almost feel as if I'm meeting Aran for the first time again today, even though it's only been four days since I last saw him. Or four days since I realized I don't know him that well. But wish I did.

I suck in air through my teeth. Ever since he poofed after the game, I worried about two things. One, that something happened to him. Two, what my reaction would be when I saw him again. Now that fear one hasn't been realized, the second one slams me with the force of a sledgehammer.

There's no dressing this up as anything other than what it is. I have a huge crush on Aran Rodriguez. And I need to swallow it down.

I can just imagine his reaction if he were to find out. He'd be weirded out at best, freaked out at worst. He'd wanted a guy tutor all along precisely to avoid being hit on while trying to study. I can't do that to him.

I pretend I'm busy with my own work, but I'm acutely aware of every move he makes. Aran takes his laptop from his backpack and settles it across from mine. One of his hands is draped around the back of the screen, and I can almost feel the touch against me.

At some point during the skating non-date, when I got too warm from the exercise, I removed my gloves and stuffed them in my pockets. Which meant, occasionally, he grabbed my bare hand with his enormous, calloused one. But his skin was soft in parts, his hand strong and as hot as the sun now bathing us in this corner. I wish I could feel it again in all its glory.

My inbox pings with an email from Aran containing the reading packet. I better focus on that instead.

After skimming it quickly, Aran and I discuss his ideas for the essay, and he gets to work. Just like that. No further comment about anything else whatsoever.

That's… good. Safer. I can try to keep this session professional, as if he were any of my other students.

It takes me several tries and emptying my water bottle until I'm able to focus on my own work. And by work, I don't mean the one for school. I mean the hockey romance book.

I've poured all my frustrations into writing for the past few days, breaking my own daily word count record two days in a row. Now I'm halfway through the book, and the main characters are going to kiss for the first time. As I build up to that climax, it occurs to me that thinking about this while sitting across from Aran may not be such a great idea.

I glance over my screen and find him concentrated on his own work. His eyes run through the screen, probably rereading a passage from the business case. He moistens his lips with his tongue, and I stab my eyes back on my own screen. I delete two whole paragraphs because two seconds of

Aran licking his lips was so much hotter than everything I've written until now.

Maybe I should use that as inspiration. Maybe the female lead should stare at the male lead as he runs his tongue across his lips after a sip of beer.

I run my fingers across my keyboard, trying that angle. Instead of making them fight right away and then kiss, there should be more hints about what's going to happen. Raise the tension that way.

A zipping sound pierces through the quiet. It's Aran, opening his black hoodie to reveal a thin gray shirt underneath. Is it just me, or are his eyes a little hooded as he watches me back?

"Feeling warm?" I blurt out.

He smirks a little but says nothing, then gets back to work.

Well, I'm not feeling warm. I'm boiling now. But unlike him, I can't unzip my flannel dress to cool down.

I attempt going back to the scene, but I hate every single word on the screen and delete them again. I feel so inadequate writing a make-out scene between a hot girl and a hot guy, being the least attractive girl on the planet and sitting across the most gorgeous male specimen in history.

Closing my eyes, I search my memory for inspiration for this scene. Obviously, my own experience won't cut it. But I've read thousands of romance books and watched countless kisses on-screen. Their success wasn't so much because of the mechanics but on how urgent the desire between the characters was. That's what I need to translate into this book.

"What's got you struggling so much?"

I nearly jump out of my skin, even though Aran doesn't shout the question. His voice is a low murmur that wraps around my senses. When I open my eyes, his attention is on me. I wish I knew for how long.

"Um, just a scene in my book."

"The hockey one?" He's leaning back in his chair, appearing bored for all intents and purposes. But the fact that he's talking means he's either procrastinating, or he's in a good mood.

I'm curious as to which one of the options it is, so I play along. "Yup."

"Need help?"

Procrastinating it is, I think as I narrow my eyes. A glint of amusement appears in his eyes, confirming my suspicions.

"Aran, get back to work."

"I can't concentrate with your squirming and sighing and lip biting."

I gasp. "I was not!"

"It's not the hockey part giving you a hard time now, is it? It's the romance part."

"Wait, how did you know?"

"It was all the squirming and sighing and lip biting." A smirk appears on his face. Probably because my face is combusting. I clear my throat. Fold my arms. His smile widens. I focus on his eyes instead.

Mistake. I hope he's not reading my mind, otherwise he'd know I was wondering what kissing him would feel like.

"Well, writing romance is hard." My voice comes out a bit too squeaky.

"Oh?" Aran leans forward. "What aspect of romance?"

"Nothing like that, you perv." Or not yet. I'm not sure I can handle writing something too spicy. I may simply die trying.

"I'm not the one thinking about *romance* in the middle of the library."

In a burst, I kick him under the table, and he doesn't even flinch.

"It's just a kissing scene! Nothing as saucy as you're implying."

"Why would it be so hard, then?"

I put my face in my hands and groan. I seem to have forgotten in the past few days how annoying Aran can get when his amusement is at my expense. Even though he also makes butterflies flit about in my stomach with that smile.

"It's just hard, okay?" I say into my hands. "Not everyone has extensive experience to write about."

"Wait, have you never been kissed?"

"Of course I've been kissed!" I roar, as if this were a matter of pride.

It takes me a moment to remember that this conversation isn't happening in my living room. I lift my head and nearly die as a trio of students down the table give me looks of pity, disbelief at my bold declaration dripping from their faces.

Slowly, I face forward. Aran's eyebrows are up as far as they go. He's biting his lips as if holding back laughter. As if he, too, didn't believe me.

"Really." Not a question. He folds his arms. His pecs tighten, and the thin fabric doesn't hide them. "That's obviously why you aren't struggling with this scene, huh?"

I purse my lips. "I'm just trying to describe the mechanics in a way that—"

"You need help. Admit it."

I suck in air before clamping my mouth shut.

Aran tilts his head and blinks slowly, as if my bravado were a boring little interlude to the truth that, yeah, I have no flipping clue what I'm doing. I bite my lip and press the enter key several times.

"Fine. *Write what you know* isn't going too well this time." I put my hands on my face again. "Ugh, I can't believe you made me admit that aloud. Anyway, it's not like I can walk up to some random guy and ask him to give me the epic kiss I need as inspiration for this scene."

"I'm not a random guy, but you can ask me."

Going by his expression, he asked me about the weather and I hallucinated the past thirty seconds.

I start laughing. At myself. That's definitely what happened. I'm finally losing my mind.

Aran's smirk comes back. "Am I not your reverse tutor?"

Just like that, my laughter snuffs out. I blink hard. Open and close my mouth. "You're kidding."

"Am I laughing?"

No. He looks amused, but I've heard him laugh before. I know he's capable of it. And if he's not doing it right now, it means he's serious.

Flashes of fire and ice travel up my body. I clear my throat once. Twice. Push my hair behind my ears. Finally, I find the words to say, "You said hockey only," and follow them up with a weak laugh.

"Well, who else are you going to ask to make out with you for book research?" Aran shrugs, arms still folded. "That's what this is, anyway. Nothing else."

"Right." I nod rapidly. Then I start shaking my head so he won't take my gesture as agreement. "No. It's one thing to ask you what icing is, it's another to…to … play tonsil hockey."

"But isn't that what your hockey tutor is for?"

"Now I know you're pulling my leg."

Aran grins. "Let me give you the inspiration you need, Maddie."

Oh my word. He has no idea what he's doing to me, does he?

A bead of sweat trickles down my temple, and I wipe it away. Then rub my hands together. The cursor keeps blinking against a completely blank page, the result of my absolute lack of a love life.

And then I remember when Aran Rodriguez first walked into my life, as if the heavens had sent him precisely so I could get off my behind and do all the things I've always been scared to do. I stood up to my bullies. I found new friends. I learned something new. Somehow, I had the courage to do all that when I was next to Aran.

I glance at him again. Maybe that's what this is. A chance to try something I otherwise would never dare to. What Aran is offering is an epic kiss. The kind I've always wanted. When else would I have the chance to kiss the guy I'm into without showing my hand?

"For my book," I say, my heart thumping wildly in my ears and almost making me dizzy.

"No strings attached."

His voice sounds weird, but that could be because I'm having trouble anchoring in reality. I grip the edge of the table hard.

"Right. Okay."

"Let's go." Aran pushes his chair back and starts to get up.

"What?" I whisper, checking our surroundings to see if anyone's paying attention to this mess. "Right now?"

He deadpans, "When else? In five days? Yeah, right now."

And then he does the thing. The one that nearly undid me when he took me skating. He bends his fingers in a *c'mon* gesture.

As if I'm having an out of body experience, I find myself standing up too. I walk around the table until Aran clasps his hand in mine and tugs me along. He faces forward, and I stare at the back of his head, at the muscles in his neck.

What the heck are we doing? Are we really going to find somewhere to make out? Just like that?

The library is almost empty, and most of the people we pass ignore us. Aran weaves through them to the middle hall-way. I feel his hand readjust its grip on mine a little tighter. The sensation rushes through my body like a lick of fire.

When he leads us down the path between two shelves, I say, "If this is a prank, it's not funny."

All I hear is a little snort.

Aran passes the narrow corridor between the windows and the end of the shelves. Pulling at my hand, he settles me against the end of the bookshelf and finally lets me go. A gasp tears out of me as he leans an arm above my head against the shelf, which brings him so close I can feel the heat radiating off his body.

On reflex, my hands push against his chest. "Wait."

He halts.

A weird giggle falls from my mouth. "I'm just wondering how epic a planned kiss like this can be, you know?"

"Oh, I'll show you. Close your eyes, Maddie."

"Maddie? Not Strawberry?"

Aran is so large he blocks out the light and casts me in shadow. Yet the closer he gets, the hotter the air becomes.

"Are you chickening out, *Maddie*?"

Yes.

No. I'll still seize the opportunity.

"Okay, fine. Show me what it's like to be thoroughly kissed, then," I say in blatant challenge, desperately hoping he takes the bait and that this isn't a bluff.

Aran's eyes fall to my lips and then his stretch into a little smile. "Brace yourself."

I take in air as if I were diving into the ocean. Then his free hand holds my neck, tilting my head back. But it's not an anchor. Instead, it makes me fall so hard and so fast, I have to close my eyes against the vertigo.

You know that *ah-ha* moment when you solve a puzzle? That's how it feels the second Aran's lips press against mine. Like I finally found the last piece I was looking for—and it fits seamlessly.

Aran's lips are oh so soft as they caress my bottom one with languid care, as if he has all the time in the world for that alone. Strength starts leaving my body at the soft pull of his lips, and I sag against the shelf. His fingers twine with my hair deliciously, another caress.

My hands travel up his chest, tracing the hard planes until I find his neck. Then I let one hand continue to the velvet soft hair at his nape.

A rumbling sound comes from his chest. Before I know it, his tongue runs across my lips and his other hand comes around my body, bringing me flush against him. Shocked at the sudden closeness, I open my mouth to gasp, and that's all he needs to deepen the kiss.

The touch of his tongue against mine tears a sound out of me that makes him smile against my mouth. But then his tongue caresses mine in a hot, wet stroke, and I die—only to come to life when he does it again. It feels like more than just one kiss. Like a promise of something more.

I don't know what comes over me, but I grab his head in both hands and try to push him closer. The wet, sucking sounds of our mouths should embarrass me, tear me back to reality.

But they don't.

Not when one of his hands is tangled in my hair, holding my head so he can have full access to my mouth. Not when his other hand presses against my lower back until there isn't a molecule of air between us.

I gasp for air when, with a sucking sound, he lets go all of a sudden. But Aran's not done. Softly, he pulls at my hair until I arch back as far as I can. I blink against the stars dancing on the ceiling. And then his mouth is on my neck.

"Was that inspiring enough?" he mumbles against the skin under my ear before placing a hot, open-mouthed kiss and gently suckling at the skin. I feel the pull all the way to my toes.

Something that sounds like the love child between a groan and a mewl comes out of my chest. My skin is on fire and my heart is pounding full throttle, and he must obviously realize all this.

Oh, this guy knows how to drive a girl wild with his mouth alone. And he hasn't even used the rest of his body.

As if reading my mind, Aran chuckles. His hold at the back of my head grows a little gentler, and he leans me back against the shelf.

He's not completely breathless like I am, but his nostrils flare with his rapid breathing, and I feel the thrum of his pulse against my hand on his chest. Aran's dark eyes are at half mast, still fixed on my lips. He licks his slowly, as if savoring the taste of mine on them.

I gasp at how strongly I felt that. Everywhere.

Aran's eyes shift back up to mine. We're suspended in silence for a long moment. Me, because my brain packed up its bags and left the building. Him, I don't know why. But then he reaches for my face. His thumb wipes at the moisture under my lower lip, and I shudder.

"And that," he says, his voice raspy and thick, "is how you get thoroughly, epically kissed, Madeline Berkley. Go write that."

"Oh." I collapse against the bookshelf.

Aran pulls away. With one last look that could melt someone's clothes off, he turns away and leaves me a mess.

CHAPTER 21
ARAN

'm back, baby.

That was all I needed. A safe outlet for my pent-up energy. I can't believe it presented itself in such a casual way. Bless hockey romance book research, am I right? One little kiss, and I'm cured of the curious case of the cranky hormonal haze I've been plagued by since the whole Kelsey mess in January.

Today is shootout practice, and I'm killing it. Twenty-three saves to two goals. I catch an easy shot from one of the JV freshmen and drop the puck back onto the ice.

"You watched the puck," I say, because Coach Green demanded I give advice during the drills. "Next."

The following guy positions himself at center ice and goes from zero to one hundred in the blink of an eye, like this is a breakaway. I crouch a little lower. His stick handling skills are pretty good. They'd fool Edwards.

Not me. I pluck the puck right from the air.

"Dayum, son!"

"Bro, did you see that?"

"Unreal."

Edwards's voice is louder from the opposite net, where he waits for his next attacker. "Why didn't he play like this last week?"

I toss the puck away, and to the slack-jawed JV forward, I say, "You would've scored against our backup goalie."

"Damn you, Rodriguez," comes from the opposite net.

I smile and wipe it off right away, not that anyone had a chance at seeing it through my gigantic mask.

"Next."

Jamal does score on me, which earns him a lot of *oohs* and *ahhs*. Two more JV players try. One of them shoots so wide even he snarls in frustration. The other one has a good slapshot on him, but my knee's faster and sends the puck bouncing away.

The whistle pierces my eardrum, followed by clapping. "All right, everyone. That's good enough for today. Keep this energy up for the next stretch of games."

"Don't forget it's the last one before regionals," Assistant Coach Thomas adds.

"Yes, sir!" the two teams chorus back, even though Varsity is the one that can almost taste the Frozen Four. That is, if I can keep playing like today and don't send everything to the crapper again.

"Now, hit the showers and get some rest. Don't let me catch you in the news tomorrow."

"Yes, sir!"

I hang back as everyone files off the ice. The coaches discuss something among themselves, and freeze up as I skate over. Can't be faulted for thinking it was about me.

I pull my mask off, and Coach Green says, "Rodriguez, good catches today, son."

"Thank you, sir."

Silence.

The two of them exchange a telepathic message. Assistant

Coach Thomas nods and says, "I'm gonna go make some notes about today. See you at the office, Glen."

"Catch you later, Jerry." Coach Green folds his arms and chews on his gum with more purpose. "You appear to want to talk. Is this a miracle?"

Not really. But I'm trying to do the right thing, even though it makes me use words, and that alone grates on my nerves.

Sighing, I say, "I've been thinking."

"Uh-oh."

"And I don't think I'm cut out to be the captain."

The *C* stitched on my jersey over my heart represents a vow I've struggled to keep. A vow I never asked to make. The team voted me captain during boot camp last summer after all the seniors were gone. I said it was a mistake then, and I'm saying it again now.

Coach Green takes off his cap and scratches his head. "Why?"

"Someone like Bracken can give the guys all the encouragement they need easily."

"Son." He snorts. "You do that without even opening your mouth. You look at one guy, then at the goal, and he goes and scores. You give another the same look you have on your face right now, and he shuts up."

"Not Edwards, though," I mumble.

"No, but that's because he's jealous of you. Where is this coming from? I thought you had taken to the role well enough."

I wipe my face with the sleeve of my jersey and grunt. "You saw me last week. I crumbled and brought the whole team down with me. But maybe if I'm not captain—"

"And you crumble again, the team will follow. Again. You're a natural leader that way, Rodriguez."

I frown.

Coach isn't cowed and plows through. "Listen, I seriously

hope you pull your shit together and play like an all-star during every game. But you're still just a kid. You need to learn to deal with failure. Both what that means for you as an individual player and how it affects your team. Because guess what?"

He waits so long to continue that I grumble, "What?"

"It will happen again," he says. "You won't have perfect games every time. Something will happen in your life or during the game itself that will get in your head. And if you want to be in the pros, you have to learn to suck it up, buttercup."

"And you're okay with letting me learn that while being the worst captain this team has ever had?" I ask, grasping at straws.

"I'll deny this if you tell anyone I said this, but you're one of the best captains the Thunder Bolts has ever had."

I frown. "Are you sure?"

"You can think whatever the hell you want." He jerks a thumb toward the walkway. "Are we gonna stand here talking about our feelings forever, or are you gonna hit the showers and let me wrap up for the day?"

"Fine, but don't blow my eardrums off if I screw up again."

"Oh, I will. That's why they pay me the big bucks."

I shake my head and almost smile. I can only admit to myself that I'm relieved he didn't agree to stripping me of the C, even though it's what I'd have done in his place. Being the captain helps me pad up my résumé for the league, especially since I'll have to start as a free agent.

"Dude, you were on fire today," Archie chirps as I drop onto the bench beside him. "Did you get laid or something while you were away?"

I drop my mitts onto the floor and run my hand over my head. The longer hair bristles against the palm of my hand. I wonder if Strawberry liked it.

And just like that, my temperature goes higher than when I

was on the receiving end of an hour-long shootout practice. I grunt as I grab the back of my jersey and pull.

"I'll be honest," he keeps saying as if we're having an actual conversation. "I did wonder if what had your panties in a wad was lack of action off the ice."

"Me too," Mark says from a few stalls down. "I haven't seen you with a new girl since Kelsey."

Shit, they're getting too close to the truth.

"Burgers at O'Malley's tonight?" I ask.

Mark pumps a fist. "Aw, yeah."

Naive fool.

But Archie narrows his eyes. Fortunately, since he came to the locker before me, he's done undressing and heads over to the showers. I breathe a little easier when he's gone.

No, I didn't get laid.

After making out with Strawberry, I had to go take a walk around the building and stop at the restroom to wash my face before facing her again. In that time, our study session officially came to an end, and when I returned to the table, she had already begun to pack up.

The glassy eyes and flushed face were gone. Instead, she was back to normal as she said, "So, uh, since we didn't work for more than half of the session, you should put in the system as if the session was canceled, and I'll do the same."

"But then you won't get paid," I said with a frown.

She wrinkled her nose. "Oh my word, Aran. I'm not going to get paid for making out with you. We'll just have to actually work tomorrow, okay?"

She said it so blatantly, without any hint of her previous awkwardness, it was as if she was ready to dismiss the whole thing.

And so was I. Since the moment I let her go, I started racking my brain for what to say to reset things. We both got what we wanted. She got her book inspo. I got my itch kind of scratched. There were no commitments. It was just a reverse-tutoring session.

"See you tomorrow," she said, hanging her full bag on her shoulder.

Grunting, I sat down to continue working. And I did. I finished the whole damn essay while she was gone. And I've stayed buzzing with energy all day.

*

I hit O'Malley's with the guys, and the second I walk in, I pick her out among the crowd.

Strawberry's sitting at a table surrounded by Strikes. She tips her head back to laugh with all her might, revealing a hell of a lot of throat. Because her clothes show a hell of a lot of cleavage. My tongue feels like a useless lump in my mouth as I stare.

I should've licked her throat. I should've committed the taste of her skin to my mind forever. I should've gone south instead of to her ear.

I wonder if I left a hickey on her neck. Her long hair cascades around it. There's no way to find out unless I get real close and personal.

"Rodriguez, move," one of the guys says behind me. "You're blocking the door."

I move away. I'm even able to walk behind the guys as we make our way through the packed place. But I'm not able to tear my eyes away from her. I now realize, like a damn fool, that one little kiss was nowhere near enough. And that the reason I was able to do my coursework, hyper focus in class, and kill it at practice, is because I flared back to life after kissing her.

"Ah, shit," I mutter.

"Don't worry. We got your back," Archie says to me, and I do a double take. Did he read my mind?

"What are you talking about?"

He jerks his head toward the left, away from the table full of Strikes and one Strawberry. I turn in the general direction he pointed and—

"Ah, shit," I repeat to myself. There's Kelsey. Sitting with Strawberry's former roommates. Because of freaking course.

"It's a shame," Archie whines. "Why are the hot ones always problematic?"

That's not true. Strawberry's not problematic.

I glance over my shoulder, and she's watching me. Not because she spotted me among the crowd like I did, but because Ryan is waving her arms frantically at us. I pat Archie's chest and point at the Strikes' table. And like the best assistant captain, he rallies the troops without me making any effort.

"Well, well, well. If it isn't the losers and their loser captain," Ryan says in greeting, squeezing against Strawberry to make room for the four of us.

Archie, being at the front of the group, takes the empty spot beside Strawberry. If I kill him here, people will start talking. Instead, I take the spot right across from her. The smile still lingers on her face, but it dims a little upon spotting me.

Is that good or bad?

Beside me, Jamal says, "Obviously that's the alcohol talking. Or did you forget we won our little friendly last summer?"

"Only by one goal," Christine says with a roll of her eyes.

"Please, we couldn't possibly go full force against a bunch of girls." Archie puts his hand on his chest, and his arm brushes against Strawberry's.

I hide my tight fists under the table.

That's when I notice the girls have gone through at least two rounds of beer. An empty glass sits directly in front of

Strawberry, blurring the view to her cleavage. Both a good and a bad thing.

"What's with all the empty glasses?" I ask, having had enough of the banter.

One of the younger Strikes sighs. I don't know her name, but Ryan points at her precisely and says, "Amber here got dumped, so we decided to celebrate our independence from men until you àll decided to crash our party."

"Hmm." I hum too low for any of them to hear over the noise.

"Or," Archie says with a shrug, "you could also celebrate your freedom to find a better guy. Am I right, Maddie?" He puts his arm around her shoulders and grins down at her, and she beams that sweet little smile of hers up at him.

"You guys want anything?" a server, appearing out of nowhere, asks beside me.

I thank the heavens for the interruption because I was just about to show my ass.

As everyone voices their orders one by one, Archie's attention shifts away from Strawberry, and he drops his arm. Which officially means he lives to see another day.

Slowly, I start to cool down until I'm back to my iceberg self. Through the table's chatter, I make a silent plan to replace the plan I made after the Kelsey debacle. There's no way I'm canceling our tutoring sessions now. Instead, I'm going to rewrite Step One to something like swearing off girls except for Strawberry's reverse tutoring—and not just on hockey.

As long as Coach never finds out about it, and I keep playing like today, it should work like a charm.

CHAPTER 22
MADDIE

shouldn't have worn this shirt. The only other time I did was for a night out with Rebs and the others. The dress code had been to wear something tight and sexy, which, in retrospect, was probably hazing, because I spent the whole night too worried about my boobs spilling out to have any fun. And that's exactly the concern I have right now.

What possessed me to wear it again?

The reason sits across the table. Him. And the fact that he awakened my hormones with a vengeance.

Not that Aran's looked at me very much since they arrived. Which is good, honestly. This morning was a glitch in the matrix. Something that won't happen again, and that did, in the first place, because he was teasing me. And because I wanted him to tease me.

Why isn't he doing that now?

Right. We're just hanging out with friends. This isn't a book research situation.

"—do you say?"

"Huh?" I turn to the source of the question. Archie's

expression is calm, but there's laughter in his eyes, and I don't know what put it there.

"Darts," he says as explanation.

"The Strikes here say they can wipe the floor with us at darts," Jamal elaborates from across the table.

"We can and we will." Ryan pushes her sleeves up. "And it's perfect. We're four against four. Let's go."

I laugh a little. "Um, I'm not a Strike, though."

"You are now, babe. We adopted you the second we met you." My roommate puts her arm around me, and I melt.

"Aww, guys. I'm so touched."

"Welcome to the Bolts and Strikes rivalry." She laughs and shoos the guys with her hand. "Go commandeer the boards while we strategize."

Mark scrunches up his face. "Why does a darts game need strategizing? All you need to do is shoot and hit the bullseye."

"And this is why you lose games. Because you all refuse to think," Christine volleys back, sticking out her tongue.

For the first time all night, Aran's eyes meet mine across the table, only to roll as if in annoyance. But there's a tiny smile playing on his lips, and when I look at them, my skin breaks into goose bumps.

"Strikes, let's huddle," Ryan commands, and I'm thankful for the distraction.

I swivel in my high-top chair to face Amber, Christine, and the ringleader.

Amber tucks her short bob behind her ears and gives a feral grin. "What's the plan, Captain? And does it involve making grown men cry? Because I'm in the mood for that."

"Oh, yes." Ryan rubs her hands together. "Okay, Christine, you pair up with the nice side of the double-A battery."

Christine nods with the kind of seriousness I'd expect if this were a hockey game, but I ask, "The what?"

They all glance at me. Ryan's face splits into a grin. "Right,

I forget you're new. Archie and Aran are the double-A battery. Rumor has it they were the last two standing during bootcamp freshman year."

"Rumor also has it that they can keep going and going at other things, if you catch my drift." Amber laughs, because the second I catch her drift, my whole body turns into a blinking red light.

"Shush, don't corrupt our sweet Maddie," Christine says, putting her hands on my ears.

"Anyway. Amber," Ryan says, pointing at the other girl. "Since you're out for blood tonight, pair up with the mean side of the double-A battery and crush him."

"Yes, ma'am!" Amber shouts and smashes a fist against her palm.

Ryan motions between us. "As for you and me, we get the MJ combo. Which one do you want?"

"Oh, they'll be easy to beat." Christine smirks. "I've seen them play darts before, and let's just say that half of the holes in the wall are theirs."

I turn to glance over my shoulder. It doesn't even shock me anymore that the only one who appears crystal clear in my vision is Aran. He's leaning against the pool table, arms crossed, listening as Jamal says something. Beyond the game area, Lori, Tiff, Rebs, plus a couple of other girls, eye him like hawks.

Well, not Lori. She's glaring at me.

Yikes.

"Um, Jamal," I say, only because it's the first name that comes to me.

"Perfect. I'll take Mark and wipe the floor with him quickly." Ryan puts her arms around me and Amber, and one by one, the rest of us do the same. "Christine, what do you think are your odds?"

"About fifty-fifty. I'm good, but Archie's also good." She

clears her throat dramatically. "I may also flirt a little. See if that distracts him. Is that okay, Maddie?"

"Whoa, why are you asking me?"

She smiles with uncertainty. "Well, it's just that I saw the two of you sitting pretty close, and I thought… Ryan, maybe Maddie and I should swap."

"No, no, no." I shake my head. "Archie and I aren't like that."

"Are you sure?"

"Yeah, go at him."

Ryan gives me one of those looks where she's trying to read my mind, but finally shifts her attention away. "Amber, Aran is a wildcard. I've never seen him play darts, but expect trouble."

Amber snorts. "Sounds about right. He's trouble personified."

Don't I know it.

I sigh, and it gets the captain's attention. She turns to me. "How are your skills, Maddie?"

"Well, I'm a bit tipsy, so I could either hit the bullseye or stab someone in the eye."

"We'll gamble," Ryan says with a fierce nod, and it makes me giggle. She puts her hand in the middle, and the other girls stack theirs on top. By turns, they stare at me, and it takes me a second to catch on. I place my hand on top of Amber's, and Ryan shouts, "Who are we?"

"Thunder Strikes!" they shout in unison. I shrink a little, because the whole bar is now watching.

Nonplussed, Ryan continues, "And what do we do?"

"We strike first! We strike fast! We strike hard!"

My hand flies up with the power of theirs. I'm equal parts pumped and embarrassed when the whole bar erupts in cheering. This must not be the first time, because soon enough, the other patrons turn back to their own conversations.

"Wow, you guys are so cool," I say, mouth agape as I

observe them. Ryan with her pixie haircut and leather jacket. Christine with her blond waves and a Barbie doll face that hides her aggressive nature. Amber with her glowing brown skin and a smile that could stop traffic. All elite athletes, the queens of this campus. And they're so freaking lovely too.

"Weeee," Ryan drags out the word and laces her arm in mine. "*We* are so cool, Maddie."

I shake my head. I know what she's trying to do, and I love her for it. But it's not like all of a sudden, I've become a varsity athlete just because I'm hanging out with them. I'm still boring little Maddie, who was stress-knitting at home when Ryan barged in, demanding I join them for a man-hangover session.

But here I am, in line for throwing darts against Jamal Amadi, a guy I'd never have seen this close if it hadn't been for how my life has so drastically changed in under two months.

"So, Maddie. You know I like you a lot, right?" Jamal grins down at me, and if it weren't because of the Latino TDH, my stomach would flutter.

"You do?" I press my lips into a small smile.

"Yes, but I just want you to know that I'm also very competitive."

This time I laugh. "I kinda figured."

"So no hard feelings when I win?" He extends his hand, and I shake it.

"Nope. No hard feelings at all," I chirp.

"Is that the best you can do, Webber?"

Ryan's taunting reaches my ears, and I lean to the side to catch the action. Poor Mark wears a grumpy expression as he allows Ryan her shot. His must be the first dart on the board, and it's almost at the edge.

"Having fun?"

Dang it, body. Stop reacting so obviously.

Aran's voice wraps around it like warm velvet. Except I'm wearing fewer layers and showing more skin than usual, and I seriously don't want this entire bar to know what he does to me. I rub the goose bumps off my arms quickly and glance up.

He's right next to me, hands in his jeans pockets. Those unreadable dark eyes of his sweep down my face, and lower still. He's not even apologetic as he checks me out down to my white Doc Martens. And hey, maybe feeling like a burrito wrap in my push-up bra, a super tight emerald top with a round, plunging neckline, and tight high-rise jeans was worth it.

Blinking slowly, he lifts his eyes up, and they linger a little on my chest. When they finally reach my face, the corner of his lips rises, and I know exactly why.

My chest, neck, and face must be as red as a ripe strawberry.

Meanwhile, Aran's amusement is obvious. And that's when I realize he did this to see if he could affect me. And like a fool, I showed him he most definitely could.

Taking a deep breath, I say, "Oh, I am. Ready to lose?"

"Hmm, careful which bear you poke, Strawberry."

"Take that, sucker!" Ryan shouts, tearing my attention away from the bear I wish I could cuddle with.

I shake my head to refocus my beer-and-hormone-addled brain. Ryan goes around high-fiving us after her victory against Mark Webber. Then it's Jamal's and my turn, but on the other board, Christine and Archie are still locked in a tie.

"Ladies first," Jamal says, which is a mistake.

"Thank you." I bat my eyelashes at him and accept the green darts from his hand, since they match my clothes.

Aran shouldn't have sobered me up with his scorching look, either. Because I stand behind the line on the floor, push my hair behind my shoulders, and shoot.

And it's a bullseye.

Silence reigns among the group.

I turn to Jamal, still smiling sweetly. "And now it's your turn."

"Dayum!"

"Girl! You weren't kidding, huh?" Amber says.

My shoulders shake with a chuckle. "No, I wasn't."

Jamal's okay. Certainly better than Mark. But I make such quick work of him that Aran and Amber step up to this board instead. On his way, Aran narrows his eyes at me, and I shrug.

"Are you a national darts champion, or something? Because that was amazing," Mark says as I join them to watch who will end up winning between Christine and Archie.

"No, I was simply a very bored kid in her room," I say without adding that I was also very lonely growing up as an outcast of society. That's why I got into reading, writing, knitting—just anything I could do to pass the time without feeling like it was all a waste.

Funny how some of those skills now got me new friends, huh?

Finally, Archie pumps a fist in the air. "Yes, baby! That's what I'm talking about!"

The Strikes groan, and the Bolts celebrate. But not for long, because Ryan steps up. "Now you're against me, Archibald."

"Bring it on, Ryan not Meg."

I snort a laugh.

A particularly strong thwack diverts my attention. It must've come from Aran, since he's at the line.

"Crap," Amber says, frowning at the board. "Looks like Maddie wasn't the only dark horse."

They only have one dart left each. Seeing as how Amber throws the green ones, I check the board to see where the red ones are and… they're so close to the bullseye there's no way Amber's revenge on men will succeed tonight.

Sure enough, Aran wins with the next throw, and the Bolts celebrate again.

"Where was all your big talk, Archie boy?" Ryan teases after the redhead Bolt throws a really bad shot.

Poor Archie's face now matches his hair color. But he doesn't let it get to him, unfortunately. After one more throw each, the clear winner is the Bolt.

As he celebrates by bumping his chest against Jamal's, Ryan heads over and puts her hands on my shoulders. "All our hopes and dreams now rest on you, Berkley."

On my right, Christine says, "You got this, Maddie."

"That's right." On my left, Amber nods. "You're amazing. Go get them, tigress."

"Gee, no pressure, huh?"

"No, there's pressure. You have to defeat the double-A battery for us." Ryan shakes me a little. "Can you do this?"

"Uh, I don't know, but I'll try?"

"With a bit more certainty next time, girl. It's called manifesting."

I burst into laughter. "Yeah, okay. I'll deplete the battery."

"That's what I'm talking about!"

"Aw, yeah!"

"Go drain them!"

They steer me toward the throw line, one of them massaging my shoulders as another gives me advice against my next opponent, who is none other than my rival dark horse.

I lick my lips. Aran's not a trash talker, but he can throw me off my game with just a glance.

And yet, I really want to win. I want to get this one not just for the Strikes, but for me. Because it's the first time I've played darts with anyone, and it's a heck of a lot more fun than playing alone in my bedroom.

Aran offers me the green darts. He must've seen me use those before. When I collect them from his open hand, my fingers brush his palm, and it twitches.

Well, maybe I affect him a bit too.

Knowing we're on even ground helps me fire a near bullseye for my first shot. The others cheer and shout as if we're in the middle of a hockey game. It's a wonder we don't get kicked out of the place.

Aran shifts a little away from me to measure his throw, giving me his profile. He's so beautiful it hurts, with his deep-set eyes, his straight nose that curves just a little at the bridge, the full, wide lips I know taste delicious, the square jaw I can now map with my hands. I wish he wouldn't wear hoodies all the time so I could get my fill of him more easily.

He throws, and tearing my eyes away from him to check the board feels like nails on a chalkboard. But his dart is a smidge farther from the center than mine.

Just one good look at him, and I'm drunk again. My feet stumble, and someone catches me. Big, warm hands grip my hips, and I don't need to wonder who it is.

Aran's breath fans against my neck, and he pushes my hair away from my ear to whisper, "I got you, little Strawberry."

He does. Like putty in his hands.

"Tripping!" Ryan screams.

Then Amber adds, "Interference! Stop trying to throw our best player off her game."

Releasing me, Aran snorts. "What, did you want me to let her crash to the floor?"

"Maddie is a grown woman who can catch herself." Christine lifts her chin. "Right?"

"Right," I say, not feeling it at all. Because I really did trip all on my own because of a pretty boy. I need to focus.

I stand behind the line and take a deep breath. This throw —no, this game—means more now. It's proof to myself that I can keep my cool around Aran. That I won't be showing the whole planet that anything he does is enough to make me swoon. Like Christine said, I'm a grown woman, and I don't need to let any man get in my way.

Thwack!

Grinning, I turn around. "Oh, you're in trouble, boy."

"Ooh!"

"Burn!"

Aran tucks his tongue against his cheek, but his eyes shine with amusement. No one would guess he's close to losing.

He steps up and doesn't think about it too hard. But his second dart is off again, almost next to his third. I throw my last one, and it's not dead center, but almost.

By this point, everyone's gathered around us. Aran's boys give him a pep talk, while Ryan heckles the crap out of him. I've gone and lost it, because I can't stop cackling like a hyena. Finally, he takes his last shot and…

"Booyah!" I throw my hands in the air.

Someone slams into me from the side, then another, until I'm in a pileup of Strikes chanting their team name. Through the commotion, I get a glimpse of Aran's grin, and I feel it like a brand. I can't get it out of my head, even after I defeat Archie to a round of applause from the whole bar.

I've never been the center of attention, but that is nothing against the high I got from being the cause of Aran's joy.

CHAPTER 23
ARAN

My phone starts ringing as I park at the library the next afternoon. I turn off the car and check the name on the dashboard. Frowning, I pick up. "What?"

"So, uh. I may have screwed up." Archie clears his throat, and since I keep quiet, he continues. "I ran into Kelsey after class and, well, I didn't want to be impolite. So we talked a bit, and your name came up."

I rub my eyes. "You should've been impolite. Often, it's better."

"But other times, it gets you slapped in the face." Very annoying that he has a point. Archie adds, "Anyway, long story short. I may have mentioned you were going to the library."

"I know where you live, Archibald Bracken," I say in a growl.

"Listen, I'm not the one who dated a menace to society."

I hate even more that he has another point, and that these are the consequences to my actions.

"Fine, I guess I won't go to the library."

"What if she shows up at practice tonight?"

I suck in air sharply. That would actually be worse. If she shows up at the gym and makes another scene, Coach is going to have my head on a pike. And it's not like I can bodily keep her away.

Shit, it's time to fess up. I need help.

"Archie," I say, somewhat reluctantly. "Last time, Kelsey got me in serious trouble with Coach."

"I'm not surprised. Is that related to why you've been acting all weird?"

"Yeah," I admit, sighing in exasperation. "Coach wants me off dating for the rest of the season. If Kelsey shows up and makes another mess, he's going to bench my ass for at least two games."

"Whoa." Archie repeats the word several times. "Bro, that's way too harsh."

"You know Coach Green, though."

"Okay, wow. So your moodiness has been a serious case of no action under threat of suspension. You could've just told me instead of acting all precious."

"Archie." There's a clear warning in my voice that he ignores, because he starts chuckling.

"I get it, don't worry. I'll make some anti-Kelsey plan with Mark and Jamal to cover your six."

"If you tell them—"

"You will murder me, I know. Trust me."

I snort. "How can I when you just told Kelsey where I was going?"

"I'll take that L and compensate you by not making too much fun of the fact that you can't get laid for at least two more months."

"Damn you. This is why I didn't want to say anything."

"'Kay, thanks, *bye*." He drags the last word out like a kid and hangs up.

I don't know why I put up with him when I want to throttle

him half the time. But right now I have a more pressing concern. I scroll through my contacts until I find my tutor and press call. I know she's already in the building because I can see her yellow Beetle a couple of rows ahead.

She picks up after too many rings. "Hey, Aran."

Her voice alone has the power to dial back my bad mood scale at least one point.

"Hi. I can't go to the library."

"Oh, okay." Is that disappointment in her voice? "We can reschedule—"

"No," I cut in, turning my car back on. "I can't go to the library, but we can go somewhere else."

After a short stretch of silence, she hums. "That's not a bad idea. The weather's too nice to be cooped up in the same place I'm in every day."

I don't add anything to that because I'm not in the library every day, but that seems to be her favorite spot to write her hockey romance. Actually, this may be the perfect excuse to ask if she needs any more tutoring. And I have the perfect place in mind for it.

Well, well. Maybe Archie didn't screw up after all.

"I'll wait for you in my car."

"Okay!" With that, she hangs up, and I wait.

The seconds feel like days until she comes out of the library. Her coat is draped over her arm, and her hair is in a loose braid over her shoulder. I hope I get the chance to undo it. I want to run my fingers through her hair, tangle it around my fists again, find the spot between her neck and shoulder and lick it.

"Buenas tardes," she says, all sunny, as she climbs to the passenger seat and shuts the door. "Did I say it okay?"

"Your *r*'s need work," I tease to distract her from the fact that I'm breathing funny.

She buckles up. "Yeah, not sure I'm ever going to get that one right."

I set the car in motion as her scent invades the cab, not helping my situation at all. She loves her strawberry shampoo and soap, but that's not all. There's something else underneath that is sweeter, warmer. That's the stuff that's making my blood thrum.

"So, are you sick and tired of the library, or…?"

With my attention on traffic, I say, "Definitely not *or*. The library's my favorite place now."

She chokes, and I hide a smile with my left hand. I knew she was thinking about yesterday when our session focused on studying each other's mouth. No matter how hard she pretends like it was no big deal, I know it affected her. It was in the way she moaned in my ear, how her eyes hooded, in the unmistakable flush in her skin.

I want to see all that again.

Clearing my throat, I pick up on her question again. "No, according to Archibald, my quasi ex was waiting for me in there."

"I take it that it didn't end well?"

"No. She marched into the locker room while we were changing and slapped me in front of everyone. Got me in trouble with Coach."

We're at a red light, so I turn. Strawberry's jaw hangs and her eyes are wide. "Whoa. Um, that's intense."

I run my hand over my freshly cut hair. "Yeah. It was like a damn telenovela."

"I can see why you'd want to avoid another episode," she says in a mumble, her eyes on the road. The light changes, and I can't pay attention to her anymore. "Erm, so, where are we going?"

I know she's uncomfortable now, but I'm not in the business of lying, even if it would make me sound like a better person than I am. All my friends know I'm a little shit, so why should it be different with Strawberry? We're just friends, after all.

Friends who shared such an amazing kiss that I can't stop thinking about it.

"We're going on a little adventure" is all I can manage to say.

Several times through the course of the drive, she tries to get it out of me. At first, she guesses a local café, then the public library. Her next guess is either of our apartments, but when I drive by them, she seems fresh out of options.

It's when I hit the country roads that she asks, "You're not taking me somewhere rural to kill me and hide my body, are you?"

"Do I look like someone who'd go through all that effort?"

"Fair. You're too straightforward for a murderer."

I flash her a deadpan expression. "Have you been reading thriller books or something?"

Strawberry gasps. "How did you know? Did you install a secret camera in my room?"

"Please." I snort. "First of all, that would be a crime and would ruin my chances at playing pro."

"Right, that's how I know for sure you're not going to kill me now."

"Second," I say, shaking my head, "if I did install a spy camera in your room, the last thing I'd care about would be what book you're reading."

I pull onto the back road to the lake just as she asks, "And what is that supposed to mean?"

"Do you sleep with clothes on or not?"

"Aran!"

"I'm just explaining what I'd care about."

She laughs and looks away. "You're absolutely terrible."

The car bounces on the rough road, but it's a short stretch, and soon, we're approaching a clearing. I'm not the only person in the world who knows about this spot, but it's not as frequented as other areas of the lake that are more manicured. This one's a bit wild, just sand and rocks, with a strip of shore that looks like a beach but has a quite steep incline past a certain point. There's nothing interesting about it other than it's peaceful and quiet.

She leans forward, hands on the dashboard as she drinks it up. I love the wonder that takes over her expression, as if this is the last thing she imagined she'd see today.

"What is this place?"

"My secret hideaway." I maneuver the car so it's parked with the back close to the lake lapping at the shore.

Slowly, she tilts her head toward me. "Is this where you disappeared to last week?"

"I was going to." I turn off the car and undo my seat belt. "Until my sister called on her way to the hospital." I get out of the car and stretch like I've been on the road for hours.

"What happened?" she asks with alarm.

"She's fine. Just scared us all with her peanut allergy."

I head to the back of the SUV and open the back door. She meets me there and says, "I'm glad she's fine. And I didn't say it before, but I'm glad you're fine too."

I freeze for a moment. She really has no idea that the reason I'm fine one second and not the next is her, huh? I expel air out of my lungs.

Pulling at the floor, I uncover a compartment that normally would house a spare tire, but now that you only need a patch kit to survive, I'm using it to store a blanket and some other things for when I come out here. Since we only have a few hours until I have to head back for practice, I leave the lamp in there. And with an abnormally warm February day like this, I don't need to get a fire going.

"How did you discover this place?" Strawberry leans

against the car, drinking in the smooth surface of the lake that is only disturbed by a soft breeze. It plays with the wisps of hair that escape her braid. A strand caresses her cheek just like my hand itches to do.

She pulls the hair behind her ear, and it snaps me back awake.

My voice comes out as rough as the gravel under our shoes. "Dad and I come fish by the lake in the summer. That's how I found it."

She cocks an eyebrow at me. "Do you bring girls often?"

"No," I admit. She's the first one I've brought here.

I make quick work of lowering the back seats and spreading the thick blanket across the cargo area. When she sees me taking out my laptop and sliding it over the blanket, she finally gets it.

"Oh. Um. Okay, so that's the plan."

I smirk. "What else did you think we came here for?"

To my surprise, she punches my arm. "Of course it's to study, you perv. What I mean is that I don't know how I'm going to climb into the back. Your car is really tall."

"Like this." I crouch under the overhead door to stand in front of her and wrap my hands around her waist.

Her brown eyes go wide. "No, Aran—"

I lift her and set her on the bed, but I don't let go of her right away. Having to bend down under the door means I'm very close to her as I say, "Like that."

"Oh." Strawberry swallows hard. "I forgot you're very strong."

"Do you need more reminders?"

"How about we start the session? We're like an hour late."

"I like it when you go all tutor on me."

"Aran, please. I'm trying to be professional here," she whines.

I feel a smile stretching my lips. I pretend like I'm pushing hair away from her face just so I can brush my fingers across her hot cheek. Making her blush feels just as good as catching a puck.

"What if we're unprofessional for a bit?"

Her eyes flutter closed, but her lips set in a stern line. "I would like to be able to pay my bills, though."

I jerk back, hitting the top of my head on the door.

"Are you okay?"

"Fine." I grunt. "And you're right. Today's session is supposed to compensate for yesterday's."

She nods too fast. "Right, and I know it's going to be harder to schedule new sessions starting next week with so many games coming up."

Sighing, I relent. "Let's get to work, then."

CHAPTER 24
MADDIE

Once I get him to stop stalling, it's surprisingly nice to sit side by side in the back of his car, shoes off, hearing the breeze, the quiet sloshing of the water at the shore, and the alternating sound of his typing or mine.

It's funny how his legs are so much longer than mine, and how tiny my chubby feet look next to his. Aran is so large he takes up most of the space, and his rock-solid arm brushes against mine every time either of us moves. It's the sweetest torture.

Fortunately, this time, I'm doing coursework. Unfortunately, that means I don't have any excuse to ask him for more reverse tutoring with his mouth. Or maybe with his hands this time. But after the conversation on the way here, I recalled when he said *no strings* yesterday, and it would definitely seem like strings if I initiate anything. I have to do whatever it takes to keep things professional during study sessions and friendly beyond them.

Wait. His hands stopped typing a while back.

Slowly, I turn. Aran's head rests against the back of the passenger seat, and his eyes are closed. It's only now that I notice how thick and long his eyelashes are. Darn him. I would love to have eyelashes like that.

"Are you staring?"

Crap. How does he know?

"I was just checking to see if you'd fallen asleep."

"Contemplating it," he murmurs in a way that makes me bite my lip. "This business case is so boring it makes me want to nap."

"Aran." I use my best admonishing voice. "Finish what you started."

He cracks an eye open. "Does that apply to things outside of this essay?"

I scramble to think of any possible innuendo behind that but come up blank.

"What are you talking about?"

"*Hmmwell.*" It comes out as one word as he sits up straighter and puts his ginormous laptop under the bend of his knees. "I started reverse tutoring you yesterday, didn't I?"

My heart leaps to my throat. I splutter but don't say anything coherent. Not when he's giving me that smirk that only means trouble.

"I should finish that session first, shouldn't I?"

"It finished quite nicely," I say, voice squeaky.

"Nicely?" He wrinkles his nose. "Is that a challenge to do better?"

"No!"

Oh, actually yes. Absolutely.

"So, here's my idea for today's session." With his hand on the blanket, he leans a little closer, which puts his nose almost against mine. "We're at a lake, right?" He stops, as if waiting for a reaction.

"Um, yes?"

"Then let's go for a dip."

I reel back with a laugh. "In February? Are you off your rocker?"

"It's really warm today. You said so yourself."

"Yeah, but not enough to swim."

"Well, I'm going in." Aran grabs the hem of his sweatshirt and pulls it off in a smooth move. His T-shirt catches on the other fabric for a moment, and I get a glimpse of cords of muscle down his side. He catches me staring and adds, "You can watch all you want."

Before I can even dream of protesting, he grabs a fistful of the back of his T-shirt and pulls it off. And just like that, my brain stops functioning.

Not true. It functions, all right. But to drink him in.

Aran leans a little away from me, twisting so his shoulder rests against the door. "Got your fill yet?"

"Not yet, actually," I respond with shocking calm compared to how fast my heart is racing. "Stay still."

His shoulders vibrate with a chuckle, but he really stays there, letting me ogle him openly.

The real deal is so much better than the training video of him I watched months ago. Aran bends one knee up and rests his elbow there, head against his fist. His bicep bulges in this position. No wonder he can pick me up easily. His arms are as thick as my thighs.

"Good gravy," I mutter like a Southern lady. "Your stomach looks like a chocolate bar."

That's not even a six-pack. He has eight defined squares of muscle that stay defined even when he's hunching over. Then they disappear into a V that starts at his hipbones. That might be more shocking than how small his waist is compared to his enormous shoulders.

He smirks. "Do you want a bite?"

That's when I gasp and cover my face. "Aran Rodriguez,

stop teasing me or I will spontaneously combust in this car and burn it to ashes."

"Fine."

It's not fine. I hear rustling, and when I open my eyes, I find him unzipping his jeans. I should look away. I really should. But I don't. Aran lifts his hips, which makes his core muscles flex so beautifully I wish I could snap a picture. And then he's sliding his jeans down.

I force myself to hide my face inside my sweater, and he must see it, because he starts chuckling.

"Don't worry, Strawberry. I'm not going to get naked for you unless you ask for it."

"Argh!"

I feel his heat move away and peek out once more.

Urgh, his back muscles have muscles, and all of them bunch and flex as he drags himself out of the car. There, he leans one arm against the open door and peers at me.

"So, what's it going to be? Are you going to keep watching or join in the fun?"

I fold my arms and try to copy his bravado. "Is this all a ploy so you can see me in my underwear?"

"Of course it is." Aran has the nerve to smile as he adds, "I mean, I've already seen your underwear, but what I'm really interested in is what's underneath."

I paw around me until I come up with his sweatshirt. Then I ball it up and throw it at him. Which was useless, since he catches it easily and tosses it back onto the blanket.

"C'mon, Maddie. Don't be a coward."

"I'm not a coward. What happened to professionalism?"

"It can get bent for all I care."

Aran leans away, giving me ample view of his incredible body, clad in only black boxers. Folding his arms, he throws a final challenge. "Don't writers need to experience a lot of things to write about? Stop being a spectator, Maddie. Do something different." And he bends his fingers in the way he must know drives me wild.

I grit my teeth, knowing he had me the second he started taking his clothes off. Knowing I'm not going to reject any chances at another tutoring session in the romance part of the hockey romance. My own body feels so hot I could melt my clothes off. Obviously, the only way to not turn into a sweaty mess is to take them off.

No! What am I doing?

Something different.

Something I want.

Something my mom would never imagine me doing.

I want to have fun with Aran. Maybe get in just a bit of trouble. Nothing terrible.

"Okay." His eyebrows rise at my response, and I motion in circles with my hand. "But turn around."

"Why?"

"Because, unlike you, I'm shy."

"But you enjoyed the full show. Why can't I?"

I don't know whether he realizes he sounds like a whiny kid right now. It's adorable and normally would make me tease the crap out of him. But not right now. Right now, I'm fighting with my insecurities.

"Aran, not all of us have zero percent body fat like you."

"I do have fat. Eight percent of it." I give him A Look and he puts his hands up. "All right, I'm turning." And he does, and I'm ashamed to find my eyes lowering to his perfect bubble butt. Unfair. The man is just perfect. If he knew I'm well into the double digits of fat percentage, he'd probably be put off.

Even then, I start taking off my clothes. A part of me is defiant. He's known I'm a chubby lady since day one, like everyone else. But on the other hand, it's different when you're wearing clothes than when you're not. Or when you're wearing as little as underwear.

Wait a second. I glance down at my bra and relax. It's a cute pink one. And I know I wore matching undies.

Oh my word. Am I really undressing in Aran's car?

Yep, I am. I pull off my leggings, and that's it. I'm semi-naked.

Slowly, I scoot to the edge of the car and lower my legs. Despite how warm the day felt earlier, now the breeze raises a chill out of me. The sand feels like snow under my bare feet as I stand.

Clearing my throat, I say, "Okay. I'm ready." Aran starts to turn, and I push my hands against his back. "No! I didn't mean you could turn yet."

"Then how can I know you're telling me the truth?" His voice sounds light, teasing. Uncharacteristic. Beautiful.

I rest my forehead against his back. "You'll have to trust me."

His body vibrates with a grunt. "So that's what today's lesson is, huh? Getting you out of your shyness."

Good luck with that. I've spent twenty-one years trying to hide myself and make myself as small as possible.

"Wrap your arms around me."

"What?" I jerk away.

"You heard me." He reaches back and grabs one of my arms, pulling me flush against him. I melt against the heat of his back and let him find my other arm. It's Aran, not me, who places my hands against his stomach. "Huh, you did undress."

I bury my face against his back, although there's no point. He must be feeling how hard my heart hammers against him.

"I am dying," I declare.

"Let's go die in the water."

Slowly, he walks us to the shore. I am way too pleased at the feeling of his velvet-soft skin against my face, at the hair on his stomach, the unrelenting hardness of his muscles. When I try to put any distance between us, his hands grab my arms tighter and pull me even closer.

But then the freezing water makes contact with my feet, and I jerk away with a yelp. And Aran turns to face me.

He doesn't flinch at the water lapping up at his ankles. Instead, he tilts his head and runs his eyes down my body.

Too late, I think about trying to cover myself. Except my hands are too small to try to hide anything.

"Why are you trying to hide yourself?" Aran takes a small step forward and slides his left hand around my waist, bringing me against him. It's exhilarating to feel all of him. "Because in case you didn't notice, I find you damn hot, Maddie."

My tongue is heavy, which makes my voice come out weird when I ask, "You do?"

"Yeah. It shouldn't take some random horndog guy for you to realize it."

"You're not random, though," I say in a voice barely above a whisper.

With his free hand, he cradles the back of my head, and I think he's going to kiss me. Instead, it keeps going down over my braid, and down still until he reaches the end of it. I feel the tug but only realize what he's doing when he pulls the hair tie off.

"What are you doing?" I ask, breathless.

"I want to feel your hair on me."

A shudder racks my body. I don't know if it's that I'm overly sensitive, or if it's him, because those words shouldn't be enough to make me feel like this. Like I'm a ball of fire and liquid all at the same time.

"That's more like it," Aran murmurs as he runs his thumb across my bottom lip. "I like this look on your face. Not the one you had before."

I bite his thumb. Pretty hard. "That's what you get for teasing me."

His eyebrows are up. "You may think you're punishing me by biting me, Strawberry, but you're not."

I squeeze my eyes shut tight, dying of embarrassment. "Are you always so forward?"

"No." I feel him lean down to my ear, and then he whispers, "I'm a goalie."

I can't believe he's making me laugh in a situation like this, but here I am. Semi-naked with a guy who knows exactly how to make me forget all my worries and fears. And I forget myself too, because I'm not even sorry when I bring my arms around his neck and stick flush to him.

"You're incorrigible."

"Wait to see what I have in store next."

"What—"

I don't finish the sentence, because next thing I know, I feel his arm slide below my knees and I'm flying. I yelp and grab him tighter, burying my face against his neck. But the clean spice of his skin gives me even more vertigo.

And then we're crashing into the icy water.

Aran himself pulls me to the surface. We both gasp as we come up for air, and now there's hair in my mouth.

"I'm going to kill you," I announce while spluttering.

Aran laughs. The nerve.

I try to push hair away from my face, but it's stuck like glue. He shifts his grip to release my legs, and I dip underwater a bit more. If it weren't for my arm around his neck, I would sink.

With his free hand, Aran brushes my hair back more effectively than I can, clearing my view of him. Drops of water trickle down his face. One of them catches on his eyelashes. His eyes are on my lips, and I'm cured, because all of a sudden, I'm not shy anymore.

"Aran," I rasp out.

"Hmm?"

"If you don't kiss me right now, I'm really going to kill you."

He smiles. "Who's the murderess now?"

But he also doesn't bother with playing any more games. Circling my waist with both arms, he lifts me up until I have no choice but to wrap my legs around him. And as gravity takes me, I let my lips crash against his.

Aran opens his mouth, and I groan, pleased I'm getting exactly what I wanted. Yesterday, he was in control. He was the only one who knew what to do. Today, I'm a little bolder.

Suddenly, I'm encased in ice again because we're underwater. But I don't let go of him. Even if I can't breathe, I'm not breaking this kiss. I gasp a little when he pulls us back up. I don't care that my hair is a curtain covering both of us, tickling in places and pulling in others. I care more that one of his hands is on my butt. That the other one is sneaking under the band of my bra.

Aran bites my lower lip softly, opening his eyes just a bit. His face is obscured by my hair, but it doesn't seem to matter. It could be storming with lightning bolts striking the water, and it wouldn't matter.

"I died and went to heaven, didn't I?" he murmurs against my lips.

"Stop talking and kiss me again."

"Yes, ma'am."

But instead of kissing my mouth, he dips his head down and kisses right under my chin. Then lower. The kisses turn into nibbles, and then he runs his tongue along the base of my throat.

I clutch at his head, gasping. "Aran."

"Yes?"

"I meant my mouth."

"Mouth, yes." He grumbles, pulling my hips lower against him until our faces are at level again. The smirk on his face makes me want to scream. "Sorry, I got a bit sidetracked there."

Annoyed, amused, and a concoction of other feelings sloshing in my belly, I bite his shoulder. Too late, I remember his words from earlier.

"Strawberry," he says, voice low and choked up. "I wasn't planning for this tutoring session to end horizontal, but it will if you keep biting me."

Lifting my head, I whisper in his ear. "How were you planning for it to go?"

Slowly, he turns until our noses touch. "Just like this. Exactly like this." And kisses me again.

CHAPTER 25
ARAN

We're on the way to the second to last game that will decide if we go to regionals. I know we will, but half of the team is collectively crapping their pants and the other half is frozen. There's little chatter on the bus, which suits me well because I'm in the mood for it even less than usual.

I sit at the very back on my own, headphones on and blasting something hardcore. My knee bounces nonstop. If anyone was paying any attention to me, they'd think I was nervous.

About the game? No. Our opponents are down their star striker. It's not like I'm underestimating them for that reason. They're just one of those teams built around a single player. Without this guy, they'll crumble against our defense. And if not, they'll have a wall between them and the net.

However, for the past two weeks, Strawberry and I haven't been able to schedule a single tutoring session.

Between studying for midterms, the midterms themselves, increased practice time, PT sessions, scheduled games, interviews with pro recruiters, cooking, and sleeping, we've seen neither hair nor hide of each other. Which is a damn shame because I like both of hers a lot.

And that's a problem.

Because I can't find another excuse for reverse tutoring. And I can't ask her out because a) I have no time, b) Coach sniffing around, and c) we're about to graduate—and then what? I don't know what she's planning to do after college. I don't know where I'm going to land either. What would be the point of starting something now?

I should've taken that damn elective a year ago. Maybe then…

I lean my head against the cold window and stare into the dark. An apt metaphor for how my future looks right now. Strawberry would be proud of me for knowing what a metaphor is.

I check my phone for the billionth time. Still no texts from her.

Except for the one time a bunch of Bolts and Strikes got together at my place, I haven't seen her since the lake. I wish we could've stayed together longer that time and that I hadn't had practice that afternoon. But maybe it would've been worse. Because we might've scored in each other's nets, and I'd be a lot more tangled now.

I stare at my bouncing knee. But maybe I wouldn't feel so restless. Maybe I wouldn't be checking my phone every five freaking seconds.

Unlocking the screen, I find Strawberry's contact and reread the last exchange—just a friendly *good luck on your next game* and *thanks*. In theory, there should be nothing more to say. With other girls, I rarely said more than this. But she's not other girls. She's…

Strawberry.

I convince myself to stop the knee-bouncing by taking action.

ME

Grunt

Time passes slower than usual as I stare the crap out of the screen. It works, though, because her three dots appear.

STRAWBERRY

Well if it isn't my favorite caveman

I spring forward so fast that I slam my forehead into the seat in front of me. A vague protest filters through the music playing in my ears, but I ignore it while I type back.

ME

Didn't know I was your favorite anything

Oh, shit. I know what I'm doing, and I can't stop myself. Probably because I don't even try. I'm flirting, and I know it.

Her three dots appear and disappear. Every time they go away, I glare at the screen as if it's the enemy. But finally, her response comes through.

STRAWBERRY

You're my favorite in two categories:

1) Caveman

2) Student

ME

What about favorite tutor

STRAWBERRY

Um, you're my only tutor, so that's not really fair to say

Maybe if I get at least one more and have a basis for comparison...

She better not. I don't want to become a murderer.

"Shit," I mutter, rubbing a hand up and down my face. I have no right to act like a possessive tool. We're not together. She can play the field if she wants. It's not my business. But the thought of some other dude putting his hands—or his mouth, or any appendages—on her, makes me want to break something. And it shouldn't.

So I change the topic.

ME

I'm bored on a bus full of panicky fools

What are you doing

Her next text comes right away.

STRAWBERRY

I'm hiding from mother dearest and an overzealous group of bridesmaids in the dressing room of a bridal shop

Definition of overzealous, I type into my browser.

Huh, is that what I'm being right now? Except I'm not sure what my objective here is, other than talking with her.

And that's a first. I've always known where I stand with the women in my life. With Mom and my sisters, it's obvious. They exist to annoy me and ignore me, and I'm here to caveman them as much as Dad does. With Ryan, it's also clear-cut. She's a friend I discuss hockey captaincy things with and also trade insults with that pack no punch. With the girls I've dated, it was even easier. They were just temporary distractions.

Maddie Berkley doesn't fit into any of those categories. And the problem is, I'm not interested in anything outside of them—but I'm interested in *her*.

ME

I have exactly an hour before we reach destination

So why hiding and why overzealous

STRAWBERRY

Sighing emoji

Don't forget you asked for details, so here
we go

The dress is HIDEOUS

It makes me look like a misshapen potato even
though it's too tight??

And Mom keeps saying I must've put on
weight, but I didn't!!

And if I did, so what? It happens!

Meanwhile the bridesmaids keep offering up
their cousins or their friends' friend who is
"totally not a creep"

ME

They're offering what?

STRAWBERRY

Their friends

For my plus-one

But it doesn't matter. I'll just ask Wyatt

The hell she will.

Before I even process what I'm doing, my fingers type up a
message lightning fast and hit send.

ME

You have a plus-one already

STRAWBERRY

I do?

ME
Your favorite tutor

Her three dots appear and stay on the screen for-freaking-ever without ever changing into coherent words. Until finally she responds.

STRAWBERRY

I don't know

"Why the hell not?" I ask myself in a grumble. Does she really want to take the Wyatt guy?

I press pause on my music and slide my headphones around my neck, because the roaring in my ears doesn't let me hear squat anyway. I'm racking my brain for ways to convince her when she messages me again.

STRAWBERRY

I don't think you want to subject yourself to my family

ME
Is there going to be free food

STRAWBERRY

Obvi

It's a wedding

ME
Then I'm in

STRAWBERRY

Uhh

Aran, I can't ask you for that favor

A favor?

It is not a damn favor. I'm not doing this out of pity. I just want to—

No, you know what? Favor it is. That way it's not a date, which I can't do unless I want Coach to bench my ass, because Murphy's Law has a thing for me.

ME

Sure you can

First, it won't be free. I will eat all the food

And hopefully *at least* eat her mouth again.

ME

Second, we can make a tutoring session out of it

STRAWBERRY

Really?

What would be the study subject?

Her thighs. I have a real curiosity about those. Instead, I steer my answer to something I know will win her over.

ME

Didn't your book have fake dating?

STRAWBERRY

Wide-eyed emoji

ME

What

I pay attention

Sometimes. Not often for things outside of hockey. And not to a lot of people. She doesn't need to know that.

STRAWBERRY

Tempting

But we all know fake dating isn't a real thing

ME

Pretty sure I just showed you how real it is

I blow a raspberry. Fake dating is the most bullshit thing I've heard of in my life. I had to work really hard to not laugh my ass off while she was telling me about it on the way back from the lake. People read that shit?

According to her, people don't just read it; they lap it up. And now I can see why. I'm desperate for her to agree to the little scheme.

STRAWBERRY

Hmm, good point

I guess it'd be better if you're my plus-one instead of a friend who has a girlfriend

ME

What

STRAWBERRY

Wyatt, he's taken, but I was this close to desperation

The noise that comes out of my mouth sounds like a cross between a snarl and a growl.

I could punch myself in the teeth. You're telling me I acted such a fool that I basically threw an entire game in the trashcan because I saw her sitting with her guy *friend*?

I put a hand on my head. Jealousy. That was the hot, blinding rage that made me miss pucks and throw punches at the millionth racist asshole I've encountered playing hockey. How am I only realizing that right now?

"Dude, what is wrong with you?"

I glue the screen of my phone to my chest and turn to Archie, who's now sitting next to me. "Where did you come from?"

"My mom." He eyes my phone. "Who you texting that has you kicking and squealing like a toddler?"

"I don't squeal. What the hell?"

"Your version of it sounds like a wild wolf."

"Go away, Archibald."

Instead, he leans closer and whispers, "Who's the girl?"

"It's your mom," I say in a deadpan.

"Tell her I don't want to have a stepfather my age and that she could do better."

I push him so hard he stumbles into the aisle. He recovers his balance quickly, and as he scoots back to the seat in front of me, he whispers, "Head in the game, Rodriguez. Not in the girl."

"Eat shit."

His chuckling abates as he sits back down, facing forward. But his words dance a jig in my head. I have to focus on tonight's game. And then the next. And then it's regionals. Four games to become the national champions. And then there's no way a pro team won't sign me. I don't need distractions.

Then I check my phone again and find more texts.

STRAWBERRY

I'll give you a chance to change your mind

Going once

Going twice

Too late. You're my plus-one now

The corner of my lips curves.

Good thing we established that Strawberry isn't *just* a distraction, huh?

ME

Don't we need to coordinate now

What color is the dress

STRAWBERRY

Oh, you're going to love it

It's pink

Of course there was a catch. I sigh as I type again.

ME

Show pic

Need exact shade

Immediately, a picture of a pink dress balanced on a weird hanger shows up. If I could roll my eyes harder, they'd get stuck.

ME

Pic of YOU wearing it

STRAWBERRY

No

ME

Yes

That's how I'll know the real shade

I couldn't give two flying turds about the color of this dress. It could be the color of baby diarrhea for all I care. I just want a picture of her. In the dress. That has very little fabric at the top.

> **STRAWBERRY**
>
> Is this for real, or are there nefarious purposes?

> **ME**
>
> Both

> **STRAWBERRY**
>
> *Blushing and laughing emoji*
>
> You COULD have been a forward with how forward you are

I grin.

> **ME**
>
> I thought you weren't so shy anymore

> **STRAWBERRY**
>
> Okay fine, let me put the dang dress on again

I hunch against the window, because no one better be watching over my shoulder for this.

> **ME**
>
> Wait a damn moment
>
> Were you texting me in the nude

> **STRAWBERRY**
>
> Obviously NOT
>
> I have underwear on

> **ME**
>
> Did I mention I also need to know the exact shade of that

To coordinate ofc

STRAWBERRY

Aran Rodriguez

Are you sexting me?

ME

Technically no. Apparently I'm the only one fully clothed

"Are you focused tonight, son?"

Slowly, as if I haven't been heavily flirting with my tutor, I slide my phone away from sight and look up at Coach Green. He stands in the aisle before me, grabbing the backrests of the seats in front of me. I know my face is impassive, but my heart races at full speed, and it's not because he showed up silent as a ghost.

"Yes, sir."

Ish. Once I suit up, I'll be Aran "the Iceberg" Rodriguez, the ice wall before the net.

"Good. Our opponent should be easy, but don't underestimate it."

"No, sir."

He chews his gum for a moment, watching me as if he can read my mind. "I made some calls, and there will be a lot of eyes on you tonight."

I nod. "I won't disappoint, sir."

"I know you won't. You've been sticking to our terms, and I plan to start you for every game as long as you don't lose your cool. This is your last chance to impress, Rodriguez."

What terms is he talking about?

And then it slams into me like a slapshot to the teeth. He's talking about the no dating, focusing only on the game little deal he coerced me into.

"Right," I say curtly.

Coach reaches down and pats my shoulder twice before heading back out to the middle of the bus to give essentially the same speech to everyone else. I'm not the only guy on this team eager to be recruited, whether as a free agent or in the draft, in the case of the younger guys. But it's a bit different for me. Goalies aren't typically the flashiest players. We're also not the bulk of a hockey team's roster, so recruiters tend to pay less attention to us.

And this is my last chance.

My phone pings with a message from Strawberry. I unlock the screen and nearly die of a heart attack right in my seat.

She took the picture without capturing her face, but there's a marked flush down her neck and across the expanse of her chest. And there's a lot of chest. The fabric puts it on glorious display without being obscene. Although maybe it is, considering what it's doing to me. I barely register anything else about the dress, other than it's the exact hue of her flushed skin and that it hugs her hips perfectly.

I rub my chest hard. What am I going to do with her?

Or, more accurately, what am I going to do with myself?

CHAPTER 26
MADDIE

should be excited to see Aran for our next actual tutoring session, but I'm not.

With every second that passes, I barely survive a new attempted murder from my uterus. Just yesterday I was an active member of society. I aced a midterm, tutored two students, hung out with Wyatt and Melinda, and made dinner with Ryan. Even went to bed early.

Today I'm more useless than a wet tissue.

I came to the Thundercloud for a strong coffee I could drink to get my ibuprofen going fast. But for an hour, I've sat at a table clutching at my stomach, unable to do anything but breathe. How am I going to even get to the library?

My phone buzzes against the table, moving dangerously close to the edge. I grab it with a shaky hand, and my heart leaps as I see Aran's name on the screen. His text asks where I am. Seems like he's already at the library.

ME

I don't know if I can make it today

Seeing that it takes me forever and a half to write such a

simple text, I question whether I can even make it home. Maybe I just need to rest for a moment. I lower my face to the table, because I can't bring myself to care about germs right now, and close my eyes.

Except my phone starts buzzing again. With a groan, I feel around until it's in my hand and open my eyes. Aran's calling. I accept the call and lean the phone against my face.

"Why not?" is his greeting.

With a thread of voice, I reply, "I don't feel well."

There's a pause on the line. Then, "What's wrong?"

"Um." I debate whether to tell him, but it's not like Aran has never seen any of my imperfections. He also probably deserves an explanation as to why his tutor is flaking out. "I've been trying to physically move myself from the Thundercloud, but I can't. My period's killing me."

"Okay." There's something so final about that one single word. I'm sure he's hung up until he adds, "I'll see you in a minute." And then the line goes dead for real.

I squeeze my eyes shut. I don't want to see him like this. I'd rather be transported back in time to the lake when we were making out on the shore, my back in the sand, him on top of me, and the water gently lapping at us.

Did I hallucinate that, or did that really happen?

Who knows what would've happened if Aran hadn't had to go to practice. Well, I know, but that all resides in my head only. And I don't think Aran meant to take the reverse tutoring that far in the first place—especially since it came with a no-strings-attached clause.

"Hey."

I open my eyes, and for a moment, I don't know where I am. My mind was replaying the study session at the lake. I lift my head, and a fresh wave of pain slams into me so hard that I groan. Is the table swimming? Or am I the one underwater?

"Whoa, Strawberry." I recognize the voice. It comes from somewhere beside me. "You look like a ghost."

"I am one," I mumble. "Pretty sure I'm dead."

A scalding hot hand touches my forehead. "You need to see a doctor."

"No." I moan. "They always tell me it's nothing and that I should lose weight instead. No doctors."

Aran is crouched beside me. This is the second time I've seen him from above. The first time was when he lifted me in the water with his arms around my butt. Funny how, instead of making my womb happier, that memory makes it hurt more. His brow furrows more.

A grunt. "Fine, then let's get you home."

"Only if you have a teleporting machine."

"It's called a car. Let's go." He stands up and gathers my bag, then circles an arm around my waist, and with his free hand, he grabs my arm to pull me up.

I stagger against him, though not on purpose. I can't feel my legs. Aran curses in my ear. We don't say anything else as he slowly walks me out of the café. I keep my head down so he doesn't see the tears trickling down my cheeks. I'm angry and embarrassed and it hurts so freaking much.

My period has always been like this. It arrives without warning, sometimes four weeks after the last one, other times two, others months later. But every time, it visits with the power of an anvil falling on my body. And everyone around me tends to think I'm overreacting, especially doctors.

"I'm sorry," I say once we're in his SUV and on the way back home.

"What the hell for?"

"Being an inconvenience." He starts to turn, and I look away.

"Who said that?"

"Well, no one," I whisper. "But you seem annoyed. And

we'll have to cancel the study session because of me. And I feel bad."

"Yeah, you feel bad because you look like a nine on the pain scale. And I am annoyed, but only because I can't do anything else to help."

"Oh." I bite my lip hard, as if it could tamp down the butterflies fluttering in my chest.

We get to the apartment complex, and I'm all too eager to unbuckle myself, since the seat belt felt like a clamp around my hips. I open the door, and slowly, I turn around until I can basically melt onto the pavement. And that's when I realize something.

"Oh no. How am I going to climb four floors like this?"

I want to cry. But not in front of Aran. I take big gasps of air, trying to not let myself.

"I'll carry you if I must," he says from the other side, shutting the door.

"No, you will not. If you get hurt because of me, I couldn't live with myself."

Sighing, he walks around the vehicle until he reaches me again and offers his arm. "First, let's try. If it doesn't work, you stay very still, and then I won't get hurt while I carry you."

"Aran—"

"Just walk, woman."

I grunt just like he does all the time and grab his arm. It takes him a few tries to match my minuscule steps, which are all I'm able to take while it feels like my insides want to push out. It takes embarrassingly long to make it just to the building entrance, and on the way, I've complained at least ten times to his zero.

Aran stays completely silent as I groan and gasp through the snail's-pace climb of the first flight of stairs. At the landing, I clutch at the banister with one hand and him with the other because everything's swaying again. And we're not even halfway.

"Yeah, that's enough. Hold still."

"What—"

The world tilts, and gravity disappears for a moment.

And then I'm in Aran's arms again. Gasping, I cinch my arms around his shoulders. He bounces me a couple of times until he gets a comfortable grip.

"Are you sure?" I whisper in his ear.

"Just don't move."

I've never met a guy who could lift me up. And I never imagined there was one who could climb stairs while doing it. But I can't enjoy even a second because the pain seems to get worse with every step he takes. My head collapses on my arm that rests on his shoulder, and that's the last thing I'm aware of for a bit.

I come to at the sound of heavy breathing and a voice calling me. Shaking my head, I focus on it until I make out the words.

"Where are your keys?"

Something incoherent comes out of my mouth. I grab Aran tighter as he slides me back down to my feet. But neither of us trust them, and I'm glad he keeps his arm around me, pressing me up against him. My head on his chest bounces with his heavy breathing as I feel around my coat's pocket. Aran takes the keys from my hand and opens the apartment door.

"Thanks. I can take it from here." I sound drowsy as I speak.

"Sure, you can." Sarcasm drips from his words. With a huff, he picks me up again, and I groan.

"Your back—"

"Stop worrying about me. I'm not the one who passed out in someone's arms."

"I did?" I slur.

Aran crouches a little to open my bedroom door. My vision blurs as he maneuvers us to enter the room sideways. With surprising gentleness, he sets me down on my bed.

"Yeah, you did." His eyes are dark as he stares down at me with a frown, hands on his hips, nostrils flaring with labored breathing. "Scared the shit out of me. I was this close to turning around and taking you to an ER."

I open and close my mouth. But I'm more surprised when he undoes the laces of my boots, chucks them off, and walks out of the room without another word. His steps recede and stop when the front door closes. And then it's silent.

I don't blame him for running away. If I could, I would.

Now groaning to my heart's content, I weasel out of my coat and push it off the bed. With just that small amount of effort, I pant harder than Aran after climbing two and a half floors with a fat girl in his arms. There is no position that can help me ease the pain, but I'm a side sleeper, so I turn and wither. Maybe if I stay like this for the rest of the afternoon, I'll start feeling better.

But then the front door opens. I wonder if it's Ryan, but on Wednesdays, she has a full schedule at school. My bedroom door opens, and Aran's deep, husky voice sounds again around my bed.

"Put this on." He appears in front of me, crouching to fiddle with something. Then he stands up holding a heating pad. "Stop giving me that look. Sometimes we get muscle cramps after training and need to alternate between hot and cold. This shit's amazing."

"I'm not judging." I smile a little.

Aran gives me the pad, and I put it against my stomach, trying to keep it upright. He moves away from the window and light streams into my face again. There's some rustling, and suddenly, my mattress dips with a heavy ball of heat and—

Aran's arm comes around me, pressing the pad against my stomach until the heat seeps through my clothes. Until I'm glued against him. He pushes his other arm under my head until I feel his hot breath fanning my neck.

I lie very still as he murmurs, "Heat helps, according to my sisters."

Yeah. It helps.

It helps accelerate my heart from normal to about to spill out of my mouth along with words he won't want to hear. I blink hard, but that doesn't stop the tears from pouring from my eyes.

We stay like that until he has to head out for practice and well past the point of no return for me. Because that afternoon, as I lie in Aran's arms, his little spoon, I'm pretty sure I've fallen in love with him.

CHAPTER 27
ARAN

This is it. The game that decides whether we go to Regionals.

Neither team has scored, and we're in the third period against the Bulldogs. We've had one PK from each side this period alone. I've been a freaking wall, but so is the other goalie. Goal attempts are fired from each side like artillery. The boards have even seen blood. The crowd roars with the intensity of a finals game.

The Thunder Bolts' home arena explodes as I bat a puck away from the net like I'm playing baseball. A group of Bulldogs who are all bark and no bite try to jostle me around while the puck's still in play. It should get them dinged for interference, but the ref's distracted. Webber and some Bulldog battle for the puck and soon forget it altogether. Gloves drop and the whistle blows, but more and more players from each team join what's now a scrum.

I smack my stick against the ice a few times, and one of my guys sees it. That's our code for *stop this shit right now before I make you regret it*. Right on, he grabs the next Bolt and pulls him away, and one by one, they leave the Bulldogs to fight each other if they want.

We end up on a four against four, and I pull up my mask and spray water on my face to clear away the sweat before the next faceoff. And off we go again.

The crowd chants, "Go, Bolts, go! Go, Bolts, go!"

But we go straight into overtime.

Bracken brakes in front of me, offering his elbow. "Ready to rumble?"

I bump my elbow with his and say, "Tell Coach not to send the first line in. Amadi's favoring his left hand and Charles looks ready to drop dead."

"Aye, Captain." He takes off for the bench to relay the info before the ref starts the game again.

I know part of my family's right behind my goal, and I can hear our adopted pet, Brooklyn, screaming his throat hoarse with various encouragements. Olivia is probably so annoyed at him she's not even focusing on the game. She can never seem to get him to shut up. Next to them are Luz and her fiancé, Max Cassiano. His team has a game nearby tomorrow, so he apparently flew in early for tiramisu. Dude is as obsessed with it as someone I know who is wild about strawberries.

Speaking of, she sits with Ryan and some of the Strikes right by the tunnel to the locker room.

I'm happy to report my concentration has stayed in mint condition all game. It could be because my green-eyed monster isn't triggered tonight, but I'd prefer to think it's because I've learned a few lessons since that game. And also because I got to make out with her while she was in her underwear and wet.

There's a party planned for after we win this game. I wonder if I'll manage to do some overtime reverse tutoring there. Maybe further her book research—both on the hockey front and the romance front. We'll see.

The puck drops, and I forget all of that.

The Bulldogs explode out of the faceoff with a breakaway. A meteor could drop in the parking lot and it wouldn't flap me, least of all some dipshit who escaped our even more dipshit defense. I don't know if he's tired or if I'm on a new plane of existence, but he's moving too slow. I can read every move of the puck as he handles it. I can see the target painted in his eyes for my fourth hole. I can see the exact angle of his wrist's bend as he goes for a slapshot.

My mitt catches it like a magnet, and the arena blows up with noise.

Surprise flashes across the Bulldog's face, and that's when I know we've already won. Whether in overtime or shootouts, it doesn't matter. This save shook the foundation of their team to the damn core.

I stay vigilant, though. The clock ticks fast and even. Though the Bulldogs keep barking, our D bites them back. Finally, our first line hits the ice, and I check the time. We have one minute and eight seconds left. Should be plenty.

The puck changes sides several times. A Bulldog ices it. It goes back into play. Webber checks a Bulldog against the boards. Bracken picks up the puck and makes a pass at Amadi, who shoots with his left hand. Even though he's a righty.

And he scores.

The buzzer goes off to a cacophony of celebration all around us. I pump my fist as the guys celebrate all the way across the ice in a way that almost gets them beat up. The final buzzer goes off, and I can't help it. I laugh. My teammates are assholes, but they're the best assholes.

My roommate is the first one to slam into me, saying, "We're going to regionals, baby!"

"Heck yeah!" Another one smashes against me from the other side, and I grunt.

And then one more. "I can't believe it!"

"What are you talking about? I knew we had this in the bag!" someone else shouts.

"Regionals! Regionals! Regionals!" That one's Amadi, and one by one, the whole team joins the chanting. Soon enough, the arena is intoxicated by it and chanting too.

My heart's hammering harder than in the middle of the game. I finally take in the audience. This is probably the first time in my Division I career that I've seen this place packed to the rafters, like finally this snobby-ass school has gotten with the program and understands that hockey's the best.

I'll make sure this team modifies St. Cloud's DNA until students and staff alike bleed Thunder Bolts blue.

As we do a victory lap around the perimeter, I catch my little sister giving me a thumbs-up. That's much more shocking than Brooklyn and Luz competing over who can jump and wave the most. Cassiano shakes his head, wearing a thick scarf and baseball cap meant to conceal his identity. I don't think it's working, because some chicks in the row below keep glancing back at him.

I take off my mask and raise my stick at them, and even Liv claps.

Following the stream of my teammates, I file off the ice into the corridor. People extend their hands for us to high-five them, but I'm not about that life. Instead, I spot the Strikes and the honorary Strike.

"Great job! Now you're not losers anymore," Ryan says with a guffaw.

Strawberry's cheeks are pink, and she beams that wide smile directly at me. A congratulations that is only for me.

As it should be.

I clamp my jaw tight and nod at her, lest my teammates see me smiling like a clown. I keep going, and at the locker room, Coach is giving a quick debrief before we hit the showers.

It hits me like a bolt. I have no right to think like this. I'm not her boyfriend. A smile from her shouldn't feel even more monumental than this win. Especially because I won't see it again once the semester ends.

"Who's ready to get wasted?" one of the guys asks in the middle of the running showers.

Another one counters with "More importantly, who's ready to get laid?"

A chorus of horny animals roars at that. I rub my face extra hard with soap because I'm dying to get into Strawberry's pants, but I shouldn't. And I don't know how to stop myself from wanting her. She deserves better than a covert and temporary friends-with-benefits situation, which is all I can offer without getting in trouble in more ways than one.

Maybe I shouldn't go to this party. Maybe I should go home and watch film from the teams we'll face at regionals. Or maybe I should go tire out my hormones with a late-night swim at the lake by myself.

But I want to see her. I want to banter with her. Make her blush. See if I can get her to gasp my name in my ear.

Mierda. I can't keep doing this, not with regionals on the horizon.

My head's still swimming when I make it out of the locker room and find my family hanging out near the training area's exit.

"Hermanito!"

Luz spreads her arms wide and squeals as if I were some celebrity. I brace because I know exactly what will happen next, and nothing in this world will stop her. She slams into me with enough power to make me stumble back a step, making me drop my duffel bag on the floor so she can squeeze the crap out of me. I don't drop my stick, though. It has to hold out until the championship game.

"I'm so awed by you," Luz says with her face buried in my chest. She pulls away to look up. "You're so much better than many pro goalies already, including the starter on Max's team."

"For real, man." I like Cassiano because he respects boundaries. He offers a fist to me, and I bump it with mine. "I got some film for my coach, by the way. His mind's going to blow away when he sees that wild save you made in overtime."

"Dude, you got shot point blank at easily a hundred miles per hour." Brooklyn opens his mouth wide, shakes his head, and runs a hand through his goldilocks. The picture of shock.

I sigh and peel my older sister off me. To her fiancé, I say, "Thanks, but I don't want to have to use connections." I'm not Edwards.

Cassiano blows a raspberry. "It's not because you're my brother-in-law. Coach literally sent me here to scout you once he knew I'd be in town."

Luz nods rapidly. "Yup. We didn't come here just to support you, although we did that too. Right, Aceituna?"

"Whatever," our younger sister says, checking her phone. "Can we go eat now? I'm starving."

"Actually, I'll agree with Aceituna for the first time in my life," I say.

She frowns until her whole face scrunches up. "When are the two of you going to stop calling me by that ridiculous name?"

"Never," Luz and I say at the same time. I can't help but exchange a grin with her. This is what older siblings are for.

Huffing, Liv whirls around and heads for the exit. Her golden retriever of a best friend follows her, talking her ear off about the game. I pick up my duffel bag and follow after Luz and Cassiano. They're just as disgusting as they were six years ago, their arms around each other's waists as if they can't stand to be apart for a single second. Cassiano glances down at my sister as if the moon itself were in her eyes, and she looks up at him as if he put it there.

I can't do that.

The thought halts me in my steps.

I can't be that guy for someone. I've never looked at anyone like that. I can't afford to bend my life over to accommodate one more person. I have enough with two reckless sisters who are regulars at the hospital and parents who can't afford those bills. It's on me to make sure the Rodriguez family has a good future, and I can only do that if I stay focused on making it to the league.

Coach was right. I needed a dating ban to understand this. Hockey isn't just something I do for fun. It's the thing I'm best at—what I need to make a living with for my family's sake and my own. I can't jeopardize it by giving priority to something else. Or someone else.

I need to really enforce the dating ban. Tonight.

With a lump in my throat, I follow after my family and spend the whole dinner thinking of how to end what has been the best part of my year.

CHAPTER 28
MADDIE

"Where's Aran?"

I glance up from the Jell-O shot I'm about to take, thinking the question is for me, but Ryan's attention is on Jamal. A flush rises up my throat because who the heck am I to think I speak for Aran?

The Nigerian-descent forward checks his phone, and above the din, he shouts, "Apparently he's having dinner with his family. His older sis and her fiancé are in town."

"Cassiano's in town? I want his autograph!" Ryan pulls out her phone and types furiously on it, probably to ask Aran for the prize.

I push down the Jell-O shot. It tastes like medicine, if medicine were like a big clump of glue that burns your esophagus as it makes the trip down.

"Geh." I stick my tongue out and pile the empty plastic cup on the stack at the coffee table.

The Strikes commandeered the big sofa in the living room of what is known as the Bolt House. Five guys from the team live here, including Jamal and Mark. Tonight, there isn't a single corner of this house that isn't teeming with players, their friends and strangers.

A beer pong tournament has taken over the kitchen, with the added twist of using cheese puffs instead of ping-pong balls. It amps up the difficulty level and also makes the beer taste like crap with piss. I tried it earlier and nearly upchucked, but fortunately, I lost on the very first round.

Behind us, people are attempting to dance to a playlist that blares out of some truly powerful speakers set on the fireplace mantel. I chose this corner of the sofa so I can be close to the roaring fire, because the dress Christine weaseled me into makes me cold. It's a little black number that is so tight I had to wear shapewear underneath, except there's no hiding my bare shoulders or the great display of cleavage happening. At least she let me wear warm tights.

I push half my hair over one shoulder and half over the other so at least I can warm them up a bit. Maybe also to cover a bit of the boobage threatening to spill over.

"We'll get you with a man tonight," she said with a wink as we got ready at Amber's before the party.

"Or two. We don't judge." Amber laughed.

But I saw Ryan narrowing her eyes at me through the mirror. I kept applying mascara as if I hadn't seen it, and as if she couldn't read my mind.

Last week, when I had the horrible cramps, Aran and I fell asleep in my bed and Ryan found us. The noise of my door opening woke me up while I was half sprawled on top of Aran, and even though he somehow didn't stir, I remember the look on Ryan's face.

First, it was true shock. Round mouth, wide eyes, eyebrows as far up as they go. And then she cringed, as if she were watching a train wreck about to happen.

We didn't talk about it afterward, which is what I was expecting. But she gets extra contemplative if I mention Aran's name. Or if someone utters it around me. I think she's waiting for me to admit I have feelings for him. Meanwhile, I'm trying to avoid showing her I'm just like every other girl on campus, salivating over our resident bad boy with the moody eyes, the velvet lips, and the chocolate bar abs.

"That was disgusting, right?" Amber says, grimacing before she shakes her head. "Let's do another."

As if we share a single brain cell, we reach for a new glass of Jell-O shots each, clink them together, and chug. Good gravy, this one tastes even worse.

Jamal holds the tray with shots away from us, making a face. "Yeah, okay. That's enough for you ladies."

"What?"

"Boo!"

"You're fired as a waiter, Amadi."

"No tip for you, sir."

At the Strikes' heckling, he shakes his head and turns away to keep distributing the nasty concoction to invitees. Normally, I wouldn't take shots in this kind of situation, but I saw Mark and Archie making them in the kitchen when we arrived an hour ago. And actually, I trust these guys. I know Aran would murder them if they stepped out of line.

I trust Aran, I guess.

For the billionth time, I scope the perimeter as discreetly as possible in hopes of sighting a certain TDH. But there are two people making out in a corner next to a group of guys who don't notice them while engaged in some sort of debate. Besides them, one of the younger Bolts is attempting a keg stand while some people record it. There's stomping down the stairs, and someone shouts about not being able to find their coat. The song changes to a club banger that makes half the living room erupt into cheers, and a girl literally jumps on a guy in the middle of the dance floor to kiss him.

Everywhere, people are having fun. Technically, so am I.

The Strikes are noisy and hilarious, and they treat me like one of their own even though we've virtually just met. But something's missing. Something shaped like a six-foot-four iceberg.

"Would you look at that! The king of the clowns finally makes an appearance," one of the Strikes says, pointing at the door.

My heart stops and then gallops at full speed as Aran Rodriguez himself walks through the front door, wearing all black, as if we'd coordinated outfits on purpose.

His eyes are on mine like he spotted me the second he walked in, but someone gets in the way to fist bump him. His attention shifts to that guy, and then the next handshake, and then to a girl who hugs him as if they know each other, even though his expression says he has no idea who she is.

Those dark eyes lift to me again, and I check my surroundings. Unless he's checking out the girl dancing behind me, he really seems to be looking at me.

Maybe I shouldn't have pushed my hair forward. He'd probably enjoy the whole boob spillage situation.

"I can see Rodriguez's ego growing with every new person who showers him with praise," Ryan says from Amber's other side.

Christine leans forward from her end of the couch. "Let's give him a pass tonight. He did make a save for the history books. But tomorrow, we go back to giving him crap."

"Fine. Rain on my parade, why don't you." But Ryan laughs. "Anyone want to play another game of beer pong with me?"

"Pass." I make a yuck face. "I can't possibly do another beer-soaked cheese puff."

"Okay, fair."

"I'm in." Amber scoots forward to dislodge herself from the depths of the couch. "Let's find some Bolts and knock them down a peg."

"Beautiful plan." Ryan jumps to her feet, and they lace arms as they make their way to the kitchen to wage war on their ancestral enemy.

Christine offers her hand over to me. "Let's go dance, Maddie."

"Um, I'm not much of a dancer."

"Not when sober, maybe."

"Hmm. Good point." Grinning, I grab her hand, and together, with stumbling feet, we round the couch to join the mass of people jumping to the beat of a '90s classic.

I have no idea what I'm doing, so I try to copy Christine's moves. Even though I'm nowhere near as graceful, I soon stop thinking about anything and just shake what my momma wishes she hadn't given me.

The whole world could be watching and making fun of me, but I'm buzzed enough that I couldn't care less. A pop song everyone knows plays next, and Christine and I sing along off-tune. My hair plasters to my sweat-coated skin, and I hope my makeup's not running. But even if it is, I'm not stopping until this song ends.

My new friend and I sing to each other as if we're recording a duet. Movement from the corner of my eye catches my attention, and I find Aran leaning against the wall by the kitchen, drinking from a beer bottle as he watches me.

A shiver racks through my whole body.

It's annoying how his eyes alone have the power to incense me.

But he's vanished by the time Christine and I finish dancing.

"Dayum, girl, you got moves." Christine elbows me as we weave through the crowd toward the kitchen. "I caught like five people thirsting over you."

"No way," I say, breathless and unsteady with the dancing and shots.

"Yes way. One of them was a certain Bolts captain. What's up with that?"

I'm glad she asks that while my back is turned to her. I keep pouring a cup of water and pretend the question doesn't shock me.

When I turn around, I say, "Christine, you must be drunk. Have some water, girl."

She smirks and pours herself some too. "I mean, if you wanna tap that, I don't blame you. But you have more choices, is all I'm saying."

I laugh awkwardly. "I don't wanna tap anything tonight."

"I'm sure that's why you let me make you wear this dress tonight." She waves a finger up and down my frame.

Tossing my empty cup into the overflowing trashcan, I rack my brain for an escape to this conversation, and nature presents me with the opportunity. After beer, shots, and water, a girl needs to heed nature's call to the bathroom.

"I need to pee," I declare as if that had been the topic of conversation.

"Actually, me too."

Together, we wrestle through the throngs of people toward the bathroom beyond the corridor. But the line of people is so long, we make a U-turn and head for the stairs.

Meanwhile, I've turned into a freaking fan, just turning this way and that in hopes of finding a certain someone. Where the heck has he gone to hide? And is he alone so I can join him?

What if he's not alone?

I half pay attention to the Strike's chatter while we're in line for the bathroom upstairs. A disheveled couple stumbles out of a bedroom with the look of having been up to no good. Heat travels up my body as the thought pops up unbidden in my mind.

That could've been Aran and me.

Finally, it's our turn for the bathroom, and Christine and I do rock, paper, scissors to decide who goes first. She wins, so I wait outside. I'm glad she's not one of those girls who does her thing in front of her friends. I always found it super uncomfortable, especially because it gave Lori another opportunity to make fun of my fat rolls.

"Well, look what we have here."

I shake my head hard. Am I hallucinating?

Nope. I really did summon her by just thinking about her.

I take a deep breath as heels click closer. Someone yells, "Hey, don't cut the line!" But Lori doesn't care.

She and the others plant themselves next to me. From the back, Rebs waves her fingers at me, and I give her a tight smile. Tiff glances down at my dress in surprise. A fourth girl I don't know checks me out with even more venom.

She asks Lori, "Are you sure this is Aran's new girl?"

I reel back.

"Believe it or not." Lori shrugs and folds her arms delicately. "I've seen them all chummy-chummy more than once."

"That's impossible." The unknown girl sneers at me. "He may be a player, but he doesn't do just any girl."

"Too right, Kelsey," Tiff says.

I don't care for this conversation, so I say, "How about you take all your assumptions somewhere else? Enjoy your night, ladies." And I turn to face the door.

But then a claw grabs my bare shoulder and forces me to turn. Kelsey laughs in my face. "You got some spunk. I'll give you that. But don't think someone like you could possibly keep Aran's interest for long. He's probably boning you out of charity."

"We're not bo—" But too late, I shut my mouth.

"Of course you're not." She squeals a laugh. "How could you be his rebound after dating *me*?"

Oh.

So this is Aran's quasi ex, whatever that means. The one

who was waiting for him at the library. Who slapped him in the face and has now left marks on my shoulder.

I back away until my back hits the door. Half the people in line are distracted by their own things, but the half paying attention to the drama doesn't contain any friendly faces.

Crap, I should've gone into the bathroom with Christine.

"Listen," I start with an exasperated voice. "I don't owe you any explanations, but I will tell you this out of the kindness of my heart. Aran and I are friends, and even if we were more than that, it's none of your business."

Rebs grabs Tiff's arm, who is closest, and says, "Guys, let's just go, okay?"

"Just friends, my ass." Lori barks a harsh laugh. "Weren't you eating his face at the library like a little pig? Oink, oink, oink."

Tiff bursts into laughter. "Oh, Lori. That's so mean. She doesn't even eat pork. She's a vegetarian."

I'm too stunned by what Lori says to even care about Tiff's weak dig.

"What did you say?"

Lori leans a hand on the wall next to me. "Oh yeah. I saw that. Did he even want to kiss you back? It looked pretty aggressive from your side."

There's murmuring down the line at that.

My heart beats so fast it makes my chest hurt. I hate that she saw that moment. Even more, I hate that she's smearing dirt on it in front of a bunch of strangers. And much more than that, I hate that I'm blinking back tears.

"Screw you. How dare you imply I would—without his consent—that's ridiculous! Of course he wanted to—You know what? It really is none of your damn business."

I try to push Lori out of the way so I can leave, but the same claw from before holds me back.

"But I thought you were friends?" Kelsey asks, tilting her

head. With a fake friendly voice, she says, "Friends don't make out at the library. Or anywhere. Right, girls?"

"Right," Tiff and Lori chorus.

"Trust me, I know Aran very well. Intimately," Kelsey says with extra emphasis on the last word. "I'm just giving you a friendly warning that you shouldn't fall in love with him just because he gives you a little attention. He'll move right on the second he realizes you have feelings for him. Because you do, huh? It's written all over your chubby little face."

"She's pathetic," Lori adds. "Falls in love with the first guy who's nice to her. Can you blame her?"

"So what if I'm in love with him? How's that any of your business?" I snap, shaking in my boots but not out of fear. No, out of how hard it is to not drop my figurative gloves and slam my fist in their noses. "What are you trying to accomplish here? To intimidate me? Well, guess what." I pause and push both Kelsey and Lori away from me with so much strength they stumble back. Lori trips on her heels and falls on her ass, and I glare down at her and at Kelsey. "Trying to bully me isn't going to make him like either of you, because you're both horrible people.

"And you," I say to Rebs. "You're turning into one of them, even if all you do is stand by and do nothing as they bully your former friend. I hope you have fun hanging out with people who will stab you in the back the second you try to think on your own again.

"And you," I snarl at Tiff. "Being a vegetarian is not an insult, you damn airhead."

Someone in the line starts clapping, and I wince. For a moment, I forgot there was an audience. And then the absolute worst thing happens.

There, at the top of the stairs, is Aran. And his expression tells me he heard some of that.

"Maddie." It weirds me out that he's not calling me by his

nickname for me. The bad feeling in my stomach takes over as he rubs his head and asks, "Are you in love with me?"

I suck in air.

My mind rewinds through the past five minutes and stops right at the moment when, like an absolute fool, I admitted my feelings for Aran Rodriguez in front of a corridor packed with strangers and foes. And apparently him.

I hear laughter. Then someone else joins. A chorus of *ooh*s echoes across the hallway. The only exit is by Aran. I turn and rush through the open door of the bedroom the couple stumbled out of earlier. But before I close it, a big foot appears between the door and the frame, and Aran pushes his way in.

"No, I—"

I jump away from him and knock my hip into the corner of some furniture. His hand grabs my arm, preventing me from falling. Or from pulling away again.

I don't dare meet his eyes.

"Maddie…"

"Don't *Maddie* me." I shake my head, breathing hard. "I'm drunk and angry. I didn't mean what I said."

"So you didn't mean to tell them to screw off to another planet?"

I jerk my arm away from his grip and hug myself tight. "No, that part I meant for sure."

"And you did great. I was just about to send them packing myself, but—" He interrupts himself with a soft little grunt. "But that's not the only part you meant."

I bite my lips hard enough that the pain sobers me. Where are words when I need them the most? Why can't I think of a combination of twenty-six letters that could get me out of this?

Because I meant it. And now everyone knows. Aran knows. Even though I've known all along that this was just a game for him. Reverse tutoring. Book research. Nothing special. One last chance at fun before college ends.

"We agreed no strings attached," he says at last, with a soft voice. The confirmation cuts through me. "I can't do relationships, Maddie. I just can't. Not until—I need to focus on regionals. I wanted to tell you this even before I heard... Please, understand."

I want to rage that *this* is when he finally learns to say please, when he's breaking up with me even though we were not even together.

I find strength from somewhere to raise my head. "Don't worry. I knew that. I tied the strings myself, and I can cut them too. I have plenty of experience to write a whole book series on that."

Aran's hand lifts toward me, and I flinch away. He squeezes it into a fist and drops it. The impassive mask on his face cracks just a bit. But I don't care to decipher the look. This time I'm the iceberg. I push past him and walk out of the room with my head held high, even though inside, there's nothing left to hold me up.

"Girl, where were you?" Christine asks from the middle of the hallway. "I know it was a very long dump but—what's wrong, Maddie?"

"Can we go home?"

Worry twists her face at whatever she sees in mine, and she nods. "Let's go get the others and blow this joint." And with her arm around me, she steers me away from the witnesses to my biggest humiliation ever.

CHAPTER 29
ARAN

climb up the stairs slowly, one by one, just going through the motions.

That's how the entire week has been through school and practice. I've managed to go to class, take notes, sit exams, and even ace my essays. And if Coach has noticed something weird, he's had too much on his plate to even look my way, what with Jamal being down with a wrist injury and a first line that doesn't work so great anymore.

Why does doing the right thing and being honest feel so shitty?

Because I went to that party last week with the sole intention of taking Maddie aside and telling her… I don't know. All the words went up in smoke the moment I saw her sitting in the living room. But I intended to hit the brakes on the book research and stay friends.

We're not even that now. She won't answer my texts. She canceled our official tutoring sessions. The one time I ran into her here, on the apartment stairs, she nearly tripped in her haste to run from me.

And I can't stop thinking about it. I'm out there catching

pucks during practice by rote, my mind churning her words over and over. I'll be calculating cashflow and remembering something we did before.

There's a before and an after. Huh.

"Rodriguez."

I lift my head. Ryan stands at the top of the stairs, a garbage bag sitting at her feet. Her arms are folded and her expression gives no warm fuzzies.

I blink slowly, frankly about to pass out from exhaustion. And I sound like it when I say, "Avery."

"We need to talk."

"Later, I'm tired," I mumble and drag my feet for the last of the climb. I walk past her for my door, and it takes me two tries to jam the key in the hole.

My plan is to order pizza and watch film from our opponents until I can't keep myself upright anymore, but I don't know if I'll even make it to dinner. At the rate I'm going, I'll drop dead asleep the second I hit the couch.

And maybe that wouldn't be such a bad idea. That way I don't have to think about how she's at her sister's wedding tonight, sans plus-one. I texted her several times, asking if she still wanted me to back her up, but since she left me on read, I assumed the answer was a big hell no.

I drop my duffel bag onto the living room floor and dump my stick on top. Leaning against the wall, I toe out of my sneakers and leave them there. Slowly, I lower myself onto the couch and rest my elbows on my knees. I try to rub the bleariness out of my face, but it's bone deep. As if I completed years' worth of practice this afternoon alone.

Of course, Ryan doesn't let me be. She makes her way into my apartment, sets her trash bag down on my floor, and makes herself comfortable on my couch.

"What did you do to Maddie?"

I draw in a deep breath and let it out before speaking. "Why do you think I did something?"

"Because now, if anyone so much as mentions your name, she looks like she's about to cry or puke or both."

I flinch, and there's no hiding it. Even then, I say nothing.

"Listen carefully, Aran. I like you, but I like Maddie more. If you hurt her, I will end you."

I glare at her. "You know damn well I'm not in the business of assaulting women."

"No, but you sure have a talent for hurting them here." She taps her chest repeatedly. "And I warned you, didn't I?"

She did, weeks ago, when she caught me walking out of Maddie's room to head to practice while she kept sleeping off her period pain. Ryan was sitting by the kitchen counter, munching on baby carrots with so much violence I suspected she was pretending they were my head.

"What's the deal between you and Maddie?" she asked point blank.

"Nothing." My response was a total lie, and we both knew it.

"That in there didn't look like nothing. It looked like some real boyfriend shit."

I remember rolling my eyes and saying, "We're just friends. Friends give a shit about each other, right?"

"Does that mean you'll cuddle Archie if he's hurting somewhere?"

I snorted. "Archie can go cuddle himself."

"Exactly. You could've ignored Maddie like you do with everyone else, but here you are. So don't give me that bullshit, son." She got up from her seat and walked over to poke my chest hard. "And if you so much as hurt a hair on her head, I'll come for you."

So here we are. I guess this is Ryan's version of coming for me.

"She won't talk, so you tell me what happened."

I scoot forward and rest my head back. Drawling, I say, "If she doesn't want to share, why should I?"

"So I can gauge what kind of bodily harm I will do to you. If I have to serve time, I want it to be fair."

"Ryan, I'm really not in the mood for this." Or for anything, really. I toss an arm over my face, wishing her away.

Softly, she asks, "Why did she go to her sister's wedding on her own when you were supposed to take her?"

The only sounds filling up the living room come from our breathing, mine heavier. Unless she can hear how loud my heart is thumping.

"Shit." I snarl the word and sit back up. Rubbing my head, I add, "Double shit."

"Spill."

"She said she's in love with me."

Ryan draws in air through her teeth. "Oh, Maddie."

"And on a scale of one to ten, I was a jerk about it."

"Of course you were."

I glare at her, but the person I really want to punch is me. "You *know* I can't do relationships, Ryan. I'm just not that kind of guy. I've spent the whole week trying to do damage control so no word about what happened at that party with Maddie gets to Coach's ears. If it does, he's going to bench my ass. And I'm so damn spent, all I want is to be left alone until the next game. Are you happy now?"

"No, you fool. Of course I'm not happy." She throws her hands in the air. "I just wish you hadn't treated her like you cared more than you did."

Through gritted teeth, I say, "I care. As her friend."

"You're pathetic." Ryan shoots to her feet and marches over to the entrance, picking up her trash bag before she opens the door. She turns around for a moment. "You're letting the best girl you'll ever meet go because you care more about what your coach thinks than about your own damn feelings. I hope it's worth it."

She slams the door shut so hard the walls rattle.

"What the hell do you know about my feelings?" I shout too late. She's probably climbing down the stairs by now.

I'm left breathing hard, like a horse that tried really hard at a race and still lost it.

A burst of energy propels me to my feet, and I pace the length of the living room back and forth. Before I make a canal on the floor, I go to the kitchen and start taking ingredients out of the fridge and the pantry. Forget the pizza. I need to move my body. That's the best way to shut down my brain. I'll make arepa con pernil and pico de gallo from scratch. I will—

No, that reminds me of her. This is what we ate the night she hit her head. Well, I did. She doesn't eat meat because of freaking course. She's too good to even hurt a fly. And I hurt her. And I don't want her out of my life.

I rest my arms on the kitchen island, just breathing deep and thinking.

Ryan's wrong. It's not that I care about what Coach says just because. We're in the middle of regionals now. Missing two games—hell, missing a single game—could mean we lose. Or let's say Edwards doesn't mess up the first two games by some miracle and I get to play the semi-final and final. Recruiters would think he did the work for me.

But I miss her. So damn much. I want to just… be in the same place without her running. I want to at least be her friend. Which is what we should've been, but I had to go and be a horndog.

"I need to talk with her," I mumble to myself.

That'd be a good first step. If I explain myself better, maybe she'll be less hurt. She'll definitely see that she didn't do anything wrong, and it's entirely a me issue caused by my past shenanigans. And that if things were different…

I shake my head. No, I can't go down that road with her. What-ifs don't change this situation. We're still graduating and parting ways soon.

Besides, I shouldn't have assumed she didn't want me at the wedding. Especially not after she shared how gross some of her family members are to her. Like I told Ryan, friends give a shit about their friends, and I shouldn't leave Maddie to the vultures. At least not the full night. I already missed the actual ceremony and at least a couple of hours of the party, but I can still salvage this.

I start putting everything away. Instead of cooking, I quickly down a protein shake from a carton. Once I'm done, I take off my sweatshirt and head into my room. The tie and handkerchief that perfectly match the shade of her dress are neatly folded in my closet. I retrieve them, along with one of the suits I wear after games and put them on the bed.

I pick up my auditing textbook from the floor and spread it open on the page where I jammed the wedding invite. I drop it on top of the suit and quickly strip off my sweats. It will take maybe fifteen minutes to get dressed and into my car, then just under an hour to make it to the farm where the wedding's being held. Should be plenty of time to think about what to say and how.

CHAPTER 30
MADDIE

"Maddie, why aren't you with the others? I'm about to toss the bouquet."

I groan into my club soda.

I made a decision before coming to Meg's wedding. Option one, get thoroughly sloshed so I could put up with the full night of torture among Mom and other equally bad, or worse, relatives. Or option two, stay sober so I could drive away at the earliest chance. I chose the second one, and I regret it, because I haven't found a window of opportunity to hightail it out of here.

Every time I try, Mom seems to read my mind and gets between the exit and me. And apparently even the bride can now read my intentions, because I was just thinking this might be it. Most of the attendees who aren't dancing or still attacking the open bar are getting ready to watch the bouquet toss, which will be followed by the garter toss.

"It's okay. Your law school friends seem to not need any further competition."

We turn to the group of women. A couple of my sister's friends from the good ole days have even removed their heels so they can maneuver. That's how committed they are. Or maybe their feet hurt and they should've worn flats like me. We'll never know.

Meg shakes her head at them and shifts her attention back to me. She runs her hand down my arm until she grabs my hand. "Don't mind them. I want you there. You've looked gorgeous but sad all night, and this should be fun."

Swinging our hands, I say, "Dude, you've had a chance to look at me all night? I thought your eyes belonged to your hubby already."

"Looking at his beard gets tiring after a while." She grins. We both know they've been making moony faces at each other since the day they met in law school and that it'll be that way until the day death do them part.

According to Mom, she and Dad were the same until death did do them part. I've always yearned for something like that, even though deep down, I've never believed I would get it. I don't want another fresh reminder of how this whole thing isn't for me, so I try gently shooting my sister down again.

"I think I'm okay, but thanks."

"Is this related to that plus-one of yours who didn't show up?"

I grimace. "That's a bold assumption."

"Not quite." She shrugs one delicate shoulder. "It's all the harpies have been talking about tonight. Not even the shrimp caused such a sensation, unfortunately."

And the shrimp were massive. Here I thought it'd capture their attention for a bit.

I fold my arms. Even if the whole… thing with Aran hadn't gone down, I'd still have probably been miserable here, and we both know it. Mom's still annoyed by the fact I'm not wearing the bolero she spent extra money on to hide my arms with. She still tells everyone my work options are open after graduation. My cousins still openly call me a loser for never having a boyfriend. One of the bridesmaids keeps pushing me to the corner spots in pictures, probably to crop me out later. And I'm really hungry, because for some reason, the vegetarian options flew off the tables first.

As if that all wasn't enough, I just had to add some severe form of heartbreak to all that, huh?

"Yeah, well. If you know, you wouldn't want to rub my eternal singlehood in my face."

"It's not that, silly. I just want to see you have a little bit of fun. Will you give me that gift tonight?" Meg has the nerve to pout all cutely, and even if I try, there's no way I could get angry at my sister. She's the only angel in this family, and to date, I don't understand how she can transform into an intense bloodhound in court.

"Fine."

"Yes!" She pumps her fist and leans forward to give me a one-armed hug, mindful of not squishing the famous bouquet between us. When she pulls away, she says, "That guy's a complete bonehead and doesn't deserve any of your time. You'll find a better one who worships the ground you walk on. You'll see."

I'm not sure if I'm smiling or grimacing. I'm sure there are better guys than Aran out there. Somewhere. Probably in Iceland or in Laos. Where I'll never meet them.

She drags me toward the fray and squeezes my hand one more time before letting go. As Meg takes her position and the cameras start rolling, I let the throng of women swallow me. The ones who show the most interest in catching the bouquet elbow their way to the front quite violently. I'm happy to hang out bruise-less at the back.

"Ready?" Meg screams, and the hyenas screech in response.

It is kind of funny. But it's also kind of sad that we're all out here desperately looking for love in a silly tradition when men are so… unavailable. Let's call it that.

My sister swings the bouquet once, twice, and throws. Amid squeals, the women struggle, trying to trace the arch. It's pretty high. The beautiful arrangement of white roses and pink peonies spins in the air, tendrils of decorative ribbon making quite a lovely swirl in the air. This will show up in the highlight reels of the night.

I frown. Goodness, Meg should've been a football quarterback. This thing is still going.

Straight to me.

"Oh, crap." The pack of hyenas skid as they try to change tack. I take a few steps back, one eye on them and one on the flowers.

One thing happens and one doesn't. The one that does is that I shut my eyes tight and extend my hands just in case, but instead of protecting me, something soft and perfumed lands in them. The one that doesn't happen is that I don't get run over.

I crack one eye open. The women groan, some glare. But no one's busting the hockey enforcer moves on me to steal the bouquet. Beyond them, Meg is doing a happy dance, as if this was her plan all along. I wouldn't put it past her.

Mom materializes right next to me. "Smile for the cameras, sweetie."

This time I'm sure there's a grimace on my face instead of a smile.

"Isn't this great, Maddie!" Meg makes her way over, grinning from ear to ear. "Can't wait to attend your wedding next."

"First she has to find a man," Mom says through a tight smile as we get pictures taken. "Any man will do at this point."

"Gee, Mom. I'm only twenty-one, and this isn't the Regency era."

She's squinting at something in the distance instead of paying attention to me, though. "Who is that?"

"Who?" Meg asks, standing on her tippy-toes to try to see around the people on the dance floor.

"Anyway, I'm going to—"

My words die in my mouth because a stirring in the crowd catches my attention too. Between the strobe lights flashing in the dark and the people coming and going or dancing out of sync to a DJ relying mostly on playlists, it's hard to see. But I see it, all right. It would be impossible to miss a guy who is a foot taller than me.

I turn into a statue, which my Mom and Meg notice immediately.

And Meg, being the smart one of the family, immediately says, "Wait, is that your plus-one?"

He's wearing the tie I got him.

I should've run away earlier.

Aran makes a determined straight line toward me, and I try to peel away, but Mom's vise grip on my arm won't let me.

"Maddie, I'm sorry I'm late," he says, as if anyone asked him. Before I can react, he extends his hand to my mom. "Hi, I'm Aran Rodriguez, Maddie's plus-one."

"Oh?" Mom looks him up and down. Twice. And then turns to me with a cocked eyebrow. "Is that so?" If disbelief turned into a human being, it would be her right now.

Meanwhile, my sister says, "So great you could come! You've missed a lot of the fun, though."

Aran is his usual impassive self, and tonight, it irritates me. I wish he had the capacity to look contrite, at least because it would mean he cares enough to feel that. But maybe I shouldn't expect feelings out of someone who hasn't committed to them. That's my fault.

"Mom, Megs. I need to talk with Aran for a moment." I hand Mom the flowers and add, "Alone."

"Of course." Meg laces her arm with Mom's and pulls her away, saying, "Let's go see if Justin's ready for the garter toss."

"But—"

"Come, Mother."

Crap, why did I send them off? As much as I didn't want them to engage with Aran, I also don't want to be alone with him. I've been avoiding it for a week for reasons. The main one being that looking into his eyes makes me want to bawl mine out.

I keep my attention on my folded arms as I ask, "What are you doing here?"

"I figured you may need a friend." If he notices my flinch, he ignores it and keeps going. "And friends are there for friends in need, right?"

"Is that what you think we are now?"

That gets me no response. Slowly, I take in his frame, pausing at the tie and the handkerchief neatly tucked into the breast pocket of his suit jacket, then continuing on until I finally reach those piercing eyes of his. And by the look of them, he's trying to read my mind.

"And who is this tall drink of water?"

Oh, great. It's my cousin Stacey, the Lori of the family, along with my cousin Leah, her lackey. I forgot that getting Mom to give us some privacy didn't extend to the rest of the family.

She slides next to us, closer to Aran. Funny enough, he slides right up to me.

"I'm Maddie's plus-one" is all he says, the fabric of his jacket brushing my arm. So close and yet so far.

Stacey's eyes ping-pong between us. "Really. Maddie, did you really have to hire an escort service to impress us?"

Leah snorts a laugh.

I check in on Aran. He doesn't seem insulted, but even so, I tell him, "I assure you not everyone in my family is as disgusting. Just about half of them."

"What did you just call me?"

Aran's lips twitch. He leans down to whisper in my ear. "I'm game if you want to give them a show."

Of course he is. As long as it's for fun only.

Well, no more. I can't go ahead with our fake dating scheme. Or the kisses that make me want more. I'm done. I don't care if my relatives think I had to hire some hot guy so I wouldn't look pathetic. I don't give a crap about what anyone else thinks anymore.

I offer a saccharine smile to my cousins. "You guys go find someone else to belittle. Heaven knows that's the only thing that makes your miserable lives keep going. My plus-one and I are leaving."

As if on cue, Aran circles my waist with his arm and leads me away. I keep going even when he stops, and he has no choice but to follow me out. At the front of the converted barn, a teenage boy asks for my coat ticket and makes a face when I fish it from my bustier. Aran doesn't give him a ticket, though, and we wait in silence until I get my coat.

Outside, his steps echo in the quiet night, the party noise well behind us.

"Why are you here, Aran?" I finally break the calm, keeping my attention ahead while crossing the expanse of grass toward the parking lot.

"I told you."

I stop and turn around, catching him in the middle of rubbing his head like he does when he's stressed out. There's a crease between his eyebrows. This is the expression I wanted to see earlier, but now it brings no satisfaction. I feel...

Empty.

"We're not friends," I say, my voice soft but surprisingly firm. "I don't know what we were, but it wasn't exactly that."

His shoulders sag when he drops his arm. "Maddie, we are friends. We've been friends all along. We can keep being friends."

"Maybe that's what you think, but I can't." I shake my head several times, my eyes lowering progressively until they fall into the abyss between us. "I can't keep seeing you if I want to have any hope of getting over you."

Aran swallows so thickly even I hear it. His voice comes out like gravel when he says, "So, what? Are we supposed to be strangers now? Is that… Is it really what you want?"

I squeeze my eyes shut, trying to contain the tears pooling in them. Bundling into my fluffy coat, I turn my back on him and say, "You can't have your cake and eat it too." And with an even more quiet voice, I add, "Sorry you came all this way for this."

And again, like that night at the Bolt House, Aran doesn't follow.

CHAPTER 31
ARAN

"**R**odriguez, what the hell is this?"

It's not so much the question as it is the anger behind it that clears some of the fog from my brain. I'm sitting at my assigned bench in the locker room at the arena belonging to our first regionals opponent. The whole place vibrates with energy from the crowd. The locker room buzzed until the moment Coach Green strode in with his phone held high, his face red, and his nostrils flaring.

I fumble with my jersey until I manage to slide it down all the way. That's when Coach shoves his phone in my face and I freeze. Every molecule in my body just turns to ice. Except for my heart. That bastard races fast.

Someone posted an Instagram video of a couple kissing in the St. Cloud library. But it's not just any couple. It's Maddie and me, the first time we kissed. The angle mostly captures me in the act of, well, basically eating her mouth like dessert. My hand's tangled in her hair. Hers are cradling my face, and my body is arched over hers.

For a week and a half, I've been so careful. Half the guys on the team basically became my bodyguards to keep Kelsey and Co away from the facilities and me. Even despite her newest attempts at contacting me, I managed to avoid her.

Of course my lies would catch up to me right when they'll hurt the must.

"You must've thought I'd never find out, huh?" Coach removes his phone from my face, and everything about his expression tells me I'm done for. Sure enough, he confirms it by saying, "You are officially benched."

"What?" Archie springs to his feet. "Coach, you can't—"

"I can, and I will!"

Noise explodes around the locker room. The prevailing comments stem from confusion.

Edwards, of course, preens like a damn rooster. "Aw, yeah. My time to shine has come." And if he didn't look so damn surprised, I'd suspect him of doing this.

But no. It must've been Kelsey. Maybe she overheard Coach's threat that time. She certainly saw the drama between Maddie and me go down. She knew this would hurt the most.

"Coach." Archie slides up to the man, speaking lower. "We're already down Amadi. We could lose this game without Rodriguez."

"We had a deal, son," Coach says to me, ignoring my assistant captain's pleas. "You broke it, so there will be consequences." Spittle flies from his mouth as he screams the words at me, pointing his finger accusingly.

As Coach turns, probably to tell the refs about the player change, Archie hits my shoulder. "Dude, don't you have anything to say?"

But all I do is shake my head. For the first time in my life, I wish I could talk, but words refuse to come out.

Of course I deserve to be punished. I went behind Coach's back. I played a game with Madeline Berkley that neither of us was truly ready for. I tried to have my cake and eat it too. I deserve to be kicked while I'm already down.

I finish suiting up by rote. As the captain, I still have to sit on the bench. The entire way out, the guys try to pry anything out of me, but I can barely focus on moving one skate first and then the other. The cold in the arena has never affected me until this moment, as I skate out just for the national anthem and back to the bench.

It's like I'm here but I'm not. Because my mind is on Maddie. And how embarrassed she must be feeling after this video was posted online.

And how she cut me out of her life, and now I have no hope of getting back in it.

And how much I hate it.

"First line, go out there and salvage this. Webber, don't let them score. Don't let your captain's mistakes ruin the rest of the season for you, do you hear me?"

The weak round of *yes, sir* stirs me. The guys look uncertain. But there's no time to even think about how to reassure them. The game starts, and I can tell from the moment the puck drops that this is the real punishment. Sitting on my ass out here, having ruined the team's mojo without even lifting a finger.

Anxiety starts building up in a way it never does when I'm on the net. My knee bounces. I can feel sweat pooling in my mitts and under my clothes. It's not that the other team is that much better; it's that we're in disarray. The first line doesn't carry the puck far enough without slamming into the other team's defense. And every time we lose the puck, Edwards overreacts about the littlest things.

I know the moment they're going to score on us before the rest of the guys do. When the buzzer goes off, only three minutes into the first period, Coach Green rips off his baseball cap and slams it onto the floor. As if maybe he's regretting his life choices too.

The puck is back in play after the cellies. There's something extra aggressive about the game now that we're down one. Two of our guys check an opponent against the boards hard, raising deafening booing from the crowd. One of the other guys tries to clear the puck and shoots it too high. My body moves by itself, and it takes me a moment to process that I just caught the flyaway puck barehanded from the bench.

My hand squeezes it hard as the play stops, and the memory of that conversation with Coach slams into me like a physical blow. Back then, I asked him if he'd hurt the team to teach me a lesson, and now it's clear he sure as shit would. And pin the full blame on me, as if he wasn't the one with the power and the full responsibility.

I tear my mask off and yell above the crowd's noise. "So you'd really see us lose this game, throw the whole damn season away, because I was seeing a girl?"

Coach looks from the puck in my hand to my face. "You're shitting me, right, Rodriguez? This isn't about some girl. It's about you not keeping your head in the game!"

"My head was fully in the damn game before you messed with it." I drop the puck back onto the ice in a full display of anger. "I have the highest save percentage in the division. And guess when I played my very best game? When I was with her!"

He jumps to his feet to push open the door to the tunnel. "Well, I don't give a shit. You broke my rules. You don't deserve to be on my team."

My throat already feels raw from screaming, but I don't care. I don't care about anything but the rage and frustration and the pit that sinks deeper and deeper in my gut. I, too, get on my feet and look down at Coach Green.

"Why the hell do I need to abide by different rules from the rest, huh? Why is it okay for the rest of the team to fool around and do whatever they please while I can't even fall in love?

Why can't I have a normal life? Why do I have to work so much damn harder?"

"Because you're different! Because guys like you have to work so much harder to prove to everyone else why you deserve a spot."

"What the hell does *guys like me* even mean?"

But we both know. Guys like Amadi and me. Guys who don't look like everyone else.

Coach's expression shifts the moment it hits me, and he tries to change tack by adding, "And on top of that, you're the captain. You're supposed to lead by example."

I'm not listening because the buzzer goes off again, and I don't need to see who scored with the way the whole place seems about to go down.

"Great, so you tried to teach me a lesson about how hard the world is for brown kids, as if I already didn't know that. Boo freaking hoo."

His face goes red. "Of course I didn't—"

"But if I'm the captain, then what are you?" Coach and I are breathing hard as we square off. I point toward the ice. "You could've blown up on my ass after we won this game, but no. You had to put me in my place in front of everyone and make a damn mess of tonight, huh? Please tell me again how this is supposed to help me."

"Don't you dare speak to me like—"

"Oh, I'm sorry. Let me say it more nicely: teaching me a lesson wasn't more important than the team. How's that for being the freaking captain?"

I push the door so hard it slams against the board and walk off the bench.

"If you walk away—"

"What?" I glare over my shoulder. "You'll kick me off the team? Good luck explaining that to the team and the boosters."

As I head to the hallway, I'm aware of many pairs of eyes on me. Blood roars in my ears. I let out my anger in a burst when I'm alone at my locker, throwing my helmet at the bench so hard it leaves a dent. And then I hit the locker with my stick for good measure.

I stand there, shaking from head to toe.

I'm the absolute stinking worst. She was right. I really wanted to have my cake and eat it too. I fooled myself into thinking what we were doing wasn't anything like dating and that no one would ever have to find out. Steps One and Two of my plan were a total bust the second I caught her making notes about me. I was drawn to her like a moth to a flame, and now I'm burning.

Because I'm in love with a girl who is obsessed with strawberries and writing and knitting and making me say *please* and *thank you*—and I realize now that I lost her while trying to keep something I already had.

Hockey will be there for the rest of my life, even if today's game is my last as a St. Cloud Thunder Bolt. I will never give up on this game, because I know I belong in it. And I'm not going to let assholes like Edwards and his connections, or Coach Green and his white savior complex, bring me down. But I gave up on her, even though, deep down, I knew I belonged with her.

I drop a mitt onto the floor and rub my eyes. This thing in my chest that's squeezing my lungs until I can barely gasp for air feels a lot like that night at the hospital after Luz took the hit.

I was just a nine-year-old kid, and I didn't understand a lot of what was going on, but I did get very well acquainted with a sense of loss. Pure dread filled me up, and I didn't know how to deal with it. So I lost my shit. Just absolutely went on a rampage in an ER waiting room, hitting chairs and people and myself, until they had to sedate me.

Somehow, I feel as if I've skipped all that now and I'm already sedated.

I feel nothing as I sit back on the bench. My ears barely register the noise from the stands above. I lean back against the closed locker and shut my eyes, wishing I could just sleep.

Is the rest of my life going to feel like this? Empty. Nauseating. Distant.

I can't.

That can't be it.

The door bursts open, and Assistant Coach Thomas sighs in relief when he sees me. "Oh, praise be. I thought you'd walked off the premises." He jerks a thumb behind him. "I cooled the hotshot down, and we're subbing you in."

"Why?"

"Because Edwards's friends in high places won't get him to actually catch a puck tonight. We need you, captain."

I rub my head. "I don't know if I can."

"What's that you said in an interview once?" He makes air quotes with his fingers and says, "'When I'm in the net, I don't think; I just am.' Some real philosophical crap that we're now banking on."

"Have I always been such a clown?" I mumble.

"C'mon, Rodriguez. Time to stop moping. Take care of your team first, and once we win this game, you can take care of whatever this mess is."

A plan.

Maybe that's what I need. A new plan. After all, I'm a numbers guy. And that sounds like a good one to me.

New Step One: win this game.

New Step Two: avoid Coach, deal with him later. Or never. Whichever one's easier.

New Step Three: …

That one stays blank for a moment. I drove an hour to some barn wedding in the middle of freaking nowhere so I could explain myself to Maddie, and she shut me down basically on sight. She's determined to get over me, and probably more so after this whole video leak.

But she needs to not see me so she can forget me, which is exactly what I don't want. Something hot explodes in my chest and imbues my limbs with renewed energy.

New Step Three: set up camp at the library until Madeline Berkley acknowledges my existence.

I jump to my feet and grab my mask and stick. To make it to Three, I first have to make it through One.

"Let's go," I say.

CHAPTER 32
MADDIE

I feel like I'm going to die for real this time.

Every time my period's early, it feels worse. As if my uterus thinks it's my freaking fault that *it* is bleeding ahead of schedule.

"Just because you're graduating soon doesn't mean your conduct should deteriorate. Do you understand me?" Melinda says, tapping her finger at the phone screen where she just played a video of Aran and me making out that I know was leaked by Lori; she said so herself at the infamous party. Or maybe she sent it to Aran's ex. I don't know.

Slowly, I nod. "Yes, ma'am."

She leans back in her chair and folds her arms. For a good moment, all she does is regard me like she's intending to paint my portrait. Finally, she smirks a little.

"Now, not as your boss or as a staff member of this illustrious institution… you go, girl. Get it."

"Huh?" My head's spinning, vacillating between confusion and sheer, self-destructive pain.

"I thought you were a goodie two-shoes, but va-va-voom."

I can't believe I have the capacity to blush in these circumstances, but here I am. My face is so hot I could melt an iceberg.

Well, apparently not "the Iceberg." That one doesn't see me as va-va-voom enough, I guess.

Whatever.

"So, um. Am I going to get reprimanded or… or fired?" I ask in a shaky voice.

She snorts. "Of course not. Your private life is your business. Just, next time, keep it behind closed doors."

"Thanks?"

"Now, I know you have a student to tutor in"—she checks the massive decorative clock on the wall that only she can read—"eighteen minutes, so I suggest you get going."

That might not even be enough to make it to the library in time, with how slowly I'm moving. As I stand, it takes Herculean effort to stifle the groan threatening to spill out of my mouth at the stab of pain in my nether regions. I sway a little and grab the back of the chair.

"'Kay, see you later, Melinda."

"Bye, kiddo." Her attention goes back to her computer screen, and I'm dismissed.

Approximately ten years later, I manage to walk out of her office. Outside, I find Wyatt sipping gross coffee from a paper cup.

"Isn't it great?" Wyatt chirps as he joins me. "We're just a month and a half away from graduation. And even better, just two weeks from your book debut."

"Yay, so exciting."

I wince with every step away from the student center. Oh, how I wish I had a golf cart to take me all the way to the library. Or better yet, that I could teleport there. Or even better still, teleport into a life where I'm not such a loser. Wouldn't that be sweet?

"Why don't you look excited, though?"

Maybe because I have two aliens trying to tear my body apart from the inside. One is obvious. The other one is my heart. This excruciating pain today is nothing compared to how I've felt since…

I sniffle. No, I don't want to cry in public. Again. Today.

I thought I caught a glimpse of Aran earlier this morning. But the buzz cut was longer than usual and the guy had a bit of a beard. Similar build, though. And just a millisecond of wondering *is it him?* was enough to activate my tear glands. It made eating alone in the cafeteria very awkward.

The worst part is that I can't write. It was so much easier to work on a romance book while my heart was still in one piece. And I hate that he took that joy from me. I wish I could sock him a good one—and then hug him so tight he can't let go of me.

What has Aran Rodriguez done to me?

Wyatt still chatters beside me as we head to the library, and I make an effort to focus on his words. Whatever he's saying has to be better than my thoughts.

"—taking him to the book launch?"

"What? Sorry, I zoned out."

He takes a deep breath. "I said, are you taking your make-out partner to the book launch?"

Nope. Never mind. My thoughts were safer.

I try to go the safe route by saying, "I don't need to take a date to my book launch."

"So, were you dating him?" He nudges me, and I'm too weak to avoid it.

"Would you look at that. At this pace, I'm going to be late. See you later!" But my traitorous body can't go any faster.

"Hmm." He falls quiet, and it makes the trip to the library more bearable. But when we get to the building and he opens the door for me, I see something in his expression I don't like. Pity. And it's not just in my head, because he says, "If you need a rebound, just let me know. One of my friends is interested."

"What?"

"Apparently, he saw you dancing at some party, and voilà, instant crush."

I grunt. The only party I danced at was the one that crushed my heart. I don't need any reminders of that night.

Wyatt chuckles. "Whoda thunk our little Maddie was such a femme fatale?"

Yeah, right. Some femme fatale I am in my cozy cardigan with pockets shaped like bunnies' heads and a dress that could be worn by my grandma. There is no vestige of the confident Maddie of that night, the one who wore a full face of makeup and a dress that hid very little. Rather, if I could wear my fluffy blanket outside the apartment, I would. I'd stay under it until my demise.

"Thanks, but I'll pass," I mumble as we enter the quiet area at the front of the library. I'm absolutely drained from this conversation, this day, and my life, in that order.

"The offer's standing. See you later, gator."

"Bye, Wyatt." My smile is more grimace than joy.

My face stays locked like that as I make my way upstairs to the study area. I'm pretty sure my student is already waiting there and is probably docking points off my rating. He's one of those pretentious freshmen who got into this school because they're a legacy and can't face up to the fact that he's not as smart as he thought he was. Sessions with him are always a hoot—and I say that with sarcasm as thick as honey.

Sure enough, my student's there. And he's sitting all the way at the back, as if he knew making me walk the entire length of the building was the perfect punishment for me.

"You're late," he says in his snooty voice.

"Which means we don't have a second to waste, right?" I say this with a sugary smile, and it's the perfect way to cut his tirade short. He mumbles something that I probably don't want to discern.

As I settle down and take my things out of my bag, I explain how I would structure the essay he has to write. This kid needs tutoring in the same kind of thing as Aran, and it makes me wonder how it's going for the Bolts captain with his new tutor. When I canceled my remaining sessions with him, I made sure Melinda shifted him over to a guy tutor like Aran intended all along.

I hope he's freaking happy now with his hockey and his tutor-dude and—

I shouldn't think like this. Aran didn't lead me on or treat me like crap. He even wanted to stay friends. I'm the one who can't see past her giant, flaming torch for him.

Sighing, I open my laptop and try to do some writing. I get as far as three words—*He doesn't want*—before my mind goes kaput. The hero of my novel is supposed to be professing his love for the heroine because he doesn't want to live without her. But she has her reservations because she's been played one too many times. It's almost like I reversed the roles without realizing it until now.

"Hey, what should I do if this happens?" my student asks, his voice grouchy.

I tear my eyes away from my screen to see what he's pointing at, but something distracts me from the corner of my eye.

It's *him*. The one who doesn't want me in real life.

Aran sits at the table in front of mine, facing me directly. He's drinking a green concoction like on the day we met. And like then, his eyes observe me from above the rim of his sports bottle.

My heart rate spikes. I follow my student's finger to where it's pointing at an error message on his computer. Apparently, I'm supposed to know IT now.

"Um, I don't know. Maybe try restarting?"

"I can't do that. I didn't save my work, you dolt!"

I frown. "Not my fault, and no need for name calling."

"Whatever." He smacks his computer a few times. I go back to mine.

Lies and deceit. My eyes go straight back to Aran instead of to my work.

This time his aren't on me. They're narrowed at my student as if he's plotting a dark academia book in his mind.

This is why I fell for him. Little things like this that made me feel like he cared. And maybe he did. But it really freaking sucks when the guy you like only cares for you as a friend. I don't know how other people cope, because I can't. I paw around the table until I find my favorite pen and my journal and make a note to consider the unrequited love trope for my next hockey book. Except my characters will get the happy ending I didn't. It'll be cathartic.

I pause. This is the first time I've felt inspired at all in weeks.

Dang Aran. He's both the sickness and the cure.

I bite my lip and put my hands on my keyboard. Let's focus on the words, not on the boy staring at me across the tables, not on the rude student next to me, not on the throbbing stabs of pain in my abdomen. Just the writing. Nothing else.

After that whole pep talk, I end up typing some gibberish. Instead of focusing, I peep over the edge of my laptop screen and almost jump out of my skin.

Aran is smiling at me. It's that slow, tiny smile that looks like a smirk from afar but warms his eyes until they're molten chocolate. The one that often preceded a kiss for the ages.

I can't take this anymore.

Without thinking, I spring to my feet and scamper away from the tables. Pure nerves give me the speed I lacked earlier, and I only stop when I'm behind one of the massive bookcases. I need a quiet moment alone to compose myself.

I breathe so hard that my head spins, and as I steady myself against the bookcase, I realize something's very wrong. And it's not that Aran is approaching this little nook.

No, my vision keeps swimming, and I can no longer control my limbs. My hands drop like lead, and my mind finally catches up to what's happening.

I'm about to pass out.

CHAPTER 33
ARAN

One moment—and for the first time in my life—I'm optimistic about starting a conversation. The next, I see Strawberry's eyes roll closed and she plummets to the floor.

The world stops as her head hits the bookshelf at a weird angle. The thud's echo reaches me halfway across the expanse.

And then she hits the floor.

I don't even think. I take off at full speed and leap over a table on the way. I grow tunnel vision, and there, all I see is her unmoving form.

Es Luz, otra vez, es Luz otra vez.

That little voice incessantly repeats that even as I kneel before her. Only when I stop do I realize several things. I'm panting like a stinking horse. She's really pale and unresponsive. There's blood trickling slowly onto the carpet.

"Shit, shit, shit. Maddie, wake up."

I know I can't move her. My hands hover in the air, frozen. But I can't let her keep bleeding. As I'm tearing off my sweatshirt, I feel someone behind me.

"What's happening?"

I fold up the fabric quickly, and with shaky hands, I press it against the back of her head. My eyes run over her frame, stopping at her chest. I see it rise and fall, and some of the adrenaline rushes out of me. Some. I should call 911, but how long would they take to get here? Should I take her to the hospital instead?

Finally, I turn and find the guy she was tutoring. His eyes are wide as boiled eggs looking at the scene.

"Get our stuff and follow me," I command.

"Um—"

"Now, man! Can't you see she's bleeding?"

"Er, okay."

I'm praying harder than I have since Luz's accident while I carefully maneuver Maddie in my arms. Her head lolls over my shoulder, and the sweatshirt falls to the floor. Hope returns to my body when I see the bloodstains are small.

"Stay with me," I whisper to her, rushing through the library with her pupil on our tail.

In record time, I bundle her into the passenger seat of my SUV and strap her in. The dude dumps all our junk in the back seat, and when we're done, I race to the driver's seat. This time my hands are steady as I turn on the car and fasten my seat belt.

A little moan echoes in the quiet, and I still. But she doesn't open her eyes yet.

By some miracle, I catch all the green lights on the way to the hospital. It's the second time in as many months that I have to go to that damn place, and the closer I get to it, the more I sweat. The more my muscles spasm. The more my chest feels like there's an elephant sitting on it. This is why I've never wanted to get involved with anyone. Somehow, I always end up coming here with the women I love. I hate it. I hate it. I hate it so damn much that I'm trying not to barf all over the dashboard.

I park sideways between two spots. Everyone will just have to deal with it. Even though my breathing's getting shorter and shorter and my vision blurs, I pick Maddie up again and settle her head safely against my shoulder.

"You're going to be fine, little Strawberry. We're going to be good."

I put one foot forward, and then the other. I can't remember whether I shut my car door, but I don't turn back until I'm in the ER. And I don't stop until someone brings a gurney for her and wheels her away. I'm aware of someone asking me shit, but all I can do is stand there, shaking like a leaf. My clothes stick to my skin while buckets of cold sweat keep pouring out. All I can see is the white of the walls. I can taste the hospital smell, that stench of chemicals and detergent and faint traces of blood.

I shut my eyes and force myself to breathe, even though I really don't want to inhale more of that scent. I ball my hands tight, and the pain of my fingers digging into my palms grounds me a bit.

This isn't like what happened to Luz. I didn't lose anyone that night. I'm not going to lose anyone today. It's going to be fine. I'll get my chance to tell Maddie how I really feel.

"—sit down?"

Those two words penetrate through my mind, and I blink hard. An older nurse gently leads me to a chair in the waiting area. I feel like I'm nine years old again, except this time, it doesn't take two people and a syringe to calm me the hell down. I comply, and the fight drains out of me when I park my ass on a chair. For a moment, I feel like I'm going to pass out too.

"That's a good boy," the woman says with a kind but firm voice. "Now, can you tell me exactly what happened? It will help us treat your friend."

I open my mouth, and nothing comes out. After shaking

my head hard enough to hurt, I tell her what I saw and what I did. She asks for her information, but all I can give is her name, age, and weight because she told me that once.

"Do you know her emergency contact? Her insurance provider?"

"I—No." I rub my forehead. "But her things are in my car."

"Bring them over, honey. We may find the information in her phone or wallet."

I do. At this point, I can't think any longer. I don't even want to. I'm terrified my mind will transport me back in time again. So I follow the woman's instructions like I wouldn't pass a Captcha. We go through Maddie's wallet and find an insurance card. Turns out she had her mom listed on her iPhone's emergency contact, and the nurse can access it without knowing the password. I bundle everything back into her purse and wait by the counter while the nurse enters the data into a computer and calls Maddie's mother.

When the nurse is done, she turns to me again and smiles. "Take a seat, honey."

Honey this, honey that. What makes her think I'm sweet? I'm so bitter right now, it's all I can taste in my mouth as I return to my chair.

Was this my fault?

If I hadn't tried to approach her… Am I such persona non grata that she can't stand the sight of me anymore? No, I'm being a damn fool. This wasn't my fault, but maybe something's wrong with her, and that's even worse to think about.

I set her bag on the chair beside me and lean my arms on my knees, bending over until my hands hold my head. I don't know how long I stay like that, but I only come out of it when a vaguely familiar voice goes off nearby.

"Where is my Maddie?"

Slowly, I lift my head. A red-haired woman stands at the

information desk. I see her in profile. Some of Maddie's features are etched on her face, and the same panic I felt earlier is there too. The nurse talks for a good moment, but I'm too far away to hear her calm voice. After a moment, though, she points at me, and Maddie's mom glances my way. Recognition flashes in her eyes, and she starts heading over. For lack of anything else to do, I get to my feet and wait.

"You're Maddie's plus-one," she says, still a few paces away. But then when I think she'll stop, she doesn't. Instead, she squeezes her arms around me hard enough to crack ribs. "Thank you, thank you, thank you."

"I—uh—"

Then she sniffles, and I have no choice but to stay still.

Fortunately, that only lasts a second before she steps away. Her chin trembles the same way as her daughter's does when she's crying. "The nurse told me what you did. Thank you so much for taking care of my Maddie."

I rub the back of my head, pressing hard. Something about the words *my Maddie* has shut down my brain.

Ironically, I'm rescued by a doctor striding over with a flip chart in her hand. "Madeline Berkley's guardians?"

Her mother basically teleports to the doctor's side and pours some verbal vomit on her. "Yes, I'm her mom! Is she okay? What happened with her? Is it bad? Will she recover?"

All questions I also want the answers to.

"Yes, she's fine. It's a mild concussion," the physician says offhandedly as she flips the chart open and checks something. "Her sugar and iron were extremely low, and there's something else in her bloodwork we've sent to a specialist to check."

A spe—

Before I can even formulate the question in my mind, Maddie's mom asks, "What kind of specialist?"

"A gynecologist."

"A what?" While she screeches, the woman turns to me. "You didn't get my daughter pregnant, did you?"

"What? No!" I gape.

"No, she's definitely not pregnant," the doctor cuts in before this can escalate. "Her hormones just look off, but it doesn't seem like a thyroid issue. Anyway, the gynecologist will diagnose her accordingly."

This is all going over my head but... it doesn't sound like Maddie's in danger.

I collapse into the chair with a great huff that catches their attention for a second. They talk some more about logistics and payments, and because they have Maddie in a busy area, only her mother is allowed to go sit with her. I give the woman her daughter's bag, and there's still a frown on her face when she looks at me. Maybe she thinks I'm relieved that her daughter's not pregnant. Little does she know I haven't done even one-quarter of the things I want to do with Maddie.

If she lets me, of course. If she even gives me the time of the day again.

Today, just the sight of me was enough to make her run, even though her tank was so empty she fainted. That's how little she wants to be in the same room as me.

But if she was completely indifferent to me, she wouldn't have run.

As I finally leave the hospital, I wonder if I'm wrong for feeling a little hope.

CHAPTER 34
MADDIE

When I open my eyes, and the first thing I see is my mother's face, I immediately know something's up.

"Whargh?"

Wow, what was that gibberish that just came out of my mouth?

I try to sit up and—nope. My body's not having it. In fact, I may not even have a body anymore. I've officially turned into a raw nerve that has been stabbed in the deepest fiber.

"Maddie, sweetie," my mother says, and I feel her cold hand grab mine. "Does your head hurt that bad? Excuse me, my daughter needs stronger—"

"Not my head. It's my freaking *uterus!*" Every word comes out as a groan, and the last one as a scream. Too late I realize I don't even know if I'm someplace where it's okay to vociferate about my lady parts.

Mom sounds perplexed as she asks, "Your what?"

It takes monumental effort to open my eyes and survey the situation. By the fluid bag hanging next to my bed, and the fact I'm in a bed, I put two and two together. Gasping, I think back to what happened. One moment, I was trying to hide from Aran behind a bookshelf in the library, and the next... nothing. Until now.

I fainted again.

Oh no. I fainted *in front of Aran*.

His name spills out of my mouth unbidden, and Mom surprises me by squeezing my hand. "Your boyfriend seems like a decent fellow—strong too, because he carried you here. But I don't want you sleeping with him nilly willy, Maddie. What if the problem is that you're pregnant? You're just twenty-one!"

"What?" A couple other patients and a nurse turn at my screech. Pulling up the thin blanket, I hide my face with it. "Mother, what the heck are you talking about?"

"Aaron, right? Your boyfriend who arrived late at Meg's wedding and whisked you away."

I could cry. Or laugh. The sound that comes from my throat is a combination.

"It's Aran, not Aaron. And he's not my boyfriend. No pregnancy. Oh my word!"

She settles back on the chair and smooths the bedsheet as far as she can reach. "Well, the doctor did say you weren't pregnant, but I just wanted to make sure."

"I'd say a doctor is even more reliable than me."

"I just worry about you. You're my baby."

Irritation surges up my throat, and I clamp my mouth tight to hold it back. I don't want to explode on my mother in the middle of what is clearly an ER, surrounded by patients and hospital staff coming and going.

After taking a few deep breaths, I say through gritted teeth, "Don't worry, Mom. It's as you suspected at Meg's wedding. Aran and I are just friends. It's inconceivable that he'd impregnate me."

"I didn't say it was inconceivable. In fact—"

"No, it was written all over your face."

She huffs. "Okay, maybe I was surprised. But not now. The way he was so eaten up with worry out there, you'd think the guy's wife was going into labor."

I bark out an awkward laugh that makes my abdomen spasm painfully. "Mom, please stop. If you keep saying absurd stuff like that, I'll have to laugh, and it makes my womb hurt."

"Then, what is wrong with your…" With a frown, she leans down and whispers, "Nether regions?"

Where's a black hole when you need one to swallow you whole?

"My uterus, mother. You know my periods are murderous."

Her whole face, so much like Meg's, with slim cheeks and a pointy nose, scrunches up. "To the point of fainting?"

I sigh. "Yes, this isn't the first time."

"What do you mean by that?"

At the edge in her voice, I realize that, uh, yeah… I made teenage Meg swear she'd never tell our mother, and Meg happens to be really good at keeping secrets. She's turned it into a professional career, even.

So, nine years later, I finally confess the whole story to Mom. One afternoon, some months after I'd gotten my first period, Meg and I were alone at home. I had a really bad pain episode and basically dropped like an anvil in the middle of a conversation with my sister. Cue her panicking, thinking I'd just spontaneously died on her, until I came to a few minutes later.

Of course, being a responsible person, Meg wanted to tell Mom the second she walked through the door. But I was twelve, okay? Everything about periods was extremely embarrassing, and we both knew Mom's capacity for making a whole mountain range out of a molehill. I begged Meg to not say anything unless it happened again, and it didn't. She sort of forgot about it.

Except I didn't. Knowing that, with every period, I could get pain so severe I could lose consciousness has made me walk on eggshells every month—or whenever my dang period does end up arriving. I have to walk closer to furniture, move slower, do less, and I've been okay taking all those precautions.

Until today, when I thought I could outrun a whole elite athlete. Or rather, not him, but my feelings for him. I simply have Mom's talent of making a whole mountain range out of a molehill. The time has come to accept that I truly am her daughter.

When I finish the tale, Mom's jaw is dropped. "Maddie! Why did you never say so?"

"I have." I know I sound like a whiny baby, and I don't care. "I've told you a million times my periods are extremely bad, and you never believed me."

"You never said they're bad enough to faint!"

"Well, you should've just taken me at my word! You and every doctor who's thought I was exaggerating for attention!"

"Shh! This is a hospital, for goodness' sake."

We both shut up at the admonishment. I hide under the blanket, but Mom has nowhere to go, so she sits there, her cheeks as red as apples and wearing an expression that says this is far from over. But as far as I'm concerned, it is. I'm done telling her my body hates me. And I'm even more done talking to her about anything and having her dismissing it.

The silence between us stretches unbearably until a doctor shows up at the foot of my bed. He grabs a chart, scans it quickly, and joins Mom at the side of the bed.

"Hi, I'm Dr. Pranad, RE."

"RE?" Mom and I ask at the same time. We exchange an annoyed glance.

"Reproductive Endocrinologist."

Mom draws in a sharp breath, and I cut in before she talks. "Mom, for the last time, I am *not* preg—"

"She's not pregnant," the doctor says with a nod. "But she may need a gynecologist who also specializes in hormones. That's me."

"Oh."

While Mom eases back in her chair, I sit up straighter. "Hormones? Do I have a problem with my hormones?"

"Maybe. We'll run some tests starting now if you're up for it."

"Oh, I am so up for it." Tears brim in my eyes as if on cue. "I'm so ready to finally figure out what the hell is wrong with me."

"Madeline, language!"

"Fine, Mother. I will express myself in clearer terms." Turning to the doctor, I ask, "Dr. Pranad, can you please help me find out what in the actual hell is wrong with me?"

"Madeline!" Mom hits me in the arm hard enough that I'm sure it's left a mark, but all I do is laugh. Especially when the physician himself looks like he's holding back his own amusement.

I thought because I landed in the ER, the test would be some fancy, bank-breaking stuff. But no. It was just a good old ultrasound and more bloodwork.

But from the ultrasound results alone, Dr. Pranad says, "Yep, you have PCOS."

Mom gasps, bringing her hands to her mouth in abject horror. I shift wide eyes between her and the doctor.

"Um, is that cancer?" I ask.

"No, no. Polycystic ovary syndrome basically means your ovaries don't work like they should."

My hand flies up to rub my nape like Aran does all the time. The sharp pain in my head makes me realize what I'm doing. I drop my hand back to my lap.

"You have some of the visible signs," the doctor keeps saying, all blasé. "More body hair than average, overweight, extreme period pain. You probably have too much androgen too, but we'll confirm that in a few days."

"Doctor." Mom is serious as she cuts in. "What does that mean for my daughter? Like, for her health and her daily life. Is she going to be okay?"

"Sure, I have many patients with PCOS." He shrugs, because obviously, this issue doesn't want to unalive him every month. "Madeline's particular case looks to be on the severe end. It's a good thing she's getting diagnosed early, before any irreversible complications."

I swallow hard. "Like what?"

"Worst case, type-two diabetes, heart issues, masses, and fertility issues."

"Oh no." Mom's pale and wringing her hands. "What should she do to manage this?"

"Eat healthy, exercise. Losing weight helps—"

"I told you—"

But before Mom finishes, the doctor adds, "But my patients often say it's extremely hard to do so, and I get it. Your weight can naturally be off range when your hormones are out of whack."

"Thank you!" I throw my hands in the air and go the extra petty way and turn to Mom. "I told *you* so!"

"But you can still eat healthy and exercise," she snips back.

"I climb four sets of stairs up and down every day. I wouldn't say I'm a freaking sloth."

"The contraceptive pill also helps," Dr. Pranad says into the ether, because Mom and I are in our dimension.

"You can't possibly call that exercising, Madeline."

"Well, do you want me to join a CrossFit gym or something? Good luck getting me to lift weights that could kill me if I faint because of my period pain."

"It doesn't have to be so extreme. Just walking every day is fine. And also layoff the takeout."

I throw my head back and laugh. "I do takeout once a week, Mom. I can't afford more than that."

"Then why are you so… so chubby?"

"It's the PCOS," the doctor says.

Mom turns sharply to him. "But didn't you say the way to treat it is by losing weight?"

"Yes."

"That makes no sense," Mom fires back.

He nods. "Yes, I know."

"What?" The question is more rhetorical, because she leans back and shifts her attention to me as if seeing me for my first time. Blinking hard, as if she can't quite believe the picture she's seeing.

I wipe a tear from my cheek. "I told you it wasn't my fault. I told you it's not like I want to be this way. It's just how I am."

"But…"

Dr. Pranad checks his watch. "Sorry to cut this short, but I have another patient waiting. Madeline, set up an appointment after your bloodwork results are in, okay?"

"Yes, sir," I say in a mumble. "Um, thank you for everything."

Mom also expresses her gratitude, and we tumble out of the office into the hallway. Well, I do. Mom grabs me by the arm and steadies me. I don't know if it's because the painkillers haven't fully kicked in yet or if it's because I'm just shaken by the whole thing.

"So the good news is that I'm not dying, even though I do feel like crap," I say too lightly.

The crease between Mom's eyebrows deepens. "Yes, that is definitely good."

"The bad news is that I'm probably going to keep being fat for the rest of my life."

As we walk down the hall, Mom sighs several times. Finally, she says, "Sweetie, I don't hate that you're fat—"

"Sure could've fooled me."

"I've just always worried that you weren't healthy."

"Funny, I always thought I was. Do you know how many salads vegetarians eat?" I snort. We exit the building at my snail's pace, and people look at the bandage around my head, probably imagining I had some terrible accident.

"Well, but you're not fully healthy, right? Otherwise, your ovaries would be normal." She stops us in the middle of the parking lot and muses aloud. "Come to think, Dr. Pranad didn't say *why* your ovaries aren't normal."

In her car, we Google PCOS and find an answer. A bull crap one: no one knows why ovaries act up and cause PCOS.

"Great." I grunt. "I basically have an unknown thing that has no specific treatment. Just peachy."

We're quiet as she drives away from the hospital. I'm so tired, even though it's barely noon and I haven't done much today—aside from making an absolute fool of myself and collecting new medical debt. What a great day.

It takes me a moment to recognize the streets, and I say, "Oh, I no longer live here. I moved."

"You what? Why the hickory am I just finding that out now?"

"Because we don't talk, Mom. Or rather, every time we do, you just want to complain about how imperfect I am and you don't care how much it hurts."

"I don't—" She splutters for a bit. "I'm your mother, Madeline. It's my job to worry about you."

"Well, just—stop worrying and accept me as I am!"

Aaand we're officially back to screaming.

"Of course I accept you! I love you more than anything else, and if I could make everything perfect for you, I would, no matter what it takes!"

"How is complaining about how my arms look or what I want to do for a living loving me? I just don't get it!"

"Because I worry!" She's breathing hard and has to stop herself. After a moment, she adds, more softly, "I worry that others are treating you badly because you look a bit different from them, and maybe if you try to look a bit more like them, they'll leave you alone."

"I'm not in middle school anymore, Mom. People in college could not care less about how I look. And actually, someone even told me I am damn hot. His words, not mine."

"Aaron?"

I clear my throat. "Aran. And maybe. What makes you think it's him?"

"That boy is absolutely smitten with you." She smiles a little. "Didn't I mention he carried you?"

I turn toward the window, hoping to hide the heat blooming in my face. "It's not the first time."

"See?"

I can't possibly explain to her how she's seeing something that isn't there. Aran made it very clear that he wants us to be friends and nothing more. And then I shot that down, so now we're nothing at all.

Rather than that, I say, "My point is, you really don't have to fret about how I look. As long as I'm as healthy as my ovaries let me be, it's fine."

"Fine. No more talking about your weight."

The way I whip toward her makes me dizzy. "For real?"

Mom grips the steering wheel tighter but nods. "Yes."

"What about complaining about my career choice?"

"That's different." Her stern frown is back. "Can you guarantee you'll always be able to support yourself with books?"

"Can you guarantee you'll always have a job as a teacher?"

"What kind of logic is that?"

I laugh. "Nothing in life is ever guaranteed. But I can tell you that there are many, many people making hundreds of thousands and even millions of dollars publishing, so... it may be tight sometimes, but I want to pursue what I love. What I'm good at."

Even though she keeps her attention on the road, she does several double takes. "Excuse me? Millions?"

"And hundreds of thousands."

"But millions?"

I nudge her. "What, do you like books now?"

"Oh, yes. Big fan." I start to laugh, but she cuts me off when she says, "I've already preordered your book. You'll sign it for me, right?"

First my mouth opens. Then my chin starts trembling.

"Y-You did?"

Mom huffs. "How could I not? You talk about it all the time."

"I, uh—I didn't think you were paying attention."

"I listen to every word you say, Maddie. And I scan every inch of you every time I see you to make sure there's not a scratch on you. Because you're my baby daughter, and I have to worry over you for your dad's share too."

"Great." I sniffle. "Now I'm crying."

Since we're at a red light, she reaches over and wipes my cheek with her thumb. Smiling softly, she says, "So, where are you living now, and why did you move?"

With a shaky breath, I explain the whole story, not just how to get there. And for the first time in as far as I remember, my mom and I have a conversation. A good one. And we don't even shout again.

CHAPTER 35
ARAN

Thwack. Chug. Thwack. Chug.

That's been the pattern for the last hour. I throw a dart, hit anywhere between bullseye and the wall, and take a big swig from a beer glass I keep getting refilled.

After sitting at my secret spot for a few hours, I hauled my ass to practice and killed it. Just like I killed it during the last game after Edwards almost blew it. But since Coach doesn't want to bend and neither do I, the varsity guys have started taking sides. The so-called Team Coach—which is really Team Edwards, in my opinion—versus the Team Captain. So now we have some weird mutiny on our hands. When people started getting in each other's grills, Assistant Coach Thomas and others from the staff sent us home.

And shockingly, I'm the only one at O'Malley's this time.

Well, Archie wanted to join me in my grouching, but he's on a date with Christine from the Strikes. Mark's down with the flu and didn't even attend practice. And Jamal's cramming for a midterm.

Being alone was probably what I needed, until Luz texted in the Rodriguez siblings' group chat that she's bored at our parents' and demands a siblings' night out. Her fiancé is back on the road, and since the remodeling she's having done for the grand opening of her PT clinic isn't finished, she's back at the parents' and bored out of her mind.

Now, she and Aceituna are on their way over to O'Malley's, and I'm on my way over to being absolutely shitfaced. There's only beer in my stomach, and that is no bueno, but all I can do is thwack and chug. Otherwise, I'll punch something.

Why? It's not because of what went down during practice. Nah. But because I sat by the lake for long enough that I got even more tanned and came up with exactly *zero* ideas for how to get into Maddie's good graces without being too pushy.

I've never been this stumped about a girl before. Because today, I realized they've always come to me. And if it makes me sound like an asshole, it's because I am one.

So, when Luz said she wanted to hang out, I agreed right away because… maybe I need the female perspective from someone other than Ryan, who still wants to murder me. And I'm nervous as shit about the prospect of this conversation, so thwack and chug.

"Excuse me, can I get another one?" I ask the waiter passing by. He pauses, staring at my empty glass. Maybe he's doing the math. I don't tell him it's my eighth. I do blurt out, "I'm not driving tonight."

He takes my glass. "One more coming."

"Thanks," I say, all polite and shit.

The only place I'm driving myself to is hangover town. I have an exam tomorrow that will be super fun, but that's a problem for future-Aran. Tonight-Aran needs beer so he can talk about feelings without socking himself in the nose.

I know the second my sisters arrive because the few people at O'Malley's on a random weeknight start cheering like they're seeing a celebrity. Because Luz is a superstar for the locals nearly as much as her future husband is. I throw one more dart and grab onto air, because the waiter hasn't come back with my refilled glass.

Sighing, I turn to face the incoming projectiles.

Luz is shaking hands and snapping selfies like a politician. Behind her, Liv rolls her eyes, already bored with everything.

Mierda, esto es una mala idea.

It's too late to run, though. As if reading my mind, they both zero in on me. Of course, this is when the waiter comes back with a new glass of beer. Which I down in one go before Luz and Liv even reach me.

"Whoa, big guy. What's up with you?"

Loaded question, to which I grunt.

"Can I even be here?" Olivia asks, glancing around. "This looks like a bar."

"Of course you can. It's not like we're here to get sloshed like this Neanderthal here." Luz pinches Liv's cheek in the way that makes her recoil and bring the claws out. Which she does.

I signal the waiter again. "One more." After a second, I add, "Please."

Both of my sisters narrow their eyes at me. Then exchange looks. They think I can't read the secret message, but I can. I grew up translating that language.

They're thinking *What's wrong with our robot?*

They're about to find out.

Slowly, I walk around them and slide into a booth. Everything spins. Maybe the ninth beer wasn't a good idea.

They sit together across from me, and the second the waiter sets the new beer down before me, Luz swipes it and says, "Can we please have three loaded double cheeseburgers, one lettuce wrapped burger with no cheese, and a jumbo basket of fries?"

"I also want a Coke," Liv adds. Luz repeats it to the waiter, as if he didn't hear it himself. The guy nods, knowing the boss of this table isn't the burly drunkard, but the first-ever captain of St. Cloud's Thunder Strikes.

After he's gone, Luz takes a healthy swig of the beer and, sighing, she says, "I'm sensing something's up with our brother. Wouldn't you agree, Olivia?"

"Oh, it's written all over his grumpy mug," my younger sister adds with a lopsided smirk. "It looks particularly grumpy today, in fact."

Speaking of, I rub my face hard and keep it in my hands for a minute. I know two out of the three cheeseburgers are for me, and honestly, I'm starving. Also, a bad midweek hangover no longer sounds appealing.

"Aran, seriously. Is there something wrong?"

"I'm in love with someone."

After that, there's silence at the table. Someone laughs at the back of the bar, beyond the pool tables. That's some excellent comedic timing, huh?

I ease my hands down and lift my face. Both of my sisters are as wide-eyed as they physically can be. If I had any willpower, I'd snap a picture for blackmail purposes. But I can't bring myself to move a muscle other than to keep talking and getting it all out before I chicken out.

"And I don't know how to go about it because I've never felt like this before. And by the way, I already messed it up with her, so I'm playing on hard mode here, and I'm losing so bad it hurts."

Wow. My chest feels tight. Like it physically hurts to say all this aloud. Like I was pretending it wasn't this bad while I kept it all bottled up.

"I…" Luz closes her mouth. Opens it again. Twice more.

I glance down at Luz's glass, but she has *both* hands firmly clasped around it. She'll never give it to me. How the hell am I going to deal with the rest of this conversation, though?

"Wait, wait." Olivia raises both hands as if Luz and I are

about to fight or something. "You're telling me that you, Aran Jose Rodriguez—best known as 'the Iceberg'—are actually capable of emotions?"

"Hardy har har."

Luz turns to her. "This is breaking news to me too."

I frown. "I told you I can pass a damn Captcha."

"Maybe what's more shocking is that there's a girl on this planet who can capture the attention of this serial dater," Liv says, resting her chin on her hand. "When can I meet her?"

"Never, if I can't get her to forgive my ass."

"What did you do, you turd?" Luz asks.

The food starts arriving, and before I can use my burger as an excuse to stay quiet for a while, Liv pulls my plate toward her and destroys my plan. Normally, neither of them could pull this off. No one's reflexes are faster than mine, and no one's ever hungrier than me. But today, I'm not normal.

Today I smell of eau de desperation.

Sucking it up, I give them the abridged version of the tale. I skip over the parts my little sister has to stay innocent about, but I don't gloss over all the parts where I screwed up. And as I explain, I realize I botched everything up from day one. Because the second I set my eyes on Madeline Berkley and her strawberry earrings, her bad spying skills, her blushing cheeks, it was like I knew this was it. I was toast. And I chose to ignore it and play my own nefarious little game.

I may be objectively depressed, but once I'm done talking, I slide my plate over and tuck into the first burger.

Luz runs a hand through her long hair, while Liv observes me like I'm a puzzle she can't crack. Joke's on her. I don't understand me either. Why couldn't I just tell Strawberry I liked her back when I had the chance? It wasn't like Coach was breathing down my neck and making me say what I said.

"Yeah, I'm a freaking coward," I say aloud while I munch. "I'm terrified of hospitals and I'm scared shitless that someone I care about will leave me. So I try not to care about others, and I freaked out when I realized I care about this girl. A lot. Pass the mustard." I motion with my fingers at Liv.

Wordlessly, she grabs the condiment bottle from the corner of the table and sets it before me. I squirt mustard on my fries and stuff a handful into my gullet.

Luz gives out a short, snorty laugh. "I can't believe you just said all that with such a straight face, and while eating as usual."

"What? Do you want me to starve?"

"Heaven forbid."

"You have such a middle child complex." Liv shakes her head and grabs her as yet uneaten lettuce wrap burger. "Abandonment and trust issues all rolled into one."

"I'm proud of you, hermanito." Luz reaches over and pats my hand. "Growing up hurts. And I know you haven't had it easy, anyway, with two whacky sisters who have always kept you busy."

Liv reaches out for one of the fries, and I smack her hand away. "Don't touch those. They fry them in peanut oil."

"What?" Liv leans back with a huff. "How dare they."

"My point exactly," Luz says, motioning between Liv and me. "Aran, you've always been such a caretaker, and it's our fault. Our parents' too, to be honest. But have you never wanted anyone to care for you?"

I freeze, the burger in my hand hovering in midair before my open mouth. My older sister's smile is a bit sad.

"I'm just saying, if you try to keep everyone else at a safe distance, you also close yourself off to that possibility."

"Dude, you're a PT, not a psychologist," our little sister says with her mouth full. Luz preens a little.

Fully grouchy now, I set my burger back down. "Whatever. Stop psychoanalyzing me. What do I do now?"

Liv opens her eyes wide. "Um, have you not considered just telling her? Communication is so sexy."

"Shut up. You're too young to think anything's sexy at all."

"*You* shut up. I'm almost eighteen now."

I roll my eyes. "As if that still didn't make you a baby in diapers."

"That is absolutely gross, but you're too far away for me to kick you under the table."

"You are both babies in diapers," Luz chimes in instead.

Our sister tells her, "No, you're just old now."

"Wow, the disrespect."

"Mujeres." I bark the word, and it silences them long enough so I can speak. "What in the hell should I do so that a) Maddie forgives me for acting like a tool, and b) goes out with me, or at least becomes my friend again?"

"Hmm."

"That's a tough one."

"Yeah."

They look at each other and start giggling. At me, obviously.

Grunting, I go back to my burger.

Liv takes a sip of her soda and then says, "I'm still a fan of communication. In fact, it's super annoying in romance books when the couple's apart only because of some silly miscommunication."

I sigh. "Did I mention Maddie's a romance book writer?"

My little sister gasps. "You're kidding me! I must meet her for real now."

"Why are you reading romance books?" Luz cocks an eyebrow at her. "I thought you hated romance."

"Real-life couples are yuck. Chief of them, you and Max. But in books, they're cool."

I can't believe I'm about to say this but… "Can we focus back on me?"

And whaddaya know, it works. It's so abnormal to have their combined attention on me that I, "the Iceberg," squirm a little. It's totally the alcohol, right?

"Okay, okay." Luz motions for the three of us to huddle, and Olivia and I lean closer. "Here's the game plan, big guy. First, you have to choose which option you're really going for. If you truly want to just be her friend, you can't give her weird signals again."

I shake my head. "No, I'm done with that. What I really want is her."

"Aww."

"Focus, woman."

Luz grins. "Okay, so we're going straight for the a and b combo. If your girl is into romance books, the best thing you can do is show her what she means to you."

Liv's eyes light up. "Oh, yes. A grand gesture."

"A what?"

"You know, flowers, chocolates—promposals are an example of a grand gesture."

I scrunch my face up and glare. "I'm not going to do a promposal."

"No, but like—" Liv gesticulates with her hands. "Just do something extraordinary, is what I mean."

I turn to our older sister. "Did Cassiano ever do some crap like this for you?"

"I guess when he proposed last year, though he didn't really need a grand gesture."

"Are you implying I'm lesser than Cassiano?"

Luz bursts out laughing. "No, you knucklehead. You're just different."

"Plus, you, yourself, said you needed ideas, so there." Liv folds her arms and lifts a shoulder like a queen who hath spoken or whatever. Maddie would know how to say that right.

I lean back, tucking my tongue against my cheek as I mull

over this half-baked idea. It's already more than I could come up with on my own.

"Okay, grand gesture. What are some examples that won't shatter my self-respect?"

"You mean you wouldn't write *I love U Maddie* across your moobs and flash her in public?" Liv cackles like a hyena, and I have to ask the heavens for a heavy dose of patience.

"Of course not. I'm not a stalker fangirl. And I don't have moobs. I have pecs of steel."

"Every grand gesture needs an event. You shape the actual gesture around that theme." Luz speaks over us as if she's the wise one here. Which couldn't be farther from the truth. Except she's making some sense now.

"Oh, good one," Liv confirms.

I rub my head and back down my neck, racking my brain for an event. I mean, the biggest one is graduation, but that's too far away. I can't wait that long. Whatever time I have left with her, I'll take. Then there would be the national championship, when the Bolts make it there, but she's not even going to our games now. And her sister's wedding already happened.

Then it hits me.

"I got it. Her debut book is launching next week."

Liv gasps, excited, as if she's reading one of her books.

Meanwhile, Luz makes us huddle again. "Okay, how about this…"

I start sobering up as we hatch a plan.

CHAPTER 36
MADDIE

"**Y**ou guys are being ridiculous."

Ryan hovers over my shoulder as she says, "We are so not. We're protecting our talent."

She's wearing a short-sleeved T-shirt that doesn't match the chilly early spring weather. But earlier, at the apartment, she said she wanted people to see her muscles and know they shouldn't mess with her, and therefore me. Because today, she's here as my bodyguard.

What she didn't know was that Justin, my brother-in-law, was coming over, thinking the same thing. Except he's in a plaid flannel that doesn't hide his massive CrossFit guns, and he's got a beard so thick anyone would think he's going to pull an axe from under the table and throw it like a lumberjack warrior. No one would guess he's the softest teddy bear and hasn't chopped a log in his life. He's a corporate lawyer who works on customer contracts at a desk every day.

Mom is also acting like I'm someone famous, asking the occasional reader who approaches me to sign my book to stay at a respectable distance. And Meg apparently really likes photography now, because all she's done is take pictures of me from every imaginable angle, both when I did a first chapter reading and while a whopping ten people lined up for a signature.

It's so embarrassing. My face has been a jalapeño all day. But I'm so touched I've cried twice in the bathroom already.

I shake my head and fiddle with my gold Sharpie that matches the pretty crown on the cover of my debut book. I've been so overwhelmed the past few weeks with school, tutoring, finishing my hockey romance so I can start preparing it for self-publishing after graduation, a PCOS diagnosis and the ensuing research, reconnecting with Mom and… and um, the whole thing with a certain boy… that the launch day crept up on me. Don't get me wrong, I did as good a preorder campaign as I could on a student budget and with limited support from my publisher. But this goal that had felt so out of reach, so far away for so long, is now realized.

It occurs to me now that graduation is just around the corner, which will put the words *The End* to the college chapter of my life. And I'm not ready to say goodbye to this life just when I was starting to have fun with it.

Great, now I'm teary again.

The doorbell chimes, signaling a new customer, and I automatically plaster on a smile, hoping it's a potential reader. But the person who walks in is the very last one I expected.

I blink really hard. "Rebs?"

She gives me a tentative smile that looks like a grimace, and something about it tells me this isn't a coincidence. She must've seen my posts about the event on my author social media pages. I figured she had unfollowed me when I moved away. I sure unfollowed her.

Stretching to glance around her and out the windows, I don't see neither hide nor hair of the other mean girls. Huh.

"Um, hi," she says as she approaches the table.

Mom, who now knows everything that went down between

Rebs and me, gets in the way with her arm raised to the side. Words dripping with sarcasm, she says, "Excuse me. Strangers must stay behind this line."

"Yeah, we have to protect the talent," Justin gruffs behind me.

"Oh, okay." Rebs clutches something against her chest, and I only catch a glimpse of what it is as she extends it toward Mom. "Can I please get an autograph?"

It's my book. Rebs preordered my book.

A gasp is all I'm capable of. I meet her eyes, and she bites her lip.

"I'm sorry, Maddie. I'm sorry it took me so long to understand that I should never have traded you for popular girls. You left my name in the acknowledgments, and it nearly broke me, you know?"

Choked up, I confess. "To be honest, it was sent to print months ago. It was too late to change it."

"And you would have?"

I cringe. "Probably."

Here she is apologizing, and maybe I could've lied for her benefit, but I'm done with lying to myself to please others.

Rebs doesn't seem offended. She nods as if she expected this answer. I reach over and hold my hand out, and for a moment, no one moves.

"I'll sign it."

She springs into action and hands me the book. Mom leans over to catch what I'm about to write, so I hunch over and use my hair as a curtain to hide my scribbles. Once I'm done, I sign with an extra flourish, set the marker down, and return the book with a salesperson smile.

"Thank you so much for coming to my signing. I hope you enjoy the book!"

Rebs picks it up, and with one final watery smile, she turns around and marches out of the bookstore with her shoulders drooped. She doesn't know yet that what I wrote is:

To Rebs,
*   The protagonist's best friend was based on you, because you were mine. We may never go back to being exactly that way, but we can start over and go on a new journey, just like the leads of this book.*
*   Your friend (and now published author—squee!),*
*   Maddie*
*   PS I miss our couch.*

I'm sure she'll text me when she reads it, and I'll read the text because I never blocked her on my phone. I always left that channel open for her, and for her only, because I always knew deep down that she was also a victim of the others.

Realizing how far I've come, I sag against my chair with a sigh. All I need now is a pizza from Romano's with my family, maybe a movie at home with Ryan, and a nap that lasts for three days.

Again, the bell chimes, and this time, a massive guy walks in. My heart leaps into my throat, but it's not *him.* This one's too white, with hair too red, and he's dragging a girl in by their joined hands. A smile forms on my face when they face forward, and Ryan speaks first.

"Well, well, well. What do we have here? The traitor and the nice half of the double-A battery."

Christine rolls her eyes. "Traitor my ass." Mom clears her throat in that teacher way of hers, and Christine straightens. "Um, my behind, I mean."

"Mom." I hiss at her. "People are free to talk how they want. Not everyone is your student."

"You're my daughter, though. So don't you use that language again, missy."

I've decided to accept her nagging me about language to

her heart's content, because since the hospital saga, she hasn't mentioned any of my fat rolls even once. Is this growth?

But also, she doesn't have to know my new hockey romance is packed with cuss words. It's not like hockey players are known for being clean-mouthed.

"Anyway, we came to support you. What do you want us to do?" Archie asks, looking around as if this is the first time he's seeing all these strange artifacts the rest of us call bookshelves and the small and curious objects in them that we know as books.

I wonder if that's how Aran looked the first time he walked into the library for his tutoring session with Wyatt.

No, I shouldn't think about him. I've been really good about it this week.

Somehow, after he took me to the hospital, I thought he might reach out to ask how I was doing or something. I anticipated it and dreaded it in equal measure. But he didn't, and that disappointment was like a brand-new heartbreak.

I had to remind myself again that he would've been a good Samaritan to anyone in that situation and that there was nothing special about that day. He was probably at the library to meet his new tutor or to study. And he sat across from me, watching me, because… well, I have no idea why. But it definitely wasn't because he has a crush on me or something. We're not in middle school.

So, anyway, we're back on the getting-over-Aran train. Choo freaking choo.

"Let me explain. It's very easy," Ryan says matter-of-factly. "You grab one of these books from this pile here. Then you ask Maddie to sign it. And then you go over there to the nice lady at the counter and pay for it."

"Bravo." Meg starts clapping. "We should've printed that and put it on a poster, to be honest."

I laugh. They're such a strange combination, and I can tell

that after this, my sister and my roommate will become besties. I'll be the third wheel, and I'll love every second of it.

It's even funnier when the two Thunder assistant captains follow the instructions to a T. As I'm signing their books, the door opens again, and another massive guy stands in line, followed by another one, followed by another girl. And they turn out to be Jamal, Mark, and Amber, who got held up finding a parking spot because they all came together.

No Aran.

My smile turns tighter, because here I am again, disappointed. What right do I have when I'm the one who excised him from my life? Being lovesick sucks.

After a few pictures and some chatter, they leave to hang out around town before the Bolts' big semifinals game later tonight. I heard through the grapevine—a.k.a. the Strikes—that the Bolts' coach started the backup goalie for the past two games, but tonight, Aran will start as usual. I wonder how he feels about that. Is he in good condition? I hope—

I shake my head hard. When am I going to stop thinking and worrying and yearning for him?

Pushing my chair back, I tell my bodyguards, "Excuse me. I need a bio break."

"Yes, of course." Ryan pretends to make way for me in the middle of an invisible crowd.

Laughing, I say, "Dork."

Ryan touches her ear and nods to herself before grinning. "Copy that. Back at you. Over."

I love her. At least Aran did right by introducing us.

Swatting her arm away, I make my way to the staff bathroom at the back and splash some cold water on my face. I smooth out my marigold dress, push my hair back so my strawberry earrings are visible, and nod to myself.

"You got this, Maddie. You're an adult now. A published author and a confident woman. This too shall pass. You'll get over him, and if not, you'll write a bestselling book about it." I pump my fists and walk back out.

And there he is.

Bulky guy. With skin the right shade of brown. The buzz cut. The square jaw. The deep-set black eyes that find me instantly. Dressed in a black suit, white button shirt, and Thunder Bolts' blue tie. My book is tucked under his arm, and he has a wooden box in his hands. It's tied with a ribbon in the exact color as my dress. I even glance down at myself to confirm. As if somewhere along the way, he realized this is the color that makes me happiest.

I can't move.

My entire family glances between Aran and me. More than once.

Justin opens his big mouth and says, "Oh, so this is Maddie's plus-one?"

And I open mine to say, "He's not my anything."

Something flashes in Aran's face, but it's gone so quick I can't guess at what it was.

"Happy book launch day," Aran says with that deep, naturally husky voice that feels like a luxurious fabric against my skin.

My legs twitch with the strongest urge to run again. Deep down, I know if I stay in his presence longer, I will fall in love with him all over again. Harder. Irreparably.

But my heart roots me to the spot, ready to get hurt again.

"Thank you," I respond breathlessly, even though I've just walked out of the bathroom.

Aran's eyes drink me in my fluttery dress that reaches my knees, my bare legs, and my wedge sandals. My toes are painted the same color as my earrings, and his eyes make the connection right away. In fact, when he sees my earrings, his lips curve ever so slightly. The movement would be imperceptible to someone who doesn't know him or isn't paying attention.

I fold my arms and almost say that yes, I even smell like strawberries. So what? I am cringe, but I am free!

"I brought you a gift," he says, cutting through my thoughts, and lifts the box just a tad.

"Well?" Mom asks me, wagging her eyebrows from behind Aran. "Aren't you going to take it, Maddie?"

I have a feeling that by *it*, she's referring to the whole man. I couldn't bring myself to tell her the minutia of the Aran saga, but she knows I have unreciprocated feelings for him, though she's convinced they're reciprocated. Captain of the ship, apparently.

Sighing, I propel myself forward. I keep my eyes on my pile of books by the corner of the table instead. He places the box in my hands when I extend them to him. One of his hands holds one of mine like he's trying to steady it under a massive weight. Except the box is light, and his hand is so warm and soft, and my whole body flares to life.

As coolly as possible, I snatch my hand away. But the brush of our skin is like lighting a match. Pretty sure my face is flaming.

Clearing my throat, I take a seat. "Thank you for the gift. Would you like me to sign your book?"

"After you open the box."

Ah, crud. I've made the mistake of looking up at him. Aran's full attention is on me like there's no one else on the entire planet. He doesn't notice that my mother is about to squeal.

"Uh, okay."

I hasten to untie the pretty bow. The sooner I look at the contents and sign the book, the sooner he'll leave and this can all be over. I slide open the box's lid and…

Inside, there's half a dozen strawberries coated in milk

chocolate and a note nestled between them. Aran motions at the note with his lips.

Breathing in deep, I grab it and unfold it. I recognize his handwriting right away. My heart starts hammering at full speed, even before I read the first word.

Strawberry,

> *I could never be the hero of one of your romance books, but if you give me a chance, I want to be the hero of your own life's romance. Friendship isn't enough. I want the whole bite, and you can bite me back (any time).*
>
> *Yours,*
>
> *Chocolate Bar.*

I shock everyone by barking a laugh. That's when I finally figure out why the strawberries are covered with chocolate, because the moment I saw his naked abs with my own eyes, I blurted out that they looked like a chocolate bar.

He's—He's saying he's all over me. That I'm the strawberry to his chocolate.

I shock everyone by bursting into tears. Even him.

"Rodriguez, you are so dead—" Ryan starts.

"Are these good tears? Bad tears?" Mom asks, the excitement melting away from her face.

"Listen, punk—"

Meg interrupts her husband. "We are lawyers. If you hurt her, we bankrupt you."

I laugh again, then sob. "Stop, everyone. Just stop."

Aran unfreezes himself. His hands hover in the air, as if he wants to reach for me, but he pulls them back. The only sign that he's nervous is that he swallows hard. But he says nothing as I regard him. Everything was in this box in my hands.

But why now? After I've worked so hard to get over him? After he only wanted to be friends? Wasn't he only a no-strings kind of guy? And what if his coach suspends him again? Will he like me if I keep becoming an obstacle in his life?

My heart wants to leap to his hand, but my brain says *hold back*. My stomach is a cocktail of emotions that makes me want to puke.

Slowly, I return the note to the box and close it delicately. Without looking up at him, I ask, "Can you give me some time to think about it?"

Aran murmurs, "As long as you need, Strawberry."

"Straw—huh?" Justin asks behind me.

After a quiet pause, I hear shuffling and see Aran turn around. He leaves with my unsigned book still tucked under his arm. And the fact that the clerk doesn't stop him means he walked in with the book. Which means he preordered it. He dressed up, wrote this note, and bought these delicate treats to… to…

To confess his feelings for me.

Aran "the Iceberg" Rodriguez has feelings for me.

Ryan crouches beside me. "Maddie, what do you want us to do? Should we tackle him to the ground so you can kick him while he's down, or do you want us to hold him down so you eat his face?"

"Is that what kids nowadays are calling it?" Mom asks.

I push to my feet, square up my shoulders, and say, "No, I got this."

Except, when I burst out of the indie bookstore, Aran is nowhere to be seen. I meander around the streets downtown, but there's no sign of him. It's like he decided to give me time and space by running as far away as possible.

But I know where Aran runs to. And so I ditch my book launch and go chase my own romance.

CHAPTER 37
ARAN

I sigh as I yank at the knot in my tie. Soon, it's wide enough that I can toss it on top of my blazer, which is strewn in the back of my SUV. I don't have a lot of patience for the shirt's buttons, so I pull the whole thing over my head and toss it on the pile. I work through the rest of my clothes and shoes until I'm down to my underwear. A swim will clear my head.

Time. She needs time. That's not a no, even though it's not the yes I hoped for.

My sisters are blowing up my phone. I don't want to have to explain this to them. I'm actually annoyed as shit that they now know for sure I'm not a robot. Their teasing before this was so much more bearable.

I work out my muscles as if this is a swimming meet. This. is the sport my parents signed me up for back when I was a kid, hoping I preferred a less dangerous sport. But I'm starting to think I have the same issue as Luz—I like to live life on the edge of disaster. If I didn't, I wouldn't have lied to Coach or to myself or to Strawberry. I'd have figured everything out earlier.

But I'll give her all the time she wants. And in a way, Coach is going to get his end of the bargain too. I can't possibly date anyone else now. Maybe now he'll be freaking happy.

I emerge from the water with a great gasp once my lungs start to burn from the hard swim. I clear the water from my face with my hand, and I'm about to tumble onto my back to float for a bit when a voice stops me.

"Aran Rodriguez! Did you break the speed limit to get here so fast?"

My hand drops, and there she is. Madeline "Strawberry" Berkley in the flesh.

Her chest rises and falls with rapid breathing, which is really bad for my health because her dress shows off her cleavage nicely. And it hugs her curves perfectly. And her hair tumbles over her shoulder. And her cheeks are a shade lighter than her lips, and I want to kiss them.

But she asked for time, so I stay still, where the water is up to my stomach.

She kicks one foot in the air, and her sandal flies off. Then she does the same for the other one. I narrow my eyes, confused, even though it's clear what she's doing.

"Why the heck did you have to be so fast?" She pushes her hair forward and stretches her arms back to fiddle with the dress. "Wait, hold on. The zipper's tricky." Then she turns her back.

I clear my throat. "Do you need help?"

"No, I got it." Her voice is far firmer than necessary, so I stay put and watch her struggle until she grabs the zipper tab and pushes it down just enough.

I blink hard as more skin gets exposed. Tilt my head to get a better view. I don't need to make an effort, because she shimmies out of the dress until it pools around her feet on the sand. Then she pulls down some tight shorts, and for a second, I think she's naked. Until I do a double take and notice that her underwear is a similar shade to her skin.

Strawberry turns around—as if suddenly remembering that the way to the lake is over here—and stands there with her hands on her hips, legs wide, breathing hard. Which draws my eyes to her chest again. And I recognize the bra. It's the lacy one I saw hanging in her bathroom the night after I met her.

Have I died and gone to heaven?

She steps out of the circle of her dress and keeps walking. Forward. And the closer she gets, the harder my heartbeat thrums in my ears. When she makes contact with the water, she flinches, and her skin breaks into goose bumps all over. I can't believe I'm jealous that it's the water that put them there.

But she continues going with a determined little frown that wrinkles her nose. Her brown eyes are trained on mine, as if trying to make sure I don't go anywhere this time. But nothing in this world could make me move away. The hard part is not reaching for her when she stops an arm's length away.

The wet ends of her hair float around her in the water. Her bra is already growing darker as it absorbs the moisture. I've never seen anyone more beautiful than Strawberry as she glares up at me.

"I said I needed time, not for you to change zip codes."

"This is a temporary change. I plan on being your neighbor for at least a few more months."

She grunts just like I would. I press my lips tight to keep from laughing. "You also left before I could sign your book."

"You can sign it whenever you want. Along with the other two I forgot in my car."

Strawberry gasps. "You bought more than one?"

"My sisters want to read it too."

"Oh." The grumpiness starts melting from her face. "So you really mean it, then? What you said on the note?"

"Every word," I say slowly, softly, earnestly. I don't know what else to do. With a shaky breath, I add, "Maddie, I'm actually a chicken shit. I hate hospitals because I hate the thought of people I care about leaving me. So I try not to care. And I—"

I interrupt myself to rub my neck, and she doesn't flinch at the sudden spray of cold water. Like she's turned into a statue.

"I cared about you so much and so fast, I panicked. But I knew I'd messed up when you kicked me to the curb. And when you hit your head…" I blow out all the air in my lungs. A shudder racks over my frame, and I swallow hard. "I was drowning."

I don't understand what's written on her face. It's almost blank except for the slight upward rise of her eyebrows. But she takes a tiny step forward, and I have to tilt my head down to meet her eyes.

Slowly, her hand rises from the water until it rests on my chest. Against my heart. Her skin is cold like ice against mine, and she splays her hand wide to really feel. If anything, my heart beats even faster.

"Oh."

"What does that *oh* mean?"

Her attention is on her hand as she says, "Well, I just wanted some proof that this was all real."

"It's very real." I close my left hand around hers, keeping it against my chest. But with my other one, I bring her closer until she's flush against me. Low and slow, I say, "It's very real."

She swallows hard, and for a long moment, just stays still.

Suddenly, she circles both arms around my neck, and now there's not a molecule of water or air between us. I run my hands down her back, past the dip of her waist, over the swell of her butt. Her lips part a little as I spread my hands and grasp her firmly. A full gasp comes out when I lift her until she's right where I want her to be. Her legs wrap around my waist, and yeah, I can die happy now.

Except I'm missing one thing.

"Strawberry?"

"What do you want, Chocolate?"

My lips twitch. "You. I want you. I want you to tell me that I can kiss you now and tomorrow and the day after that, for a very long time."

Her fingers knead at the muscles at my nape, like she's seen me do, but better. With more care. And that's almost enough to undo me. I start to turn into a noodle and have to hold her tighter so she doesn't sink.

Smiling as if she knows what she's doing to me, she whispers, "With one condition."

"Consider it done."

"Before you even hear it?"

"If I don't get to kiss you in the next ten seconds, I'll die here, woman."

"Hmm." She caresses the side of my face like this isn't the first time, as if already knowing every plane and dip. "Fine, I'll be quick. The condition is that you have to give yourself to me too."

"Oh, I'm so ready."

She presses her lips. "Not just like *that*. I mean all your fears and worries, and your hopes and your laughs and your tears. Because I'm sure you cry sometimes too."

"Never," I joke.

She ignores it. "*Everything*. That's what it means to be the hero of my romance. No hiding or lying or pretending to be okay when you're not. Are you ready for that task?"

"No," I admit with a soft voice, inhaling deep. "I'm not. I don't know how. But I want to figure it out with you. And, uh, disclaimer: I'll probably mess up a few times along the way, but you can't be a hockey goalie if you give up easily."

She nods solemnly. "I'll make a mental note of that for a future book."

"Don't worry, Strawberry. I have endless inspiration to give you."

"I have no doubt."

"Can we keep bantering later? My mouth misses yours."

She snorts, and I think she's going to say something, but instead, she presses her lips against mine in a soft kiss that lasts exactly one second. Strawberry herself is the one who pushes my mouth open and sucks at my tongue as if it's my lips instead.

The moan that comes out of my throat is very obvious. I am now fire itself. I press her hips tighter against me, and with my other hand, I push her head down a little more. This kiss might bruise. But we're both hungry for each other.

As I let her devour my mouth, I slide my hand up from her ass to her hip and squeeze. I break the kiss to speak against her lips. "Yes, I'll give you all of me. And when you're ready, you'll give me all of you too. Seems like a fair trade."

"So fair."

She presses that smile right against mine. Then she bites my lower lip, and I might just be a little late to tonight's semifinal, because there's no way I'm cutting this moment short. I'll savor every second of it, along with every inch of my Strawberry's lips, until we're both out of breath.

CHAPTER 38
MADDIE

"Are you sure about this? It's a pretty bold statement."

From the kitchen of my apartment, Aran says, "As sure as I am about how my name's actually pronounced."

I pad out of my room in socks and stop in front of him. He's tossing a banana into the blender, but he pauses when I raise my arms out to the sides. Surprisingly, his jersey is ginormous on me. Not surprisingly, he's never getting it back. But it's one thing to wear the piece of fabric with the *C* on my chest and *Rodriguez* with a big number1 on the back when I'm at home with Ryan. It's quite another to wear it tonight at the national championship game to watch him play.

"We've only been dating for two days, you know?" I explain so he thinks about it carefully.

His eyes roam down my body and stop at my legs. That's when I remember I haven't put on my jeans yet. Maybe I'm getting a bit too comfortable showing skin in front of my brand-new boyfriend.

Slowly, he lifts his eyes. "What's under the jersey?"

My lips twitch. "What do you think?"

"Hopefully nothing. Say it's nothing."

"Underwear, Aran. I wouldn't go out wearing your jersey and nothing else."

"That's a good point. Let's keep the nudity only between us." Aran dumps the rest of the ingredients into the blender and turns it on. I feel like that's a metaphor that applies to me too.

Shaking my head, I head back to my room and put on the jeans I should've been wearing all along. It's not like Aran is a one-track-mind kind of guy, but it's very easy to send it into the gutter. The problem, I'm finding, is that when he gets *my* mind in the gutter, it can get very dangerous. Like at the lake this time around. If it hadn't been for his semifinal game, we would've taken things a step further right there in the wild.

Which… maybe wouldn't have been so bad.

I shake my head and smack my cheeks, looking at myself in the mirror. Maybe the perv has been me all along.

"Focus, Maddie," I whisper at my reflection. "We're here to get studying done before his big game. Nothing else."

"Why not?" I jump out of my skin. Aran's leaning against the doorframe, arms folded. "We could study our mouths some more. And so many other parts that we could study with our hands or our mouths—preferably both. According to research, such activities help athletes focus before their games."

"Are you trying to sound academic while pitching sex to me?"

His eyebrows go up. "Is it working?"

"No."

"That's fine. Academic research is all about trying again and again." Aran shrugs.

"Good gravy," I mutter, barely biting back my smile. "Let's go put your mind on your very last essay, okay?"

He stretches out one hand, and I immediately slide my fingers between his. They're so big they stretch mine out a bit.

Yet there's nothing more perfect than when we hold hands like this. Not with a weak grip that can be broken easily, but all in. Tight. As if our lives depend on it.

I pull him to the living room, and we settle on the floor with our backs against the couch. Aran lets my hand go only to put his arm around my shoulders and pull me against his side. With the other hand, he fires his laptop back up. He'll have to type one-handed, because there's no way I'm getting out of this embrace. I lean my head on his shoulder and pick up my reading packet from the coffee table.

We get maybe ten minutes of actual work done, with Aran reading his business case and me studying the material for my advanced creative writing elective, before he decides my neck is more interesting. He brushes my hair away, and I feel his breath against my skin.

"Aran."

"Maddie?" he whispers against my ear.

I can't possibly think of what to say when he closes his teeth softly around my earlobe. Turns out we both like to bite and, um, be bitten. Because I shudder so hard it makes him chuckle.

I grab his knee, but it's not the warning I was hoping for. Not when his muscles feel so delectable under his sweatpants. And the fabric is very thin. I knead, trying to map them all in my mind.

"Careful with that hand, Strawberry."

"Or what?"

I feel him curl a finger into the jersey's neck and pull, brushing my skin until it hits the strap of my bra. Then he pulls on that too. My eyes roll shut as he kisses my shoulder. Softly. So softly it's barely a whisper. And now every inch of my skin has goose bumps.

My tongue's heavy, and my words come out weird. "Aran, we only have a couple of hours before your game."

He smiles against my neck. "You're right. This deserves a lot more time."

I clear my throat. Twice. "Right. So can we get back to studying?"

"No."

Not only was I not expecting that answer, but I also wasn't expecting him to pull me up and against him, grabbing my thighs and spreading them apart until I'm on his lap. Straddling him. And facing him. With his hands all cozy on my hips. Under the jersey.

I'm going to combust as he looks at me with those deep eyes that see right through me. And his smirk tells me he knows I'm putty in his hands.

"How about this?" he says in that low voice of his that hits me like a lightning bolt. "We study each other a little now, and then we do some serious overtime after the game."

"Would that be considered a reverse-tutoring session?"

"Of course. I plan to teach my favorite student many things."

"Like what?" I ask against his lips just as his hand travels up my back, ever so slowly, leaving a trail of goose bumps until it settles under the strap of my bra.

He shows me with a kiss that feels like so much more, and it tears strange sounds from my throat I've never heard before.

It feels unfair to have his hands on my bare skin, though, so I take advantage of the fact that he's busy with my mouth to sneak my own hands under his sweatshirt. The chocolate abs tense as I blatantly grope them. I take my time exploring every plane and groove, but it's when I touch his sides that he growls.

"So you're sensitive there?"

"Do that again and I'll flip you onto your back and do the same to you." Aran's voice is basically a growl, which I appreciate. Means I'm on the right path.

"Oh yeah?"

Aran narrows his eyes. I feel him grab me tighter, about to follow through—when the door opens.

We both turn. Ryan's eyes and mouth are as wide as they go. She clutches a bag from the grocery story against her chest and says, "Yeah, I'm gonna go puke over the railing. Bye."

With that, she walks right back out and shuts the door.

Slowly, I turn back to Aran. "So, um. I guess she now knows we're officially together, huh?"

Mirth dances in his eyes. "And she's about to tell everyone else. You can safely wear the jersey tonight."

"I see." I nod to myself. "Guess I will. And I should probably get my hands off you now so Ryan can come into her own apartment."

"But I like your hands on me."

Laughing, I lean forward and press a little kiss on the tip of his nose. "Let's leave that for the overtime study after you win the championship."

The grin that blooms on Aran's face is enough to make me fall in love with him all over again. It's the one he keeps hidden from everyone but me. When we're happy together. I can't wait to see it for the rest of my life.

"Looking forward to it, Strawberry."

EPILOGUE

M ADDIE

I'm used to my body rioting every month in all sorts of ways, but this is something else.

Tonight is game seven of the playoff finals, the very last game of the season. My husband has played every single game of this round and about half of them throughout the entire playoff run. And that's after an intense season that saw us battling for the number one spot in the conference with tonight's rival. The physical exertion and the mental intensity required to get to this point have made him lose almost twenty pounds.

Meanwhile, I wonder if he just passed them along to me.

My stomach is a complete disaster zone of nerves not only because of the game but because of the big secret I'm keeping from him. I didn't think it'd be a good idea to drop a massive bomb like this on him during the playoffs, so here I am, eating our combined weight in popcorn so I have something to do.

"Easy there, sis. You're gonna choke." Meg passes over the cup of soda, and I stretch over to sip from the straw.

"It's totally fine," Luz, my husband's older sister, says from my other side. "I was also buzzing with nerves the first time Max made it to the playoffs." She offers a placid laugh as if her husband didn't win the cup on his first playoff run. Yet she also dips a hand into her own popcorn bucket and eats a massive handful. Like maybe she's also nervous for her brother.

Next to her, Aran's youngest sister is the picture of indifference. She's been texting someone nonstop since the players hit the ice for warmups, nonplussed by all the lights or cameras recording the scene. She hasn't even noticed that we've appeared on the Jumbotron a couple of times since we're sitting together in the WAGs section.

The wives and girlfriends of Aran's teammates are actually really nice, but most of them are pregaming hard in the family room, and while normally I'd join them, tonight I can't. I'd rather sit with Aran's family and mine.

"When does this start?" Mom asks behind me.

Before I can respond, Aran's mom answers. "I think in five minutes."

"Is anyone recording this?" his dad asks, his voice breathless even though he's been parked in his seat for exactly an hour.

"It's going to be available on demand, Dad," Luz shouts without turning around.

Meanwhile, my eyes have been fixed on *RODRIGUEZ 31* emblazoned on the back of my husband's jersey. I forwent the WAGs jacket and donned my matching jersey over a hoodie. This turned out to be a good choice, because the nerves have drained me of any body heat.

Aran finishes stretching his legs and gets back up, turning around to grab his water bottle hanging from the back of the net. He lifts his mask, which is adorned in the team colors and multiple lightning bolts that pay homage to his college team, and sprays water on his face and hair.

"Ugh," I grunt to myself. He looks so dang hot when he does that. No wonder he's amassed a whole fan club by himself. There is *nothing* like a goalie with swagger.

And Aran has it in spades. He's practically guaranteed the Vezina Trophy, even if his team doesn't bag the whole show, and there are strong rumors that he may also get this season's Hart Memorial Trophy.

Yeah, his fan club isn't just women in the audience. Everyone in the league is going bananas over the guy who's been dubbed this generation's wall. Sounds a bit cooler than "the Iceberg" if you ask me.

His eyes catch mine from clear across the ice. I'm in the corner between his net and our team bench, in the front row, so it's not hard. We've been keeping tabs on each other the whole time. And every single time, my stomach jumps like it's the first time our eyes have ever met.

Yes, I'm the number one member of his fan club. Aran still makes my belly flutter just as it did when we met at the library years ago. It's kind of embarrassing, but what can I say? I'm a romance girlie to the core, and he's my TDH brought to life just for me.

My heart hammers harder as he pushes away from the net and glides over to the glass partition separating us. I toss my popcorn bucket haphazardly to my sister and jump to my feet.

"Hey, wife," he says louder than his usual grumbly tone.

"Husband." I smile at him. "Don't forget the reward I have for you tonight, no matter what happens."

The corner of his delectable lips rises. "I won't." And maybe that was all he needed, because he pivots around and heads back to his net.

"Ew." Olivia, his younger sister, elongates the word until her voice gives out.

Luz makes a grimace, complete with her tongue sticking out. "Yeah, I totally didn't have to know that."

"Know what?" I frown as I retake my seat.

Meg offers my popcorn back to me. "They think you were talking about boinking."

I jump. "What? No! I learned to make pabellón criollo for him," I explain. I completely botch the pronunciation, but it's enough for my sisters-in-law to relax.

"Oh."

"Whew."

I roll my eyes. Please, as if Luz isn't married to an objectively hot man, and as if Olivia doesn't have a boyfriend too. They know about the birds and the bees. It shouldn't be shocking if my bee-husband really loves my flower.

"What are you youth talking about?" Mom kind of yells from behind us.

It occurs to me now to be extra thankful that the place is packed full and noisy. Mom still likes to pretend that there's no such thing as bees and flowers between Aran and me, even though we've been married for a couple of years. I think it's her way of masking the disappointment that I haven't been able to give her more grandbabies to add to the collection Meg and Justin have produced.

"Nothing, Mom," Meg and I chorus.

"Please stand for the national anthem," a voice finally booms, and everyone who is able in the arena scrambles to do so.

Well, no matter what happens with the game, everything is going to change tonight.

The game starts with a bang… ish. The opponent wins the initial faceoff, one of their forwards breaking away for an aggressive slapshot, and Aran plucks it from the air as easy as popping a soap bubble. We're on home ice, and I'm not exaggerating when I say the entire place almost goes down from shock.

Not me. All I do is smirk like the villainess of my next book.

It's really bold to try to frazzle the best goalie in the whole dang league like that when that gives him plenty of opportunity to demoralize the other team.

Plus, the way he drops the puck back onto the ice like this isn't a biggie is going to get him more than just food as a reward tonight.

The first period ends up scoreless. During the intermission, my whole body itches with the desire to run and find him outside the locker room, or to at least text him. But he doesn't like getting out of the zone during important games like this. He doesn't even accept intermission interviews from the team's marketing people. All I can do is wait. Wait to see how the game goes, and wait until after the game to drop the mother of all news.

But the second period ends in the same way. Both teams are exhausted after the long season, but they're battling for the puck with their reserves. They're truly a marvel of what the human body is capable of. Aran's drinking more water than he normally does. I can only imagine how heavy his pads must be with sweat.

By the time the third period's reaching its last minutes and the scoreboard is still a grand total of zero for both teams, I'm the one sweating buckets.

"Come!" Luz sucks in air. "On!"

My sister is paralyzed in her seat, eyes wide and trying to catch the action without daring to utter a word. Aran's parents grab each other in a vise grip, but their status is otherwise the same as Meg's.

Olivia and I are stuck to the glass. She bangs it with enough strength to make it rattle. "Aren't you all tired? Just finish the damn game! I wanna go home!"

I shout something very different. "You got this, Aran! Don't let them shake you!" I doubt he can even pick my voice apart from the deafening noise around the arena, but this is all I can do for him, so I keep screaming encouragements. I keep crossing my fingers that our forwards score, that our defense stays strong. That we don't have to take this to overtime, or worse, to shootouts.

My eyes keep shifting from him to the clock ticking away on the Jumbotron. The popcorn and soda in my belly war with one another over who can rise up my esophagus faster. I swallow hard and keep it all down somehow. The numbers on the screen seem to accelerate unnaturally, propelling all of us closer to zero. Closer to an overtime.

A buzzing goes off, and I jump. Did someone score? But there are no lights going off, and now the screens above announce that we're going into overtime.

"No." I melt into my seat. "I can't do this."

"You have to, Strawberry." Luz grabs my hand, using the nickname Aran gave me that has now spread to his entire family. "You got this."

"I don't got this. This is too painful." I squeeze my eyes shut tight.

"Be brave, Maddie." I feel my sister's slimmer hand hold my other one. "Take deep breaths."

There's a snort, followed by Olivia's voice. "You guys, she's not about to give birth, you know."

Aran glances our way. I straighten up and pump my fists in the air at him. He gives a minuscule nod and turns back to the front, ready for overtime to begin.

"Water," I demand. "Someone give me water or I'm going to barf all over the glass and the cameras will catch it all and I'll go viral online because of this instead of my books. Water!"

"Geez, calm down, woman." Meg twists to dig in her purse under the chair and produces a water bottle. "Here."

I uncap it and down the whole thing in one go as the game

resumes. I should've taken some medication for the nerves, but I don't know how that works now.

I forget all about my stomach as the other team attacks. We all lean forward. Our defense intercepts their top forward, stealing the puck for a second, only to get it stolen right back. And through the legs too. I grip the armrests hard enough that my muscles tremble. A melee's forming right in front of Aran. Luz's voice screaming interference sounds garbled, like I'm underwater. Aran's being jostled, but he stays put. The puck moves faster than I can track it, between skates, bouncing off sticks. Suddenly people are screaming, and players in the wrong color jerseys are pumping their fists in the air.

I don't breathe.

There's no way he lost.

No way. Impossible. All his hard work doesn't end here. My heart wants to tumble out of my mouth.

And then the refs whistle and gesticulate.

The arena grows deathly quiet as one of the refs skates to center ice, fiddling with his microphone equipment at his waist, and says, "It was deemed goalie interference. No goal."

I break my personal speed record by becoming the first person in my entire section to jump to their feet, screeching. The four of us at the front row become a tangle of limbs as we hug and jump.

It's not lost! He hasn't lost!

Play resumes amid cheering and booing. We glue ourselves to the glass, watching with growing excitement how our team rallies under the power play. Aran watches just as intently from his crease as his teammates eat up the ice.

And he's the first one to celebrate when his team scores the winning goal.

I'm screaming and crying, and I literally have my hands against my mouth so I don't throw the hell up.

Now the one being jostled is me, but I can't focus on

anything but Aran. He drops his stick, gloves, and mask wherever they fall, picking himself up to leave the net. His teammates intercept him, more of them pouring from the bench beside us and turning into a mass of the same colors. I lose sight of him for a solid moment while he's enveloped by bodies.

But then he pushes his way through, skating away from the main celebration. And he keeps going.

"Oh, he's coming this way." Meg shifts us around to allow me space. "Go, Maddie."

I park myself against the barrier separating us from the corridor by the team bench. Aran pushes the half door open with his knee pads, and then, without a word, we're kissing. He has to stretch to reach me, and I grab on to his sweaty face to steady us. I don't care that the fence is digging into my belly in a super uncomfortable way. I kiss him like this is our living room and we have all day, open mouthed, tongue and all, gambling that my long hair may not be hiding any of this from onlookers or cameras.

He groans, and that's when I pull away, our lips making a smacking sound. Aran wears that little smile that is only mine, the one that lights up his eyes brighter than the lights in the rafters.

And out of the million things I could say, what tumbles out is "I'm pregnant. Now go get your cup, champ."

His jaw drops.

Much later, when we watch the footage from the award ceremony, the whole family gets a kick out of how the great Aran Rodriguez openly weeps for the cameras. What fans and reporters alike don't know is that the real reason for the tears is because he's really wanted to be a dad.

ARAN

I hate the hell out of hospitals. My sole life goal after winning a Stanley Cup last year was to not step foot in one ever again. I kinda forgot that's necessary when your wife is pregnant with your child.

"Easy there, big man. It's all going to be fine," says Max Cassiano from the vantage point of having gone through this already.

Grunting is all he gets from me. *He* wasn't kicked out of the labor room for making both wife and staff too nervous. I'd scream that it's discrimination against big, intimidating-looking guys, but I did pass out once her contractions started.

Thankfully, no one out here knows that's what happened. They all think I was just escorted out, and that's all they'll ever know. I'll make sure of that.

First, I have to survive this horrible wait. My mom's been calling these nine months a dulce espera, and for the most part, it's been pretty damn sweet. Maddie suffered no complications other than bizarre cravings she'd wake me up in the middle of the night for—pickles and frozen strawberries with chocolate drizzle was a popular one.

It was also completely awing and humbling to watch her body grow our child more and more with every passing day. I wish I could've shared that burden somehow, but I've made sure she's been extremely pampered—bathing together in our massive tub was also a popular one.

But now? This isn't a sweet wait. This is a horrible wait. Excruciating. My mind keeps running through every damn scenario where this can go wrong, and in all of them, I can do exactly jack shit to prevent it. My clothes are soaked through in more sweat than if I was in the middle of the playoffs final. I've never been more scared in my life.

The two people I love the most in my whole life are fighting without me because all I can physically do is sit in a tiny hospital chair, doing breathing exercises like I'm the pregnant woman.

My mom rubs circles on my back, and I think Dad's retelling the story of the birth of one of my sisters, or maybe it's mine, for the millionth time. I can't focus on his words. Luz keeps flagging every staff employee who walks by to see if they can get us some news. Olivia's flying over, and Meg and her husband are taking care of their kids and the Cassiano-Rodriguez brats. I clasp my hands and pray harder than ever before.

"Mr. Rodriguez?"

Dad shuts up, and I look up. A nurse pokes her head out from the door to the room where my wife has been delivering our baby with her mother's support.

"Yes?" My voice sounds nothing like me. I don't care.

"Would you like to come in and meet your son?"

"A son?" I blink. Hard.

We kept this as a surprise. It hits me now: I have a son.

"Congratulations, big man!" Cassiano grabs me by the shoulder.

"Oh no, I'm not sure the world is ready for a second Aran." My older sister grins down at me from the hallway.

One by one, the rest pass along their congratulations. Little by little, I manage to rise from my chair. My legs shake like a newborn calf's as I follow after the nurse. I'm vaguely aware of Maddie's mom stopping me for a hug. My attention is solely trained on my wife, hair stuck to her sweaty forehead, her cheeks and nose redder than a ripe strawberry, and a big smile contrasting the tears trickling from her sparkling eyes.

And then there's a tiny bundle in her arms.

I rush over, braking by the bed as if I'm on skates.

She looks up. "Aran."

"My love." I wrap my arm around her carefully, bringing her against my chest and dropping a kiss on her forehead. My free hand trembles in the air, but Maddie takes it and places it against the warm bundle of our baby. The little gurgle that comes from him almost drops me to my knees. "My other love," I mumble with a shaky voice.

Slowly, I tug at the swaddling until his face is revealed, all red and pudgy and so tiny—I think all of him fits in my hand. The next thing I know, I'm weeping like I'm the baby.

My wife chuckles against my chest, convulsing with sobs. "See? Some good things come out of hospitals."

"You. This is all you," I say, sniffling, kissing her hair, her nose, her forehead. "You're my joy, and now so is he."

"And you are ours." She tries to snuggle against my chest. I don't care if they try to kick me out again. I climb my huge ass onto the tiny hospital bed so my wife and son can snooze against me.

Much, much better than winning the cup in overtime, I think and close my eyes.

THE END

*

*Thank you for reading **Overtime**! I hope you can take a brief moment to leave a review on Amazon.*

Here are my other works if you're craving more closed door sports romance:

*Book one in the St. Cloud Hockey Series, **Faceoff**, is a rivals to lovers romance.*

*Book three and the last in the St. Cloud Hockey Series, **Shutout**, is a childhood friends to enemies to lovers romance.*

***Mistlefoe** is an office rivals to lovers Christmas romance, loosely linked to Faceoff.*

*Preorder **Wild Pitch**, book one in my upcoming Wild Baseball*

Romance series where the team's hot pitcher becomes our heroine's dating coach.

Sign up for my newsletter at MARILOYAL.COM to download **Set Me Up**, a free volleyball romance novella.

Happy reading!

GLOSSARY OF SPANISH VOCABS

Chapter 1

- Mierda: shit.

Chapter 3

- Bienvenida al club, fresita: Welcome to the club, little strawberry.

Chapter 5

- Mierda: (see glossary note from Chapter 1).

Chapter 13

- Cojones: men's dangly bits.
- Incluyéndome a mí: Including myself.

Chapter 15

- Pico de gallo: the literal translation "rooster's beak" has no actual related meaning to the subject, which is a simple salad of chopped tomatoes, onions, cilantro, dressed with vinegar, olive oil, salt and pepper.
- Ya te puedes casar: You can get married now.

Chapter 19

- Mijo: mijo is a colloquialism of "mi hijo" or my son but used widely beyond parent/son relationships.
- Chao: a form of goodbye.
- Te odio: I hate you.

Chapter 27

- Mierda: (see glossary note from Chapter 1).
- Hermanito: little brother.
- Aceituna: olive.

Chapter 29

- Arepa con pernil and pico de gallo: arepa is one of the national dishes of Venezuela and has no English translation, it's a corn flour "bread" that can be filled with basically anything. Pernil is pork, often pulled or sliced. See glossary note from Chapter 15 for pico de gallo.

Chapter 33

- Es Luz otra vez, es Luz otra vez: It's Luz, again. It's Luz, again.

Chapter 35

- No bueno: incorrect translation for "not good" commonly adopted by non-native speakers.
- Mierda, esto es una mala idea: Shit, this is a bad idea.
- Hermanito: (see glossary note from Chapter 27).
- Mujeres: Women.

Epilogue

- Pabellón criollo: translated would be "creole pavilion," which means absolutely nothing to us, except that this is the name of the national main dish in Venezuela (white rice, black beans, marinated pulled beef, side of arepa and fried sweet plantain). Yes, we have two national dishes.
- Dulce espera: sweet wait.

ACKNOWLEDGMENTS

Oh wow, I get to do this a second time. That's bananas!

First, *always*, thank you Lord. Contigo todo, sin ti nada.

The number of times I slide to my text messages to ask unhinged and/or hyper specific questions, panic about something random and possibly not too important, or send cute animal videos—and the fact that you remain so patient and welcoming every time—means I have to dedicate a special thanks to you both: Tamara Lush and Avery Keelan. What would I do without you?

To my cuzzy Melissa, who was the first person ever to put up with my over-the-top crush on a real-life goalie. I finally got to write about one!

Speaking of extremely patient people, Enni at Yummy Book Covers deserves an award. So does Beth at VB Edits. You two make me a sharper professional.

Thank you to all my Faceoff readers, and especially to my ARC team. Giving me that first chance encouraged me to keep going. You may not know this, but you're changing my life.

Last but not least, I want to thank my mom and my sister, and my dad up in heaven. You always believe in me and are on my corner, and thanks to do that I have the confidence to *try*. Los amo con todo.

ABOUT THE AUTHOR

Mari Loyal was born and raised in Venezuela, a baseball country that only cared about another sport, football soccer, every four years. As such, she decided to make hockey her whole personality because she had to make a point of being different. These days she no longer suffers from Not Like Other Girls syndrome and is very happy to be in the sports romance fandom. She writes closed door romance with a Latin American flair and an abundance of cinnamon rolls heroes. She also enjoys eating cinnamon rolls (the confections), in her spare time.

Sign up to my newsletter at MARILOYAL.COM